GORDON R. DICKSON

THE DRAGON AT WAR

ACE BOOKS, NEW YORK

This Ace Book contains the complete
text of the original hardcover edition.

THE DRAGON AT WAR

An Ace Book / published by arrangement with
the author

PRINTING HISTORY
Ace hardcover edition / November 1992
Ace paperback edition / November 1993

ISBN: 0-441-16611-3

ACE®
Ace Books are published by The Berkley Publishing Group,
200 Madison Avenue, New York, NY 10016.
ACE and the "A" design are trademarks
belonging to Charter Communications, Inc.

PRINTED IN THE UNITED STATES OF AMERICA

10 9 8 7 6 5 4 3 2 1

To Kay McCauley,
who puts up with me,
for the many years of
help and friendship

CHAPTER 1

The copper tea kettle skittered at its magic-given top speed through the woodland track. It had already polished its bottom shiny on the alternate turf and bare earth it skidded across. Its owner, the AAA+ magician S. Carolinus, had once, many years ago, commanded it always to be three-quarters full of water for tea; and to have that water on the boil. In spite of its mission, it was faithfully three-quarters full and on the boil, now.

"*On the boil*," in Carolinus's terms, meant that the kettle water was just below the boiling point; so that Carolinus could have his cup of tea when he wanted it, night or day.

So now the kettle continued to skitter and almost boil. Only as it bounced over the uneven ground, it occasionally splashed some of that water high against its hotter, dry, higher-up sides; and that water burst in steam out of its spout.

When this happened it gave a sharp, brief whistle. It could not help whistling, any more than it could help being on the boil, or going to Carolinus's rescue—which was what it was doing now. It was only a kettle. But if, as some folk suspected, the articles of Carolinus's cottage had personalities of their own, this kettle's heart was in its present task.

So, it skittered through the wood—at the best speed with which Carolinus had endowed it—giving voice occasionally

1

to its sharp whistle; and the creatures of the woodland it passed reacted accordingly.

A bear feeding on all four legs stood up suddenly with a "*Whuf!*" of surprise as it went by. Aargh, the English wolf, who feared nothing but had an ordinary wolf's prudence where unknown things were concerned, leaped abruptly to cover behind a tree as it went by, in order to observe it from relative safety. A boar, farther down the path, who was in the habit of charging anything in sight, on general principles, blinked his eyes at it, his curly tusks gleaming in the sunlight, got ready to charge—then thought better of it, in this case.

He backed away, off the path, and let the little kettle pass.

So it proceeded. Deer fled from it; small burrowing creatures dived into their burrows at the sight of it. In short, it spread consternation in every direction as it passed. But, this was only the beginning, the preamble to what happened when at last it broke out of the trees into the cleared area surrounding the Castle de Bois de Malencontri, the castle of that gentleman, the famous Dragon Knight: Baron Sir James Eckert de Bois de Malencontri et Riveroak (currently not in residence).

The kettle skittered across the cleared area, mounted the bridge over the moat, and shot through the open great gates in the curtain wall of the castle. There was a guard on duty at the gate. But he did not see the kettle until it began to clatter across the logs which made up the bridge. When he did, he nearly dropped his spear. He was under orders never to leave his post for any reason—as fourteenth-century guards on the front gates of castles always were. But in this particular case he held on frantically to his spear and ran full speed ahead of the kettle into the courtyard, shouting at the top of his voice.

"Gone mad! I always said he would!" muttered the castle blacksmith, glancing up briefly from the open shelter above his forge in the courtyard, carefully built away from anything else it might set fire to. The blacksmith had lowered his eyes again by the time the kettle went by, and he dismissed the sharp whistles he heard as merely a ringing in his ears.

Meanwhile the guard had fled through the open door of the castle into the Great Hall, still shouting.

"*A witch-kettle! A witch-kettle. Help!*" His voice rang against the walls of the Great Hall and back into the castle itself, bringing other servants flooding out. "It's following me! Help! Help!"

His voice reached even to the kitchen of the castle where the Lady Angela de Bois de Malencontri et Riveroak was telling the cook—for the several hundredth time—that after returning from the outhouse she must wash her hands before cutting up meat.

The Lady Angela was a winsome sight, in a blue and silver gown, had either she or the cook cared about that at the moment; but neither of them did. Picking up her skirts with a resigned fury—resigned, because it seemed there was always something around the castle for her, as Chatelaine, to be furious about—Lady Angela headed in the direction of the shouting voice.

When she got to the Great Hall, she discovered the men-at-arms there, with other servants, were all plastered back against its walls; while the little kettle had somehow managed to mount the high table, set itself in the very center, and begun whistling steadily, as if it was tea-time—not only for Carolinus but for anyone else who was around.

"M'lady! M'lady!" babbled the gate guard, as she passed him where he was clinging to one of the pillars of the halls about four feet off the floor. "It is a witch-kettle! Ware! Go no closer! It is a witch-kettle—"

"Nonsense!" said the Lady Angela, who was from an alternate world in the twentieth century where they no longer believed in witch-kettles.

She strode decisively past the guard toward the high table.

CHAPTER 2

Meanwhile, less than a mile and a half from this scene, there was the Dragon Knight, himself. He was the good knight Sir James Eckert, Baron—and in the King's name—Lord of the High Justice and the Low, for the lands of le Bois de Malencontri et Riveroak—though where Riveroak was, only James and the Lady Angela knew.

Actually, it was the name of the small town holding the twentieth-century college in which they had both been teaching assistants, before they had ended up back here, dimensions away, in an alternate *fourteenth*-century world—with dragons, ogres, sand-mirks and other suchlike interesting characters.

To everyone else here, Riveroak was a place unknown; probably far, far away over the western sea.

At the moment, Sir James, being in direct fief from the King, and with a tendency to avoid administering any justice, High or Low, to the people of his lands, was presently engaged in picking flowers.

He was on his way back from an over-long stay up at the border between England and Scotland, in the north. He had stopped for the flowers, hoping that a bouquet, presented to his wife, might allay part of her understandable annoyance at his somewhat overdue reappearance.

He had been led to these flowers by his neighbor and closest friend, the also good knight Sir Brian Neville-Smythe. Sir

4

Brian was unfortunately only a knight banneret, with a ruined castle which he was hard put to keep livable; but he had a name in the land; not only as a Companion of the Dragon Knight, but in his own right as a master of the lance, at the many tournaments held about the English land in this time.

Sir Brian, full of happiness, was by this time a good four miles off; on his way to his lady-love, the beauteous Lady Geronde Isabel de Chaney, current Chatelaine of Castle de Chaney; since her father, the Lord of same, had been gone now some years in Crusade to the Holy Land.

She and Sir Brian could not marry until her father returned and gave permission. But they could most certainly get together—and did at every opportunity. Sir Brian (and Dafydd ap Hywel, the Master archer—another close friend and Companion) had been with Sir James up at the Scottish border, visiting the castle of Sir Giles de Mer, a fourth true Companion and good knight. Like James, Dafydd was also only now returning to his home, a half-day's ride away, with the outlaw band of his father-in-law, Giles o'the Wold.

Since Sir Brian knew all this countryside like the back of his hand, and Sir James was only a latecomer of barely three years, it had taken Sir Brian to direct him to this place where summer flowers might be gathered nearest to Jim's castle.

Sir Brian's knowledge had been excellent. On the water-rich ground of a marshy-edged lake there was indeed a proliferation of plants in flower, with rather loose petals of a sort of orangey-yellow color.

They were not exactly in the same class with roses, of which James—or Jim, as he still thought of himself—had vaguely been thinking. But they were undeniably flowers; and a large bouquet of them could certainly not make matters worse concerning Angie's reaction to his delayed homecoming.

He had his arms half-filled with lengths of twig with blossoms on them—for the flowers grew on a sort of bush, rather than individually—when he was interrupted by a bubbling sound from the lake before him. Lifting his eyes from the flowers, he suddenly froze in position.

The water in the center of the pond was disturbed. It was mounding upward into large water bubbles that finally burst and let a round shape poke through. The round shape grew and grew and grew . . .

Jim stared. Because it seemed that the round shape would never stop growing. Finally, it emerged to the point of revealing itself as ten feet across; and looked like nothing so much as short, wet, blond hair plastered to an enormous round skull.

It continued to come up; rising until it revealed a huge forehead, a pair of rather innocent-looking blue eyes under thick blond eyebrows, a massive nose and an even more massive mouth and jaw—a face that would have been heavy-boned even if it had been the face of a man of normal size. But what it was, in fact, was the face of an incredible giant. If the head was any indication, the whole person to whom it belonged must be nearly a hundred feet in height; and Jim would have guessed, from his acquaintance with such small lakes as this, that the water in it was nowhere deeper than eight feet.

Jim had no time to speculate on this, however, because just then the head began to forge toward him with its chin just above water; creating a considerable bow wave with a muscular neck thoroughly in proportion with the head. The bow wave ran ahead, leaped the margin of the lake, and splashed Jim to the knees. Meanwhile, more and more of the body belonging to the face had risen above the water to reveal a giant not as tall, but even more remarkable than Jim had expected.

Towering, this monster eventually stepped out on to the margin of the lake, to stand dripping, and staring down at Jim. Jim's estimate had indeed been wrong. Thirty feet was more like the actual height of this stranger.

Giant as he was, he still seemed perfectly human in every other respect. He wore some sort of massive piece of gray-colored hide, or skin with no fur on it. This hung from one shoulder, dropping to his knees and wrapped around him in the fashion of Tarzan's clothing in old movies. Or, thought Jim a little wildly, the way cavemen were normally pictured as being dressed in animal skins.

But there were two differences between this and a caveman. No, three. The first was his enormous size. The second was that he was apparently as at home on the land and breathing air as he presumably had been under the lake and breathing water. But the third was the most amazing of all. The man, or creature, or whatever he was, tapered downward.

In short, below that enormous head he had a relatively narrow, by giant standards, pair of shoulders, and a chest only slightly smaller in proportion to the shoulders. But he continued to taper on downward from there, until he ended up in feet that were probably no more than four times as large as Jim's.

The same could not be said of his hands, which looked not merely large enough to be buckets for a derrick, but to seem capable of picking up a derrick itself in each fist.

"Wait!" boomed the giant. Or at least that was what Jim thought he heard.

"Wait?" echoed Jim, startled into speech. "What for . . . ?"

Then he realized, out of his earlier years in the twentieth century when he had been an associate teacher at Riveroak in the English department, that what he had just heard was not "*wait*." He was being addressed in Old English; and what he had actually heard was "*Hwaet!*"

The only reason he made this identification with his whirling mind was because that same word happened to be the first one in the Old English poem of *Beowulf*, created some fourteen hundred years before Jim's own original time, on his own world.

He tried to remember what "*Hwaet!*" meant—evidently it was some form of greeting or call to attention—but he was too bewildered at the moment to fish up any of the Old English he had once painfully learned. It was a shock to be addressed so, here on this world; where up until now every human being, and those of the animals who also inexplicably talked, including the dragons, spoke the same tongue.

"I'm—I'm sorry," he stammered, "but I don't speak—"

The giant interrupted him, talking now in the same language everyone else did.

"Of course!" he boomed. "Been two thousand years, if me memory serves—or was it three? A long time, anyhow, since last I was here. The way folk speak was bound to change. No, it's all right, wee man, I can also speak the way you little folk do. Easy as *that*!"

—And he snapped the thumb and middle finger of his right hand together, with a noise like that of a cannon going off.

Jim shook the ringing out of his ears, and broke out with the first thought that came into his still-stunned mind. He looked from the inversely pyramidal giant to the lake, which now seemed, by comparison, very small indeed.

"But—" he said. "Where'd you come from? How did you get—"

"Lost me way!" boomed the giant, interrupting him again. "Many centuries it is since my last faring hither. Mislaid me way among the underground waters of this isle."

Jim's only thought was that now the other was beginning to sound even more like *Beowulf*—but *Beowulf* translated, with a sort of old-seamanlike flavor.

Standing only a dozen feet apart as they were, Jim had to crane his neck to look up at the giant's face; and he got a very foreshortened view of it, even at that. To see the other more fairly, he backed off about twelve paces.

"Fear not!" boomed the giant. "Know that I am Rrrnlf, a Sea Devil. Call me 'Ranulf,' as you wee folk did the last time I was here. As then, by the Sirens, I mean you and your kind no ill. It's another I seek. How do you call yourself, lad?"

"I—er—" Jim, on the verge of introducing himself simply as "Jim Eckert," caught himself just in time, "am Sir James Eckert, Baron of Malencontri—"

"Strange names you small folk do have!" rumbled the giant. "Only one 'R' and no 'L' anywhere. However, no matter. Whereaway's the sea?"

Jim pointed westward.

"Ah," said the Sea Devil with satisfaction, "then I'm lost no longer." His speech was becoming more normal with every sentence. "From here I can go anywhere beneath the ground and not be lost again. But why hold those—whatever they be?"

"Flowers for my wife," Jim told him.

"She eats flowers?" boomed Rrrnlf, staring.

"Noooo . . ." said Jim, wondering how to explain himself. "She just likes to keep them—to look at them, you know."

"Why doesn't she come here, then, to get them?" demanded Rrrnlf.

Jim was beginning to get a little annoyed with all this questioning. What blasted business of this human-shaped mammoth was it anyway about Angie and the flowers?—On the other hand, no point in making someone his size angry.

"Because she'd rather have them close at hand!" he said.

At the same moment, an idea exploded in his mind like a shower-of-stars rocket on the Fourth of July. He had been completely forgetting the—admittedly limited—magical ability he had picked up in coming to this feudal world. What was the use of being able to do magic, if a magician like himself couldn't use magic to take care of a little situation like this?

Quickly, he wrote a spell on the inside of his forehead.

MAKE ME AND MY CLOTHES→ SEA DEVIL SIZE

Immediately he found himself looking into the giant's face on a level. As usual there had been no particular sensation; but he was now thirty feet or so tall himself and gazing at the other from what seemed to be only a couple of feet away.

Seen straight on this way by someone the same size, the Sea Devil appeared rather a pleasant-faced, if still heavy-boned, blond character, with only the shape peculiarity about him, except the intense, deep blue of his eyes. They were eyes which irresistibly reminded Jim of the greatest depths of sea water at which he had ever gazed, with sunlight glancing off it.

Surprisingly, Rrrnlf did not seem at all startled by Jim's sudden growth.

"Ah. A wee mage!" he said.

His voice still boomed. But now it did not seem to have the thunderous quality that Jim had thought he had heard in it, while listening to Rrrnlf from his own normal height above the ground. The other went on.

"Well met, Mage!" said Rrrnlf. "Fear not. I know magic and those who do it."

He beamed at Jim.

"—A great luck meeting you!" His voice was jubilant. "A mage is the very one to aid me. It happens I'm in search of a foul robber, whose limbs I will tear from his body when I find him; leaving him to wriggle in the sea mud like the worm he is! Only, use your magic and tell me where to find him."

"I'm afraid," said Jim, "my magic's not that good yet. I'm just starting out as a magician. I'm sorry to hear you've been robbed, though—"

"Most foully and unfairly robbed!" burst out Rrrnlf, suddenly looking very dangerous. "My Lady taken from me!"

"Your Lady?" said Jim. He tried to imagine a female equivalent of Rrrnlf, but his mind boggled at the idea. "You mean—your wife?"

"Wife? Never that!" boomed Rrrnlf. "What does a Sea Devil need with a wife? This was a Lady I took from a sunken ship—from the prow of a sunken ship; and was the image of my own lost love. A most fair Lady, with golden hair and a trident in one little hand. She had been fixed to a ship sunk some time past. I broke her free and took her to safety. For the last fifteen hundred years I have gilded and adorned her with gems. But now she is stolen—and I know by who. It was one of the sea serpents! Aye, a wicked sea serpent, who envied me her; and stole her away when I wasn't there, to keep in his own hoard!"

Jim's head spun. It was bad enough to try to imagine a female Sea Devil. It was infinitely worse to juggle all the information thrown at him in Rrrnlf's last words. He knew of the existence of sea serpents. The granduncle of the dragon in whose body he had found himself, when he had first landed in this time and world, had told him once of a dragon ancestor who had once slain a sea serpent in single combat.

He tried to think of the name of both the ancestor and the sea serpent. He found he could not remember any name for the serpent—perhaps he had not been told any—but the name of his dragon ancestor had been Gleingul. According to his dragon granduncle, what Gleingul had done in winning a one-on-one fight with the sea serpent had been something like the equivalent of the original St. George slaying the original dragon.

Just why Gleingul and the serpent had been fighting had never been explained to him. But if sea serpents were something like undersea dragons, in that they believed in accumulating hoards of gold and gems, what Rrrnlf was saying made sense.

"I see," he said, after a moment, "but I'm afraid I can't help you. I haven't seen any sea serpents around here—"

"You have already helped me by giving me the direction of the sea!" said Rrrnlf. "I shall return to my search now; and—fear not—I will find him. Granfer said that for some reason the sea serpents were all headed toward this isle. The one I seek may have sought to hide underground on this island; though they like not fresh water and avoid it by any means. We Sea

Devils care not whether water be salt or fresh—or even that we stand in open air as now I do. So, I bid you farewell. I'm in your debt, wee mage. Call on me if ever you need me."

With that he turned about, stepped back into the lake and strode toward the middle of it, the water swallowing him up vertically as it grew deeper. Jim suddenly thought of something.

"But how would I find you?" Jim called after him.

Rrrnlf looked back over his shoulder briefly.

"Call for me at the seashore!" he boomed back. "Even a wee man should know that much. Send your message by the surf. I shall hear!"

"But . . . what if you're on the other side of the world?" called Jim. Living in this fourteenth-century society had taught him to seize on any friendships that came his way. He had no idea how Rrrnlf could ever be useful to him; but it would do no harm to be able to call on him. But the other had already submerged.

"Wherever in the ocean-sea I am, your words will reach me!" said Rrrnlf, suddenly bobbing up again. "The sea is full of voices and they go on forever. If you call for me I will hear you no matter where I am. Farewell!"

He disappeared once more under the surface.

Jim stood staring at the lake until the disturbed water finally smoothed out, leaving no sign that the giant had ever been there. Bemusedly, he turned himself back to his actual size; and went back to gathering a full armful of the blossoms. Then he mounted his war horse, Gorp, who had been standing by, comfortably munching on some of the soft and sweet grass of the lake margin, and rode off toward his castle.

It took him only a short time to reach it. He frowned as he rode across the open space—kept open for defense purposes— between it and the surrounding trees. There was something of a desolate look about the castle that bothered him. He urged Gorp to a trot; and within a few moments clattered over the logs of the drawbridge and into the courtyard.

The courtyard was apparently empty. His original feeling of uneasiness became a full-blown foreboding. He dismounted hastily from Gorp and started toward the front door of the castle. Instantly he was almost knocked off his feet by being—for all practical purposes—tackled around the knees. He looked down and saw the agonized face of the castle blacksmith, who was still embracing his knees in the powerful grip of his sleeveless, burn-scarred arms.

"My Lord!" cried the blacksmith, who had finally become aware of what was going on since he had seen the guard running for the castle and shouting about a witch-kettle. "Go not in! The castle is held in a thrall by a witch-kettle! We are all doomed if you are caught in that thralldom, too! Stand out here in safety and counter that evil with your magic. Otherwise we are all destroyed forevermore!"

"Don't be sil—" began Jim; then he remembered just in time that the word "silly" had a different meaning in the middle ages. It meant "innocent" or "blessed"—which was not what he meant at the moment. He decided that the best way out of this situation was the direct, or medieval, method.

"Unhand, dog!" he snapped, in his best baronial manner. "Do you think I fear thralldom by any witch-device?"

"You . . . d—don't?" stammered the blacksmith.

"Absolutely not!" said Jim. "Now, stay here and I'll take care of the matter."

The blacksmith's arms fell away from around his knees and the expression on his face changed to one of hope as Jim stalked off.

About halfway to the castle door, however, a first small doubt began to nibble at Jim. This was a world where nothing could be taken for granted; and magic was very much a part of it. Perhaps there actually were such things as witch-kettles? Perhaps they could indeed hold people in thrall . . . ?

He shrugged the thought off. He was angry with himself for even thinking it. After all, he reminded himself, he was a magician, if only a C rated one.

He strode forward and in through the doorway into the Great Hall, continuing on toward the high table at the Hall's far end.

Within, the walls were crowded with the castle's servitors. But they were all deathly silent; and all pressed as far back against the sides of the hall as they could get. On the high table there was indeed a kettle, that appeared to be steaming; and also—although he could hardly believe it—singing with that steam in a breathy little voice that nonetheless carried its melody, at least, clearly through the hall.

Standing motionless, looking down at it with the tip of her

right forefinger most uncharacteristically in her mouth, was his wife, the Lady Angela.

No more than those pressed against the wall all around them, did she move or make a sound.

CHAPTER 3

J im broke into a run toward the high table. No one had seemed to notice his presence until now, but now he felt as if all eyes were on him. He was almost to the kettle now, anyway.

The Lady Angela turned at the sound of his running feet. She took the tip of her finger from her mouth and stared at him as if he was a ghost. He vaulted up to the level of the high table and enfolded her in his arms.

"Angie!" he said.

For a moment she did nothing; then she enclosed him in her own arms and kissed him fiercely.

"Jim!" she said. "Oh, Jim!"

They hung together for a few moments; and then Jim felt himself pushed away from her, with her hands on his chest. A dark frown was gathering over her eyes.

"And just where have you been all this time—" she began.

Hastily, he shoved the flowers, which he had been unconsciously carrying all this time in his left hand, into her arms.

"For you!" he said.

"Jim, I don't care—" She broke off again and looked down at the flowers. After a second she took a long deep sniff at them. "Oh, Jim—" She broke off with an entirely different note in her voice. She lowered her head and sniffed deeply again at the flowers, then she put her arms around him once again, hugging him to her.

"Damn you!" she whispered in his ear; then kissed him again, both angrily and lovingly. Then they both let go and stood back from each other.

"But are you all right?" demanded Jim. "Your finger was in your mouth—"

"Oh, I burned it on this kettle," said Angie vexedly. "I couldn't believe that it was boiling with no heat under it, so I touched. Stupid thing to do! But Jim—how does it happen you turn up at just this moment? Did you use magic, or something?"

"Not to get here at just this moment," said Jim. "Why is getting here at just this moment so important?"

"Because the kettle just got here, too, and it wants to talk to you!"

"The kettle?" Jim stared from her to the utensil, steaming and singing away on the table. "A kettle wants to talk to me?"

"Yes! Don't you hear it?" demanded Angie. "Listen!"

Jim listened.

The kettle was still singing away in its breathy little voice; and up close, as Jim was now, he found its singing made recognizable words. The song was a brief refrain, but repeated over and over again.

> *This is an emergency.*
> *Fetch Jim Eckert here to me.*
> *He is needed desperately!*
> *Fetch Jim Eckert here to me!*

Jim blinked as the kettle went back to its first line and began to sing the quatrain all over again. He listened to it halfway through again before he came out of his daze.

"I'm here!" he told the kettle. "This is Jim Eckert. I'm here. What do you want to tell me?"

The kettle immediately switched its song.

It sang:

> *Carolinus needs you, Jim,*
> *You must swiftly rescue him!*
> *He is sick, in living hell—*
> *From nurses who would make him well!*

Two "wisewomen," from Hill Farm
Not really wise, but strong of arm.
Dose and poultice him to death.
Haste, before his final breath!

Rescue Carolinus!
Rescue Carolinus!
Rescue Caro—

"All right! All right, I've got the message!" snapped Jim; since it seemed the kettle was prepared to go on singing "*Rescue Carolinus!*" indefinitely.

The kettle fell silent. A small puff of white steam did manage to escape from its spout after he had spoken—but it was absolutely noiseless. The kettle's copper sides seemed to gleam at him in apology, but also in mute reproach. Inexplicably, Jim felt guilty for his outburst at it.

"Sorry," he said aloud, without thinking.

"You idiot!" Angie hugged him once more, affectionately. "It's only a kettle. It doesn't understand an apology."

"I suppose you're right." There was a cold feeling in the pit of Jim's stomach. "But evidently Carolinus is sick and being mistreated by these people who think they're helping him get well—as I can well believe could happen in this particular here and now. I'll have to go to him right away."

"We'll both go to him right away!" said Angie. "And didn't the kettle sing something about these women being strong of arm? I think we better take a few men-at-arms along with us. Theoluf!"

Jim's squire detached himself from the wall and came forward.

"Yes, m'Lady? M'Lord?" he asked. He was a most unusual-looking squire, having been one of Jim's men-at-arms until he had been promoted to this new rank. Above the half-coat of armor he wore on his upper body, his dark face under its slightly graying shock of hair—though he was probably no more than in his early thirties—and the scar on his face made him look as if he had been around for years.

"Pick out eight of the men-at-arms; and you and they come along with us," commanded Angie. "Also see to the horses and all other preparations for the trip. We'll leave immediately."

She looked past him.

"Solange!" she called.

The castle cook, a tall woman well into her forties and about fifty pounds overweight—although a lot of that looked as if it might be muscle—also came forward from the wall. She was a bit on the stout side to be curtsying; but she gave a sort of a bob.

"Yes, m'Lady?"

"See food is made up for the men's saddle bags and for m'Lord and myself," said Angie. "In my absence you are in charge of the inside servants. Yves? Yves Mortain! Oh, there you are. As chief man-at-arms, you'll be in command of the castle while we're gone. You both understand?"

"Yes, m'Lady," said Yves. With Solange, he turned away. She was not from France, in spite of her name, but actually from the island of Guernsey.

"One moment!" snapped Angie. "Who do we have that knows something about these two sisters from what was it— Hill Farm?"

"Margot might," said Solange, turning back. "She comes from near there, m'Lady."

"Margot!" called Angie. But it seemed that Margot was not among those in the Hall. "Solange, have her fetched at once and sent to us!"

"Right away, m'Lady," said Solange.

Margot made an appearance within a few moments after Solange disappeared through the doorway back into the keep and its ground-floor kitchen. Apparently she had been back there at some duty or other when the kettle came in, and had prudently stayed out of sight.

"Yes, m'Lady," she said, curtsying. She also was tall, but narrow, with a wide mouth and graying blonde hair.

"What do you know about two sisters who act as nurses and help sick people—for a fee undoubtedly—from a place called Hill Farm?"

"Oh that'd be Elly and Eldra, m'Lady," said Margot. "They were the only two children of old Tom Eldred, who was the biggest and strongest man around the neighborhood. Both Elly and Eldra took after him—looked like him, I mean, m'Lady. As a result no man would have them for fear of being beaten

by his wife; instead of the other way around. Young Tom
Davely even left home and ran off, when Eldred told him he
was going to take Elly to wife whether he liked it or not—"

"Thank you, Margot," said Angie, decisively, for Margot had
dropped into a comfortable, confidential tone which seemed to
threaten a complete history of her neighborhood. "That tells us
all we need to know. You can get back to whatever you were
doing, now."

She turned to Jim.

"I've got a few other arrangements to make, to be sure
the castle doesn't fall apart while I'm gone," she said to
Jim. "You'd better take a fresh horse. Even if you've ridden
him easily, Gorp's been carrying you for some days now, I
imagine."

"You're right," said Jim. "I'll go take care of that right
now."

He and Angie went off in opposite directions, Jim to make
his way back out the front of the Great Hall, from which the
servants were rapidly dispersing, under the sensible servant
doctrine that if those in authority couldn't see them, they were
much less likely to be put to work.

In less than half an hour the expedition to rescue Carolinus
was on horseback and on its way. Jim and Angie rode first,
with Theoluf and eight of his best men-at-arms behind them.
The kettle had been left, looking a little forlorn, the only
occupant of the Great Hall. Servants were normally passing
to and fro through that large space; but the feeling that the
kettle might after all still have something of witchery about
it was enough to make them keep their distance.

Jim and Angie were busily comparing notes. Her part consisted of bringing him up to date on affairs around the castle.
But she listened closely as he told her about the Sea Devil;
and then to his earlier adventures up near the Scottish border.
These involved the Hollow Men (who were a form of ghost)
and the Borderers, those Northumbrian knights and others of
authority who lived next to the Scottish border; and—last but
not least—the Little Men.

She had been fascinated that the Little Men had taken to
Dafydd, which was why they had wanted him to act as their
leader; and Jim ended up very nearly telling her that on which
Dafydd had sworn him to silence—the fact that the bowman
had been related to an ancient royalty that the Little Men

remembered, even if no one else did.

"I'd tell you the whole story, but I promised Dafydd," said Jim finally.

"That's all right," said Angie. "I know there are some things you can't tell me. As long as it's nothing to do with your own health and safety, I don't worry about it. Do you think the Little Men could be what's left of the Picts who were there when the Romans built the wall?"

"I don't know. We could ask Dafydd; but I promised to forget his connection with them—so I don't like to go asking him questions."

He reached across from his horse, took her hand and squeezed it. They looked into each other's eyes.

"You're marvelous, you know that?" said Jim.

"Of course I know it," said Angie lightly. She gave Jim's hand an extra squeeze and let it go. They went back to riding side by side in perfectly decorous fashion.

The Tinkling Water, which was the place of Carolinus's residence, was not far away, and they were there before they had run out of things to tell each other. Its pool, turf and trees, at least, were unchanged.

It had always been in a peacefully empty, open circle of grass surrounded by tall elms. The grass had always been close and lush without any sign of a weed in it. It had been like a carpet surrounding the pool and small, peaked-roofed house that Jim knew from experience had only two rooms—one upstairs and one down.

The front door was approached by a gravel path that was always magically raked, up to its single step to the entrance. Beside the path was the small, round pool of beautifully blue water, from the exact center of which a jet spouted some four or five feet into the air, before breaking into drops and falling back into the pool with a tinkling sound that was very much like that of the wind gently clashing some oriental glass chimes. It was this particular element that gave the location the name of The Tinkling Water.

In Jim's opinion it had always been a very beautiful place. But it was not a beautiful place now.

The reason for this was some thirty to forty people who were now camped around the cottage. Their tattered shelters— it would have been flattering them to call them tents—were scattered over the lush, green lawn. Litter was everywhere;

and the people themselves—mainly men, but with some women and a few children—were more dirty and ragged than usual, even for the fourteenth century.

It was very clear what had happened. Carolinus's place had been surrounded by one of the roving bands of vagabonds and ruffians who were continually on the move up and down the roads, working when they had to, stealing when they could, and belonging to no particular Lord or Master.

It was equally clear that they were here at this present time like vultures at a carcass, in the hopes that Carolinus would not survive, and that they might find valuable pickings inside his house and property. Right now, of course, they were merely waiting to see what would develop.

Angie, Jim saw, recognized them as quickly as Jim himself had—and he was sure that the men-at-arms behind him had done so even more quickly. He heard the slight rattle and clink of metal on metal as his eight men-at-arms and Theoluf made sure their weapons were close at hand and in position for quick use.

Ignoring them all, Jim led the way, riding his horse through the crowd, forcing it to scatter and clear before him until he came to the gravel path. Then he dismounted, and Angie with him. Among the sullen muttering of the mob a voice could be heard explaining this was the dragon who was a knight.

"No, Angie!" he said urgently, in a voice low enough for her to hear but not loud enough to carry to those around. "Stay on horseback. It's safer. I'll go in alone."

"You certainly will not go in alone!" said Angie. "I want to look at these so-called nurses!"

She had dismounted and started up the gravel walk before Jim had a chance to do anything but hurry after her. They reached the door and Jim flung it open without knocking.

A gush of ill-scented air struck them in the face, and for a moment the gloom inside confounded their eyes, adjusted to the outside sunlight. Then they saw that Carolinus was lying on his bed, the head of which was against a far wall of the downstairs room. One woman was standing over him with folded arms while another stood across the room, both looking around with startled faces at Jim and Angie.

Margot's description had not exaggerated. Both of these "wisewomen" had three or four inches of height on Jim; and they probably outweighed him by something like fifty pounds apiece. They were as broad-shouldered as they were tall; and the folded bare arms of the woman who stood by Carolinus's bed showed muscles like those in the arms of Jim's blacksmith. It was this woman who was the first to react to their entrance.

"Who be ye?" she snapped in a baritone voice. "This be a sick house. Out with ye! Out!"

And she freed one of her arms to wave them away as if they were flies.

Jim felt himself brushed against from behind and Theoluf suddenly appeared beside himself and Angie. The squire had for the moment reverted back to being the chief man-at-arms he had once been; and not merely his face, but his whole manner, was anything but friendly toward the two women.

"Silence!" he snarled. "And show proper respect for the Baron and Lady of Malencontri." He laid a hand on his sword hilt and took a step forward. "Did the two of you hear me? Let's hear some courtesy from you!"

"Elly!" cried the woman across the room, shrinking back against the wall. " 'Tis Sir Dragon and his Lady!"

"Dragon Knight or no," said Elly, unmoved, still standing by the bed with her arms still folded, "this is no part of their domain; but land that belongs only to the Mage, whom we are here to tend. Here, we give the orders. Out with the two of you! Out! Out!"

Theoluf's sword rasped out of its scabbard.

"How say you, m'Lord?" he said. His eyes glittered. "Shall I call the lads and take these two out and hang them?"

"Hang them?" cried Angie in her ringing voice. "No! They must be witches. Burn them! Take them and burn them—both of them!"

The one against the wall, who was obviously the sister named Eldra, gave a shriek and crammed herself even further back against the wall. Even Elly, by the bed, seemed shaken. Jim stared at Angie. He had never heard that tone of voice from Angie before, or expected her to express such sentiments before. This was his gentle Angie, talking about burning people alive? Then he realized that Angie did not mean the threat. She was merely trying to crack the composure of Elly, the stronger-minded sister.

Elly, however, remained stoutly by the bed, although even in the relatively dim light of the house with its few narrow windows, it could be seen that she had turned pale.

"Talking of burning's one thing. Doing it's another!" she said stoutly. "Happens we have a few friends outside who might have a word to say if your armed men try to harm us, m'Lord—"

"Excuse me, m'Lord, m'Lady," interrupted a new voice; and a small man wearing the tattered rags of a brown robe with a rope girdle tied in three knots at the waist—the dress of a Franciscan Friar, came out of the shadows beneath the stairs to the cottage's upper floor. His hair was black, dirty and shaggy; but the crown of his head had been shaved bare to give him a tonsure. "Indeed, gentles, the good women here are only doing the best they can for the Mage, who is badly ill."

He walked around to confront both Jim and Angie, ignoring Theoluf and his bared sword.

"I am Friar Morel," he said, "shepherd to the little flock you see outside."

He crossed himself.

"—Which God protect, along with the Mage and these two good women and your noble selves." He crossed himself again. "*Dominus vobiscum.*"

In spite of Jim's general lack of religion, he had not spent a good chunk of his graduate time learning medieval church Latin without being able to understand and respond to the friar's pious, "*The Lord be with you.*"

"*Et cum spiritu tuo,*" he said. "*With you as well.*"

He was aware that the friar had brought up the Latin exchange more by way of proving his credentials than anything else. But now the little tonsured man was speaking again, this time to Angie.

"M'Lady," he was saying reproachfully, "you could not really have meant what you said about burning these two good women. I can tell you in the Lord's name that they are not witches, but only wisewomen who lend their help to the sick and troubled. Only by their efforts has the Mage remained alive until now."

"Is that so?" asked Jim. He strode forward, elbowing Elly aside. In spite of her words, she backed off without protest. He laid one hand on Carolinus's forehead. It was cold and clammy rather than hot. But the old man seemed unconscious. Then the aged eyelids lifted briefly and words whispered from Carolinus's lips.

"Get me out of here—"

"Don't worry, Carolinus," Jim answered him. "We'll do just that. You'll be much better back at Malencontri in the castle. What have they been doing to you?"

"Everything . . ." whispered Carolinus, and then evidently ran out of strength. His eyes closed.

"Why, 'tis a foul lie!" broke out Elly. "Delirium, I say, brought on by his sickness! We've given him nothing but wholesome purges and drenches, and only bled him twice."

"That's enough to kill him!" snarled Angie.

She had joined Jim and was now standing by his side. She spoke over her shoulder.

"Theoluf, have a couple of men make a litter. Let them get poles from anywhere and we'll use blankets or whatever cloth we have around to carry Carolinus on."

"Yes, m'Lady." Theoluf sheathed his sword, turned about and went out through the bright sunlit rectangle of the doorway. They could hear him giving orders to the other men-at-arms.

" 'Twill be his death!" cried Elly. "To take him from our care, when we have barely kept him alive all this time. He will not even survive the ride to your castle!"

"Oh, I think he will," said Angie fiercely to the larger woman. She too had been feeling Carolinus's forehead. "He may not have been very sick to start off with; but you two have brought him close to death with the way you've been feeding him all sorts of rotten things!"

"He is ours!" replied Elly fiercely. "Lady, you may be; but this, as I say, is not in your domain! The Mage's last sensible wish was to stay with us. And we will keep him here at whatever cost there may be to it!"

"Indeed," said Friar Morel smoothly, "not merely these two good women, but all of my flock would be sad to see you try to take the Mage from here to die on the way to your castle. In God's name, we would have to resist any such attempt!"

"M'Lord!" called Theoluf's voice from beyond the doorway. "Could you come speak with me for a moment?"

"Be right there!" said Jim. He swept his gaze around through the two women and to the friar. "If I find anything has been done while I step outside to either m'Lady or Carolinus, none of you will see another sunrise!"

He was surprised to realize he meant it.

He stepped to the doorway. Just outside on the front step, Theoluf was standing, while beyond him, with their horses facing outward and their hands close to their weapons were the eight men-at-arms they had brought with them. Effectively, these kept the scruffy crowd around them from getting close enough to overhear. Theoluf murmured in Jim's ear.

"These ditch-rats," muttered Theoluf, "who are clearly here for the pickings they may gain from the Mage's house, are only waiting until they can make free of it. All there is that is here now will be warded with magic; but the magic dies when the Mage dies. They are clearly of a mind to keep us from taking him away from here and saving his life. I would we had brought another dozen of the lads! There will be long knives hidden about all of them, and even not a few swords."

Jim ran his eyes over the now-scowling group, peering out from among their bright-colored, dirty rags of tent and clothing. It called for the death penalty by Royal Decree to carry a sword; unless you were of a rank, or authorized by someone of rank, to do so. But these people's lives could be forfeit on half a dozen other excuses at any moment. Yes, there would be swords among them. Clearly, also there were closer to forty than thirty of them. He, Theoluf and the men-at-arms would be outnumbered four to one; and while those against them might be untrained, they would certainly have had some experience with their weapons. It was not good.

Not that that made any difference, Jim suddenly realized. This was the fourteenth century and he was a Baron and a knight. The very idea of giving in to any rabble like this would disgrace him forever in the eyes of his neighbors, including those of his best friends. In particular, Sir Brian Neville-Smythe, as his best friend, would take the shame personally. Brian, in his own right, would not have hesitated to attack an army by himself. In fact, Jim had occasionally thought Brian would probably have enjoyed the chance.

So, the only question was not whether to attack and try to carry Carolinus out—but when and how.

It occurred to him fleetingly that he could use his own magic to seem to multiply the numbers of his men or else make them several times as big so as to overawe the rabble. Then he remembered that if Friar Morel was actually a member of any order of the clergy, no matter how minor, while existing magic could not be erased, no new magic could be made to work here; particularly if Morel had prayed against its use.

In fact, Jim realized abruptly, he must already have done so. Otherwise Carolinus would have used his own magic to transport himself in a twinkling from the hands of these nurses to Jim's castle—where, of course, he knew he would be well taken care of, even if Angie was there without Jim.

Nor was there any doubt that there was some connection between the two nurses and those camped outside. Whatever had made Carolinus sick in the first place must have been something strange. Because Carolinus never got sick; although he had more than once pointed out to Jim that while magic could heal wounds, it could not cure sickness.

So, it had probably been something not dangerous by itself, but enough of an excuse for the two women to move in on him. Then somehow those outside must have heard of it, and moved in also; since Elly and Eldra could hardly not have known that their treatments could only make Carolinus's condition worse.

They knew that he was an old man and frail; and therefore his body would not be able to stand much abuse without giving up entirely. It was a good thing Jim, Angie and Jim's men-at-arms had gotten to him in time. In fact, it was a good thing the kettle had brought the message in time. Morel would not have been able to stop the kettle since his prayers could only block *new* magic.

But, any magic Jim might try would be blocked. So, the use of it by him was out. That meant they would simply have to fight their way through with what they had. To do so, carrying Carolinus, would be no easy task; since those outside would be looking for an opportunity to kill him in the heat of battle.

Come to think of it, however, it would be best to make sure that magic would not work before giving up on it. He beckoned Angie and Theoluf to him, frowning at Friar Morel who, uninvited, moved forward also. The frown stopped Morel.

With Theoluf and Angie leaning close Jim whispered.

"Stand back and give me room," he said. "I'm going to try changing myself into dragon shape."

The two nodded and stepped away from him. Morel peered out through the front door and would have approached them then, but Theoluf put out a hand and thrust the smaller man back with no gentleness whatsoever. Jim wrote the accustomed spell in his mind.

ME DRAGON SHAPE, CLOTHES TO VANISH
UNHARMED→ NOW!

He stood where he was. Nothing happened. He remained Jim Eckert, with nothing about him resembling a dragon.

Well, that was that, then. He looked at Angie and Theoluf, both of them gazing back at him in expectation.

"I'll explain later," he said out loud and quite openly.

They couldn't magic their way out; but also they could hardly take on odds of four to one and fight their way out, carrying Carolinus in a litter at the same time.

It was swords or wits that were left to solve this situation. What would a good fourteenth-century knight like Sir Brian do in a fix like this?

CHAPTER 4

Of course!
    Jim's mind woke to a sudden inspiration. What Brian
would do, would be to take a hostage!

It was doubtful whether either of the two nurses would be
particularly valuable as hostages. On the other hand there was
Friar Morel.

Jim pulled Angie aside and spoke into her ear in too low a
tone for anybody else in the room to hear.

"Did you arrange for anyone to come after us if we weren't
back right away?" he asked.

She shook her head and turned to whisper in his ear.

"No," she said. "Certainly Yves Mortain is going to send
somebody by tomorrow morning; in fact, I'll bet he'll send
a considerable force, if we aren't back by that time. But I
don't like the idea of spending the night here; particularly
with Carolinus in the state he's in. I think we've got to get
him back to the castle just as fast as we can. Get him warm,
get some food into him, and start taking care of him."

Jim nodded and Angie went back to paying attention to
Carolinus with Theoluf, naked sword in hand, scowling at
Elly, just in case either she or the other sister might think
to interfere.

Jim thought.

He could pull the men-at-arms from outside to inside the

house, then simply close the door and lock it. The magical wards Carolinus had put not merely around this house, but around the whole clearing, were better than the defenses of the most stout castle imaginable. Those outside would not simply be able to break their way in, even though the walls looked as if they would give way to a punched fist. A magician's dwelling simply did not yield like that.

But there was this other point—Angie's feeling that they should get Carolinus away as soon as possible. Jim tended to agree. The old magician looked next to death. He was pale as a corpse already, lying on the bed in the uncleaned, grayish gown he was wearing.

But could they get away simply by using Morel as a hostage? Undoubtedly, the vagabonds outside would have little love for Morel, personally—any more than they had for each other. The kind of people of which these groups were composed had put affections behind them a long time ago. They might not want to protect the friar for his own sake; but he was undoubtedly highly useful to them.

Not only did he throw a cloak of semirespectability over them as a group, but he was probably the shrewdest one among them and could well be their leader.

At this point the door opened and one of the men-at-arms from outside stuck his head in.

"We have the litter ready, m'Lord," he said. "Shall we bring it in?"

"In a minute," said Jim. The head disappeared and the door closed. Jim turned back to Friar Morel. "We're going to carry Carolinus out of here. Now, if any of those people outside give us trouble we'll cut your throat; because we'll be taking you along with us as a hostage."

"You cannot!" Morel drew himself up to what must be his full five feet five of height. "I am in Minor Orders and under the protection of clergy. Whoso harms me imperils his immortal soul."

Jim had not thought of this. He was not sure that there was that severe a penalty for harming someone in Minor Orders; to one of which Morel almost undoubtedly belonged. Still . . . he had been about to give an order to Theoluf, and have the squire hold his poignard at the priest's throat.

Glancing at his squire now, however, he saw that Theoluf had very definitely gone pale. Morel's claim was clearly nothing but that, backed up by the ragged robe he wore. But Theoluf was as clearly not ready to take a chance on what the friar threatened; and that meant that none of the other men-at-arms would be willing to lay hands on the friar, either.

It would be up to Jim himself.

He braced himself for the effort, and put on the most ferocious grin he could contrive.

"I care naught for such threats!" he said, putting his face down close to the smaller man's. "I will be the one to cut your throat, if necessary! Be sure I will do it!"

Now it was the turn of Morel's face to lose color. Jim could almost hear him thinking that the Dragon Knight might well have sold his immortal soul to Satan, long since.

To emphasize the point, Jim drew his own poignard and, reaching around to the back of Morel's head, took a firm grip on the other's lank, greasy hair below the tonsure there, and jerked him around so that his back was to Jim. He placed the sharp edge of his naked blade against the other's throat.

"*Now!*" said Jim.

But with that, a new source of opposition appeared.

"Ye'll not be taking a sick man from us!" cried Elly.

Jim turned his head to look at her and saw that from somewhere among her balloonist clothing she had produced a good-sized knife of her own which she now held at Carolinus's throat.

"Sooner would I see him dead, than in the hands of those who cannot cure him!" Elly went on.

It threatened to be a standoff. But a sudden inspiration erupted in the back of Jim's mind.

"You think you can cure him?" said Jim fiercely. "Do you know that you, yourself, now stand on the very brink of death from being this close to him? You little understand what terrible illness you've exposed yourself to!"

Using Morel's hair as a handgrip he forced the other over to the side of Carolinus's bed. "Look at him, Friar!" Jim said. "You know your Latin! What you're looking at is a man in the last stages of *phytophthora infestans*! You know what that means, of course?"

"Er—y—yes. Yes, of course!" said Morel, his teeth suddenly chattering with fear. "Why didn't I see it myself? The nurses are doomed!"

There was a shriek from Eldra, across the room. Elly's face went ugly with sudden fear; but she still stood fiercely with the knife in her hand and her arms folded.

"You are a magician, not a man of medicine—" she said to Jim accusingly. But her voice was abruptly unsure.

"I am also a man of medicine!" snarled Jim. "You know what those Latin words mean, Friar. Is it not the most deadly disease on the face of the earth—worse than leprosy?"

"Yes—yes—yes . . ." stammered Morel, giving at the knees, and trying to back away from the bed but being prevented by Jim's standing behind him.

Jim turned to Elly and Eldra.

"You heard the friar," he said. "Let me tell you what's going to happen next to Carolinus; and to you—if you've caught it from him. There will start to grow ugly black fringes, like hairs, coming out on the skin all over. When you see those, you know you're already starting to rot inside."

Eldra shrieked again. Elly's knife had disappeared.

"Sir—m'Lord, magician . . ." stammered Eldra, "if we have caught it, can we come to your castle? Will you help us?"

"I'll think about it," said Jim harshly. "Now, I'll keep hold of the friar here, just to be on the safe side, but you two go outside and start telling those people out there what they're up against—what may happen to them if they get too close to any of us."

"M'Lord . . ." faltered Elly. "I cannot say those Latin words. Would you tell me once more?"

Jim sounded out the various syllables of the words.

"Fy-top-era in-fes-stans."

Elly's eyes lit up. Jim was satisfied. The medieval memory, which in all these people needed to be able to stick like glue to whatever it heard because of the general lack of ability to write, had just come through again. Outside, Elly would be able to parrot the sounds she had just heard, whether she understood them or not. She headed toward the door; but her sister already had it open and was out it before she disappeared through herself.

"M'Lord," said Theoluf shakily, "I'm your squire now; and with you to the death. But the other lads may be as little willing as the scum without to be close to the mage; if he has such a dread disease and we cannot carry him by litter, just the three of us."

Jim had not thought of that. For a moment he stood, still half holding up the sag-kneed friar by the bedside—and then a further inspiration came to him. He beckoned Angie over to him; and, holding the friar at arm's length with one hand, with the other turned her sideways so he could whisper privately in her ear.

"Potato blight!" he breathed.

"What?" said Angie out loud in a startled tone of voice. "Po—"

"Shhh," whispered Jim. "Careful, don't say it out loud— even though those words probably wouldn't mean anything to these people either. I tried to think of some horrendous disease, the Latin name of which the friar wouldn't understand; but one he would automatically go along with. All I could think of was the Latin name for the disease that hit the potatoes in Ireland during the potato famine there. You remember? In eighteen hundred forty-six and eighteen forty-seven, Ireland's potatoes were ravaged by this disease— it's also called the 'late blight.' A million people are supposed to have died of starvation."

"Oh," said Angie. "Yes. Of course."

"Good. Now go whisper in Theoluf's ear and explain to him that it's all a fake; that I'm simply using a disease for a vegetable that they don't even have here, yet. Then the two of you go outside; and you tell each one of the men-at-arms by whispering in his ear—individually. They may not believe Theoluf if he simply passes the message on. But they have to believe their Lady Angela de Malencontri et Riveroak. That gang outside will simply think you're giving the men special instructions you don't want overheard. Will you do that?"

"Right now!" said Angie—and in the same instant she was gone through the door.

It was nearly ten minutes before she reappeared, but this time she brought in four of the men-at-arms with a litter between them that they had made from two poles, probably taken from the people outside, since they were of dry and weathered wood; and fitted with several layers of cloth, securely tied to the poles to make a temporary litter-bed on which Carolinus could be carried.

"Now," said Jim to the men-at-arms with the litter, "we want to ease Carolinus gently onto this. One of you take the litter at each end; and Theoluf, you and the others pick up the bed sheet by its corners. Then lift sheet, Carolinus and all onto the litter."

So they did, with Jim and Angie supervising. Carolinus groaned softly, once, as he was being moved, but otherwise gave no sign of awareness. He still seemed to be either unconscious, or, at best, only semiconscious.

They all moved outside, Jim still holding his poignard at Morel's throat. He closed the front door of Carolinus's cottage behind him, knowing that it would lock magically and automatically. The other four men-at-arms were in their saddles, now, and the ones who were going to carry Carolinus were seated, ready to take the handles of the litter as it was transferred to them.

The vagabonds outside had drawn back from the entrance and opened a path of sorts to the wood, but they had not drawn back as far as Jim had hoped they would, nor was the path all that wide or open. They had simply moved those shelters that stood directly in the way—the shelters that Jim and his men had more or less trampled down with their horses' hooves on their way in.

It had made Jim a little uncomfortable to simply break his way through even such temporary structures; but he knew very well that such was the fourteenth-century way of doing things by men of rank like himself. Not only his men-at-arms, but the vagabonds themselves, would have figured it for a weakness in him, if he had not.

The little troop formed up, with Carolinus surrounded by extra men-at-arms. So that there was a double thickness of armed men between him and the vagabonds; counting those who were carrying the litter, each of whom had already tied his particular wooden pole end to the high cantle of his medieval saddle. Angie mounted, and Jim mounted with Morel astride the horse before its saddle.

"All right," said Jim. "Move out now at an easy walk, so Carolinus is jolted as little as possible. Angie, you ride next to him so you can keep an eye on him—"

This was something of a trick on Jim's part. But he wanted Angie as well as Carolinus surrounded by armed men. Angie moved accordingly; and Jim took up the tail of the procession with Morel astride the shoulders of Jim's horse and Jim's poignard still at his throat. Theoluf was at the head. They moved slowly out through the crowd.

At first they were allowed to pass with silence; but a murmuring began among the vagabonds that began to escalate. Then suddenly, there was a cry of rage behind Jim; and he looked back over his shoulder to see some of them trying to open the door to Carolinus's cottage and failing. Of course, Carolinus's magical wards would still be holding it secure against anything up to and including a battering ram. Jim smiled internally, and turned his attention back to their passage through the crowd.

The vagabonds were now obviously very unwilling to let Carolinus, let alone Friar Morel, be taken from them. They were beginning to crowd in and close up the passage to the trees. The glint of knives was visible among them; and, as Jim watched, first one, then several, swords appeared and there was a general movement toward the small mounted group.

"Ye've got no right to take him!" shrilled the voice of Elly suddenly behind them. "Ye're taking him to his death—and we could save him. Only we!"

Jim felt a sinking feeling. Apparently the fear he thought he had infused in them by mentioning the Latin name of the potato blight was losing its terrors. He looked forward and saw that the end of their way out from among the crowd had now been closed off; and the vagabonds on each side were moving in. The voices around him rose in tone until they were in the center of a clamoring group and steel was showing on every hand.

"Forward!" ordered Jim grimly.

Up front, Theoluf echoed the command; and the men-at-arms drew their own swords.

The crowd closed in. They were forced to halt. Theoluf turned to Jim for orders.

"Cut your way through if necessary!" shouted Jim.

But—before they could move, a sound rang out that froze everybody as they stood.

It was the silvery peal of a trumpet. Not the mere raucous voice of a cowhorn, or even one fitted with a sounding nipple, but the pure note from the kind of rare musical instrument that was made of metal and used only by such as royal heralds and important officers of the King.

It cried from the edge of the woods, a little to the right of where Jim and his small group had been heading. Looking, Jim saw three figures on horseback. One, slighter than the rest, bore a staff with a forked pennon on it and was just taking a bronze trumpet from the lips beneath his lifted visor. He was all in armor, fourteenth-century style, which was a combination of chain and plate.

On the other side of the central one of three was a short, but broad, figure in the same type of armor, also with a forked pennon; but in this case the pennon was attached to the lance sitting upright in its socket attached to his saddle. In between was a tall figure with its visor down, wearing full plate armor—something very rarely seen. As Jim watched, the center figure raised its visor; and a voice that was familiar to Jim echoed out over the crowd.

"In the King's name!"

CHAPTER 5

❧

The openly waved swords and knives of the vagabonds had disappeared suddenly. Jim released Friar Morel, who jumped down and ran to join the vagabonds at the cottage door. The friar gone, Jim reined his horse about and rode directly toward the three figures on horseback, and the rest of his small group followed him.

The vagabonds scrambled aside, abruptly silent. Even Elly's voice was still.

As Jim got closer he recognized the shorter, wider figure—and the figure just then raised the visor of his helmet, revealing the luxuriant curling blond mustache and magnificent nose of Sir Giles de Mer.

It was the same Sir Giles that Jim, with Sir Brian and Dafydd ap Hywel, the Welsh archer, had just spent a month visiting at the de Mer Castle, up by the Scottish border. Jim stared a little to see the smiling face of the other man. Giles must have been almost at the heels of Jim, Brian and Dafydd all during their long trip home, if the short knight was here now. If that was the case, though, how had he managed to pick up his two companions?

The armored figure with the trumpet was clearly a squire. The tall figure in plate armor Jim had already identified. He was as clearly in command; not only here, but of whatever military force was out of sight behind him in the trees of the forest.

The military force could only be assumed to be there. But the virtual certainty of that, plus the trumpet blast and the sounding of the King's name, was enough to immediately change the attitude of the vagabonds. It would be good Norman practice to hang them all from the nearest trees, on principle; and well the crowd knew it.

Jim rode up to the central figure and stopped.

"Happily met again, Sir John!" he said. "I'd be glad to see Giles again, in any case; but the sight of you makes it doubly welcome. Can I take it that you'll be coming back with us to Malencontri, for whatever sort of poor entertainment my castle affords?"

"It was there I was headed originally, Sir James," answered Sir John Chandos. Famous as he was, the man seated on a tall and powerful roan war horse before Jim had refused all offers of higher rank; and insisted on remaining merely a knight-banneret, like Brian and Giles. But the lean, regular features spoke of power and command, without any need for titles or blazonry.

He smiled, now, looking at Angie.

"Can I take it that this is Lady Angela, your fair wife?" he said. "Not only you, but she, has been spoken of at court."

Jim looked at Angie and could almost swear that there was a trace of a blush on her face for a second.

"I can only hope they speak well of me, Sir John," she murmured.

"Be sure they do," the knight answered. He looked back at Jim, lowering his voice. "Those ruffians behind you know it not, but there are only the three of us. Perhaps we should move out as quickly as possible."

"Absolutely, Sir John!" said Jim fervently. "Will you do us the honor to lead?"

"Let us say we will ride in company; and, with your permission, Sir James, perhaps the Lady Angela will agree to accompany me," said Sir John, bringing his horse forward and turning it about to line it up on the other side of Angie. "Will you do me the courtesy to follow with Sir James, then, Sir Giles?"

"Gladly!" said Giles. "And glad I am to see you again, James!"

"And I you," answered Jim.

Giles and Jim, with Chandos's squire following alongside
Theoluf, and the mounted men-at-arms behind, turned their
horses around and led off into the woods, cutting back on an
angle into the track that acted as a road between the Castle
Malencontri and the Tinkling Water. As the shade of the trees
fell upon them, the men-at-arms resheathed their swords. A
moment later, the wood had swallowed them up.

"How did you happen to appear just when we needed you?"
Jim asked Giles.

"The answer could hardly be simpler, James," answered
Giles. "Sir John and I reached the edge of your domain.
There we found a plowman who told us that you had just
left for this place called The Tinkling Water. He gave us
directions to get here; but faith, they were hardly needed. It
was a short distance and a straight one."

"I hadn't expected to see you again so soon, Giles," said
Jim.

"There are sad things afoot, James," said Sir John, but
without turning his head. Obviously he had been listening,
even while keeping up a conversation with Angie. "But let
us not talk about them until we are safely in your castle and
can speak privily among ourselves."

He did turn his head now, to look at Giles; who was riding
directly behind him.

"Giles," said the older knight, "I would you not speak to
Sir James of it, either; until we can be secret in our talk."

"Certainly, if you wish it so, Sir John," said Giles.

He turned a cheerful face to Jim.

"I wagered you would not expect to see me so soon!" he
said to Jim. "I had agreed with Brian to come down for the
Christmas holidays, but not until then. Will you not be at the
Earl's Christmas too, James?"

"That depends," answered Jim.

The truth of the matter was that he had dodged as much
as possible those Christmas festivities, which both Brian and
Giles clearly loved. They consisted of childish games, dangerous sports and a great deal of trying to get somebody else's
wife in bed with you—with, on top of all this, a tremendous
amount of food and alcoholic drink to be consumed. None of
these things were particularly attractive to Jim.

On the other hand, it was socially desirable that he and
Angie show up eventually. He was still trying to think of

a good excuse that would allow them to dodge it, this year, too.

The thought made him pay attention with half an ear to what was going on ahead of him. There, Sir John, in the best of courtly manners, was devoting all his attention to flattering, and—in a word—politely going through the motions of seducing Angie. Angie seemed to be fielding his courtesies fairly well; but Jim found his admiration for the other knight at war with his resentment at such advances being paid to his wife under his very nose. Yet, here, this was a common and accepted occurrence.

But there was nothing he could do about it; and no immediate danger as long as they were all on horseback riding back to the castle. His hope was that Sir John was gentleman enough merely to play at the game, without trying to push it through to its logical conclusion. The instinctive feeling in him was that Sir John was, indeed, that sort. But he could not be sure; and his instinct did not completely relieve his anxieties on the subject.

Meanwhile, Giles was chattering away to him.

"—What ails the Mage, think you?" Giles was asking. "Though I had the honor of meeting him only briefly in France and up at our castle, I would be sad indeed to hear that he had been brought low by anything serious—or indeed dangerous to his life."

"I think he's just been overdosed with medicines, that's all," said Jim, a little more shortly than he intended, because his attentions were still on Angie and Sir John. He made an effort to pull them back to Giles, and smooth out his voice.

"There were two women back there who call themselves 'nurses,'" he went on. "They generally do midwifery and tend sick people around their neighborhood, I guess. I don't think they were really, seriously, in league with that rabble you saw outside. They were simply cramming one medicine after another down Carolinus because that was their way. But the end of that sort of treatment in his case could only be that he would die—he's an old man, after all—and they had to know that. Then the magic wards on his house and everything around Tinkling Water would be gone with his death; and the nurses as well as the vagabonds looked forward to finding good plunder inside that little house of his."

"What sort of plunder?" asked Giles.

"I don't know," said Jim. "Probably there are some ordinary valuables there, in the shape of jewels and things like that—or even some money. But the real values would be in Carolinus's tools, such as his scrying glass and other things that could be resold to younger magicians who needed them. Altogether, they'd probably have found enough inside the cottage to make getting in well worthwhile. But if we can take Carolinus safely back to the castle, keep him warm and comfortable, and feed him on some wholesome food of the sort he needs, I think he may come out of it all right."

"Now, that is right good to hear!" said Giles. "I said I had never met him until we were in France; but like the rest of the world, I have heard of him. He is spoken of as one of the great magicians; not merely of our time, but of all time."

"I believe that," said Jim sincerely. "Now I've got to know him."

They went at a walk, to spare Carolinus as much jolting in his horseback-carried litter as possible. But even at that they were back at Malencontri Castle in a very short time. As they pulled their mounts to a stop in the courtyard, the column of their movement disintegrated into a close body; and stable hands came running.

"If you would be so kind, Sir James," said Chandos as they all dismounted, "would you send for the good Sir Brian Neville-Smythe, the bowman and the wolf who joined you in France last year? I would like them to join us as well."

"Theoluf!" said Jim, looking over at his squire. "Would you send immediately to Castle de Chaney—or wherever—and have Sir Brian made acquainted with the fact the most honorable knight, Sir John Chandos, is guesting with us here; and would like to speak with him right away?"

"Yes, m'Lord," answered Theoluf and turned to one of the men-at-arms who had been their escorts and began giving him directions.

"—And send a carrier pigeon to Dafydd. Sir John wants him, too. Now get these people who have no business down here out of the courtyard, will you?" added Jim. "We'll have the whole castle down here next."

Indeed, there was real danger of that. The people of the castle, all those who could contrive any excuse at all to get away from their work and come out, were gaping at Sir John Chandos. They did not recognize him, of course—he lived in a different world than theirs—but they were fascinated by the plate armor, of which they had all heard but which none of their rank, of course, had ever seen; it being restricted to Kings, high nobility and other both wealthy and noble personages at this time in history—a very rare thing to behold, indeed.

The castle blacksmith, in fact, had drawn so close to the fascinatingly shaped solid metal that he was almost in amongst them. Jim glared at him, and the man backed off with a mumbled, "Sorry, m'Lord." But he did not go back to his forge, where one of the plowmen was waiting impatiently to have a horseshoe finished.

"As for the wolf, Sir John," said Jim, turning back to the older knight, "I will do what I can, but he can be any place; and there is no telling whether he would come if asked or not. He is a very independent creature."

"So I understand." Sir John smiled. "It is a characteristic of wolves, they tell me. Still, will you do what you may? Meanwhile, I wonder if you would join me and Sir Giles in some privy place for a discussion of the matter that's occasioned this visit. I will just say a word or two now, until Sir Brian and, hopefully, the wolf arrive, then leave Sir Giles to fill you in on the rest, while perhaps—"

He glanced over to meet the gaze of Angie.

"—Lady Angela would be good enough to show me about your castle." He smiled winsomely at her. "We military captains are always interested in fortifications."

"I'm afraid showing you around will have to wait a little while, Sir John," said Angie crisply. "I—and I think m'Lord should come with me—must see to Carolinus first. It'll be necessary to make sure he's decently bedded down in a clean room; and provided with those who will care for him. After that, maybe you and I can do a tour of the castle."

"How could I object to such a sense of duty?" said Sir John. "I accept being overruled. By all means, I must confess the seriousness of the Mage's case had slipped my mind. Indeed, he must be taken care of first, and with all necessary effort and time. My business can wait."

"Thank you, Sir John," said Jim. "I'll go along with Angie, then. I'll join you as soon as Carolinus is settled."

By this time Theoluf had managed to chase most of the idlers out of the courtyard, except those who had at least a passable excuse for being there. Jim and Angie headed the procession in through the front door of the castle to its Great Hall. They headed toward the Hall's inner end; where, on a low dais, the high table sat cross-wise to the lower table which ran the length of the room.

To Jim's surprise, the high table was not empty, although with both himself and Angie absent, he knew of no one in the castle with the rank enough to be seated there. But as they got closer he recognized the stout, half-armored figure seated at the high table with a pitcher—undoubtedly of wine—and a cup before him.

This figure bounced to his feet as Jim approached the dais with the rest of the company.

"Two cows! Two fine, young milk cows!" shouted the figure. It was, Jim saw, Sir Hubert Whitby, another neighbor of his. By the time Whitby had finished shouting, Jim was close enough for him to speak in a normal voice; but the other knight did not. Sir Hubert never let pass an opportunity for shouting. It was simply a habit of his.

He continued, at close to the top of his voice.

"It's your dragons who've done it!" he roared. "Nothing left but horns and a scrap of bone or so, not even the hides, and a lot of torn-up, bloody dirt. It's your dragons, I say! You've got to make them stop it—and pay me back for those two cows!"

"They're not my dragons," said Jim in the most reasonable voice he could manage. He had found that nothing lowered Sir Hubert's voice down as effectively as being spoken to softly. The other was not the tallest knight thereabout, and even standing below the dais Jim was almost eye to eye with him. Jim went on. "Besides, there isn't one of them that'd do anything I ordered him or her to. They're as independent as we humans. What makes you think—"

He was about to go on and ask Sir Hubert why the other thought that he, Jim, should bear any responsibility at all even if the dragons were doing it, when he heard something like the faint husk of a breath from Carolinus in the litter, and looking down saw the old man had his eyes open.

Once Jim's eyes were on him Carolinus's head moved slightly from left to right and back again in an undeniable shake of the head.

"All right," said Jim in his most conciliatory manner, "I'll see what can be done. Meanwhile, let me introduce you to our honorable guests."

He turned to the plate armored figure just behind him.

"Sir John," he said to it, "this is the good knight Sir Hubert Whitby, a close neighbor of mine." He turned back to Sir Hubert. "Sir Hubert, may I introduce the most noble and famous Sir John Chandos, who has come to pay us a short visit here at Malencontri."

Sir Hubert's jaw dropped. He had plump, reddish cheeks, gray-to-white eyebrows that were very bushy, some more white hairs sprouting out of his nose. There was also at least a day's white stubble of beard on his face. The hair on his head covered all the scalp there, but was also turning from gray to white. Altogether he would have made a potentially good Santa Claus; if he had only looked genial instead of outraged, as he did most of the time—his favorite occupation being to find something to get angry about, corner someone and bellow about it.

"Sir—Sir John?" he stammered now. "Sir John Chandos? I—er—forgive me, sir, for seeming somewhat annoyed—"

His voice had dropped—not exactly to a cooing level, but as close as a voice entirely unused to simpering politeness could come—

"Perhaps we could talk further—" he was continuing. He was looking at Jim. But Jim had had enough of Whitbyness. He'd be damned if he gave Sir Hubert the dinner invitation for which the other was obviously angling.

"If you'll forgive us, Hubert," he said, "we have to look after Carolinus, now. After that, Sir John, Sir Giles and myself were looking forward to a private chat—just the three of us. I'll get in touch with you about your cows in a few days."

"But—but—" Sir Hubert was stammering. He could hardly go into an explosion over Jim's lack of neighborly hospitality with Sir John Chandos there. In any case, Jim, with Angie and the men carrying the litter, had begun to move toward the tower entrance and the rooms above, one of which could be made over into a place for Carolinus.

As the little cavalcade carrying Carolinus left the others behind, they passed the end of the high table and Jim reached out to snatch up the kettle. He was careful to grasp it by the wooden handle, because the rest of it was as hot as ever, keeping the water within it on the boil.

"Now what do you want that for?" asked Angie, as they left the Great Hall for the serving room, where dishes from the outside kitchen were brought to be served at the proper time, and began to start up the circular staircase to the floors above where the private rooms were.

Jim felt stubborn.

"I just think it'll be happier in the same room with Carolinus, that's all," he said, staring straight ahead at the stairs as they mounted them.

"Oh, for heaven's sake!" said Angie. "You're treating that thing as if it was alive. You can't seriously think that a kettle has feelings, even a magic kettle!"

"Well, I do," said Jim, still staring straight ahead. "I can't tell you why—maybe it's because I've been dealing with magic myself—but I just feel it's going to be happier in the same room next to Carolinus, keeping itself ready, as it always has, in case he calls for it to provide boiling water for a cup of tea."

Angie sighed, and fell silent.

They laid Carolinus down gently at last on the bed in the one small room Angie always insisted be kept furnished and ready, dusted and cleaned for a chance late-night traveler. Once the old magician was laid down there, Angie ruthlessly stripped off his night gown, and they saw that he had acquired several bad bed sores, which was not surprising considering the care he had been getting.

"May Heather," said Angie, decisively; for the youngest member of the kitchen staff had been picked up as they went through the serving room to act as a general messenger for whatever they should need once they had Carolinus settled, "fetch me Margot, Edwina, and Mary. Tell them to start some cloths to boiling for bandages and bring me some fresh lard that hasn't been touched, as well as a couple of the clean kitchen buckets full of the boiling water that should be ready there at all times. If it isn't, I'm going to have somebody's hide!"

She turned on the men-at-arms.

"One of you stay here," she commanded. "The others can take off."

They went.

She looked at Jim.

"You might as well take off too, Jim. Get back down to

your guests. I just wanted to tell you—be polite, but keep them away from this room. Carolinus needs rest, most of all. I've got a lot to do here, and you can't help. Carolinus is going to have to be washed and those bed sores paid some attention to. Now, everybody, off you go!"

Off they went—including Jim.

As he went back down the stairs by himself, he found himself puzzling a little over his feeling of empathy toward the kettle. Perhaps Angie was right and it was simply foolish of him. On the other hand, possibly there was something to what he had said without really thinking—that his exposure and involvement in magic had caused him to see magicked things in a new light. He would ask Carolinus, as soon as the other was well enough for questions.

He shied away from the possibility that Carolinus might never be available for those questions. That thought came to him belatedly, and left him with a cold feeling. Life here in this alternate, magical world, without Carolinus, brusque and irritable as the old Mage was most of the time, would be unthinkable.

Jim put the thought from him; and found his mind occupied with another question. It must have taken a great effort on Carolinus's part a short while ago when they were down in the Great Hall to open his eyes and signal Jim, even as slightly as he had done it, not to get into a discussion with Sir Hubert about Sir Hubert's cows and the dragons.

Why Carolinus should not want him to do this was another question. Something serious was going on. Carolinus saw, heard and knew a great many things about what was going on in the world; even though he seemed almost never to leave his cottage. If Carolinus was concerned, there was probably good reason for Jim to be concerned also.

The cold feeling in Jim's stomach, which had gone away with his stern dismissal of the idea that Carolinus might not recover, returned to him and stayed until he got back to the high table in the Hall; at which he found both Giles and Sir John Chandos seated with cups and jugs of wine, chatting. They were seated close together, Chandos at the very end of the table and Sir Giles on the back side, half facing him.

"Hah, Sir James," said Chandos, breaking off his words to Giles as Jim sat down next to the other knight. "It's good to have you back this quickly. I was afraid our friend the.

magician might occupy you for some time. Perhaps now we could find a place where we can discuss matters of import."

"How private do you need it, Sir John?" asked Jim, running his mind over the available places in the castle. Establishments like his in the fourteenth century were not over-supplied with rooms available for private talks; unless one was kept specifically for that purpose.

The servants were used to walking into any room, except Jim and Angie's, without warning; and few doors had bolts. What few private rooms there were, were either in use or thoroughly dirty, and crammed to the ceiling with everything from weapons to broken furniture. One of these now would already, at Angie's orders, be in process of clearing, cleaning and furnishing as a bedroom for Sir John and Giles.

So there was really only that one place available for what Sir John needed, Jim thought with an inaudible sigh—now that Carolinus had taken over the visitor's room.

"There's the solar," he went on, "which is the room Lady Angela and I keep for ourselves. Suppose we move up there?"

CHAPTER 6

"You must forgive me," said Sir John Chandos, some minutes later, "for coming on you thus unannounced and requiring the use of your personal chamber. But there are reasons."

"Not at all," said Jim. "You're welcome to anything I have."

It was the truth. He thought highly of Chandos. At the same time, as he sat with Sir John and Giles in the solar chamber that had been his and Angie's private territory alone—except for the intrusions of the servants occasionally to clean or even possibly bring them something to eat—he could not help feeling a mild sense of violation.

Into this room alone, they had allowed some touches of the comforts of the twentieth century to creep. The chairs he and Sir John sat in had not only backrests and armrests, but were padded in a fair imitation of twentieth-century furniture; and the stool that Sir Giles sat on, although it was like any other stool that might be found around a medieval castle, also had a padded seat and a backrest.

It was not a great space, but it had been solely Angie's and his; a place where, in a way, they could escape from this parallel, fourteenth-century world, which—as much as they liked it and however much they remained firm in the idea of spending the rest of their lives in it—was not what they had grown up with and come to take for granted. As long as it was his and Angie's, it had been that private place. Now it was no longer.

"—But I must explain," went on Sir John, unheeding, "that what I have to say to you deals with matters of the utmost secrecy."

Sir Giles could hardly echo this pledge, as he might have with someone else of lesser renown, but Jim saw—out of eyeshot of the elderly knight—his friend nod vigorously so that the ends of his heavy, but silky, mustache waved.

"I must say, though," went on Sir John, with a smile, "but you do seem to attract the troubles of this kingdom the way a steeple attracts lightning, Sir James. Beyond that I have no more on that subject to say. I will tell you of our current troubles."

"Whatever you will, Sir John," said Jim.

"Thank you, m'Lord," said Chandos. "Well, to begin with, I learned by methods, knowledge of which must remain mine alone, of your visit to Sir Giles up at the Scottish border. I would naturally be interested in the two of you getting together; but even more than that was the fact that you, yourself would be on the Scottish border. It seemed to me inevitable that up there you must be drawn into the matter of the possible Scottish invasion of England, timed to coincide with one from France. And so it proved to be true; as I discovered after arriving at the Castle de Mer very shortly after you had left."

Jim nodded.

"I explained matters to Sir Giles," continued Sir John, "and Sir Giles set out with me immediately. We had hoped to overtake you. But since we did not know the exact route you would return home, we went somewhat astray and I only caught up with you finally in that moment in which you saw me, near the magician's cottage."

"And very glad I was to see you, Sir John," said Jim.

"Thank you, m'Lord," said Sir John, "but our aid was a trick—a paltry trick at that. Nonetheless, the circumstances required it; and it had its effect in allowing us all to come away easily and be together here now."

"But why search me out this way?" asked Jim. "I'd think you might have sent for me from London, from the King's palace for that matter—"

Sir John waved a dismissive hand.

"It is impossible to speak at court without fear of being overheard. For that matter," he said, "it would be impossible for us to speak anywhere in London or in any other place where I am well known, without the danger of others listening."

Jim nodded. This was only too understandable. His own castle had no safe place for keeping secrets either—except for a few rare exceptions like this solar and the privately occupied rooms—like the one that would be Carolinus's.

"At the Castle de Mer, or here in yours of Malencontri," Chandos continued, "I can feel more sure that our words will not be carried away to do us harm. Even if they were passed on merely in idle, innocent gossip, by a servant. To begin with, I must honor you for your good work with the Hollow Men and the frustration of the Scottish intent to invade. The word that reaches me is that the Scottish Crown has abandoned that idea for the moment, completely."

"I'm glad to hear it," murmured Jim.

"As am I," said Sir John. "Nonetheless, while it was a great achievement, it did not solve all the troubles that face us. King Jean was still determined in spite of all to move an army across the Channel; such as had not been done since King William invaded and defeated the Saxons that then held this land. I am unhappy to tell you that his French Majesty still holds to that intention."

"You think a French invasion's still a serious possibility?" Jim said, thinking of the problems faced by the Germans under Hitler, in Jim's own twentieth century, to invade across the Channel waters.

"The danger is there," said Sir John, "if he can land an army. True, the Channel is not all that easy to cross, particularly with craft loaded with fighting men and horses and other articles of war. But, there is word that he may have assistance from some source outside our knowledge."

"Source?" echoed Jim. Giles looked solemn.

"Yes," said Chandos. "What source it could be puzzles us. The Lowlanders would not choose to be of any assistance to him, nor would they of Sweden and Norway. No, our information hints at something beyond this. Something that may make his invasion almost certain."

"How sure is all this?" asked Jim.

Sir John looked grim.

"At the present moment," he said, "boats are building and men mustering on the shores of Normandy and Brittany, notably at Brest and Calais, to make such an invasion."

"You mean," said Jim, a little incredulously, "he's persisting in this idea of invading all by himself? No matter how many men he brings in, he'd have all England against him!"

"All England?" Sir John smiled a little sadly. "True, every Englishman will fight; from the King himself down to the lowest serf, once French invaders ride onto their own land. Attacked in their homes, they will fight. Or, our people of gentle blood and others who have the training for war will cheerfully muster to a levy. It's the second of these, that French King Jean expects mainly to contend with—"

"It's beaten him before—" said Jim. "At Crécy and Poitiers."

"True," said Chandos, "but such a levy, called by the King, gathers men swiftly—men of all ranks and weapons—but they are held together by law for only forty days. After that they're free to return home. Now, look you, this invasion threatens; but no man knows when it will come. If an English host be mustered and held in readiness, it must be fed and cared for while it waits. That will be a great expense. Also, no man knows the day it might come; not even King Jean himself; because he must wait on the proper winds. You see the problem?"

"I think so," said Jim, thoughtfully but a little doubtfully.

"There is great danger that a levy will be pulled together, but will wait their forty days with no invasion made; and start to return home—and what force is there to stop them if they do this? What arguments will sway them except immediate pay for the extra days?"

"True," said Giles, as Chandos paused. "They will see the summer advancing, they will see harvest time approaching; and feel the call of their own fields and their own home duties."

"Yes," said Chandos. "But for King Jean's soldiers it is otherwise."

"Otherwise?" echoed Jim. "Why?"

"Because our English royal purse is not over-heavy at the moment. Indeed, it is more often empty than full, and our King and his Court live on promises, rather than ready coin," said

Chandos, "while King Jean has a deep pocket. France trades south and east; and taxes flow back to him."

"That is true," put in Giles. "—Er, pardon me, Sir John."

"Not at all," answered Chandos. "I wish both of you to speak freely as you will, in this matter. But to go on—also, there are many French nobles willing to pledge large amounts toward such an adventure as this invasion. Bear in mind, they pledge not for the love of their King himself. They pledge it for the adventure of it; and the lands they may win in England. You know our knights. In France they are likewise!"

"Indeed, I do," said Jim. And indeed he did after three years now of living side by side with them. The noble class lived to fight. This was one of the problems during the long winters. There was a limit to eating and drinking, and even to sex, that made the warrior class long to be out doing what they had been taught to do since childhood, exchanging blows with their enemies.

"So," said Chandos, "it is necessary I learn, as soon as possible, what this unknown help is that King Jean expects, that he goes on building for invasion so confidently and expensively. I have had experience with yourself and Sir Giles before, Sir James, in the matter of the rescue of our Royal Prince from France. Since then, if anything, I have come to value you even more. I would that the two of you go to France quietly and under different names; swiftly as possible, and find out for me what this other force is."

There was silence in the solar. Angie, Jim was thinking sarcastically, would love the idea of his leaving again, so soon.

"Well, Sir John," he said, "I'll have to speak of my leaving with my Lady-wife. Would you and Sir Giles care to move down to the Great Hall and have a few cups of wine while I see about other duties? Then we can all gather there for supper."

"Of course. At your service, m'Lord," said Chandos smoothly. He got to his feet.

They had all discarded their armor and weapons once they were in the solar; and Chandos's lay in an untidy heap in one corner. Like most knights of his time, he simply dropped things he took off, confident that sooner or later some servant would come along to bring them to wherever he would need them next—in this case to the room that would be prepared for him and Giles.

"I quite understand that this is not a matter on which you can give me an answer immediately. Will you join me, then, Sir Giles?"

"Willingly, Sir John," said Giles.

All three of them left the solar; and Jim went with the other two to the high table in the Great Hall. There he left them, to give orders that their armor be taken to their room as soon as that was ready. Then he headed out on an errand of his own.

Outside, it was already twilight. In the woods it would be dark, and getting darker. He picked up a man-at-arms along the way.

"Amyth," he told him, "fetch two torches of bound twigs and bring them to me. I'll be waiting at the front gate."

"Yes, m'Lord," answered Amyth. He was a hard-bitten man in his early thirties with a sallow face and lank black hair.

He left at a run and caught up with Jim at the front gate, carrying not only the torches, but armed and wearing his steel cap.

They headed out together across the open space around the castle, into the woods, with Jim leading. He saw that the reddish sun was already almost behind the tops of the trees. It seemed to descend into them as they got closer to the woods; and the upper branches of these seemed to rise blackly to block the last light of day.

Glancing at Amyth beside him, one bundle of twigs fastened to his belt, the other in his hand but unlit, Jim saw that the man's face was more pale than usual. Once upon a time this would have puzzled Jim. It no longer did. To these people the darkness was full of dangers running from the real to the unknown and horrible.

There was always the chance of dangerous animals, stumbled across in the dark—boar or bear. But the real fear was of any number of all sorts of supernatural beings, night-trolls, ghosts, monsters of unknown kind and variety, lying in wait for the evening traveler.

Alone, Amyth would have been very unwilling to venture into the evening woods, even with a torch. But with his feudal Lord, a magician, behind him, the man's fear was allayed—almost.

You never could tell what was in the darkness.

Underneath the trees it was already the beginnings of night. They stopped and Amyth set the first of his torches afire with a pinch of tinder, flint and steel. He held it up as they went forward; and immediately its light made the darkness darker around them, so that they seemed to travel in a globe of flickering, yellow illumination, while on every side of them tree trunks, rocks and bushes loomed up unexpectedly out of the darkness, were passed, and left behind.

It was, Jim had to admit, eerie enough—even to him, since he knew that, at least in this alternate Earth, there were indeed beings besides animals that they could encounter. They were not, strictly speaking, supernatural beings. They belonged to that group of creatures Carolinus called "Naturals."

But most were not particularly dangerous to an armed man, like the man-at-arms at his side, holding the torch high and glancing fearfully around as they went. Many of them, like the dryads, were actually friendly or harmless to human beings. There were, indeed, night-trolls, and a large, mature one of these could be a threat, perhaps; since they were easily the weight of a full-grown man and equipped with dangerous teeth and nails. But that was the extent of it.

The Naturals were somewhere in between humans and the natural forces of this world. They were credited with owning magic by those like the man-at-arms beside him. But they really had only what might be called a single more-than-human talent apiece, which they could turn on and off, like a dog wagging its tail—but that was the extent of their abilities.

In fact, as Carolinus had pointed out, Naturals were completely incapable of doing real magic. Only normal living creatures could do this; and of normal living creatures, the only ones who had the ability and were interested were humans—and pretty rare humans at that, Jim had gathered. Most of the people of this world were like Aargh, the wolf, who saw no good in the ability to do magic; and would just as soon not have anything to do with it.

The only difference was that Aargh was not afraid of the dark, while the man-at-arms with him was.

Thinking of all this had brought Jim's attention to the fact that a small wind was working its way through the woods. They must have encountered it also in the cleared space between the castle and the first of the trees; but until now, Jim at least had paid no attention to it.

Now he was aware of its passage among the tree limbs, evidenced by soft moaning sounds that seemed to approach them from several sides at once. It was only a wind, and Jim himself was not—he told himself—in the least superstitious; but certainly the situation was one that was not exactly comforting.

However, they were almost to their goal. It was less than a five-minute walk into the woods; and even as he thought this, they reached it.

It was the stump of a young elm sapling, broken off about four feet above the ground and dead. A crack ran down the center of it. Jim and Amyth halted before it, and Jim reached into one of the inner pockets of his doublet. It was one of the inside pockets that Angie herself had sewn there, in most unmedieval fashion, to give him the convenience of carrying things unobviously. This world was still in the stage of carrying most articles in bags or purses, which were usually attached to belt or shoulder strap.

From the pocket he drew a piece of red-dyed cloth fourteen inches long and about four inches wide. He tied this around the top of the elm stump, wedging a part of it firmly into a crack in the top of the stump, so that it could not simply be blown loose.

"Now," he said to the man-at-arms, "we back off a few steps. I'm going to work a little magic—"

Looking at the man, he saw stark fear suddenly depicted on the other man's face. It was bad enough to be in these woods at night. But to be around the working of magic, even done by his own Lord, was pushing Amyth's courage to the limit.

"Light the other torch," said Jim compassionately, "and leave me the one you've got. Then you can back away."

"Thank you, m'Lord," Amyth said, relieved.

The man's teeth were literally chattering. He got the second torch alight and went off. Jim was a little amused to see that he went as far away as he could without being lost to sight in the trees, a good thirty yards or so. Jim could see the light of his torch; but that was all. Jim turned back to the stump.

Taking the original torch, which was about three-quarters burnt down, Jim backed off from the stump himself, but only about four paces. In spite of his C rating with the Accounting Office—which Carolinus had got that high by sheer threat of withdrawing his own account—Jim knew how little he was of a real magician. But he was slowly learning more.

He had been able to give it more study during this last winter; and been amazed at how much there was to be learned. It was something like mathematics, he thought now. As you moved up from arithmetic to algebra and on into the higher mathematics, the solution to a problem became a more complicated statement. In the case of magic, that translated into something more than the one-line commands he had been using most of the time—and would probably still go on using when possible.

The fact was the one-line commands had been the final line of magic so elementary that the final line was all that was needed. But in this particular case, there were things to be stated before that line.

Luckily, there was a certain amount of freedom in the way he could build the earlier parts of the command. All that was needed here was some sort of chant to use. He would chant it as he paced out a ward, a protective circle around the stick; so that only Aargh, the wolf—for whom it was intended— himself, and Angie, could come close to it.

What Jim needed was essentially the same kind of ward Carolinus had used to protect his house from the vagabonds. He thought for a moment and then summoned up out of his memory the lines that began Alfred Noyes's poem *The Highwayman*.

He began to pace out a circle about the stump, intoning the first lines of the poem. It was too bad he had to speak loud enough so that Amyth, in spite of his moving back, would hear him; and probably have his fears intensified. But that was the only way wards could be commanded into existence—at least as far as he understood, from the book titled *Encyclopedie Necromantick*, which Carolinus had made him swallow in taking him on as apprentice. Probably someone of Carolinus's ability could set up a ward silently; but Jim could not, at least so far.

He chanted:

"The wind was a torrent of darkness among the gusty trees,
The moon was a ghostly galleon tossed upon cloudy seas,
The road was a ribbon of moonlight over the purple moor
*   and the Highwayman came riding—riding—riding—*
The Highwayman came riding, up to the old inn door . . ."

To these words he added some of his own:

> " . . . *So shall this ward keep all without,*
> *Until Aargh, Angie or I'm about."*

It was pretty bad poetry; and he had needed to stretch out the last two lines, to come to the end of his chant just as he completed the circle. At that moment, however, there was an interruption—but it came too late to keep him from completing a spell.

It was a scream from behind him.

He whirled about and held his torch high; but the light it threw showed him nothing. Cursing the man-at-arms for finally giving in to his night-fears, Jim stalked toward where Amyth's torch still burned.

—Just then it dawned on him that it was lower down than it should be. When he reached it, he saw why. It was lying on the ground, burning with difficulty only on its uppermost side. Beside it lay Amyth's naked sword. But of Amyth, himself, there was no sign.

CHAPTER 7

❧

"Oh, by the way," said Jim to Yves Mortain, the chief man-at-arms, when he returned to the castle, "I've sent Amyth off with a special message. He'll be gone several weeks. Keep the matter to yourself as much as possible, will you?"

"Yes, m'Lord," replied Yves.

The scar-faced man's answer was perfectly automatic and obedient, but he looked at Jim penetratingly; and Jim had a strong feeling that Yves was puzzled and curious. A touch of anger kindled in Jim. If any other medieval lord had told his chief man-at-arms something, that man-at-arms would simply have accepted it. Yves's reaction was one more bit of evidence that Jim kept slipping in his efforts to act like a true knight and a Baron.

He was always forgetting it was not the twentieth century, and treating his inferiors as if there was no difference between him and them. A lot of those on his land, consequently, had begun to react in very unmedieval fashion, as if they were in a position to question him about what he said. Well, he said to himself, what he had just told Yves was what he had told him—and Yves could make the best of it.

Jim stalked off.

All the same, he thought, it was a good thing he had smuggled Amyth's sword up into the solar, before any of the other men-at-arms saw and recognized it. He refused to think at the moment what might have snatched Amyth away. Nothing small, at any rate.

At this point he reached the serving room, toward which he had been headed. This was the room in which the dishes were held after being brought from the kitchen, which was necessarily outside the castle, so that its wooden structure, if it caught fire, should not also set fire to the rest of the castle. This room was presided over by a fortyish, stout, and rather stern woman named Gwynneth Plyseth, and she curtsied at the sight of him.

"Gwynneth," he said, "I'll be joining Sir Giles, and our other guest Sir John, at the high table. As soon as Lady Angela can join the rest of us, serving of dinner can begin. Will you send a message to the kitchen about that; and another message off to tell Lady Angela the rest of us are waiting?"

"Yes, m'Lord," said Gwynneth, bobbing again.

Jim left and went back into the Great Hall and the high table.

"Oh, by the way," he said to Sir John as he sat down, "I haven't had time to speak to my wife yet. If you wouldn't mind not mentioning this trip to France for the moment . . ."

Sir John smiled.

"Not at all, Sir James," he said. "These things take time, as I know from my experience with my own Lady-wife. I'm in no hurry. I would gladly spend a day or two with you, taking advantage of your interesting company and that of Sir Giles, to say nothing of that of Lady Angela, herself."

"Er—yes," said Jim. He was still a little disturbed by Sir John's attention to Angie; and not too sure that the knight did not intend a further intimacy than Jim would have found comfortable.

"Drink some wine, James," said Giles, pushing in front of Jim a cup he had just filled from his pitcher.

"Oh, by the way," said Jim, late that evening, some little time after he and Angie had gone to bed and they were both relaxed and happy, "Sir John would like Giles and me to take a quick trip over to France; to look at what's going on in the way of getting ready for an invasion the French King is evidently at work on."

Jim felt Angie stiffen under the coverings beside him.

"Go to France?" Angie echoed slowly and icily. "When?"

"Well," said Jim, as lightly as he could, "he was talking about our going pretty much right away—just a short trip, you understand—"

He broke off, for Angie had sat upright in the bed, spilling bedcovers off both herself and Jim; and had begun to pound on his chest with both fists.

"Ouch!" said Jim, catching her arms to stop her from continuing to do this. "You've put on more muscle while we've been here than you realize."

"I wish I had twice as much!" shouted Angie furiously. "You're not going!"

"But just a short trip—" Jim was beginning.

"No! No! Not for a day! Not for an hour! Not for another minute! You're not leaving! No! No! NO!" she shouted furiously. "*Notgoing!*"

"But let me explain," Jim pleaded, still holding her wrists. "There's danger of an invasion. It could affect us, right here at Malencontri. We could have French soldiers on our land, attacking our castle—"

"I don't care! I don't care!" said Angie. "You just got back from one trip! And who had everything to handle while you were gone? I did. I had to be Lord and Lady too! I had to take care of all the things that you'd let run wild and put a stop to them. I had to order one of the men-at-arms whipped. You wouldn't. You didn't when you should. Yves Mortain came to me and told me that it had to be done. So I had to do it. Because you weren't here to do it. And that's not my duty. It's yours—as Lord of this barony! What if it had been somebody who had to be hung? How do you suppose I'd have felt about that, when it was your job?"

"What had the man-at-arms done?" Jim asked.

"I don't remember. What difference does it make?" demanded Angie. "The point is you weren't here; and here it's the fourteenth century. I've had to handle the castle and lands all alone. I've had to stop the fights between the servants. I've had to rule the serfs and freemen. I've had to make them all work, when they wanted to lie down on the job. I've had to do everything, my job *and* yours! While you've been off, having all sorts of fun no doubt, and never even bothering to think about your castle or your wife! We've hardly had a chance to say hello to each other, except for a few months after Christmas! And that was months ago. Why can't you stay around and take care of your responsibilities? Let alone take care of me. I need a little taking care of, now and then—if it'd ever cross your mind! You're off someplace with all sorts of other women around. You probably don't even think of me!"

"I do too!" said Jim, incensed. "I think of you—at night, at morning, in the daytime, at all sorts of times! I do a lot of thinking about you. It's just that I'm not in a position to get in touch with you and tell you so. I did send you a message by Carolinus that I'd be delayed getting back."

Angie's arms in his grip relaxed slightly, but only slightly.

"You did?" she asked. "Carolinus didn't come to me with any message."

"Maybe he was getting sick already," said Jim. "Oh, by the way, I haven't seen anything of Carolinus, since I left you with him after he'd first been brought in. How's he doing?"

But the effort to change the subject was a sad failure. Angie had pulled her wrists free, lay down again and rolled over on her farther side. Her back was to him. She did not respond; and Jim knew there was no point in repeating his question— or any other for that matter. The Great Wall of Silence had been erected; and at least until some future time—hopefully sometime tomorrow—Angie would not be speaking to him.

Jim sighed. There was a resentment kindling inside him. Certainly, Angie had a point. She had indeed had to carry a double load all the time he had been gone, every time he had been gone. Ideally, he *should* be around this place, twelve months a year. But that was simply not the way this feudal world worked for knights, particularly knights like himself who had picked up an added importance, one way or another. Chandos, he knew, was always on the move, as now, about some business connected with the affairs of the Crown.

The more he thought about it the more his resentment grew. After a moment he got up, dressed and went downstairs. As he had suspected, Sir John and Sir Giles were still at the table talking and drinking. Jim had left them early, on the plea that he had not seen his wife in a long time; and after some jokes that were not much broader than he would have encountered from his male friends in the twentieth century, they had said good night and let him go.

Now, when he returned, they had the good sense not to question him. Giles shoved another full cup of wine in front of him. And **Jim** drank deeply from it.

He continued to drink deeply. In fact, he got drunk. He had a vague memory of being carried up the stairs by a couple of panting servants; and not worrying at all about the fact that one of them might slip and all three, including himself, go plunging off the unguarded side of the stone steps that wound up the circular wall of the tower—down several stories to bloody death.

They even took him clear into the solar, undressed him, put him in bed, and covered him up. All the time this was going on, Angie lay where she was, on the other side of the bed, in complete silence; as if no one was within forty miles of her—including Jim.

This was the last thing he remembered. He woke to a splitting headache, a touch of nausea in the pit of his stomach and light coming through the narrow windows that indicated it was much later in the day than he was used to getting up. Both he and Angie had fallen into the medieval habit of rising with the sun, if not before it. His mouth was dry, he had a terrible thirst—and then he noticed that the bed beside him was empty. Of course, Angie would have gotten up, dressed and left some hours ago.

The thirst was overwhelming. He struggled to his feet and stumbled over to the table holding pitchers of drink, yearning for water. At the last second he remembered that drinking the local water would make him sick. So, carefully averting his head from the smell and sight of the pitcher of wine that was there, he located the pitcher containing small beer and poured some into a cup.

It tasted terrible, but it was wet. For a moment he was not sure that he could keep down what he had just swallowed; then it turned out that he could; and he drank some more. Gradually and thirstily he worked his way down until he had the pitcher almost empty.

He dropped into a chair at the table, with a cup holding the last of the small beer, and tried to pull his wits together. To make the trip to France in the face of Angie's absolute opposition was impossible.

On the other hand, he was in direct fief to the King. He would not be at all surprised—in fact he would be surprised only if the contrary were true—if Sir John was not carrying a paper stamped with the Royal Seal, that put him, with Giles, under Sir John's orders. Sir John would probably prefer not to *order* him to France if he could help it. That was not the way to get the best out of whomever you sent on such a duty. He was trying first to get Jim's agreement to go willingly. Plainly, Giles had already agreed to go.

Jim felt caught between two fires. Two impossibilities. Angie's refusal to let him go; and Sir John's hidden, but doubtless present, authority that could make him go whether he wanted to or not. The worst of all solutions would be for him to let himself be ordered with Angie still persisting in her opposition.

It might be that she would cave in, once she saw that he had no choice. But, knowing Angie, that was no certainty. Also, he would not feel he had the freedom of action in France, if he went there under orders but against Angie's wishes. Only if he went there of his own free will could he be confident of doing as Sir John would expect, as he saw fit in whatever circumstances he faced.

He finished off the last of the small beer. He was still thirsty. But downstairs, there were duties waiting for him that he should have been at several hours ago. He dressed and went down.

The Great Hall, as he had expected, was empty. Judging by the light coming through the window slits here, it must be nine A.M. at least.

Since the thought of breakfast did not appeal to him, he did not sit down at the high table himself and call a servant, but simply passed on through the hall and was just about to emerge from the door when he was waylaid by the blacksmith.

"M'Lord—please, m'Lord—" The blacksmith tugged at a forelock that was the scanty remnant of his brown-gray hair, and made an attempt at a bow.

Jim stopped, suddenly very conscious of his aching head and queasy stomach. But—noblesse oblige. Or, in other words, always keep on good terms with the servants, if possible.

"Yes?" he asked.

"M'Lord, if you would be so kind—" The blacksmith gave him an ingratiating, gap-toothed grin. "It occurred to me I might be of some small use in examining and fixing any little damage that the noble Sir John's armor might have suffered. I didn't want to ask him myself . . ."

The sentence trailed off, leaving Jim to supply its unsaid finish.

"I'll mention it to him," said Jim shortly and pushed past the man. A moment later he was out through the door and the sunlight hit him in both eyes like the blades of swords.

He blinked, and stood for a few seconds, letting his gaze adjust to the brightness. Then, looking around the courtyard, he saw both Sir John and Sir Giles examining one of the horses that had been brought out from the stables for them. It was Jim's own Gorp—the closest thing he had to a real destrier, or war horse.

A kitchen servant stood by the two knights, patiently holding a pitcher which undoubtedly contained wine, since both knights had cups in their hands. A couple of other cups were hooked to the servant's belt.

Jim walked toward the three men and the horse, his head throbbing with the jar of each foot hitting the cementlike hardness of the pounded earth that was the courtyard floor.

"Ah, Sir James," said Sir John as he approached, and both knights turned toward him. "A stablehand was just walking this magnificent beast of yours; and we stopped him to look the animal over."

Now that Sir John spoke, Jim saw a diminutive stable servant that had been more or less hidden from his sight by the two knights and Gorp himself, holding the end of the halter around Gorp's neck.

"So I see," said Jim as he met them and stopped. "Yes."

Even through the fog of his hangover, he was keenly aware that a couple of knights like Sir John and Sir Giles knew very well that Gorp was no "magnificent beast." But at the moment his aching head was not up to coming up with a more satisfactory answer to Sir John's statement.

"But what are you thinking of, fellow!" said Sir John, turning on the servant with a pitcher. "Standing there like a post without offering your Lord a cup?"

The servant started hastily, jerked one of the empty cups from his belt, filled it and held it out to Jim with a "very sorry, m'Lord."

Jim was too slow to stop him. Silently he accepted the brimming cup of wine, the very sight and smell of which threatened to make his stomach turn over—when he noticed that both of the other two knights were watching him keenly.

Foggy-headed as he was, he suddenly became aware that this was another of those little tests which people of the class he had ended up in loved to indulge.

They knew in what state he had gone upstairs to bed the night before. They must have a very good idea of how he was feeling right now; and, particularly, how he was feeling toward the idea of another cup of wine. There was nothing unfriendly about their interest; but it was part of the general pattern, along with the tournaments and the other rough sports of the period—a sort of general testing that went on all the time, of everybody by everybody. It was as if everyone wanted to make sure that the people around him or her still had all the strengths they had originally been given credit for. Whatever happened, he was going to have to drink this cup of wine.

He could cheat by removing the wine as he pretended to swallow; but somehow he was ashamed to do this.

He dared not close his eyes. He put the cup to his lips and simply began swallowing. For a moment his stomach hovered on the edge of revolt; but again, as with the small beer, the fact that he was pouring liquid into his dehydrated body seemed to save him. He drained the cup to the bottom and handed it back to the kitchen servant, who promptly refilled it to the top and handed it once more back to him.

This time, Jim felt he had safely passed the test. He took a sip or two from the second cup, finding it not at all hard to get it down, and made himself smile at Giles and Sir John—who smiled back.

"About the beast here," said Sir John, turning back to Gorp. "Is he schooled?"

Jim felt a strong touch of embarrassment. Gorp was about as unschooled as any horse ever ridden into combat could be. But Jim's wits seemed unexpectedly sharpened by the sudden jolt of the near-pint of wine within him on top of the small beer—though that had had almost no alcohol in it at all.

He backed off half a dozen paces and spoke to the stablehand holding the end of Gorp's halter.

"Womar!" he said to the man. "Let him go."

The stablehand dropped the end of the halter rope and Jim whistled.

Gorp looked around, mildly surprised. He spotted Jim; and, turning leisurely, plodded over to lower his head and snuffle at Jim's chest for the reward that usually followed his answering that whistle. At the moment, however, Jim had nothing to give him. Sugar was unknown, so the sugar cube he might have offered a horse as a reward back in the twentieth century was impossible. This spring's carrots were not grown yet and last year's were long gone. As were last year's oats.

Jim patted and stroked the horse a little bit, speaking to him to try and make up for the lack of a gift, then stood back and gave him another order.

"Up, Gorp!" he cried. "Up, boy!"

Gorp went into his only other trick—which was to rise on his hind legs with his front hooves pawing dangerously at the air before him. It was a false but good imitation of a war horse fighting along with his rider. Then he dropped back to all four legs.

"There. Very good, Gorp. Good horse," said Jim.

After some more petting, stroking and praising he took the halter rope and led him back to Womar.

"Indeed—" Sir John was beginning approvingly, when the howl of a wolf from some not too distant spot suddenly split the bright morning air. Sir John broke off speaking, Gorp jerked so strongly at his head rope that Womar almost lost his grip on it, and Womar himself turned pale.

"The second time this morning, m'Lord," he murmured shakily to Jim. "Evil thing 'tis, hearing a wolf howl like that in broad daylight. Night's the time for wolf howls. Some evil's about!"

Jim was suddenly aware of the eyes of both Sir John and Giles bright and knowingly upon him.

"I wouldn't worry about it, Womar," said Jim, as briskly as he could. "I believe I know that wolf and why he's howling. If you'll saddle a couple of horses for these two gentlemen and one for me—not Gorp here—"

"Gorp?" echoed Sir John, with the first note of surprise Jim had ever heard in the voice of that urbane and knowledgeable knight.

"—Er, yes," said Jim to him, "the horse's name, you know. Well, go along, Womar, and saddle those horses as I said."

Womar went off with unusual speed, towing along a Gorp who seemed only too happy to trot back to the comfort of the stables.

Fifteen minutes later they rode through the woods to the little clearing where the stump stood, with its red cloth still stuck by one end into the split at the top of the broken wood. Jim dismounted. Sir John and Giles did also, Sir Giles with a somewhat puzzled look on his aristocratic face.

"Why are we here, Sir James?" asked the older knight. "There seems to be nothing of a wolf in the vicinity."

"Oh yes, there is," said a harsh voice immediately behind them. "Turn around and you'll see me."

They turned. Aargh was standing on all four legs facing them, not more than a dozen paces away. He was a dark-haired wolf, and nearly as large as a small pony. Altogether he made a rather impressive sight, this close and appearing apparently out of thin air without any sound or other warning.

"Where—" began Sir John, and broke off—evidently aware he was betraying his surprise. Jim felt a twinge of guilt. Knowing Aargh's fondness for seeing others before they saw him, he had deliberately come in upwind, so that Aargh would have plenty of time to circle around behind them.

"Aargh," said Jim, "you know Sir Giles. This other gentleman with me is Sir John Chandos."

"Is he now?" said Aargh. "And what's that to me?"

CHAPTER 8

❧

"Sir wolf," said Sir John smoothly, having made a good recovery and speaking as urbanely as usual, "you've never met me before, of course. But it was I who requested Sir Giles and Sir James here to go to France last year to rescue our Crown Prince—that quest in which you yourself joined and played such an honorable part."

"Keep your useless words to yourself, Sir Knight," growled Aargh. "I have never done anything honorable in my life and never will. I do things for only two reasons. It is necessary they be done, or I want to do them. All else is nonsense."

"Might I ask you then, Sir Wolf," said Sir John, "what caused you to involve yourself with Sir James and Sir Giles in France last time?"

"I wanted to!" Aargh snapped his jaws shut on the last word.

"Then, may I ask," said Sir John, "is it possible you might want to assist these two gentlemen again in another such trip to that same country—"

"No." Aargh's interruption was almost reflexive.

"I see," said Sir John easily. "But if you would listen to some things I have to tell you, it's possible that you might change your mind?"

"I doubt it," said Aargh.

"You see," went on Sir John, still companionably, "the King of France intends to invade England. For some reason he seems to be very sure of his ability to land an army across the Channel on our shores. If such an army landed, of course it would come through here, devastating all in its path. Including, come to think of it, this territory of yours—just what are its boundaries?"

"This wood and the next one eastward and the one beyond that," said Aargh, "and westward to the Meres and the seashore. Even to the Loathly Tower, of which you'll have heard, and down to the water beside and beyond it. What is there is still there. So far, it has not challenged me, and I have not challenged it. True, the sand-mirks rule that territory, but they move out of my way when I come. It is mine."

"But you could leave it for a little while," said Sir John.

"I could. But I won't," said Aargh. "All this is mine because none can take it from me. To the east, to the north and even to the south there are others of my own kind who watch and wait. In time I will grow old and stiff and slower than I am now. Then the time will come when, one by one, they'll start to challenge me. In the end one will kill me and this land will be his. That's as it should be. But if I leave it empty I may come back to find some other of them already in occupation—one or even a pack. That would cause me trouble; and I see no reason to go to trouble for you, Sir Knight."

"But how about the French army?" said Sir John. "You may be ready to meet all challengers, but surely you realize you can't defeat an army. The French will slay you."

Aargh opened his jaws in one of his silent laughs. When he was done he closed the jaws again with another snap.

"They must find me first, Sir Knight," he said. "And I tell you that a thousand such as you could comb these woods and never find me. More than several thousand would fail. I am a wolf, Sir Knight; and wolves are not easily found when they do not want to be found. That would not stop me from finding them, by one and one; and the ones I found would be left dead. I am no boar or bear to be driven, cornered and brought to battle."

"Ah," said Sir John, still in the same calm, engaging voice, "your help—those things which you can do which no one else can do—will, I'm sure, be sorely missed by Sir Giles and Sir

James. I am sure we will all be sad that you won't accompany them."

"Sad or happy, what difference does it make to me?" snarled Aargh. "I am not one of your tame curs to whine and lick your hand because you are unhappy."

He turned to Jim.

"Was it for this, you called me?" he asked Jim. "You might have known better, if so."

"It wasn't the entire reason," said Jim. "I also wanted to tell you that Carolinus is safe in my castle now and we hope to have him well again, shortly."

"That is interesting," said Aargh, "though of no great import. All creatures die. But I will say that, like all we who go on four legs, I like the Mage. I wish him well; and with you and Angela his chance is best."

"Thanks," said Jim, more touched than he dared allow himself to show in the tone of his words. Aargh was as disdainful of emotion in others as he was of it in himself.

"Leave your cloth where it is in the stump, then," said Aargh. "I'll keep my eye on it and not be far distant at any time. If I see it gone, I will know that the Mage is well again. If you need me for his sake, double it and tuck both ends of the cloth in."

"I'll do that," said Jim.

"Then farewell," said Aargh, and left.

"Remarkable," said Sir John, staring at the empty space where Aargh had been, it seemed, a moment before. "It is almost as if the wolf could vanish like a magician, himself."

"It's a habit of his," admitted Jim. "I think all wolves can do it."

Sir John sighed.

"Well, gentlemen," he said, "it seems we might as well return to the castle."

He glanced at Jim.

"—Or will the wolf return?"

"No. Not without some reason," said Jim.

They remounted and rode somberly back to the castle. They had barely dismounted in the courtyard, however, before a castle servant came rushing up to Jim.

"M'Lord! M'Lord!" he said. "The Lady Angela bids you come to the room where the magician Carolinus lies, with all haste!"

"Go ahead!" Jim told him. "I'll be right there."

"Should we go with you, James?" asked Giles.

Jim shook his head.

"I don't think so," he said rapidly. "If my Lady-wife wished anyone else, she'd have asked for them, too. Would you mind waiting for me at the high table in the Great Hall? If it turns out I'm delayed, I'll send to let you know."

The other men nodded. Jim turned, and headed toward the Great Hall himself as fast as his rank would allow. As Lord of the castle he could not be seen running like a common servant—at least, not without more reason than there had been in the message that just reached him. But he walked as swiftly as he could into the castle. Only, mounting the stairway of the tower—with no one watching—he allowed himself to run. He was imagining Carolinus suddenly gone in a very bad state indeed. If so, heaven hope he was in time to do whatever he could, or at least to be there.

But when he burst through Carolinus's door, with tottery legs, and out of breath from the long, winding, stone staircase that circled the inside of the tower, it was to find no emergency in progress.

In fact, quite the reverse. Angie was sitting with her arms folded, in a chair a little back from the bedside. There were no servants in the room. Another empty chair sat close beside the bed. In the bed itself was Carolinus, propped up on pillows and drinking tea from a cup and saucer. Both were of the kind of fine china that Jim was absolutely positive was not ordinarily to be found in fourteenth-century England, either in the past of his own old world or in the present of this one. Clearly, Carolinus was not only better, but able to work his magic again.

He had even recovered the customary bristle to his mustaches and the snappish look of his expression.

"Well, here you are," he said to Jim. "High time! Sit down there, by the bed."

Jim took the empty chair.

"It's marvelous to see you looking so good, Carolinus," Jim said. "I could almost believe you weren't telling me all of it, when you said that magic could help wounds but not cure ills."

"Well, my damnable bed sores were wounds, weren't they?" said Carolinus. "As far as the ills go, I was probably over that a week ago, but I never got a chance to know it, the way those two were feeding me with purges and emetics and the like."

"Actually," said Jim, "I've been waiting for the time when you'd get well enough that I could talk to you about something rather strange that happened to me just before I got back here—"

"Never mind that!" said Carolinus. He was his old imperious self; but there was something—something *missing* about him, that Jim could not seem to put his finger on. "There are more important things I want to talk about. Are you listening?"

Jim cast a hopeful glance at Angie; but she looked icily back at him over folded arms as she sat in her chair. Clearly she had not got over the way she had been feeling toward him the previous evening. Jim turned his attention back to Carolinus.

"I'm listening," he said.

"Very well," said Carolinus, and took a sip of tea. He frowned over at the kettle.

"Not warm enough!" he said.

The kettle gave a short, apologetic whistle.

"Never mind, this time," said Carolinus. "I've warmed it up myself and made sure the milk and sugar in it are the right proportions. But keep the temperature in mind. Now, Jim—"

Jim gave the elderly magician all his attention.

"I'm afraid I had to mislead you," he said. "But at the time I spoke to you first about this, you weren't involved in magic to any real extent—I must say you're hardly involved even now, but you'll have to learn to use it, anyway—I told you there were no sorcerers, only magicians who had gone wrong. You've since experienced a case of that in the matter of the AAA magician of France, Malvinne; and you remember his end."

Jim did. Jim shuddered. He remembered a limp Malvinne being drawn up to the great shadowy figures of the King and Queen of Death, like a rag doll on a string.

"Now, I have no choice," continued Carolinus. "You must be enlightened. Jim, there *are* sorcerers."

"Oh?" said Jim.

"Oh?" snorted Carolinus. "Is that all you have to say? I tell you of a fact that shakes the world, and all you say is—'oh'!"

"I'm—I'm wordless," said Jim.

"Well, that's good," went on Carolinus. "In any case, there are sorcerers. In some ways, they appear just like magicians. But they aren't. They've no Accounting Office to keep their records straight, they're strictly single operators, and they begin by selling themselves to the Dark Powers in return for learning magic. They do learn a sort of magic; but it is not the kind you and I know. It's magic which can be turned only to evil purposes."

Jim felt a chill run down his back. For the first time the potential of what Carolinus was telling him had begun to register on him. Clearly, Carolinus did not take these sorcerers lightly. And if Carolinus didn't take them lightly— what should they mean to someone like himself, a mere C rated magician? So this was the reason behind what Carolinus wanted to tell him.

"The kind of magic that these sorcerers learn is called counter-magic," said Carolinus. "To distinguish it from that which you and I use. Now, our magic is created and designed to be used only for good purposes. It can't be used for evil, or for gain, personal gain that is—you're aware that you're not allowed to sell your magical services until you're at least A rank?"

"No," answered Jim, "you never told me."

"Strange," said Carolinus, frowning. "I distinctly had the impression I had. However, you've been told now. Officially, at any rank up to an A you're still within the apprentice bounds. However, back to the point. A qualified magician, A or above, can receive fees for his magical services in order to keep a roof over his head and food on his table and such, but anything more than this is frowned on, as in Malvinne's case."

Jim was frowning a little himself. The first time he had seen Carolinus was when he had been in the body of a dragon. And his dragon granduncle, Smrgol, had needed to bargain Carolinus down from fifteen pounds of gold to four pounds of gold, one pound of silver and a large flawed emerald—just for some information.

"What do you do with the gold and jewels you get in fees?" asked Jim, suddenly curious; for Carolinus lived simply in his little cottage and apparently had no large expenses.

"None of your business!" snapped Carolinus. "There's a great deal you don't understand about the use of magic. When you're A class, come and talk to me again about it."

"Oh, all right," said Jim.

"Now, where was I? Oh, yes—sorcerers," went on Carolinus. "As I was saying, there are sorcerers. When the King of France lost Malvinne as his private royal magician and minister, he hunted around for a substitute; and came up with not a magician at all, but a sorcerer named Ecotti. Who, being deeply hated and feared in his native Italy, was only too glad to move into the French royal palace and take up where Malvinne had left off. But, of course, his magic is all dark magic. Destructive magic. He readily fell in with the King of France's plan to invade England—"

"Oh, you know about that?" said Jim.

"Of course!" said Carolinus. "I wish you'd stop interrupting. The point is, Ecotti realized what King Jean of France did not; and that any invasion of England must naturally find me helping its defense. There are, as you know, only two others like me in the world. Ecotti alone could never hope to face me."

Carolinus frowned darkly.

"So," he said, "someone else was at work behind what happened to me—and that involves you, Jim."

CHAPTER 9

"What do you mean?" Jim demanded.

Carolinus ignored the question.

"Whoever it is, is clever, there's no doubt about it," he said, grimly. "To attack me! Not by counter-magical means, except possibly in one slight measure. That was to introduce an uncomfortable, but by no means dangerous, illness into the kettle you see before me."

The kettle gave an unhappy little whistle.

"I'm not blaming you!" Carolinus snapped at it. "You're only an inanimate object, though you seem to forget that from time to time. There's no way you could defend yourself, or even be aware of what was being done to you."

He cleared his throat and continued to Jim.

"At any rate, as you know, I was made sick; and meanwhile, by completely nonmagical means, word I was ill was passed to that particular gaggle of vagabonds you saw about my cottage; and to those two female torturers you saw. The results, you know. Those women were well on the way to wearing me down to where someone of my mature years couldn't survive. If it'd worked, I'd have been dead; and a fine mess that would have left all of you, and England, in."

He glared at Jim, as if it was Jim's fault.

"Happily, I smelled a rat," he said. "I investigated and found the trace of magic on my kettle. From that, by methods you'll not be learning for some time, I was able not only to cleanse the kettle, but to trace back and realize evil was at work."

He paused to take a sip of tea.

"It wasn't easy," he went on. "You'll find for yourself the concepts necessary to making full-scale magic—our type of magic—takes a certain amount of strength; and my strength had been drained just then. I'd barely enough to cleanse the magic from the kettle and send it to you. Little did I know that you'd be dallying to pick flowers; and so the kettle got to your castle and found you not there. Being merely a magic-touched inanimate object, as I keep reminding it—"

He threw a severe glance at the kettle. This time, it accepted this in silence.

"—It had no more capacity than to wait to deliver the message I had sent until you got there. Happily, when you did, you came and got me."

"Of course!" said Jim and Angie both together.

"It was a special case, you understand," said Carolinus gruffly. "Ordinarily, I'd scarcely need the help of people like yourselves. I'm fond of you, true; but that doesn't close my eyes to the fact that you're rather in the case of midgets helping a giant."

"Speaking of giants," said Jim, seizing on the opening, "that's the very thing I wanted to speak to you about. When I was gathering some flowers for Angie a very strange thing happened—"

"If you don't mind," snapped Carolinus, "we'll stick to the point. I was speaking. The point is that I was supposed to die; so that the French invasion would find no strong magical opposition to its sweeping through England. Believe me, this time it would have been able to do so—even without the help of the Scots; whom the French King plans to conquer as soon as he has England subdued, anyway."

"Ah!" said Jim.

"Bleating 'ah' isn't necessary," retorted Carolinus. "Any child could reason that much. But back to more important things. The point is I've survived. But I'm still hampered."

He looked fiercely at Jim.

"The difficulty," he said, "is that real magic—the magic we use—is by definition not punitive. I can use it to defend, as I use wards about my cottage and grounds; but I can't use it to attack, without a very clear and obvious reason—such as that if I do not attack now, I will be attacked myself, inevitably."

"I don't understand," said Jim.

"I understand," said Angie, behind him. "He means he can't attack this—whoever—without clear evidence that 'whoever' is going to attack him. But Carolinus—"

She looked directly at the magician.

"—Whoever it was did try to kill you!" she went on. "Even if by roundabout ways. Isn't that enough to justify your doing something back?"

"Not as long as I survived; as I now have," said Carolinus. "Unless there's evidence it'll be tried again."

"Well if the French invade, aren't you likely to be killed?" asked Angie.

"Yes—and no," said Carolinus. "They'd need magical help, no matter how large their army, to get at me behind my magical defenses. You two and the other landholders around here won't be as lucky."

"Well then," said Jim, "what's to be done?"

"I'll tell you what's to be done!" said Carolinus. "I've got to find who's the real power behind Ecotti, and plotting to get me. Counter-magic alone could infect my kettle, but not without some real magic to keep me from immediately discovering it—otherwise, it couldn't be done without my knowing it. That points to a real magician at work, helping Ecotti. But the Accounting Office assures me none were involved."

"I see," said Jim.

"I hope so, for your sake," said Carolinus. "Because whoever is behind it is also forwarding the invasion. This is all beyond your level of magic, Jim; but I have a perfect conviction that there is a hidden Mastermind there. Ecotti is nothing by himself. He's found some partner or partners who make the invasion possible. To cross the Channel, except in the best of weather, without losing dozens of troop ships and having even many more blown off course, so that the French forces land scattered and out of touch with each other, is something that's daunted, and will daunt, a great many people both in the past and the future."

He frowned at Jim.

"You have knowledge of attempts that were made after our time, in the world you came from."

"That's right," said Jim. "The Nazis were going to try a cross-Channel invasion in World War II. It never came off."

"And King Jean wouldn't be so confident, if he didn't have help. Now, that necessary help can only come from the sea itself," said Carolinus. "I've discovered that Jean's found, through Ecotti, some unholy alliance with the tribe of sea serpents that populate all the seas; and some leader among the serpents themselves has risen who can bring the rest together to act as a group. Normally they have little to do with one another once they're mature. Do you know anything about sea serpents, Jim?"

"Only," said Jim thoughtfully, "that the dragon Smrgol reminded me, just before we had our fight at the Loathly Tower, that Gorbash had an ancestor who'd met a sea serpent in single combat and won. Apparently, this was an unusual thing for a dragon to be able to do."

Carolinus snorted.

"Indeed!" said Carolinus. "As a dragon, you're large, Jim. But an ordinary sea serpent is easily twice your weight and at least double your length. It's simply much bigger and stronger than you. They've always taken it for granted that no dragon can stand up to one of them. Also, in fact, the battle to which you're referring is one I remember very well. It's rankled in the minds of all sea serpents ever since. Possibly that's why they were so quick to agree to help the invasion. The land doesn't matter to them, but the dragons of the land do. They want revenge—to say nothing of the fact that, like the dragons, each has a hoard. They also look forward to plundering dragon hoards. To that end, once in England they'll try to kill off every dragon here."

He drained his cup and glared aside at the kettle.

"Refill!" he snapped.

The kettle floated over through the air to him and poured what appeared to be water into his cup, but which changed to a dark tea-color as soon as it hit the cup. The liquid stopped a fraction of an inch short of the rim. Carolinus glared at the cup itself again.

"Milk and sugar," he said.

The liquid immediately turned milky. He sipped at it. "Right temperature this time," he remarked.

"Ecotti," echoed Jim, frowning. "It's a funny name."

"Not at all funny!" growled Carolinus. "It's a typical name in the mountains in Italy from which he comes. The people there have taken a sort of sneaking pride in themselves, for the sorcerers and witches they've produced over the centuries. He's no match for someone like myself, as I say; but as a sorcerer he's potent, very potent. I'd rate him in the very top rank of sorcerers—far above your level, Jim. Keep that in mind. Now, also keep in mind that as far as the sea serpents are concerned that invasion's already begun. There'll possibly be some in England, right now."

"England!" said Jim, starting. "Of course! That would explain what happened to poor Amyth. And Hubert's cows! That'd make the serpents a lot closer than just in the sea around us."

"Amyth? Hubert? What about Amyth and Hubert?" queried Angie sharply.

"It could well have been a sea serpent that ate Sir Hubert's cows," said Jim, "and got Amyth. Swallowed him whole at one gulp, I'd guess. That's another thing I wanted to talk to you about, Carolinus—"

"A sea serpent got Amyth, you say!" interrupted Carolinus. "Here?"

"I think so. See what you think," said Jim. "I had him carry torches for me, last night when I put the signal cloth out for Aargh. It was dark enough so we couldn't see beyond the torchlight. But he was afraid of being too close to magic—I put a ward around the post and the cloth, so no other animal or person would come along and pull it out. Only Angie, myself or Aargh. Anyway, Amyth backed off. I had my back turned. I heard him scream—"

He broke off at the memory.

"When I went to look," he said, "I could only find his sword. Nothing else. I hid the sword."

"Jim!" Angie said. "Oh, poor Amyth."

"He wasn't necessarily the nicest person, you know," Jim said to her. "Few of our men-at-arms are."

"I don't care," said Angie. "It's horrible, anyone being swallowed like that!"

"Indeed, what you did was very foolish of you, Jim," said Carolinus. "Going looking practically into the mouth of a sea serpent. What if he'd still been there?"

"How could it be foolish if I didn't know then that sea serpents were around?" retorted Jim with some heat. "As far as I knew then, the largest things here were dragons. I can't see a dragon coming and getting Amyth. For one thing, a dragon can't swallow or even lift a full-grown man or woman, and fly off. Besides, dragons don't like to fly at night. I'm the only exception to that I know of. I didn't know—and that's what I've been trying to ask you about! There's also the matter of this giant—"

"Will you stop maundering about giants!" snapped Carolinus. "We've got serious things to talk about here."

"I WILL NOT!" roared Jim suddenly.

Carolinus, he was glad to see, was startled. So was Angie. Jim had never shouted at Carolinus before. In fact, he seldom shouted at anyone. He took advantage of the moment to go on.

"This giant," he said clearly and firmly, "called himself a Sea Devil; and, from what you tell me about sea serpents, Carolinus, he may be part of the whole business. But you haven't let me get a word in edgewise about him. He came out of a pond near where I was picking flowers. He was at least twice the height of a dragon—maybe three times the height. And he was built like a wedge, point down. He had a great big head, enormous shoulders and he sort of tapered to a pair of feet that were—oh, maybe three or four times the size of mine."

"A Sea Devil. Hmm," said Carolinus, suddenly thoughtful. "Did he say what his name was?"

"Rrrnlf," said Jim, trying to trill the first letter of the Sea Devil's name. He was not very successful. He tried it again, with a Scot-like roll to his tongue; and came out with something a little closer to what he had heard from the Sea Devil himself. "Actually, he didn't seem a bad sort. He just wanted to know in which direction the sea was, and I told him. He was hunting somebody who had stolen some lady or other from him, he said. I'm not quite sure what he was talking about."

"Neither am I," said Carolinus mildly. "The Sea Devils are Naturals, of course. The most powerful creatures in the ocean, and the most intelligent—with one exception. You said he struck you as a not unfriendly type of individual?"

"That's right," said Jim. "In fact, he struck me as very friendly. He told me he was in my debt for my pointing out to him where the sea was; and said that now he would know his way all through the underground waters of this island. He said I could call on him if I ever needed him. I didn't know the underground waters were connected."

"They aren't—the surface waters aren't," said Carolinus. "But the Sea Devils, with a combination of their strength and their superhuman abilities as Naturals, can go right through earth, as well as water, without any trouble at all. He'd have been talking about the deep-down layers of water trapped between rock levels as much as thousands of feet underground."

Jim and Angie both stared at him. Carolinus went on, as if this ability was not at all startling.

"Yes," he said, "they've actually made themselves a sort of underground, water-filled tunnel between the Mediterranean and the Red Sea, that gives them a short route to the Indian Ocean. I wonder what kind of lady it was he was talking about; and who'd have the courage to steal her from him? Even a sea serpent will back off from a Sea Devil. One of the great whales, of course, would outweigh a Sea Devil many times over; but whales never go looking for trouble. I'm under the impression they and the Sea Devils get along very well together—even the killer whales and the Sea Devils. Of course, the Sea Devil is really too big a mouthful for any killer whale. Even a male killer whale is only about thirty feet long; and even if it's a carnivore, there's still plenty of dolphins and sea lions and such that the killers can take with relative ease."

He seemed to come back to present problems with a jerk.

"I'm intrigued," he said, putting his cup and saucer aside to hang in empty air, "by his being here at this particular time, though. I wonder if there's a connection between him and the sea serpents helping the King of France. But the point is, there'd be nothing in it for the Sea Devils. Unlike the sea serpents, they can stay out of water as long as they like; but they've really nothing against dragons—or humans."

He checked himself.

"But—back to what I was talking about," he said. "The Mastermind behind this Ecotti must be found, and I can't do it. So, Jim, it's up to you—with that future-trained mind of yours—to sniff out whoever it is!"

CHAPTER 10

❧

"**N**o!" roared Angie.

It is not easy for women to roar. To raise their voices, yes; but to roar—difficult. It is largely a matter of the deepness of their voice tones. Jim had just roared a few minutes before—somewhat to his surprise—but then he was a fairly passable baritone. Angie was not even a contralto. Nonetheless, there was no mistaking on the part of her two hearers in that small room. Angie had roared.

Jim started and turned to see his wife's face. But, instead of the daggers in her glance being directed at him, he was deeply relieved to see that they were all directed now at Carolinus. He looked at Carolinus and saw the old magician also looking startled. Whether he had also jumped or not, it was too late to tell. Jim had been looking the other way at the time.

"I beg your pardon?" said Carolinus, in a somewhat stunned voice.

"I say he's not going to uncover whoever this is that you're talking about!" said Angie. She was no longer roaring but she was very definitely furious. "It's always Jim! Jim! Are we in danger of having the Scots invade England? Send Jim to fix it!"

"I didn't—" Carolinus was beginning.

"Well, you had a hand in it somewhere. I'm sure of that!" snapped Angie. "Is the Crown Prince of England missing?

Send Jim! Send Jim and his friends to France to recover the Prince! Have I been stolen away from the Loathly Tower, in a move by the Dark Powers that threatens everybody? Let Jim find Companions to fight with him and handle it!"

"But," said Carolinus, regaining some of his self-possession, "I've just finished explaining why I can't be the one. And there's only myself or Jim."

"I don't care—" Angie was beginning; but this time Carolinus interrupted.

"You'd rather have this castle burned about your ears, by licentious French soldiery?" asked Carolinus. "All the men within it slaughtered and the women killed in unmentionable ways?"

There was a moment's silence. Jim stole a glance at his wife again. She had been stopped; but the fire was not out. They had both been in the fourteenth century long enough to know what Carolinus meant by the type of unmentionable deaths that were visited on women—and, to a certain extent, men as well. Vertical impalement was one example.

She glanced for a moment at Jim; but Jim was suddenly glad to see that all anger was gone from that glance. The Great Wall of Silence had evidently gone down; and they were once more on the same side.

"There must be some way that doesn't involve Jim," Angie said, after the long moment of silence. "You're the one with all the magic, all the knowledge. You grew up on this world. You've lived here for I don't know how many years. You should be the one with the answers."

All these words were addressed to Carolinus. The feeling of something missing in the older man that Jim had sensed once before came back on him now, more strongly. Carolinus shook his head slowly—but at that moment Jim had an inspiration of his own.

"As a matter of fact, Carolinus," he said, "I wouldn't be able to do anything for you right away, anyway. Sir John Chandos is here, along with Sir Giles. In fact—though you probably don't remember it—they were the ones who helped us get away from that bunch of vagabonds. Chandos wants Giles and me to go to France for him and find out why the King of France is so certain that he can have a successful invasion. Apparently he's going right on building ships and gathering men, as if it was a settled matter—when everybody knows that a Channel crossing isn't the easiest thing in the world."

"I knew that," said Carolinus, suddenly so mild that Jim immediately became wary. "It's part of the same thing."

"I don't understand you," said Jim.

"Neither do I," chimed in Angie.

"It's quite simple," said Carolinus. "Sir John is after exactly the same information I'm after. But he's aiming at the box. I want the key to that box. You're going to have to go after the key first, Jim. I repeat, I can't. I'm older, now. My diminished strength, many things, keep me from doing what you could do. Not only are you from another place, another time, you also are still—as I pointed out earlier—within the bounds of apprenticeship. You can be pardoned for doing some things. I couldn't. And that's exactly what you may have to do."

"I still don't understand you," said Jim. "What exactly do you want me to do?"

"I want to find out who put Ecotti in touch with the sea serpents and got them to agree to an invasion. He could never have done it, alone. Why, three of those monsters could tow one of King Jean's ships out of trouble; and there's more sea serpents in the oceans than there are dragons in the world."

"How are all these sea serpents going to get here?" asked Angie.

"Sea serpents come from the sea," snapped Carolinus. He had evidently recovered completely from her roar.

Jim looked at Angie. Angie looked back at him wordlessly.

"All right," said Jim, "how do I go about looking for this whoever-it-is?"

"You go to the bottom of the sea," said Carolinus.

Angie and Jim started at him.

"Bottom of the sea?" echoed Angie.

"I'm afraid so," said Carolinus. "There's only one individual whom all the creatures of the sea—including the serpents—have always listened to, even if not all the time; and that's the oldest kraken—you'd call him a squid. The oldest and largest in the ocean. I've no idea what his name was to begin with; but your friend the Sea Devil and the sea serpents call him Granfer."

"Granfer . . ." said Jim wonderingly. The name rang a bell. Hadn't Rrrnlf mentioned something about a Granfer?

"You'll find him on the sea bottom; well away from shore but not in too deep water, since he's so big now that he has to eat steadily just to keep himself alive; even though with ten tentacles, some of which are two or three hundred feet long, he can snare anything that comes reasonably close to him. That includes some fairly good-sized creatures indeed—those killer whales I mentioned earlier, for example—one of those would make just a decent meal for Granfer."

Carolinus paused, thoughtfully.

"In fact," he went on, "even one of the largest whales isn't too big for Granfer to tackle. But I think his diet mainly consists of quantities of such fish as two-hundred-pound tuna; and others on down to smaller fish. You'd make a sort of minimum-sized bite for Granfer, Jim."

"He's not going," said Angie quickly.

"He *will*!" snapped Carolinus. "He's a magician; and even Granfer knows better than to touch one of our people. Besides, Granfer will find him and his questions much more interesting than appetizing. Oh, he'll ramble a bit. All older creatures do . . . except me, that is—"

He was interrupted. Noise was floating in through the unglazed arrow slits of his room—which naturally overlooked the courtyard, though from a lofty height. These noises were the shouts and cries of men and the hammering of metal on metal—noises Jim had heard before when multiple swords had been at work on other swords, shields and armor.

Jim started for the door.

"Wait!" cried Angie.

"Never mind that out there," said Carolinus quickly. "You said Sir John is here. I'll talk to him. Help me down to the high table right away."

"Don't be silly!" said Angie, turning on him. "You're in no condition to go anywhere."

"Oh, no?" said Carolinus, and vanished. So did his bed.

Jim and Angie looked at each other again and together ran out into the corridor and down the tower stairs, through the Great Hall past an empty high table beside which Carolinus was sitting in his bed, looking annoyed, and out into the courtyard.

Before them there was a swirl of men in close combat. Chandos was one, as was Sir Giles. But so also was Sir Brian Neville-Smythe, Jim's closest friend and Companion, whom

Chandos had expressed a wish to see, in connection with the present matter that concerned him.

Sir Brian and Giles, with some of the castle's men-at-arms, seemed to be attacking the entrance to the Great Hall. They were trying to break through Sir John and some of the other men-at-arms, who were stoutly defending it.

Standing watching, from a safe distance, were some of the other men-at-arms and a great many of the servants. With them, and towering a head or more above the tallest of them, was Dafydd ap Hywel, the fourth of Jim's human Companions, who had been with Jim at the Loathly Tower and on the expedition to France to rescue England's Crown Prince. He must, thought Jim, have ridden fast to make the nearly day's journey from the outlaw camp this quickly.

Dafydd was standing well back and leaning casually on his tall bow stave. His slim body, deceptive beneath the wide, powerful shoulders above it, showed an almost laziness, at sharp odds with the intent professionalism of his handsome face, as he studied the combatants. He showed no sign of joining either side of the fray, however; unlike Brian and Giles, who—unthinkable as it was—seemed to have become determined to force their way back into the castle.

But Jim and Angie had now begun to be noticed by those watching. Cries of "M'Lord!" and "M'Lady!" were heard, and the servants began to vanish almost as expertly as Aargh was able to do.

The voices reached through to those who were fighting; slowly it ceased. Their faces turned to look up at the doorway end of the portcullis.

They were definitely shame-faced, as they recognized Jim and Angie. Neither Giles nor Brian could meet his eye, and even Sir John's still-handsome face looked somewhat abashed. Jim's gaze grew more bleak as he looked beyond them and saw several of his men-at-arms, lying either unconscious or dead on the ground a little farther out.

He stepped out into the courtyard, growing more angry with every moment.

"What's going on here—"

He got no further. John Chandos had already pushed back his visor and was smiling at him.

"My deepest apologies, Sir James!" Chandos's voice rang out. "If fault is involved in this, it is mine. It was my suggestion in a moment of thoughtlessness, on seeing Sir Brian here, again—since I have known him at many tourneys and think so highly of him. It was merely a bit of game playing; a bit of exercise in which I, and some of those of your men-at-arms who were also interested in a bit of play, should hold the door of your hall with blunted arms, while Sir Giles and Sir Brian and an equal number of others should make an effort to break through us."

"I see," said Jim grimly.

"Yes," went on Chandos. "If any attacking were able to touch the first timber of the portcullis, they would have been deemed to have won. But I take it, we have somehow earned your disapproval; and I most abjectly beg your pardon and that of your Lady whom I see at the entrance to the Hall, there. It was foolish of us, perhaps, to arouse an alarum within the castle. In any case, as I say, you must blame me entirely—"

He broke off, because Carolinus, still sitting propped up with pillows on his bed, had just now appeared in the courtyard, behind Jim.

As Jim swung around to face him, Carolinus snapped at the senior knight.

"Well?" he said. "I'm waiting. John Chandos, a word with you!"

CHAPTER 11

J im looked away from the Mage, out over the hard-pounded ground of the courtyard, past those who had been fighting to where the still forms of his men-at-arms lay. He turned back to Carolinus.

"There are wounded who need help," he said.

"Oh, that," said Carolinus. "A few knocked heads!"

He waved a hand.

The bodies in the field stirred, raised their heads, sat up and looked around them—then pulled themselves slowly to their feet.

"We were using blunted weapons, James," said Brian. "Surely you didn't think we wished to hurt any?"

Jim looked at him grimly, then suddenly the anger went out of him, like air out of an opened balloon. This was the way these people were built. Fighting was fun to them and fun was fighting. You could no more change that than you could change the path of the Earth in its orbit about the sun. It was just something you had to get used to.

"None dead, thankfully," Carolinus was saying cheerfully behind him. "I can do nothing with the dead. Come! To the high table!"

Jim looked at him sourly.

"Don't you think," he said, "that if you're able to hop around like this, carrying your bed with you, you could put yourself in some ordinary clothes?"

Carolinus glanced down with a look of surprise at the nightgown that he had insisted on. It was not the ordinary custom in the fourteenth century to wear nightgowns to bed. Most people slept naked—or in their daytime clothes. But Carolinus didn't. He also usually wore nightcaps.

"You're quite right, my boy," he said; and vanished again, bed and all.

The spectators had disappeared by this time, and even those who had been in the battle were edging off to where they might be out of Jim's field of vision.

"You can all go," Jim told them harshly, speaking over the heads of the knights before him. "And next time don't get into anything like this without my permission."

There was a chorus of "Yes, m'Lord!" and the men-at-arms scattered like guilty school children. Jim turned and led the way back into the hall. When they sat down at the high table, Carolinus was already there, seated on a bench wearing one of his usual robes of deep red. His bed was nowhere in sight.

Whether the elder magician had contrived it deliberately or not, Jim found that, once seated, he was on one side of Carolinus, Sir John was at the end of the table on the other side and across the table from Jim were Sir Giles and Sir Brian, in that order; so that Sir Brian faced Jim. Dafydd ap Hywel was a little ways down the bench from Brian.

Jim, meanwhile, was already beginning to regret the way he had acted outside the front door. He was a generous-hearted person. He seldom lost his temper; and always afterwards regretted that he had done so—even when he still felt he had been in the right. Sir Brian was smiling hopefully at him now and so he smiled back as cheerfully as he could.

"You were doing well out there, Brian," he said. "And Dafydd, it's good to see you both again, even if we did just part yesterday!"

He extended his hands across the table. Brian gripped one strongly, as did Dafydd the other—if only briefly.

"Indeed Sir Brian was!" said Sir John. "I swear before God that I was the only one left between him and the doorway; and I have little doubt that he would have overcome me and touched it, with at least his foot, shortly."

Jim felt a little jump inside him. Invoking the name of God made Sir John's words almost a legal statement. Most ordinary swearing was with the names of Saints or martyrs. Chandos was reputed to be one of the best swords in the kingdom. If Brian could hold his own with him, let alone overcome the older knight, Chandos was acknowledging Jim's friend as also a first sword of the kingdom. All the remnants of annoyance inside Jim were swept away.

"By—" He checked himself just in time. He had been about to say "by God" also; but he realized it would mean something different to these men than it did to himself. "—the—er—Curriculum! Brian, I am overwhelmed to hear that!"

Brian's face was suddenly humble and appealing.

"I pray you, James," he said, "take not too seriously what Sir John says. He had to keep one foot on the lintel of the door; and so, since this could not be his shield side, else he would be facing me with sword alone, he must stand at an angle to me. This meant he had to reach around his own shield to match swords with me; and this put him at a considerable disadvantage—"

"Have done, have done!" interrupted Chandos with a laugh. "You'll end up proving you lost, instead of near-winning, Sir Brian. I meant what I said."

He filled a cup from the pitcher of wine that stood already on the table.

"But let us to business, gentlemen, since we are all together," he said. He looked down the table. "Mage—"

"And high time, too!" interrupted Carolinus fussily. He looked directly at Chandos. "There is more to this situation than you understand, John."

"Oh, by the way," interposed Jim quickly, "Sir John, may I make you acquainted with S. Carolinus, one of the three greatest magicians in the world."

"Thank you, Sir James," answered Chandos, but without taking his eyes off those of Carolinus, "but I know the Mage well. Why do you tell me this, Carolinus?"

"Can you imagine a situation which you *do* know more about than I?" returned Carolinus bluntly.

There was a pause. Chandos shook his head slowly.

"You're concerned about a French invasion," Carolinus went on. "You should know that the French themselves are not to be feared by England at the present, without allies. But this time they have allies—who aren't human ones. They're sea serpents from the sea-depths. Creatures twice the size of any dragon; and there are many of them. More than that, they can make a safe crossing of the Channel by King Jean's army a virtual certainty."

Sir John looked at him for a long moment.

"No," he said slowly, at last, "as you say, I can't imagine a situation you would not know more about than I, Mage," he said, "and you have just proved that. But why should these serpents have any interest in aiding King Jean or ravaging this fair island of ours?"

"The serpents don't give a groat for us or our island," said Carolinus snappishly. "But they want to exterminate every dragon on it and plunder the dragons' hoards. It's a long story—too long to go into at this time—but the sea serpents have been itching to do something about the British dragons for a long time. The two creatures are natural enemies. They seldom meet, of course, since one lives entirely on land and very seldom goes near the sea; and the other lives in the sea and seldom goes near the land. Still, they are rivals for gold and gems; and each hates the other."

"I see—" Chandos was beginning, when he broke off abruptly. "Er, good morning, m'Lady. It is always an honor and a great pleasure to see you; but we are having something of a council of war here and—"

"—And women aren't invited?" responded Angie tartly, seating herself at the end of the bench beside Jim. "Oh, I perfectly understand, Sir John. Moreover, although I'd originally determined to be along on this expedition you're all planning, I've come to the conclusion after all that we have a home here in Malencontri; and if Jim goes, somebody has to be here to hold it together and once more that person will have to be me. I don't like it. I tell you plainly I don't like it. But I'm going to accept it. That doesn't mean I'm not going to know as much of what's going on as there is to know. So, simply count me as one of your council, gentlemen."

Jim looked at her gratefully. Angie glared back at him for a second, then softened. Jim prolonged his grateful smile until Chandos's words drew his attention back to the end of the table where the senior knight sat.

"As you will, my Lady," said Chandos. He turned back to Carolinus. "Now, as I was saying to you, Mage, I understand now why the sea serpents would want to get at our dragons.

But why be in league with King Jean? The reason for that must be discovered—"

"Precisely," broke in Carolinus, "and that is why—"

"—Must be discovered," interrupted Chandos firmly, in his turn, "in a hurry, by the going of these gentlemen to France itself, to where the expedition is being readied; since our advice is that King Jean is there, himself, with his court."

"John," said Carolinus, "you're a fool!"

Sir John was considered the first courtier of Europe. His urbanity, his coolness, and his politeness to other gentlemen, and anyone else worthy of respect, was a byword. But he was still a knight, and he reacted as any knight would to Carolinus's words.

"*Sir!*" said Chandos. And the tone of the word was matched by the glare from his angry gray eyes.

"You must listen to me, John," plowed on Carolinus, unmoved. "The truth is that the answer does not lie at the French King's court, but elsewhere. You know he has made a first minister of the Italian, Ecotti?"

"Oh, yes," said Chandos. His face was back under control again, but his voice still had an angry edge to it. "Yes, that Italian, er, magician. Of course I know who you mean!"

"Sorcerer, John, sorcerer!" said Carolinus. "A rare breed, but a despicable one. They are not magicians but men or women who have sold themselves to the Dark Powers to learn a sort of dark magic. A magic that is dangerous—but limited. Ecotti alone could not bring sea serpents to the aid of King Jean; even with the enticement of their own advantage— a chance to get at all the dragons of England."

"If not Ecotti," said Chandos—he had got his voice and face completely back under control now, and was as if his momentary burst of dangerous fury had never been, "who, then?"

"The short answer to that," answered Carolinus, "is I don't know yet. But, what you and I had better find out first is how many of these gentlemen are prepared to take on the task of finding out. James, of course is not only committed but indispensable."

Jim found a small coal of anger suddenly bursting into flame inside him. Carolinus was taking him very much for granted. Then he remembered his dragon connections, which left him with little choice in the matter. The coal faded and died.

"—Giles also, I take it, has agreed to go," Carolinus was continuing.

"Most assuredly," said Sir Giles, twisting the right-hand point of his massive blond mustache with a tinge of excitement.

Carolinus's eyes moved to Brian's.

"And you, Brian?"

"I will be at Jim's side, as always," said Brian simply.

Carolinus looked farther down the table.

"Dafydd?"

"Ah, now, there's nothing I'd like better than to be one of those on this small adventure," said Dafydd, in his soft voice. "But my wife is carrying a second child. She was very plain, look you, about what I might do; and told me so before I set out. *'To Malencontri you can go,'* she said, *'but no further. And return to me within two days.'* "

Dafydd sighed a little.

"So it seems that I must stay at home. Perhaps"—his face brightened—"it is all for the best. I feel that I shall have a girl, this coming Christmastide, to add to the boy to whom my wife has already given birth—and a bouncing little lad he is. In truth, gentlemen, much as I wish to accompany you, it would take a braver man than myself to go against my wife's wishes in this matter."

"Three!" said Carolinus. "Leaving out Dafydd and of course Aargh. That should be more than enough—"

"And I, too, would be going with them!" said Angie, fiercely. "If there was only anyone at all I could trust to leave in charge here."

She looked angrily at Carolinus.

"You would plan to send these gentlemen, then, into the sea somewhere?" asked Chandos. "Could I ask where and why; and looking for what?"

"Yes," said Carolinus. "They're going to find a kraken named Granfer, the oldest living individual in all the seas; and see if he can't help point them toward the guilty party."

"A what?" said Chandos.

"A kraken," said Carolinus. "You understand what a kraken is?"

"Yes—yes, I've heard of krakens," said Sir John. "But why should this one be able to tell them anything of worth?"

"He can. Take my word for it."

"I take your word for much indeed, Mage," said Chandos. "But I can hardly risk the King's business, and the hope of survival for our English race, on as slight a thing as the trust of one man like myself for another like yourself. Sir James and his friends must go to France. If necessary I have authority from the King to order them to do so."

"Oh?" said Carolinus.

He said nothing more. Chandos stared at him for a second, before realizing that suddenly at the table there were only himself, Carolinus, Dafydd and Angie. Jim, Brian and Giles had vanished.

"Send them to France by all means, John," said Carolinus icily. "On the King's business and under the King's authority. But you will have to find them first; and they have already started on their way to do my bidding in the sea."

CHAPTER 12

"Where are we?" asked Giles.

He, Jim and Brian were standing in the center of a little bay at the seashore, with stony cliffs some thirty feet high, crowned with a rim of dark earth and rough grass, behind them and enclosing a semicircle of stony beach perhaps three hundred yards in length.

The powerful, white-maned, icy waves of the Atlantic pounded on the stones of that shore, coming in one after the other—Jim could not remember who had said it originally, possibly it was the Vikings—"the Wild White Horses," someone had called them.

"About five miles north of the Loathly Tower, I should judge," Brian answered Giles. "James, if we're supposed to start doing something or other, we're damned short of equipment. I'm wearing my sword, but outside of that I'm a naked man. I need armor and a horse. Also, it would probably be prudent to have some provisions."

This was entirely true. Jim himself had been fully conscious of this aspect of Carolinus's sudden sending of them off this way. Well, it was Carolinus himself who had reminded them all of the fact that Jim was also a magician.

"You're quite right, Brian. Anything particular you want, Giles?" Jim said, turning to Giles. "In addition to what Brian mentioned for himself, that is?"

"Merely my horse, weapons and saddle goods," answered Giles, referring to the blanket-roll of personal property that most servantless traveling knights carried with them behind their saddle for emergency living.

"Oh, I'll need my saddle goods too, James," put in Brian.

"I'll be back in an hour with all of them," said Jim.

For himself, there was something more than the other two had mentioned that he personally wanted to go back for. He concentrated and wrote on what seemed to be the inside of his forehead:

TAKE ME TO ANGIE—→ NOW

He felt once more in him the curious generative sensation that Carolinus insisted was the magical form of creativity at work; but was different from any creativity feeling Jim had ever experienced before. Suddenly he found himself immediately behind Angie as she was entering their solar from the corridor outside and the tower staircase just beyond.

"Angie—" he began.

Angie gave a small shriek, jumped and rotated—it seemed in mid-air—to face him. Seeing him, she backed away from him for several steps, before catching herself. But she still stared at him as if he were a ghost.

"Angie, it's all right. It's just me," Jim said, following her into the solar. "I had to use magic to come back to see you. I just couldn't take off like that without a word. It's all right—it's me—the flesh-and-blood me."

To prove it, he put his arms around her.

She was stiff when he first touched her, but melted almost immediately into his arms.

"Oh, Jim!" she murmured after a moment; and unexpectedly burst into tears.

"I at least wanted a chance to say goodbye," Jim said.

"Oh, yes!" Angie sobbed against his chest. "It would have been—on top of everything else, it would have been too cruel! I hate them all! Chandos and Carolinus and all of them!"

"But you'll forgive them, won't you—Carolinus, anyway?" asked Jim.

Angie stood back from him and carefully wiped the corners of her eyes.

"I suppose so," she said in a shaky voice. "Carolinus, anyway—eventually. But it was too cruel! And I've treated you just terribly these last two days. I always treat you terribly!"

"No you don't," said Jim soothingly, "just—"

He broke off, aware that he was about to step into a verbal quagmire.

"Just most of the time, I suppose," said Angie ominously.

"No—no!" said Jim hastily. "I was just going to say—ah—just put the whole thing out of your mind."

"It doesn't bother you that I'm angry with you, then?" asked Angie.

"Well, of course it does—" Jim was beginning when Angie suddenly threw herself into his arms again.

"What am I doing?" she said. "Pay no attention to me—to what I say, I mean!"

She lifted her head and kissed Jim firmly and long upon the lips.

He kissed her back.

It was some little while later before they got around to talking about the things that Jim needed to take back with him to Brian and Giles.

"They won't need their horses," Jim was saying. "Horses won't do any good under water."

"How are you ever going to go safely under water?" asked Angie.

"It'll have to be done by magic, of course," said Jim. "You know how hard I practiced up here all winter. Carolinus was quite right, essentially you have to teach yourself. I told you about him having me swallow a shrunken-down copy of the *Encyclopedie Necromantick*, didn't I?"

"Yes, you did," Angie shuddered. "How big did you say that was before you swallowed it?"

"I didn't have a chance to measure it," said Jim, "but it was the biggest and heaviest book I've ever seen."

Angie shuddered again.

"But he shrunk it down to almost a speck," Jim told her. "I was surprised at how easy it was to swallow. Anyhow, with that in me, and practicing at it, I've begun to get a better grasp of magic. To start off with I was just using sort of kindergarten magic. Now I'm beginning to put together simpler enchantments. One of those will give me something to make the trip. I'll enclose all of us in a bubble of air, kept continually fresh. I've done it before."

"You have?" Angie sat up suddenly in the bed and looked narrowly down at him. "When? Where?"

Jim saw another quagmire in front of him. *When* had been when he was held in thrall by a particularly beautiful, female, French water fairy. He had used the magic to escape from her.

"Oh just a lake I had to cross by walking along the bottom of it and up the other side," he said carelessly. "Also, this time if I'm delayed, I'll find some way of sending you messages."

"Good!" said Angie. She jumped off the bed. "Now, what do you need to take back to Giles and Brian? Let me help you get it together."

Some two hours later, Jim reappeared on the pebbly shore of the beach, leading a single horse with all the personal belongings, armor, weapons and food for each knight. Happily, Brian had arrived at the castle on his destrier, and leading a baggage horse in expectation of some adventure, for like most knights he was able to get by with very little. Nevertheless, the faces of both knights fell as they approached Jim and saw what his single horse carried.

"Where's my lance? Where's Blanchard, my horse?" demanded Brian, as he reached Jim.

"And my lance, and my horse?" said Giles, right behind him. "To say nothing of your own, James?"

"You won't be needing them where we're going," said Jim. "Remember, a horse can't travel under water. And even if it was, it couldn't get up enough speed against the water to make your lance-work useful. So we'll save ourselves trouble all around by leaving them behind."

"Won't feel the same," grumbled Brian. Nonetheless, he began to check what was on the baggage horse's back, and remove pieces of his armor, preparatory to putting them on.

Jim himself was putting off the business of getting on his armor and weapons. Instead he was pacing the shingle of the beach while he worked out the magic needed to take them safely to their destination.

This involved not one, but a number of incantations; and even though what he finally worked out seemed to cover everything necessary, he had a vague feeling something was missing. He returned to the others and began to put on armor and weapons.

"What made you wait till now, James?" asked Brian curiously. "You seemed to have something on your mind, the way you were walking to and fro, over there."

"I was solving a magical problem," said Jim.

Brian was completely satisfied with the answer, as Jim had known he would be. In any case, it would have done no good to tell them what he had figured out, since none of it would have made much sense to either of them.

He proceeded, accordingly, to armor and arm himself with the help of the other two, as the other two had helped each other, into their respective armor. Even fourteenth-century armor was almost impossible for a man to put on completely by himself; and be sure it was firmly tied, hooked, or otherwise fastened in place.

Finally ready, Jim lifted up his visor—which had managed to fall down as they fastened his leg greaves—and looked into the other two faces, peering back at him from under their own raised visors.

All this putting on of armor, Jim knew, was probably unnecessary. But it would be impossible to convince the other two of that. They were going into an unknown situation, and the thought in either knight's head of doing any such thing without armor and weapons would have struck them as unthinkable.

There was only one more thing to be done; and that was to magically send the baggage horse back to the stables of Castle Malencontri.

He did so.

"Now," said Jim, "I'm going to summon our guide to where we're going."

"Forgive me for asking, m'Lord," said Brian. His use of the title emphasized the formality and therefore the importance of his question. "But where is that, exactly?"

"I've no idea," answered Jim, "but our guide will. He knows this kraken; and he'll take us to him. Now, all I've got to do is call him. His name's Rrrnlf."

Once more, he tried to trill the initial R, and succeeded well enough so that Giles looked at him with a glance of both puzzlement and approval.

"Rrrnlf," said Giles, doing a much better job of it than Jim had been able to do. Giles's Northumbrian background, obviously, Jim thought.

"That's right," he said.

He turned and walked down and away from them to where the waves smashed against the shore closest to them. He stood for a moment watching; and noticed that the waves came up different distances. In fact he was forced to move back a few feet, when one of the waves came up to the point where it would have splashed over the armor of his feet and lower legs. He found himself wondering if it was actually true that the ninth wave always came farthest up the beach. He had read that someplace. Some story by Rudyard Kipling, he thought.

Having retreated, he cupped his gauntleted hands about his mouth and shouted as loudly as he could.

"*Rrrnlf!*"

He repeated the call half a dozen times, but only the waves smashing on the beach responded. He was not at all surprised at this. Rrrnlf might be anywhere; and his notions of time were unguessable.

Jim went back to Giles and Brian.

"Now," he said, "I've called our guide. He's called a Sea Devil, by the way. But I've no way of knowing whether he's going to get here in fifteen minutes or fifteen days. So we'll just have to be patient. If it turns out to be a matter of days, we'll set up a camp here."

The other two nodded. They were no strangers to having to live outdoors for days, or more, if necessary. It was part of ordinary travel.

"Meanwhile," Jim went on, "I'll start on the magic that'll make it safe for us to go down with him to see this kraken. If you don't mind I'll just go off a little distance to do that."

"By all means, James," said Brian, almost hastily; and Giles nodded again vigorously beside him. They had a healthy respect for magic and believed in being a polite distance from it when a magician was at work.

Accordingly, Jim walked down the beach about fifty yards, though actually this was not necessary at all, and began to form the various magical commands that would need to be put together to create the vehicle that would take them safely under water.

Giles, of course, having silkie blood and able to become a seal, could have dived to a considerable depth. But Jim suspected Granfer would be a lot deeper than a seal could go with just the air in his lungs. Pressure would increase rapidly;

and, seal or not, he would have to return to the surface for more oxygen, then dive again to join them.

Altogether, an impractical way of traveling along with the other two.

Jim cogitated; then, after a moment, he came up with the last line of the incantations he had worked while pacing the beach.

MAKE TRANSPARENT BUBBLE WITH ALL
NECESSARY AMENITIES TWELVE FEET
IN DIAMETER→ NOW

Something almost invisible appeared immediately in front of him. It was the bubble, all right, for it shimmered. He could barely make out its shape from the fact that the farther beach seen through it was distorted. It looked like a very satisfactory submersible.

He was proceeding with other incantations, to make doubly sure the air in it would always be fresh and that it would resist any depth of water pressure they should encounter, when a sudden roar from seaward interrupted his attention and made him look in that direction as he recognized the roar for the single word it had been.

"Hail!"

Sure enough, now that he looked, the familiar head of Rrrnlf was beginning to protrude from the waves only about fifty feet offshore. As Jim watched the Sea Devil waded forward, appearing to grow as he emerged from the sea.

"Muddy bottom here, but nicely shelving," he boomed. "Don't like the feel of mud underfoot, though!"

By the time he had finished this sentence he was striding through the last of the surf and up onto the shore itself, where he stopped, about a dozen feet down the shore from where Jim was.

"How can I help you, wee Mage?" His deep voice echoed over Jim's head.

But Jim was staring in fascination at the sort of half boots tied up around his massive thighs with thongs.

"But your feet aren't muddy at all!" he said.

"Oh I was careful to walk above the mud, not in it," said Rrrnlf. "Always do that. Don't like mud at all. No, no, I don't like it. Or silt."

"But—" Jim looked at the towering thirty-foot figure, which seemed to be bearing down on the stones of the beach beneath its feet with entirely normal ponderousness for a body of that size. "How did you manage to walk *above* the mud? I mean, without touching it?"

"No trick, wee man," boomed Rrrnlf. "I just thought light. Think light and then you don't need to touch what's underfoot. Just a matter of thinking."

"Oh, I see," said Jim. The trick must be part of the abilities of Sea Devils as Naturals. Now that he stopped to think of it, it would be handy not only for mud, but for walking over coral, or something like it which would quickly slice any sort of boots, shoes or feet to ribbons.

He suddenly remembered Brian and Giles. When something the size of Rrrnlf hove on the scene, there was a tendency to forget about smaller objects. Jim hurried to amend the matter.

"If you'll turn around," he said to the Sea Devil, "you'll allow me to present to you Sir Brian Neville-Smythe of Smythe Castle; and Sir Giles de Mer of Northumberland. Two worthy gentlemen, and Companions of mine who will be accompanying me."

Rrrnlf turned, looked down at the two men and boomed genially.

"Good to meet both you wee knights," he said. "Which one's Brian and which's Giles?"

"I am Sir Brian!" said Brian with an edge to his voice. Clearly, Rrrnlf's size was not intimidating him. Giles looked almost equally ready to challenge the Sea Devil to single combat. But Rrrnlf had spoken in pleasant terms, and the least they could do in courtesy was to reply.

"And I am Sir Giles," said Giles.

"Well, well, well, well," said Rrrnlf, turning back to Jim. "Now what was it you wanted from me, wee Mage?"

"I want you to take us, all three of us, to meet Granfer. We need to talk to him," said Jim. "Can you find him?"

"I know where everything in all of the oceans are, of course," said Rrrnlf. "What sort of Sea Devil would I be if I didn't? Shall we go?"

"I've got a few things to do first," said Jim. He had not expected the other anywhere near this swiftly; and the magic on the vehicle he had built for Giles, Brian and himself was still incomplete.

"Oh, working some of your wee magic, I see," said Rrrnlf. "Go ahead, by all means. Take your time. I have all the time in the world. Centuries. Millennia, if necessary."

"It won't take anything like that long," said Jim a little shortly. He knew Rrrnlf meant well, but the Sea Devil seemed unable to help rubbing others the wrong way. He found himself feeling a little bit like the way Giles and Brian must be feeling after Rrrnlf's condescending greeting of them.

CHAPTER 13

❧

They dropped swiftly at a shallow angle through a translucent blue darkness—or was it a translucent blue lightness? They were very far beneath the surface of the ocean now, and the light had grown less and less; until finally it had given way to this strange bluish illumination, which was very dim but at the same time seemed to illuminate remarkably.

They were moving at what Jim estimated to be a terrific speed. He could only measure it and their drop by the sensations in his stomach, like those of someone in an elevator that was dropping rapidly; and the occasional flash of the form of some sea life that they passed. They were moving at this speed to keep up with Rrrnlf, beside them.

How the Sea Devil was managing to travel so fast was a mystery; because he was not visibly swimming or moving his body. He seemed to progress the same way someone who was able to do so might levitate himself through the air—except that for some reason Jim was certain that they were traveling at about the speed of a commercial airliner, back on his original world.

It was impossible for Rrrnlf to move without moving, so to speak. But it was also impossible for their bubble to travel this fast through as thick a medium as water, without making that water effectively as solid as concrete. Unless the answer for them lay in one of Jim's magic incantations.

He had, in building the bubble, taken the precaution to make it "uncrushable," at any pressure.

But it was an eerie, and an uncomfortable, situation. Jim sat on a stool on the leveled floor he had created, along with the stools, inside the bubble. Rrrnlf was just outside the bubble to his right, now; and Giles and Brian sat on other stools, facing him.

The two knights looked as uncomfortable as Jim felt. Their present situation was undeniably unnatural and frightening.

Jim forced his own emotions down under control. At all costs, he thought, he must keep up the spirits of the other two; because while they were both men who normally feared nothing, this was the type of unreasonable, magical situation that could make flinders of even their courage.

Jim put on a grin for their benefit.

"Well, well," he said to them, "we're on our way!"

Neither of the others responded. It was obvious that they were on their way. Jim tried again.

"Strange, isn't it?" he said. He went on grinning determinedly. "But then we've been in a lot of strange situations, haven't we? Remember how Malvinne's magic tricked us into blundering into the Kingdom of the Dead when we were trying to escape from Malvinne's castle?"

"I remember," said Brian, "but there the magic just got us into it. Here we're right in the middle of the magic and it keeps on going. This light is unGodly."

"As a matter of fact, I think it's perfectly natural. Indeed, I know it is," said Jim, thinking back. "I remember reading once about a man who went down in an iron ball into the very deep ocean and he had a window in the iron ball. He saw this same blue light when he got very, very deep indeed. So it's really not unGodly. It's just the way the ocean is."

"I'd not disagree with you, James," said Giles. "But I have to confess I've got this terrific urge to turn into my sea form as a seal, and break loose for the surface. Whatever else is true, it is not safe to be at this depth."

"Well, this is where we have to look for the kraken," answered Jim.

"In shallower water," boomed a deep bass voice from outside. Rrrnlf had a habit of intruding on a conversation any time he felt like saying something; and since his voice, in volume and tone, could simply override theirs, there was no way of stopping him. "Why do you call Granfer—what was it you called him—a kraken, wee Mage?"

"That's what people on land call such as Granfer," Jim answered.

Rrrnlf could evidently speak to them quite easily from outside; and he seemed to hear equally well when one of them spoke back to him, so Jim had not raised his voice— although the booming tones tempted him to shout in return, in spite of himself. But he told himself that doing so would be giving away an edge to the Sea Devil; and Rrrnlf had edge enough, already.

"Where is Granfer?" Jim asked. "Aren't we starting to get close to him now?"

"Not too far off," said Rrrnlf. "We're getting near. It's one of the shallow banks he likes, where the cod school. Likes cod a lot, does Granfer."

The angle of their travel turned sharply upward. Also they began to slow toward a more normal speed. As they did, they began to glimpse the fish and other sea life they were passing. But even slowed to this speed, these forms of sea life were visible only for fractions of a second—so that the effect was weirdly kaleidoscopic.

Still, the upward motion and the slowing continued.

"We're getting close now to the bank where Granfer is?" asked Jim, speaking through the wall of the bubble to Rrrnlf.

"That is so," boomed Rrrnlf, without looking at him. "It is a bank close to the large land area far to the west of your little island; and much frequented by a number of all kinds of fish."

Jim was interested. A "large land far to the west of your little island" sounded very much like North America. He wondered if the place they were coming to after traveling at such speed would be the Newfoundland banks. It was possible, at least. He knew of no banks in the mid-Atlantic that had such a reputation as a gathering place for fish.

If that was true, they had been traveling not merely as fast as a commercial airliner but at a speed more than the equivalent of supersonic speed in air, which made their quick passage all the more amazing.

The weirdly transparent blue light had been left behind now. The light in the water outside the bubble was clearly getting stronger; and Giles, at least, was beginning to look more cheerful.

They seemed to be slowing almost as fast as they must have gathered speed. Jim could feel the slowing, though he had not been aware of the acceleration that must have been needed to get them up to the tremendous rate at which they had crossed the ocean—if that, indeed, was what they had done.

They were now leveling off in water that certainly did not lack fish up to fairly good size—four and five hundred pounds and even more, although Jim's knowledge of fish was not good enough to identify clearly the ones they passed.

Looking down now through the bottom part of the bubble, he had a moment of vertigo. A sea bottom was visible, toward which they seemed to be descending, even though the motion he felt of the bubble gave him the impression that they were still headed upward at an angle. Clearly, the sea was shallowing faster than they were rising above it.

It was not a very attractive underseascape. There was no evidence of the plantlike sea creatures that populated more tropical waters. The sharply upward-angled slopes below were bare, except for occasional large boulders. Sometimes an open rock-face would be visible, but usually the surface had the sort of soft, dark, unchanging aspect of mud or silt.

They were slowing steadily now, to a speed that left them sometimes outpaced by the fish that passed them; and Giles was definitely looking cheerful.

"James!" he said. "We aren't more than six hundred feet under the surface now. Easily, I could swim up from here."

"It's good to know that, Giles," answered Jim. "Let's just hope you don't have to."

Laughter suddenly rumbled through the wall of the bubble. Rrrnlf was amused with them.

"You mean to say you didn't know how deep you were until now?" he said. "Little Mage, I'd thought better of you than that!"

"As it happened," said Jim icily, "I had ways of finding out. I have ways of doing many things. No offense meant; but it'd do you no harm to remember that!"

Rrrnlf sobered immediately.

"Now, now," he said, "no Sea Devil doubts the mighty powers that we know wee Mages can wield on occasion. It just struck me funny for a moment."

"All right," said Jim.

He spoke as placatingly as possible. He had plans that might involve Rrrnlf in the future. The last thing in the world he wanted to do was make an enemy of the Sea Devil. "Also we use those powers to help others. To our friends we are always helpful."

"That's true," boomed Rrrnlf thoughtfully. "Over the last thousand years I can think of a number of times when such as you helped one of us. I am indeed your friend, wee Mage, as witness I have brought you here. You may count on me."

"Thank you Rrrnlf," said Jim. "I do."

Suddenly, they were enveloped by a school of fish running from half a foot to a couple of feet in length.

Jim thought they might be cod, but could not be sure. He had always thought cod were a bottom-dwelling fish.

When they came out of the school it became apparent that their forward motion had stopped and they were sinking toward the silt plain below them. Jim strained his eyes to see what was underneath the bubble but had trouble making out exactly what was there. For a moment he was baffled; then he wrote himself a quick incantation:

GIVE ME VISION LIKE THE $\longrightarrow$ FISH

Immediately, staring through the bottom of the bubble, he saw that they were headed toward what looked like about a quarter acre of huge tumbled boulders, a sort of small Badlands in the midst of the silt—but also somewhat covered by silt itself. There seemed no particular reason for going down there; but then, as they got closer, he began to make out a shape which became clear as that of a large squid. It was a very large squid; and it lay with the tips of its ten tentacles buried in the silt among the rocks.

As they got closer, the squid seemed to grow in size, until Jim began to realize how truly enormous he was. His longest tentacles alone must be something like two to three hundred feet in length, and his body was as big as that of a submarine from Jim's world.

"Is that Granfer?" Jim asked Rrrnlf—and he had to struggle to keep a tone of awe out of his voice.

"That's the old fellow," said Rrrnlf. "Sitting there as usual, waiting for his food to come to him. Oh, he can move around if he wants. You'd be surprised at how he can move. But after some hundreds or thousands of years, he seems to feel—why bother?"

Suddenly, while they still seemed to be a fully safe distance from Granfer, the tip of a huge tentacle seemed to appear out of nowhere and wrapped itself around the bubble.

There was a squeaking noise as the massive suckers took hold and the tentacle tightened, trying to crush or break through the bubble. But since Jim had enchanted it to resist any pressure whatsoever, it resisted this now. After a moment the tentacle slipped off, fell downward and apparently disappeared somewhere among the rocks and silt.

"You've a Mage with you, I see, Rrrnlf," said a clear, surprisingly high-pitched voice from below them.

Rrrnlf roared with gargantuan laughter, again.

"Now, how did you guess that, Granfer?" he boomed.

"Don't make fun of a feeble old creature like me," squeaked the voice. "I have to feed to stay alive, you know."

They had continued dropping steadily toward the enormous squid body. As they got close, Jim stared; for the tips of two tentacles were holding something up in front of the one massive eye that was visible.

Whatever they held was dark and small. It was a second before Jim realized that this was only an apparent smallness. It came from the object being next to Granfer's enormous bulk. The object was a book, held open. It looked like a postage stamp beside the rest of that huge creature; but the evidence of Jim's eyes were undeniable.

Granfer was reading.

CHAPTER 14

Even as Jim tried to estimate the probable size of the book—which must be very big indeed, now that he realized its actual proportions—it disappeared.

Jim blinked. He had not even seen the flick of a moving tentacle to tuck it out of sight. He was left almost doubting that he had seen a book at all. But his memory of the sight was sharp and clear. The only solution he could imagine was that during his blink Granfer had snatched the book out of view beneath his enormous body.

But what, he wondered, would this sea creature be doing with such an enormous heavy and thick volume, that had to have been of obvious human origin? It could only have come from some sunken ship . . .

Some books, handwritten and hand-bound in the Middle Ages, were that size. Although books of any dimensions were very scarce, indeed. The labor involved in writing one by hand was mind-boggling.

They continued down until they hovered directly above the great eye of Granfer himself. It looked larger than Jim had ever imagined an eye could be. It would have made a small swimming pool, he thought. How was it looking at them now? Jim wondered. Evilly, or simply hungrily?

Their bubble halted just above it, at Jim's voiceless magical command, on his seeing Rrrnlf stop.

"You shouldn't try to eat the wee Mage and his friends," boomed Rrrnlf to Granfer.

"You're right. They should pardon me," said the high-pitched voice of Granfer.

Jim could not quite make out from where Granfer's speech was coming. Possibly from out of sight, down where the tentacles joined the body, and the mouth must be. But there was no guarantee of that. "I'm just so hungry all the time. It was sheer habit."

In fact, at this time Granfer was dragging in what looked like a manta ray about a dozen feet across, though it was hard to tell what it would be, stretched out, since it was compressed by the tentacle that held it. It disappeared underneath the tower of Granfer's body where Jim had suspected the mouth of the cephalopod to be.

It was an almost absent-minded capture and swallow. Jim wrote a quick new magical command on the inside of his fore-head to the effect that Granfer should feel himself becoming nauseated at even the thought of eating humans. If Granfer could swallow something the size of a killer whale, as Carolinus had mentioned, he could probably swallow their whole bubble with a little more effort.

"Indeed, indeed," Granfer was going on, "it's a great thing for me to meet living land dwellers, except on the surface of the sea; and I seldom go there. I suppose you came because you wanted to see me for some reason, wee Mage?"

Jim had been about to point out to Granfer that he was not really entitled to the title of Mage. But on second thought, it would do no harm if Granfer gave him credit for as much control of magic as possible.

"Oh, mainly just simple curiosity," he said. "I'd heard you were the oldest and wisest creature in all the seas. I wanted to talk to someone like that."

"Ah well, you know," said Granfer, absent-mindedly hauling in and swallowing a fish that looked as if it weighed about two hundred pounds and was almost the shape of a basketball. "It's just a matter of having so many memories, you know, and remembering so many things. But what could I remember that would be of any great interest to you, wee Mage?"

"Well," said Jim. He had intended to feel his way gradu-ally, but it was difficult to simply make conversation, some hundreds of feet under the sea surface, with the largest squid the world had probably ever seen. He and Granfer had too little in common for chit-chat. "It happens we've been seeing evidence of sea serpents on the island where I and these two Companions of mine live."

"One of those two Companions is a silkie, isn't he?" asked Granfer.

"I am!" said Giles belligerently. He was not the least ashamed of his silkie blood. He simply did not go around advertising the fact that it was there.

"Thought so. Yes, I thought so," said Granfer, hauling in and swallowing another large fish. In order to get them, Jim noticed his tentacles reached out beyond where Jim could see even with the fish-vision he now had. "I know the sign of the blood. Yes, I'd recognize it in any land dweller."

"I was talking about sea serpents," said Jim.

"Oh yes, serpents," said Granfer. "One of those is always dropping by to talk to me, too, you know. Not so fearful of me as most because of their size. And to tell the truth, I don't think I'd like the taste of one too well, in any case. Give me cod, any day. There's nothing like cod. Delicious!"

"So," said Jim, "perhaps you know why we're seeing more of them around this island of ours."

"It's that odd-shaped island, rather good-sized," put in Rrrnlf to the squid. "The one right next to the big land mass that stretches forever and ever—almost."

"Yes, yes, I rather guessed that was the island the wee Mage was talking about," said Granfer. He sighed. It was a strange, groaning sound that Jim had to puzzle over for a second before recognizing it. "Solitary individuals, the serpents. Almost as solitary as the Sea Devils—eh, Rrrnlf?"

"Much worse than us. When they gather together, it's against their nature; or there's some strong reason."

"Which reason is it this time?" Jim asked Granfer bluntly.

"Oh, just a reason, I understand," said Granfer. "Dear, dear! I tried to calm them down, you know. But it was no use. Only the other day a dragon from that same land that you come from, wee Mage—a dragon named Gleingul—managed to kill a serpent all by himself on some tide banks of a place called the Gray Sands—"

"It was about a century or so, ago, Granfer," put in Rrrnlf.

"Eh? That long? Anyway, it's worked on them. One of the troubles with serpents—and I always tell them this, too, when

I talk to them—is that they take things too much to heart. But no, they're determined to clean the dragons off that piece of high land. Of course, there's the dragons' hoards they have in mind, too—"

"Odd," rumbled Rrrnlf, "both dragons and serpents having hoards, like that."

"—Anyway," went on Granfer, "there's no stopping the serpents, this time. So for once they're all going to work together, and be helped by some kind of land dweller like yourself, wee Mage; only he lives on the large piece of land that Rrrnlf was just mentioning that went on forever and ever."

"I believe I know who," said Jim.

"Happens, he's near the western shore of it, close to your island," went on Granfer, "and he, with some of his people want your island for themselves. I understand he's the lander who's spoken to the sea serpents about assaulting your island at the same time his friends do—he and his friends to destroy your friends, and the serpents to destroy the dragons."

"I see," said Jim. Granfer was a smooth liar. Carolinus had said Ecotti could not be the Mastermind. "That raises a number of questions."

"Perhaps I can answer one without your asking," said Granfer. "This lander is also a magician."

"I know who you mean," said Jim sharply. "But he's not a magician. He's a sorcerer. That's different."

"Different, is it?" echoed Granfer. "Well, well. It's seldom nowadays that I learn anything new; but now I've just learned something. I didn't know there were different kinds of magicians."

"There aren't," said Jim. "There's magicians and sorcerers."

"Yet they both use magic; or so I thought," said Granfer. "What makes them different?"

"I'm afraid it'd take a magician with more learning than I have to explain it properly," said Jim. "But I know who you're referring to. His name's Ecotti."

"Ah," said Granfer on another sigh, "how you magicians astound me. Wee Mage, it's amazing the way you can reach out and pluck a name out of nowhere like that and be right."

"Now, for another question," said Jim. "Just how does Ecotti contact the sea serpents?"

"You know," said Granfer, "I told them not to do this. I said it wouldn't work. You'll run into another magician, I said. That island's bound to have at least one magician. And then what'll happen to you? But would he listen? No."

"Who do you mean by he?" asked Jim.

"Ah, well now," said Granfer, "I don't know whether he'd like me to tell you who he is or not. What use would it be to you to know, any way?"

"If I knew who he was, Rrrnlf could probably help me find him—"

"I can find anyone or anything in any of the oceans," said Rrrnlf grimly. "On any place on high land too, given time enough. Nothing stops a Sea Devil."

"Would you do that, Rrrnlf?" said Granfer in a tone as close to wistfulness as a creature weighing a matter of tons could come.

"I'm indebted to the Mage. And besides, he may be able to help me find who stole my Lady. I know it was a serpent. And I'll find whoever it was. When I do . . . !"

"No doubt you will, lad," said Granfer soothingly. "I've no doubt of it at all—"

"Just a minute, Granfer," said Jim. "You still haven't told me how Ecotti made his contact and agreement with the sea serpents to help the French forces—for those are the ones on the larger land that you're talking about—attack England, which is our island."

"Dear, dear, dear," said Granfer, "so many questions. And I've answered so many over the centuries that it's hard to remember where or when I am. Sometimes I think—"

Once again, Granfer's tentacles had moved like lightning. This time they came out of nowhere linked and woven together like a net, that caught the bubble, pushed it down and under Granfer. The darkness of the silt closed around Jim and the others utterly, so that suddenly they were in inky darkness.

"I'll think about that question for a while." Granfer's voice filtered down to them, muffled by the silt above them and by the mass of his own body. Jim ordered the bubble to move. It stirred slightly, but between the silt and Granfer's weight holding it down it seemed trapped.

Which was all wrong. Because it was supposed to ignore any pressure upon it; and yet the pressure of Granfer's admittedly massive body and the silt were holding it trapped.

Jim was stunned. Granfer was not a Natural, and therefore did not have instinctive, unconscious built-in superhuman abilities, like that which had allowed the Sea Devil to move at great speed with them through the water.

Neither, of course, could he have the kind of powers that the sorcerer Ecotti had obtained from the Dark Powers, unless—and this was too far-fetched to really consider—Granfer could have sold himself to the Dark Powers.

It was unthinkable, because while some humans had been known to do this, no animal that Jim knew of ever had, except the dragon Bryagh who had stolen Angie away to the Loathly Tower; and the great squid above them was an animal.

At any rate, they were stuck. Through the silt they could not quite make out the voices of Granfer and Rrrnlf, who could be either congratulating each other at having trapped the three Companions; or arguing with each other because Rrrnlf had brought Jim and the others there with every honest intention and belief in their safety.

But at any rate, the bubble would not move. Well, thought Jim, first things first.

"Light!" he said, meanwhile writing inwardly on his forehead the brief enchantment necessary to make the bubble be illuminated.

Suddenly there was light all around them. However, it was a very considerate light; for it started out low and brightened as their eyes adjusted to it. The first thing Jim did was look at Brian and Giles to see how they might be taking it.

To his happy surprise, they looked very well indeed. Excited, and almost eager. It was puzzling, seeing how downcast and fearful they had seemed to be while the bubble was going through the zone of blue illumination.

Then Jim understood. Then, there had been nothing they could do about anything, on the trip here. Worse, they did not have any idea how long that situation was going to continue. All their skills were useless.

On the other hand, here, even if their skills still seemed—at least for the moment—useless, things were happening. The fact that Granfer had decided to sit upon them and had done so was entirely understandable. It might be hopeless for them to try to do something about it—or it might not. But at least they had the alternative to die bravely, which to them was reassuring.

"For some reason," Jim told them, "I can't seem to use my magic directly, here. But there's no reason I can't use it indirectly."

For a moment he yearned to simply turn the bubble red hot, to make Granfer so uncomfortable he would move off them. But he was not sufficiently trained, evidently; for he could not summon up the necessary incantation.

Then suddenly, he had another idea.

"Hang on," he said to Brian and Giles. "I'm going to put a couple of digging hands on the bottom of this bubble."

What he had in mind actually called for two equations. He wrote them, accordingly.

1) TWO DIGGING HANDS ON
BOTTOM OF→ BUBBLE
AND
2) DIGGING HANDS BIG ENOUGH
TO MAKE TUNNEL FOR→ BUBBLE

A glow came from beneath their feet. Looking down, Jim saw what looked like two pieces of metal extending from the bottom of the bubble into the silt; and in the direction they extended, the silt glowed for a distance that the eye could not measure against the obscurity.

"Now," said Jim, writing the command into a further incantation:

DIG STRAIGHT DOWN→ TWENTY FEET

The hands dug. Behind the hands, the bubble drifted gently downward like a feather in still air, but without the sideways slipping motion of a falling feather. Then they halted. The sound of the two voices above them had become almost inaudible.

"Right!" Jim thought, writing equations madly on the inside of his forehead:

ROTATE HANDS TO→ HORIZONTAL

DIG BUBBLE-SIZED TUNNEL→ FIFTY FEET

MOVE BUBBLE TO→ END OF TUNNEL

ROTATE DIGGING HANDS TO→ TOP OF BUBBLE

DIG→ UPW—

He broke off, suddenly remembering something. It was a form of incantation that Malvinne, the former magician-minister of the King of France, had used on them when he caught them in his castle.

Jim pointed with his hand back and up in the direction in which Granfer must be. He wrote the equation on his forehead.

STILL

They had been out of hearing of the voices for some seconds now. But suddenly a faint noise that could have been a high-pitched screech or shriek came to them.

Jim grinned to himself.

DIG→ UPWARDS INTO OPEN WATER

The bubble went up.

Jim grinned agin, this time openly. He had first encountered the *still* command when it had been used on him by Malvinne, who had been not a sorcerer, but—as Carolinus had put it—"a magician gone wrong." He had been a AAA rated, account-able magician until he had sold himself to the Dark Powers.

Therefore, he had only had the regular magician's, non-aggressive, magic at his fingertips. But the command *still* was not necessarily a punitive command. It could be used, for example, to stop someone about to step into deadly danger. At any rate, it had worked now with Granfer.

They popped out of the top of the tunnel and floated up into open water.

LIGHTS→ OFF

commanded Jim; for the interior illumination was making all the sea outside an utter blackness.

It took a moment for their eyes to readjust.

When they did, they saw the Sea Devil facing them with his mouth open in astonishment; and Granfer just as he had been—except that he was absolutely not moving a tentacle or any other muscle of his huge body. Jim ordered the bubble back close to both Rrrnlf and the motionless Granfer.

"Now," he said to Granfer, "what about this business of how Ecotti managed to get into contact with the sea serpents?"

There was no response from Granfer; and Jim suddenly remembered that *still* meant exactly what it said. He made the necessary minor adjustment that would allow Granfer to speak—but nothing else.

" . . . How could you do this—do this to a poor old person like myself?" burst out the voice of Granfer, plainly made audible in mid-sentence. "A poor old creature who just wants to lie still and eat his food and not bother anyone! I'll starve!"

"Tell me what I asked," said Jim sternly—or thought he said it. To his own surprise the words did not come. Clearly *still* could not be connected to making people talk, or else it became aggressive magic. Jim tried approaching the question from a more oblique angle; and this time his voice worked.

"Come now, Granfer," he said. "If you please me, I'll release you. If you think, you can certainly guess what would please me."

He stopped speaking. Granfer said nothing for a long moment.

"As a matter of fact," said Granfer, at last, sadly, "I told him—"

"Him? Who, him?" demanded Rrrnlf with all the power of his bass voice.

"Essessili," said Granfer.

"That serpent! I knew it!" roared Rrrnlf. "Did he have my Lady with him when he spoke to you?"

"Alas, no," said Granfer. "He just came to me, like they all do, and talked to me about how he and all the sea serpents wanted to get rid of all the dragons on your island. I told him it wasn't right. I told him he was foolish. But he kept insisting. So finally I told him to get in touch with this Frenchman, who was a magician but not a magician."

"A sorcerer," said Jim coldly.

"Oh yes, you must forgive this old brain," said Granfer. "I think this sorcerer had some name like—Eketry, Etoki—you said it yourself, earlier."

"And how did you tell Essessili how to get the other sea serpents to work with Ecotti?"

"Dear, dear me," said Granfer, in something so plainly close to a whimper that Jim was for a moment touched by it. "I, who never betrayed a confidence in all these many centuries, am asked to do so now. And if I don't, I stay forever fixed here. I can't catch fish and feed myself. I'll starve and die. Dear, dear me!"

"Well?" asked Jim.

"If you must know, I told him to promise Ecotti your Lady, Rrrnlf. You had put a fortune—as landers count it—in jewels on her!" cried Granfer. "Oh, he didn't really mean to ever give her to him, Rrrnlf. He just promised."

"So," said Rrrnlf, "that's why he stole her from me!"

"No, no, not just that!" Granfer's voice rose timorously. "He'd told me how he had long envied you, Rrrnlf, in your possession of your Lady; and how he wanted to steal it, but didn't know how he could do it safely. He wanted me to give him some suggestions."

"And you did?" demanded Rrrnlf, dangerously.

"For a price. For a price for the good of all," said Granfer, whimperingly again. "I had tried to talk him out of this nonsense of gathering the other sea serpents—he's possibly the only one who could do it, since if the rest of them would listen to anyone else of their own kind, they'd listen to him. But he wouldn't. He took my advice about your Lady, and said he was all for the serpents invading!"

"Why?" demanded Jim.

"He said he was going to show them the Lady, and explain how much gold and jewels they could win from the dragons of your island."

"I see," said Jim. "So—"

But Rrrnlf drowned him out.

"So that's it!" he snarled. "I remember now. There was a sea serpent voice that called me from somewhere out of sight. It surprised me so much I left her for just a second. And when I looked back—she was gone."

"Essessili probably got another serpent to help him," explained Granfer.

"I'll find him. I'll find them both!" said Rrrnlf. "There'll be no place in all the seas or on high land where they can hide from me! I'll get her back!"

To Jim's surprise there were actually tears in the Sea Devil's eyes.

"She was so lovely!" said Rrrnlf brokenly, in a softer voice. "To think of him putting his dirty, serpenty paws on her!"

"All right," said Jim. He released Granfer from the *still* hold he had placed on him. "That's what I wanted to know. You're free now."

Granfer's tentacles stirred and spread out until their tips were lost to sight in the silted water which had been stirred up by their movement.

"Ah," said Granfer, in a tone of relief.

"Well, Rrrnlf," said Jim, "we better go now. Thanks for the information, Granfer, even if I had to twist it out of you."

"Maybe it was all for the best," said Granfer, hauling in a four-hundred-pound grouper, and popping it into his mouth as a human being might pop a peanut.

"Let's go, Rrrnlf," said Jim.

Immediately, the Sea Devil was moving again; and they were moving with him. Again, the acceleration could not be felt, but they were plainly headed downward; and while that downward movement was on a slant, once more it was swift enough to produce the stomach-floating sensation that a fast elevator does when it drops with its passengers inside.

CHAPTER 15

"Eek!" cried Angie.

"It's only me," said Jim. He advanced to take her in his arms, but she fended him off.

"What are you doing here?" she demanded.

"Well, I came back. That is, I—ah—" Jim suddenly realized that she had a good deal of right on her side. The natural thing for her to imagine was that he might be any place in the world right now except back here in their own solar bedroom. "It's not something easily explained in just a few words."

But he tried. What had happened was that as long as the bubble had turned out to be such a good vehicle for traveling swiftly under the seas, it suddenly occurred to him there was no reason why it should not be equally useful taking the three of them to his castle. Rrrnlf might have been able to bring them here faster; but Rrrnlf had left them at the seashore to go look for Essessili.

The idea of using the bubble had been simple enough. The problems involved in turning it into reality had been somewhat larger than he had expected.

So Jim had figured out the magic to propel the bubble through the air at a high altitude, where its transparency and their relative tininess, seen from the ground, would make them effectively invisible. He finally set the bubble down at the very top of the castle, where only a single man-at-arms, on watch, was standing.

A magic command caused the man-at-arms to forget that he had seen them or could see the bubble. They had gone down the stairs to the interior of the castle and Jim had turned left into the short corridor that led to his own solar bedroom; meanwhile sending Brian and Giles down one floor to Giles's room with orders to stay hidden there.

It had been a stroke of luck, he thought at first, finding Angie there. She relaxed as he told her the whole story of what had happened.

"So now you'll stay this time," she said. "Thank goodness."

"Well, no," said Jim awkwardly. "You remember John Chandos wanted us to go to France. We've still got to do that. But I wanted to tell Carolinus about what I heard from Granfer. He may be able now to tell us something more that'll help us in our search over there."

Angie tensed up again immediately. Her hands formed into fists at her side.

"I knew it!" she said. "And you didn't have to jump at me like that without warning when I thought you were thousands of miles away!"

"Well," said Jim, in the most soothing voice he could imagine. He had had time to think of an answer to this one. "If I'd known you were in here, I'd have shouted from the corridor, 'Angie, I'm back!' but since I didn't know you were here I just walked in, expecting to find the room empty. So I frightened you."

"You didn't *frighten* me!" said Angie angrily. "You *startled* me!"

"Startled you—I mean," said Jim. "At any rate, the point is, I'm back. So are Brian and Giles. I sent them to Giles's room to stay hidden. I thought it'd be wiser not to let anyone but you and Carolinus know I was back. Possibly, Sir John too—if he's still here?"

"He left," said Angie. "Shortly after you did. I don't think he was too happy with Carolinus."

She hesitated.

"You know, Jim," she said, "about telling Carolinus—I think that sickness must have done something to him. He's better now. But—for example, he's never sounded so . . . *sour* with people as he did with Sir John."

"Oh, I don't think that'll bother Sir John too much," said Jim. "In any case, Carolinus—is Carolinus. Is he able to walk around, or is he still in bed?" asked Jim. "He was sitting up all right down at the table when I last saw him."

"Oh, he's still in bed," said Angie irritatedly. "Though he can walk. But any real physical effort is a problem for him. If the rest of you want to see him, you should go to him. Why do you have to go to France, anyway?"

"I told you before I left the first time," said Jim. "I'm in direct fief to the King—"

"Oh, I know all that!" interrupted Angie. "It still seems to me Sir John simply wants some information and doesn't care what happens to you. I do!"

"How about Brian and Giles?" asked Jim cunningly. "I'm a lot safer with them along, you know."

"Of course I care about Brian and Giles too," said Angie. "Brian because he's a friend, and Giles because you've told me how much a friend he is of yours. But that's beside the—"

She broke off abruptly.

"—Oh, I forgot to tell you. Dafydd will be around the castle someplace. You'll want to include him when you talk to Carolinus, won't you?"

"What's he doing here? I'd thought he'd leave the minute we were gone," said Jim.

"He did. I don't know if you know it or not, but you've been gone about four days—"

"I have?" said Jim, astonished.

Subjectively, the time they had spent under water, crossing the ocean and talking to Granfer, had seemed like hours rather than a matter of days.

But of course, magic was strange stuff, whether it was Carolinus's or the kind that Rrrnlf used. In fact, now that he thought of it since Rrrnlf was a Natural, and could do things like moving at better than jet plane speed under water and taking others with him, maybe he could play tricks with time too.

Perhaps it had actually taken them a day or so to cross the ocean even at top speed. Maybe that was why Rrrnlf was able to answer his call so quickly. He should have asked Rrrnlf where he had been when he first heard Jim calling for him.

"—I'm telling you," Angie was saying, "as I say, Dafydd left right after you did. But when he got back home, it turned out Danielle turned him loose after all, because he was moping around so at being left out. She got so sick of that, that she kicked him out. Anyway, he came back here, hoping that Carolinus could send him to you, wherever you were. So he could join you."

"That's marvelous!" said Jim.

Dafydd not only increased their strength by a full quarter—in fact, counting his bow, he multiplied it by an unknown amount—but his particular cool and calm temperament was a great antidote to the free-flying emotions of both Brian and Giles. These, like most knights, tended to act and speak in whatever way they happened to feel at the moment. They were difficult to reason with. Dafydd would listen, at least until you finished explaining something.

"But why didn't Carolinus send him after us, then?" said Jim, getting his questions backward and asking the second one first. "When did he get back here, anyway?"

"About a day ago," said Angie. "He did ask Carolinus. But Carolinus said he should wait here, and you'd be back. Dafydd's been waiting ever since. You know him. When he has time to kill he simply sits and makes arrows. Of course, he occasionally makes a bow, too, but generally it's just more arrows. I've had to jump on most of our female staff to leave him alone. You know how he is. He attracts women like flies."

"Did he ever attract you?" demanded Jim, suddenly jealous.

"Of course he did," said Angie. She smiled a little evilly. "But of course I'm in love with you."

"You better be!" growled Jim.

He reached for her, and this time she came to meet him.

"What you'd better do," said Jim, when their mouths were free for talking again, "is go find a servant to locate Dafydd and bring him to you. Is Carolinus in his room?"

"Yes," said Angie.

"Good," said Jim. "We'll get together there. Any servant is going to scratch on the door first, before daring to enter a magician's room. Don't say anything to Dafydd about Carolinus's room until you two are alone. Meanwhile, I'll go get Giles and Brian and we'll all go to Carolinus's room, so we'll be there when you show up with Dafydd. That way nobody but you and Carolinus will know that we're here."

"All right," said Angie. But the tone of her voice said that she still hadn't reconciled herself to Jim's going to France. "Dafydd and I will meet you at Carolinus's room."

"Good," said Jim. "Here we go, then."

They left the solar together and parted on the stairway. Jim went down to Giles's room that now held both Brian and Giles. They were seated at the table there, each on a stool, rolling dice for small coins. The small amounts must be either because they were both low on funds; or else Giles was simply accommodating himself to Brian's financial straits. Brian's ancient Castle Smythe was badly in need of repair, and he had no means of income except for what he won at tilting tourneys with his lance-work.

At the sight of him they both got to their feet and Giles put the dice away in the purse at his sword belt.

"We're going to get together with Carolinus now," announced Jim, "—and Dafydd . . ."

He explained what Angie had told him about the bowman. The faces of the other two lit up. They liked Dafydd as well as he did; although occasionally one or the other of them would feel uncomfortable in social situations in which Dafydd had to be treated before company in a manner that was above his station. They could not help such feeling, in spite of the fact the Little Men on the Scottish border remembered Dafydd's connection with an ancient royalty. It was part of their training. Bowmen did not socialize with knights.

Jim explained the situation.

" . . . So, we should go to Carolinus, now," he wound up.

The others nodded and followed him.

Carolinus, when they got to his room, was sitting on the side of his bed, wearing his red robe, magician's peaked hat, and for whatever occult reason, building with clay on his table a sort of small castle; it was not unlike the peel tower that had been the original form of Giles's family home, the Castle de Mer. The table was a duplicate of the one that Giles and Brian had been dicing on back in the other room.

"Ah, here you are!" said Carolinus, calmly adding another little dab of clay to his handiwork. "Well, sit down and tell me what happened."

In his everyday robe, he looked, as Angie had said, for all practical purposes as well as ever. Jim, however, could not resist a teasing remark.

"I thought you'd know all that already," he said. "—With your magic, that is."

"Jim," snapped Carolinus, "for a C class magician, what you know about magic—"

There was a tinge of querulous anger in his voice that Jim could not remember having heard before. But . . .

But then, having checked himself in mid-sentence, Carolinus went on, sounding no different than he usually did.

"Suffice it to say," he added, "that I want you to tell me what happened."

So Jim did, his report interrupted by only an occasional "hmm" from Carolinus.

When Jim had finished there was a silence. Jim himself broke it.

"I really didn't learn a lot," he said, "as you know now."

"On the contrary, my boy." Carolinus stroked his mustache with an air of satisfaction. "We now know a great deal. We know we've got *two* individuals to find. One is this Essessili, the sea serpent—"

"Rrrnlf has already gone off to do that," said Jim. "He left us at the beach and said he would bring the sea serpent to us; and hold off taking him to pieces until we had a chance to ask him questions. Actually, I'm a little puzzled as to how he could take a sea serpent to pieces. One of them must outweigh him at least a couple of times."

"Ah, but he's a Natural!" said Carolinus. He was, Jim noticed, now sounding like his old self. "And don't interrupt. As I was saying, we need two individuals, the sea serpent—this Essessili—and Ecotti. Rrrnlf will find the sea serpent, all right. You've got to find Ecotti and question him."

"What about?" asked Jim, but before Carolinus could answer, the door to the room opened and Angie entered with Dafydd right behind her.

"Would you like me to leave, Carolinus?" she asked the magician.

"Not at all, my dear," said Carolinus. "In fact it probably wouldn't be a bad thing if you stayed around for at least the first part of our little talk."

"Dafydd!" cried Brian, starting up from his stool, and Giles echoed the name, getting up himself. They charged across the room and (since they were in private) the ritual greeting process of embracing and back-slapping went on—all of which Dafydd accepted with a pleased smile, but a slightly pained expression around the eyes. He was not a demonstrative person himself; and this demonstration so close to the last time they had been together, Jim suspected, embarrassed him.

However, with the welcomings over, the knights reseated themselves and Brian motioned Dafydd to sit also. There were no more stools. He dropped into a cross-legged position on the floor. All attention was turned back on Carolinus.

"You haven't answered my question, Carolinus," said Jim.

"I thought I had," said Carolinus. "However, if you must have it spelled out for you, I repeat what I told you once before: physical strength is required for the creativity involved in working magic. And I need all I have at the moment. For one thing, I'll need to transport you all, and your gear and horses to France by magic."

There was a moment's long pause in the room.

"As it happens," said Jim, "I think I told you I still have the bubble—"

"That I know!" snapped Carolinus. "But, as it happens, I've already destroyed it. It may not have been visible to mortal eyes; but too many unmortal and trans-mortal eyes could be watching us now. And listening—watch out for any spells that don't seem to work the way you expected them to. It'll mean the Mastermind is interfering. In any case, time is of the essence; and your bubble would have to be hidden once it was over there. No, no, the thing to do is for me to just deliver you all at once into Brest—I believe you were there the last time you were in France, weren't you?"

"Yes," said Jim.

"And you definitely are going with the rest, now, are you, Dafydd?" asked Carolinus.

"I am," said Dafydd. "Danielle said I was moping. I said I was just a little regretful, that was all, look you. But you know my wife—she said she wasn't about to live with me the way I was; but I'd better come back safe and sound."

"Well then," said Carolinus, "it's simply a matter of getting you all there. Do you have everything you need to take?"

Brian, Giles and Dafydd all nodded.

"I've got to get some gear out of the solar—" began Jim.

"It's outside in the hall, Jim," said Angie.

"Oh? Fine," said Jim. "But aren't we moving too fast, Carolinus? We don't have a very clear idea of exactly what we're trying to find out over there. Tell me, what did you learn, if anything, from Granfer?"

"One thing, very clearly," said Carolinus. "Granfer did not give you all the links in the chain. I gather he doesn't know them himself. The Mastermind can't be Ecotti. He simply doesn't have the capability, as I told you. Nor could this one sea serpent—Essessili—get so many of the other sea serpents to join him that easily."

"So?" asked Jim.

"So," snapped Carolinus. That unusual note of querulous anger was in his first words, once more. "You're going to France to find out who the missing link is! Who is the Mastermind behind the use of the sea serpents in the invasion? It's a role that can only be filled by somebody not only very wise, but very well versed in magic—much more than Ecotti is."

"But you told us—beg pardon," said Jim, "you told me— that the Accounting Office said no magicians were involved. And if Ecotti's only a sorcerer, and there's only magicians or sorcerers who know magic, who could it be?"

"If I knew," said Carolinus, "I wouldn't be sending you to France, would I?"

"Well, how do we start?" asked Jim. "After we get there, I mean. What if we're asked why we're there?"

"Tell everyone you're exiles expelled from England by the King. The fact one of you has a Northumbrian accent—"

He looked at Giles.

"—Will make it all the more believable," went on Carolinus. "Then, at the first opportunity, and as quietly as you can, get hold of Ecotti and question him."

"That'll be no small order, Mage," said Brian mildly. "Now, if it was just a matter of killing him—"

"No, no, no!" said Carolinus irritably. "Above all, you mustn't kill Ecotti. If you do we'll never find out who the really responsible party is. Just manage to get him apart and question him."

"As Brian says," put in Jim, "that is not as easy to do as it is to say."

"I know that!" said Carolinus. "That's why I'm sending you four. Believe me, I don't know of anyone else who could do it. It'll take the individual talents of all of you, put together, but it must be done! Either Ecotti has the answer or this sea serpent—I've forgotten his name now—"

"Essessili," ventured Giles, who up till now had been respectfully silent. He pronounced the name as Rrrnlf and Granfer had.

"That's right, what's his name," said Carolinus. "Just what you said, Giles. Either he or Ecotti can tell us who the Mastermind is. One of them must have been in direct contact with him. Now, any more questions? Otherwise, off you go."

Jim looked at Brian, Giles and Dafydd and beyond them at Angie.

They all looked back at him wordlessly.

"I guess none of us have," said Jim, a little sourly.

Abruptly, they were standing in a street in Brest, dismounted from their horses and holding the reins of those horses. They were just outside the Inn of the Green Door, the inn they had stayed in on their previous visit to this port city in France.

CHAPTER 16

"**M**y Lords!"

Jim would have jumped, just like Angie, if the weight of his armor had not kept him from making that sort of betraying gesture.

He turned to see the same landlord they had had before. His name was René Peran. He was a young man, but fattish rather than stout, with a stubble of dark beard that apparently had not been shaved too recently. There was an equally dark suspiciousness about his eyes. He gave the impression of mistrusting them on sight. Perhaps he did not like foreigners. Why, Jim wondered, had they ended up at this very place where they were known? Carolinus would have no reason for putting them here. Perhaps this was a case of what he had warned Jim against. The Mastermind altering others' spells.

At any rate, if Peran didn't like foreigners, he was doing his best verbally at the moment to hide the fact.

"Welcome back, my Lords!" he said, with a sort of whining geniality. "Well I remember you from last year! But then you left and we heard no more of you. You're English, no? Yes, I remember. So, and how has it been with you, my Lords?"

"Passing well, passing well," Brian answered for the three of them. "We've been in the east, fighting the heathen. A bloody time for many poor gentlemen, alas! We are fortunate to all be together and back with you again."

Jim had never suspected Brian of being so swift and facile at dissembling. When Brian so said "east" he was probably referring to an area somewhere beyond where modern Poland would have been in Jim's time and world. In the fourteenth century there had been non-Christians in that area; and it was true that knights from all over Europe went out there looking for a chance to fight them.

Jim felt a sudden itch on the right side of his head and reached up to scratch it, only to have his fingers bump themselves on the hard surface of his helm. They were all still dressed in full armor. This could not be taken by those around them in this French city as an intent to cause trouble, since most knights tended to travel in their armor; particularly if they had wild areas to traverse, where there might be any kind of unsuspected dangers. Besides, the safest way to carry your armor on a trip was to wear it.

"But come in, my Lords," said the innkeeper, stepping forward and taking the bridles of their horses. "Come in and you shall be brought a pitcher of our best wine immediately. I'll see your steeds into the hands of the stable workers myself!"

So invited, Jim and the rest moved past the landlord, who had gone off into the courtyard behind him, at an angle toward the stables, that partly flanked and were partly behind the inn. They followed him into the cobblestoned courtyard. The itch came again, but Jim was helpless to do anything about it. It struck him that they had been wearing their armor for a little too long.

The same feeling did not seem to have occurred to either Giles or Brian, who, in typical fashion for men of their kind, never complained about the weight or troublesomeness of their armor; and, as far as Jim could tell, never even thought about it. They could probably lie down and sleep in it without realizing they had forgotten to take it off.

Within the inn, everything was as Jim remembered it from before. Smelly, but cool—for which Jim at least was grateful; and evidently the itch was, also, for it went away.

Brest was at its summer now, where it had been spring when they had visited the year before. Then, the temperature had been comfortable. Now, outdoors, in the sun especially, it was entirely too warm for comfort, particularly in this blasted armor. Jim would have liked nothing better than to get up to his room, even now, and get the armor off. But after the landlord's effusive welcome, politeness must be served. Since the innkeeper had made a fuss over them, it was their duty to accept it in proper fashion. This established on both sides that such treatment was their due, no less.

A servant had already been waiting for them, evidently, for the pitcher was on the table in the common-room to which he ushered them and the thick-walled, greenish glasses were laid out. He poured the wine for them and Jim drank from his rather hastily. It was magnificently cellar-cool and he was more thirsty than he had expected. The servant refilled glasses all around—Brian and Giles had simply emptied their glasses at a draught. Bottoms up. The servant refilled them all around and went off.

Brian sprawled out his legs and put his elbows on the table.

"We are well housed in France once more!" he said.

"Yes," said Jim. He glanced around to make sure no servants were close enough to hear. "That was quick thinking of yours outside, Brian."

"Ha! What else would three English knights have been doing out of England, if they were not to be found in France? Except in the east fighting heathens?" he said; and half drained his glass again.

Brian's mention of three knights reminded Jim of Dafydd. He looked around the common-room of the inn; and, sure enough, at one of the long, community tables Dafydd was seated by himself, with his own pitcher and cup. He had remembered their difference in rank, even if Jim had forgotten it. In fact, he told himself, he seemed to have been the only one to forget it. Both Brian and Giles had taken as perfectly natural that the bowman should go and sit apart from them.

His mind came back to the business at hand.

"I'd like to get up to my room," he said, "and get this armor off. Don't you two want to get out of your armor, too? We've been wearing it for I don't know how many hours, or days."

"Hours only, surely," said Brian.

"Angie told me we'd been gone several days."

Brian shook his head.

Magic, he was obviously thinking. Jim could see it as clearly as if the word was printed on his forehead.

"Also," Jim went on, "we'd better make some plans—and those plans had better be made in secrecy."

"You're quite right, James," said Brian, peering into the pitcher. "There's no wine left here, at any rate. We'll order some more sent up as we go."

They got up. Brian went off to attend to ordering some wine sent up as well as finding a servant to show them to their room. Jim beckoned Dafydd to come with the rest of them.

They had had the common-room to themselves, it being the middle of the day, but past the lunch hour. A servant came to lead them up to the room; and in a moment they were there. It was a good-sized room and their baggage was already there. A better room than they had had the time before. Jim frowned.

"Our bowman will sleep across the threshold inside the door," he told the servant who had showed them the way up. Just at that moment another servant with pitchers and cups came in. "Oh, and another cup for him."

The servant looked a little surprised; but knights were a law unto themselves, when you got right down to it. He went off without a word. Still, Dafydd hunkered down by the door and stayed apart from them until the servant returned with the extra cup and left again. Jim closed the door behind him.

"Let's all sit at the table," Jim said. "You come join us, Dafydd."

There were only three stools in the room, but by moving the small, square, bare-wood table over to the—as usual—single bed, they made a fourth sitting place. Dafydd took this, just so none of the others would be embarrassed at not knowing who belonged where. Brian seated himself on Jim's right, with Giles on his left and Dafydd across the table.

"You seem concerned about something, James," Brian said, pouring their cups full and putting down the pitcher before glancing keenly at Jim.

"I'm a little suspicious about our landlord, if you want to know," said Jim. "I wondered that he'd recognize us so quickly after our short visit, a year ago."

"Not at all," answered Brian. "It's a trick of the innkeeping trade to remember the faces of your guests, so you can welcome them as old friends if they ever come back again. It's even a good trick to pretend you know them—but I think he actually did recognize us. After all, we're English in a French town."

"We speak the same language," Jim could not help saying.

That was one of the amazing things. Not only all the human beings but all the animals including the dragons, the wolves and even someone like Granfer spoke the same language. It was disconcerting to somebody from a world which, even if it had been five hundred years and more in the future, was a welter of different languages.

"Ah," said Giles, "but our horses, armor, weapons, everything about us, shouts that we are English and they are but Frenchmen."

"There's that, of course," said Jim dryly. "Thank you for reminding me. You don't think I should be concerned about it, then?"

"No," said Giles.

Brian shook his head.

"As I say, such things are part of an innkeeper's tricks. But I thought you wanted to talk about what we were to do here."

"That's exactly what I wanted to talk about—and just among ourselves," said Jim. "But I've got to get out of this damn armor. Give me a moment or two."

"We could all be more comfortable with less of our metal," said Brian, rising himself. Jim was already up and Giles was not slow to follow.

Dafydd turned about on his stool and watched them with a cool amusement.

"Look you, now," he observed as pieces of armor began to litter the floor. "All that weight and trouble for so short a time when it must be used."

"All right if you're able to stand off at two hundred yards from your enemy!" grunted Brian. "But if your business is getting in close—Giles, will you help me with the side lacings of this breastplate? You tied a bloody knot there at the seashore that I don't believe I'd get undone in a month of Sundays."

"I double-tied it, that's all," said Giles; but began to untie it, anyway.

Finally, out of their armor and back once more at the table, they got down to business.

"Our problem is going to be finding Ecotti," Jim said. "Because that's what we'll have to do. Locate him first; then figure out some way to get hold of him in spite of his magic; and hold him helpless enough so that we can question him.

The more I think of it, the more impossible it seems to me."

"Faint hearts are for ladies," said Brian, refilling his cup. "Finding him—that should be no task. Let me just wander around town and see what other Englishmen I can find. There's also a good chance that English—or French; I may find someone shortly with whom I've had to do in the past at tourneys—can tell us much about matters here. Your good lance travels all over in search of tiltings."

"And, come to think of it," put in Giles, "I might look around myself for a fellow Northumbrian. If I can find one such, he will be like a brother in this foreign land. I should be able to learn a great deal from him."

"But will he have knowledge of the French court—which is undoubtedly where Ecotti is?" said Brian. "Whereas, one I bump into who's a tilting buff may well be a resident of the court himself. Either at the King's command, or because he has been retained for the use of his services."

"Well, in any case," said Giles, "the chances are good of one of us, at least, finding someone of either kind here in town, since your fighting man gets quickly bored with the velvets of a court."

Dafydd stretched and got up from his stool.

"As for myself, now," he said, "I believe I will do what I often do. I will sit in the common-room all day long; and find what knowledge comes to my ears that way. Often it is best to wait for a quarry rather than hunt him. And indeed, I do believe that is true of all knowledge—knowledge of any kind."

He went out. Giles and Brian were now down to varying dress of hose and cote-hardie, with the minimal addition of a chain mail shirt over the cote-hardie; and, of course, their knight's belts and swords were once more strapped around them—with counterbalancing dagger on the opposite side from the sword. They finished the wine and also went out.

Jim was finding himself unusually tired. Almost as if he had gone four days without sleep. Whether it was indeed this, or the wine, or the two combined, he found that right now he yearned for sleep.

He got out of his travel supplies the clean mattress Angie had made him, and unrolled it on the floor. It was the only safe way of having something to sleep on that was not alive with vermin. That small bed over there that was supposed to accommodate three grown men was probably a pest house in miniature.

He took off his clothes and put them to one side and then stretched out on the mattress. Using one of his saddlebags as a pillow and covering himself with his clothes and his travel cloak, he dropped instantly into slumber.

He dreamed that he heard a deep booming noise. No, even in his dream, he decided it was not just a noise, it was the voice of a dragon speaking to him. But what dragon . . . ?

He opened his eyes.

Standing over him were three large dragons, one even larger than the rest. The largest one was also darker of skin; and had, Jim thought, although he could not pin down why, a vaguely sadistic look. It was this dragon that was speaking to him.

"—Well, dragon?" the largest dragon was saying. "You are in our France, and you are English. Where's your passport?"

"But I'm not—" Jim was stopped by the sound of his own voice, which was not the sound of his own voice but the booming sound of his voice when he was in his dragon shape. He suddenly became aware of something. He was indeed in his dragon shape. The cloak and the clothing that had covered him were scattered around him. Once again, something magical had happened without reason.

He struggled to his feet, feeling absurdly awkward in his dragon shape.

"You don't understand," he began. "I—"

"We aren't here to understand," boomed the large dragon, who was almost as large as Jim himself. "We know who and what you are. You are the george-dragon who deals in magic. You were here once before; but that time you had a passport. You'd better have a passport with you now, too!"

"But what I'm trying to explain—" Jim began.

He was cut off by the sound of a new voice, a familiar voice, even though it was a dragon voice. It was somewhat higher than the voice of any of the other dragons in the room, including himself.

"Did your ambassadorship want your passport now, or later?" asked the voice from behind the three dragons.

CHAPTER 17

The three spun around, revealing—of all individuals—
Secoh, the mere-dragon, the stunted result of many dragon
generations who had been blasted by the Dark Powers in the
Loathly Tower, on the mere that was their home area. Right
now, however, it was not his size that was important but the
fact that he was holding a large, bulging leather bag. He had
an innocent look on his face.

"Your honor told me to keep your passport until I was called
for it," said Secoh, still innocently, "but I was afraid of being
responsible for it all by myself all night long. So I was just
bringing it to you—"

Jim was not slow to take the hint.

"Of course!" he boomed, shoving his way between two of
the dragons.

He took the bag from Secoh and was agreeably surprised
at its weight. If anything it was larger and heavier than the
passport he had carried before. He held it out; and the largest
dragon took it, loosening the thong that held its top shut and
pouring some of the gems out into his great horny palm to look
at them. The first one out was the enormous pearl that was
Secoh's only treasure and heirloom. But the diamonds, rubies
and emeralds behind it were equally large and fascinating.

The biggest dragon poured the gems back in the pouch,
tightened its top and looked suspiciously down at Secoh.

"Who are you? Where'd you come from? Or are *you* the george-dragon who deals in magic?"

"Oh, no," said Secoh. "I just happened to step through the door just now. I'm a mere assistant to his ambassadorship here, who's come to save your lives."

Save their lives? Jim thought fast.

"Yes!" he boomed; and the three turned back to face him. "I am the dragon you thought me to be. I am also the magician you thought me to be. Behold!"

He wrote the proper spell on the inside of his forehead, and was instantly back in his shape as a human—unfortunately completely naked now. He snatched up his cloak and wrapped it around him. Not only because he thought that it gave him a certain amount of dignity; but because it was cold in the room. Outside the window it was night and blackness was all that could be seen. A rush-light, possibly brought in by one of the obviously French dragons, was illuminating the room.

"My assistant is only too correct," he went on. His human voice was much more high-pitched and less impressive than his dragon one; but, nonetheless, he could see his human form producing a strong impression on the three dragons. Like most people and most dragons he had met, these seemed to feel an immediate sense of awe and caution on facing a magician. If he actually was a worker of magic, Jim could see them thinking, what might he not do, besides what they had just seen him do?

"How did you three get in here?" he went on fiercely, seizing the advantage. "Here in this inn in the heart of a city belonging to georges?"

The three French dragons shuffled their feet.

"Well, you see—Mage," said the large one, awkwardly, after a moment, "we have an arrangement with this innkeeper. He brings in cloths of a strange, soft material, and other things that you—er—that georges prize highly, from far in the east; and the wagons bringing it to him pass through some very open territory. We've guaranteed the safe passage of those wagons, in return for some casks of wine; which he sends out by the wagonload for us, every so often. Because we need to talk to him from time to time, he made doors in the roof of this wooden box of his, so we could get in. And that's how we got in tonight."

"He didn't happen to send you a message that he needed you?" asked Jim. "He didn't tell you to come here tonight?"

The three shuffled their feet a little more.

"Yes," admitted the largest French dragon finally. "He said there might be an English dragon coming in without a passport."

"He knows that much about dragons, does he?" demanded Jim. "That a dragon from England would need a passport to come to France?"

"Yes, Mage," said the large dragon, and added hastily, "but he doesn't know what the passport is. We were too clever to tell him that."

Jim reflected that if the word hadn't already gotten out that dragons used gems from their hoards to make up a "passport," then the human race was vastly less aware than he had thought it to be.

"I see," he said. "Well, now that you know that I am here as an ambassador from all the dragons of England with a message for all the dragons of France, I must talk to your leaders immediately."

"Mage, you know we don't have any leaders," said the large dragon. "But you could tell us. We all represent different parts of France. Mine name's Lethane, and I represent all the north and northwest of France right down to the sea. Iren, at my left here, represents the south coast and all the far south of France. And Reall, on the other side of me, represents all the rest."

"Very well, I will!" said Jim ominously. "You all know of the sea serpents, little as France has been bothered by them because it is not an island country like our England."

"The sea serpents know better than to bother us much," said Lethane.

"Don't be so sure," said Jim. "In England no part of the island is far from the sea. You know as well as I do of the deadly hatred sea serpents have for all dragons; and you keep hoards which the serpents covet, like any other dragons. You'd better understand now that all of them, from all the seas, are planning to exterminate all dragons and get those hoards."

There was a moment's uneasy silence from the three French dragons. Then Lethane spoke up again, a little sharply.

"We are French dragons!" he said. "And admittedly our experience with these serpents is slight. But even if you're right about this, none of them have ever come more than a short way in from the coast, and that for a short time only. Yes, we know they hate us. We hate them. Still, Mage, you tell us this; but how do we know it's true?"

All dragons, Jim knew, were difficult to rouse; but Lethane seemed more hard-headed even than most.

"Would I be handing you a passport like that if the danger wasn't real?" Jim asked.

"Well," said Lethane grudgingly, "it might be—for you. The serpents may be getting together to threaten *your* island; but it's beyond belief that they would dare attack France!"

"You know they're capable of anything," said Jim. "You know they outnumber all the dragons in the world—at least twenty to one."

He had pulled the ratio out of his imagination, but Lethane would not know the exact ratio either. He went on.

"If they swarm over England, while your georges are busy keeping our English georges busy, they'll find, root out and slay every dragon there. Flushed with victory, and riches, do you think that they won't want to get even richer by attacking you? No! They will look immediately at France, and decide to plunder it."

"They might not," said Reall, speaking up for the first time.

"Would you stop, if you French dragons attacked them and wiped out a whole area of them?" asked Jim. Three pairs of eyes turned red. Of course, they wouldn't stop.

"Besides," went on Jim, "as long as they keep winning, they'll go on attacking. They'll attack around the world like that. In the end, because there's so many of them to so few of us; and because, one on one, they are bigger and stronger than we are, there'll be no dragons left."

"But, Mage—" began Lethane, and stopped, apparently at a loss for words.

"Think about it," said Jim.

They did. Obviously, they did. They stood looking at each other, closing their lids or turning their eyes inward, then opening their eyes to look at each other again. It was something much appreciated by dragons, the matter of thinking something over. Normally, the only danger was that they would go on thinking it over until it was too late for action.

"In this case, the time is short," said Jim. "Your george King Jean hopes to sail against England soon; and the sea serpents will invade then. You've got little enough time, even now, to get the message back to your fellow French dragons and make them ready. You can tell them I've a plan by which the sea serpents may be turned back; without a drop of dragon blood being spilled. But, to make that plan work, the French dragons will have to fly over to England and join the English dragons in making a common front against the serpents!"

"Oh, we couldn't do that!" said Reall, and looked up at Lethane.

But he and Iren were silent.

They hesitated for a long moment; then Lethane spoke up.

"Mage," he said, "I don't think we can get that word to everybody and get together and get over to England in just a few weeks. We're not like you English, you know. We don't gather together to live, the way you do. We're scattered over the countryside, as your Mageness knows, though of course we can be pulled together by a message being passed. But we'll need to be able to tell them what this plan of yours is."

"No!" said Jim. "I'll tell that to them only once they have committed themselves to going to England. And they will guarantee that commitment by handing back to me the equivalent of a passport—but it will have to hold not one, but at least five of the best gems from each dragon's hoard."

"F-five?" stuttered Lethane. The two others seemed frozen in place, staring at Jim.

"You heard me," said Jim.

"But—but—that's impossible!" said the largest dragon. "I couldn't—none of us could part with our five best gems and risk our lives as well."

"Then stay here," said Jim. "Leave the English dragons to defend themselves. And when there is not one English dragon left, then you and your five best gems apiece can stand alone to face the overwhelming horde of serpents from the sea!"

There was another long moment of indecision in which the three dragons did nothing but look at each other.

"How can we tell? How do we know—" The biggest dragon ran out of words again.

"You have my own guarantee in your hand," said Jim. "Look at those gems. How many of you have even one gem that's their equal? All of those in that bag are of the same size

and color and worth. Do you think I would be handing you
something like this if the situation were not as desperate as
I put it?"

Once more, the large dragon slowly loosened the thong
that bound the bag that held the passport; and poured the
gems into one of his hands until the hand was filled with all
it could hold.

All three stared again at the diamonds, rubies and emeralds
in his hand and audibly drew in their breaths. Clearly, they
had never seen anything like this.

The large dragon put the gems back, tightened the thong
and looked at Jim.

"Mage," he said, "I can promise you nothing. If we are
going to be there by your side when the sea serpents come
in, we will be there. I will be there, anyway! Otherwise—
we'll have failed with the others."

"That's all I need to hear," said Jim. "I well know, all our
English dragons well know, the mettle of their French cousins,
once aroused!"

The three dragons straightened up and slightly spread their
folded wings.

"You need not remind us of that," said the large one. "We
will do what we can. Farewell, Mage."

They turned and went out, having to squeeze painfully
through the small door of the room with their large bodies.
When they were gone Jim closed the door behind them and
turned to Secoh.

"Now tell me," he said, "just how did you happen to turn
up just at the right moment—and with that passport?"

"Oh, Carolinus did it all—" Secoh broke off. "But I should
start at the beginning, m'Lord."

"Go ahead," said Jim resignedly. Secoh was being himself
now, and showing off; by using the george term that under-
scored the fact he understood Jim merited "m'Lord" as an
address.

Secoh might be stunted and a mere-dragon; but he had all
the ordinary dragon's usual ways, including a desire to start
at the beginning of a story and work his way up to the climax,
even if that made a long process out of something that could
otherwise be pretty short.

In this case, thought Jim, it would be uncharitable to hurry
him; and besides, it was still dark outside, although he thought

the darkness was beginning to pale a little bit—perhaps the night was getting on toward dawn. In any case Secoh should have his way, this once.

"Tell me the story from the beginning then, Secoh," he said. As the other started talking, he took off his cloak and began to dress. There was no point in trying to go back to sleep now.

"Well, I heard Carolinus had been ill but was at your castle and getting better and I thought I might just go see him," said Secoh earnestly. "I admire the Mage very much; and as a fellow Companion with you and him, I thought—"

"Quite all right, Secoh," said Jim, pulling on his hose. "Go ahead."

"Well, anyway, I went," said Secoh. "By the time I got there Carolinus was already much better; and you, Giles, Brian and Dafydd had already left. After congratulating Carolinus on regaining his health, I asked about the rest of you, and he told me that your destination was France and that you had already gone.

" '*Without a passport?*' I asked.

" '*Passport? What passport?*' he said to me," Secoh went on, "and I explained to him that you couldn't possibly go into France, being a dragon as well as a Mage, without having a passport from your own community of dragons here in England—that passport to be the best gem from each dragon's hoard. And no dragon liked to part with any gem from his hoard, let alone the best one. It was very hard for you and I to get it from them the last time.

" '*Well, that's no problem!*' said the Mage. You know that snappish way of talking he has?"

"I do indeed," said Jim.

" '*Well, that's no problem,*' he said," Secoh went on. " '*You just fly up there and tell them I said they were to give you the gems, right away!*'

" '*But, Mage,*' I said, '*they won't just give up their gems that quickly or that easily. Even if you went up there yourself and argued with them, it still might take several days. We were just lucky, the last time, the Lord James and I, to get our passport when we went before.*'

" '*Oh, they will, will they? I'll just—*' and then he stopped, suddenly, just like that," said Secoh. "And then he said, '*No, why go to all that bother? I'll make you a passport. How many gems should there be in it, and what size should they be? All kinds, I suppose?'*

" *'There are eighty-seven dragons old enough to have collected hoards; so we need eighty-seven gems. Almost as big as this.'* " Secoh held out two claws several inches apart. "And also I showed him my pearl, for size and beauty, which I happened to carry always with me, for safety."

Jim was now dressed and unconsciously tapping the toe of his right shoe on the floor of the room in impatience.

"Well, to make a long story short," said Secoh hurriedly, "he made the gems; but after he had them done he said it needed one real gem in with them to make them come alive—and indeed, they were kind of dull until he added my pearl to them. Then they seemed to glitter the way you saw them do, just now. So, that's what I brought to France to be your passport; and that's what you handed over to . . . Lethane, I think his name was.

"Oh, and by the way," added Secoh, "the Mage said that the gems would '*evaporate*'—I don't know exactly what that means. Sort of go away, I understand, in thirty days; so we have to have them back at that time."

"Hmm," said Jim. "I'm really cheating the French dragons, as well as falsely representing my own community of the Cliffside dragons."

"Well, yes," said Secoh. "But you'd have to go back to England with me to get the real passport. Even if they'd give it to you a second time."

"True," said Jim, frowning.

"Anyway," went on Secoh, "then Carolinus told me where to find you and he was just about to send me, when he said, '*No, wait! Stay with me. I'll tell you when it's time for me to send you over to them.'* "

"Ah," said Jim. "He must have scented that something was going to happen; and that someone might interfere with his magic."

"Oh, he did. I'm sure of it," said Secoh. "He may not have known exactly what, but he knew something would happen. Anyway, I waited with him until he suddenly said, '*Now you go!'* and all of a sudden I found myself outside your door, here. So I came in."

"Did he tell you to say to the French dragons that I was an ambassador?"

"Yes, he did," said Secoh, brightening. "I forgot that part."

"Well, thank you," said Jim. "All his magic and my magic wouldn't have done the trick, if it hadn't been for you coming in at just the right moment and saying just the right things."

"Oh, thank you, m'Lord!" said Secoh.

"So, we now have something stirring with the French dragons—something I hadn't counted on before. It might pay off," said Jim. "The only trouble is the fact that your pearl is one of the gems that Lethane carried off with him."

Jim happened to know that the pearl was the single item left in Secoh's hoard. It was his single heirloom and most precious possession. His father had told him never to sell it; and he never had, no matter how hungry he had gotten, out on the meres. Now it was in a French dragon's possession.

"Yes," said Secoh simply.

Jim noticed the faint sheen of moisture in the little dragon's eyes.

"Don't worry, Secoh," he said. "You'll get your pearl back. I give you my word on it, both as a knight and as a magician. I'll get you back that pearl if everything else has to go smash!"

"Oh, thank you, your Lordship!" said Secoh. "Thank you!"

He dithered with the claws of his forepaws, obviously tempted to take Jim's hand and kiss it, after the george fashion; but uncertain what damage he might do with his claws if he tried it. Jim found himself feeling very guilty.

"We'll say no more about it, then," he said gruffly.

"Yes, m'Lord," said Secoh, gratefully dropping his forepaws back into a comfortable position close to his body.

But if Secoh was now radiating reassurance and comfort, Jim was beginning to feel the first sharp point of more than a small uneasiness and apprehension. Between the slats of the shutters that closed the window, the pale light of first day was definitely now showing.

"Giles and Brian have been out all night," he said to Secoh— but more to himself. It was somehow a comfort to hear his vague fears given shape by his spoken words. "In fact, come to think of it, I haven't seen them since late yesterday. Also, come to think of it, Dafydd hasn't shown up all night. He was going to sit down in the common-room. I better go hunting for them."

"I'll go with you!" offered Secoh eagerly.

The other's words brought Jim up short. He had not stopped to think of what it would do to have Secoh discovered by anyone in the inn, let alone half the population of Brest in broad daylight.

"You can't—" he was beginning. He thought for a moment. "You definitely can't be seen by people here in the inn or in the city, the way you are now. Seeing a dragon moving about the streets would really draw attention to us, even if it didn't cause a lot more trouble than that. I'm going to have to disguise you."

"Oh!" said Secoh. "What does 'disguise' mean?"

"I'll show you," said Jim.

He wrote on the inside of his forehead:

SECOH CHANGE TO HUMAN → SHAPE

Before him, there stood suddenly—naked of course—a rather wizened, small man who was quite young, but whose face and body showed the evidence of years of privation. His hair was the color of dark dragon's hide. His nose was long and thin. His mouth was wide and his chin firm but small. His shoulders were narrow and his arms and legs were as thin as his body. He stood perhaps five feet two inches in height.

He looked down at himself.

"Oh, no!" he cried on a note of anguish.

CHAPTER 18

Jim realized instantly what he had done. He had forgotten entirely about that one aspect of the dragon character that even he had come to realize only some time after getting to this world.

The dragons were not remarkable for their intelligence. Also, in many ways, though they could talk like humans, they were pretty well an animal equivalent of the medieval man and woman that Jim had to do with every day. They were primarily concerned with their individual survival and their own possessions, although they paid lip service to more important virtues.

But there was one thing about them that Jim had simply stumbled across, late; possibly because the dragons themselves never talked about it. Apparently they simply took it for granted in themselves and other dragons, that they were immensely proud of being what they were—dragons.

To defend that pride, they would even throw themselves into a fight that otherwise they would go to great lengths to avoid.

In retrospect, after finding this out, Jim had been better able to understand how Smrgol—the grand-uncle of Gorbash, half-crippled by a stroke in his old age—and Secoh, a mere waif of a dragon, could launch themselves into battle against a dragon as large and fierce as Bryagh, the Cliffside dragon who had been seduced into the services of the Dark Powers, at that fight Jim and the others had had against the creatures of the Loathly Tower.

"I'm sorry, Secoh," said Jim. "But there's no other way, you see. The only way you can go around this town with me and stay with us safely in this inn is if you seem to be a human being. I promise I'll turn you back into a dragon just the very moment I can. You know me, don't you? You know I keep my promises!"

The anguish lessened in the face of the human that was Secoh, but did not go entirely. Jim was already puzzling over another problem.

"Come to think of it," he said, "I'm going to have to get some clothes for you."

At first thought, the problem seemed insurmountable. He could magically put some clothes on Secoh, but, here in France, he was not sure of what a servant, such as Secoh would seem, would wear. And Jim wanted the other not to attract attention.

Then Jim remembered, as he so often had to do, that this was the fourteenth century, that he was an English Baron; a guest of the inn, and by the contemporary standards here, a rich man who had rank and authority. It was daylight outside, therefore the servants of the inn had to be stirring. He walked past Secoh, opened the door of his room and walked down the hall to the top of the stairs that led to the floor below.

"Ho!" he shouted. "A servant here for Lord James! Immediately! A servant!"

He went back to the room, closed the door behind him and spoke to Secoh quickly.

"Now, listen closely, Secoh," he said. "I've just called for a servant. When he gets up here I'm going to send him out with you to buy some clothes. Now, I'll give you the money. Don't give it to the servant. Merely pass it over after they've fitted you with the clothes, and say in a haughty voice, '*Take care of this for me*.' Then turn around and stroll outside as if you simply wanted some fresh air. Wait for him outside. He won't know you don't know what the money's worth. He won't know you don't know what the clothes actually ought to be priced at—for that matter, I don't know myself."

"You don't?" said Secoh, astounded. Jim ignored the question and went on.

"—But if you hand him the money and walk away, then he'll be too afraid of not bringing back a proper amount of change to try keeping everything that's left over for himself. He'll try to drive the best possible bargain he can with the shopkeeper, and steal a little bit of it, but he'll give back to you most of what you ought to get back. You hang on to it until you get back here. Then I'll toss him a coin or something like that; and we'll be all set."

"Y-yes," said Secoh slowly. "I understand."

"I'm sorry you have to walk around the town without any clothes on until he buys some for you—" Jim was beginning, when the surprise on Secoh's face halted him.

"Why?" asked Secoh.

Jim mentally pounded his head with his closed fist for being stupid. Of course, as a dragon, Secoh knew nothing about clothes, and saw nothing wrong about going without them, in public view or otherwise. He knew that georges wore clothes; but never having been a george before, he was still thinking like a dragon, who was perfectly content just to be in his skin. Luckily, the medieval world was not shocked by naked men the way the modern world would be.

"It's not important," said Jim. "Forget I mentioned it."

"Yes, m'Lord," said Secoh, a little wonderingly.

It was only a few moments until the servant arrived; Jim gave him his orders. He had already passed a gold coin to Secoh, who held it hidden in one skinny fist.

"Now remember," Jim said sternly to the servant, "this is my personal servant, who just caught up with me. I want you to treat him with respect. He's not one of your ordinary kind!"

"Yes, m'Lord," said the servant.

Awed enough by Jim's being able to get what was probably the best room in the house for himself and his friends, the inn servant did not even attempt a subtle sneer as he answered. Possibly, knowing Jim was English, he might not be too sure that Jim would not haul out his sword and slash him with it, if he was at all insolent.

They went out, and Jim paced the floor, opening the shutters and watching the brightening day, until the servant returned with Secoh, dressed in gray hose and shirt and blue jerkin, with a flat cap on his head. The hat was somewhat similar in style to what people of knightly rank and upwards wore themselves, but different enough so that it would be perfectly plain that Secoh was only a servant.

"Everything went all right?" Jim asked eagerly, once the servant had been tipped with a couple of copper coins from the change Secoh had brought back, clutched as firmly in his fist as the gold coin had been when he left. "Did he try to talk to you? What did you say to him?"

"Oh, he tried talking," said Secoh, sticking his nose in the air, probably in imitation of how he had done so when the servant had spoken to him. As a dragon, there was at least one humanlike thing Secoh knew almost instinctively; and that was how to be haughty. "I simply said, '*Don't bother me with your chatter!*' "

"Good!" said Jim. "That would shut him up."

"Well, not exactly," said Secoh. He wriggled inside his clothes. "Do georges wear these all the time? They don't feel natural. They itch. But they do wear them all the time, is that right?"

"Except when they go to bed," said Jim. "But you said he did some more talking. What'd he say?"

"Oh, something about how the landlord at this inn beats his servants all the time. They say he likes doing it. Anyway," Secoh said, "this one wanted to run away. He said something about it being against something else called a '*city law*' to leave without getting permission from your master. But he said he and I could both take this chance to run off, with the money I had; and we'd practically be rich until we found a better place to live and work. I told him I liked being with you. He mumbled something about '*All right then, don't let me stick with you, and you can end up in the cellar, too.*' "

"The cellar?" said Jim.

Brian and Giles could have been overpowered and locked up in the inn cellar. But surely not without the kind of noise that would have alerted him even up here in the room.

"The man did say '*too*'?" said Jim.

"That's what he said, m'Lord," said Secoh. "Did he mean something by it? What was it he meant, then?"

"Perhaps our Companions are locked up in the cellar," said Jim.

"Oh! Then we'd better go get them out right away!" said Secoh.

He had already taken a step toward the door when he noticed that Jim wasn't coming along with him. He turned around with a curious look on his face.

"It's not that easy," Jim told him. "We can't just go down there and break open the cellar door, or whatever we have to do, without rousing the whole inn. We could easily find ourselves fighting more people than we could handle. Particularly if some of the other guests join in—as they undoubtedly would—on the side of the landlord, just for the fun of the fight."

"Might be," said Secoh. "In that case, you better get me one of those long, sharp things like you have hanging from your belt. Not one of the short, sharp things but the longer one—you know!"

"It's called a sword," said Jim absently. "But I only have one spare one; and anyway, it wouldn't do you any good unless you knew how to use it."

"I thought you just hit other georges and everyone else with it," said Secoh. "I think I could do that all right."

"It isn't simple hitting. Take my word for it," said Jim, a little grimly. Brian had been trying to teach him about the sword for two years now, and he was still nowhere near fit to stand in front of a person with Brian's training and survive for more than a minute or two.

"I know," he went on. "A leg off that table would make a pretty good club. And that you can just hit people with."

"Oh? Good." Secoh was already across the room and tugging at one of the legs. "It won't come off!" he said, puzzled.

"You don't have your ordinary dragon strength," explained Jim. "Here, I'll help you."

Together, tugging at the end of the table leg, they managed to wrench it loose from its joint with the table by breaking off the part of it that had been pounded or glued into the thick wood of the top. Secoh took it in one hand and swung it. Then took two hands and swung it.

"I think I'll do it this way," he said to Jim confidentially.

"Good. Then," said Jim, "I'll tell you what we're going to do. You and I will go downstairs together. I'll order some wine; and I'll keep you by me, supposedly because I may need you, or something like that. Then, when nobody is paying much attention to us, I'll get up as if I was going out back to the jakes; and we'll hunt around for the entrance to the basement. If it's locked we'll try to figure out some way of breaking the lock and getting in."

"I'm all ready!" said Secoh, brightly hefting his table leg.

"You're not to use that until I tell you, now," said Jim severely. "In fact, it's going to make people wonder seeing you carrying a broken-off table leg downstairs. I'll have to think of some way—"

He was suddenly struck by an inspiration.

"I've got it!" he said. "It'll not only explain the leg, it'll also make it easier for you to stick by me when I head back, apparently looking for the jakes. I can wear my sword, all right. No one's going to think twice about that. I can carry the other sword by sticking it under my shirt and down my pant-leg; and then just walk stiffly as if I had a limp. Now, come to think of it, that'll help explain the table leg. I'll use the table leg as a sort of makeshift cane to lean on. I'll take it. Then I'll give it back to you when it's time for you to use it."

"Oh," said Secoh. There was a definite note of disappointment in his voice. "But you will give it to me then?"

"Just as fast as I can," said Jim, "because I'll want you to start using it just as fast as you can."

"Oh, I will," said Secoh.

"That's it. My leg will be stiff because I've turned my ankle and I'm walking with the cane for the same reason; and it's all their fault because I fell because their inn is so ramshackle!" said Jim. "I couldn't have come up with a better plan if I'd sat up all night to think of it. Let's go!"

He took the table leg from Secoh, hunted around among his things for the extra sword that he, like Brian and Giles, and almost any other traveling knight, would carry against damage happening to his ordinary blade. It fitted all right, down inside his hose; which, being made of knitted material, stretched easily. The blade made a noticeable bulge there, and felt coldly uncomfortable against the skin of his leg; but the bulge itself he could always blame on bandaging.

"All right, now," he said to Secoh. "Here we go."

They left the room, Jim limping and also leaning on Secoh's shoulder as if he needed support. Secoh held the arm that leaned on his shoulder as if to help steady him in that position. Slowly they descended the stairs. At the bottom a servant had stopped going wherever he was going and stood open-mouthed, watching them descend.

"Is m'Lord hurt?" he asked when they reached him.

"Yes, damn it!" Jim roared. "I've turned my ankle and wrenched my knee on your damn, bloody . . ." He went on stringing together as many profanities and obscenities as he could think of. The servant watched with admiration. On the continent the English were known to be great swearers; but Jim may have been setting a new record—at least for that particular inn. " . . . stairs!" he finally concluded.

"I'm—I'm very sorry, m'Lord . . ." said the servant. "Shall I get the landlord? Do you need a chirurgeon?"

"Do you think I want my damn leg sawn off?" roared Jim. "No! I want wine! The strongest wine you've got. As quick as you can get it! James—"

He turned to Secoh beside him and Secoh blinked his eyes at being addressed by this strange name.

"Get me to a table, James. Oh, and you there—"

He had raised his voice to a shout on the last few words; and the servant, who was already on the run toward the back of the room to get the wine, skidded to a halt and turned around.

"Yes, m'Lord?"

"And get a stool for this servant of mine!" yelled Jim. "He needs to sit by me and hold me up. That way I can put my foot up on something."

"Yes, m'Lord," said the servant, and vanished.

He was back in a remarkably short time with a stool, a glass for Jim and a brimming pitcher. Secoh looked wistfully at the single glass, but said nothing. Jim noticed it.

"Bring another glass!" Jim shouted after the servant, who was again turning away. "I'm going to drink with both hands!"

Impressed once more, the servant hurried off for the second time.

"That'll make him believe my leg is hurting like hell," said Jim, pouring the first glass he'd been given full from the pitcher.

Lifting it to his nose he realized that he had indeed been given strong wine. What was in his glass reeked of what seemed to be a combination of wine and brandy—or some other distilled liquor. He took a swallow and almost choked. He had been right. The wine had evidently been blended with some sort of raw alcoholic liquid. Interesting, he thought.

Distillation was not unknown in the fourteenth century; but it was rare.

Also, one thing more the wine was not, obviously—and that was properly aged. Evidently they thought that with the raw spirit added, the taste was ruined anyway. Whatever this stuff was that had been added, it was obviously the equivalent of pure moonshine whiskey; as that had been, back on Jim's original world.

At any rate, he managed to down a good half of a glass before the servant got back again with a second glass. Still pretending to drink from the glass in his hand, Jim waved at the pitcher and took the glass from his lips long enough to order. "Fill up the other one so it's ready."

The servant did so; and stayed there, ready to continue being of service.

"You don't need to stand around!" snarled Jim at him. "James will keep it filled for me. James—" He turned his head to look at Secoh, who gave a start. Slowly Secoh reached out and refilled the other glass. The servant had turned and gone, and Secoh leaned close to Jim's ear.

"I forgot I was James," he murmured in Jim's ear in as low a tone as his human voice could manage.

"Right you are, James!" said Jim loudly, then quickly lowered his voice. "That's all right. Drink the other glass yourself. That's what it's for. I may have you drink most of the pitcher. I can't risk drinking much, but if you get drunk, they'll just figure you were sneaking drinks when I wasn't looking, and you can't hold your alcohol as well as I can."

"What's drunk?" asked Secoh, eagerly taking the other filled glass and pouring it down his throat. He blinked his eyes. "That was good!"

"Remember," said Jim, looking at him closely, "you're not in your dragon body now. You can't hold as much wine as you could ordinarily. And that's particularly strong wine. They've added some raw alcohol to it."

"What's alcohol?" asked Secoh.

"Alcohol is what—" Jim paused. "There's no time to explain that now. But just remember you can't drink as much as you were used to drinking. If you do you'll get drunk. If you get drunk, from then on you'll know what '*drunk*' means."

He continued to eye Secoh a little cautiously as he refilled both glasses and Secoh eagerly tossed off a second one after smuggling it down below the top of the table and bending down to hide the process of getting it into his mouth and down his throat.

Dragons, Jim knew—unfortunately, from his own experience—could hold unimaginable quantities of wine and never had hangovers. But Secoh now could not weigh much more than about a hundred and thirty-five or forty pounds. There was no telling what would happen to him.

Still, if one of them had to get drunk—then it had better be Secoh rather than Jim.

They managed to empty the pitcher between them; and Jim called the servant for another. He had drunk about a glass and a half himself, and he could already feel the effect of it; but he did not think it was enough to interfere with him greatly. Secoh had drunk all the rest and showed no sign of reaction to it whatsoever.

When the servant returned with a new pitcher Jim asked him where the jakes was. The servant looked surprised. Most men or women of the upper class used the chamber pot in their room, rather than the common jakes. But the servant pointed, as Jim had expected, toward the back of the inn and went off.

Jim waited until he was out of sight, then laboriously got to his feet. Thankfully, since it was early in the day, once more they had the common-room to themselves. Stumping along with the table leg as a makeshift cane in one hand and leaning with the other hand heavily on Secoh's left shoulder, Jim made his way toward the back of the inn.

There was a door to the left, there, that he knew to be the door to the kitchen. It was through this that the servant had vanished, and it was from it which nearly all servants came.

To his right, at a short distance, were the bottom steps of the stairs he had just come down; and along a short corridor behind the stairs were two more doors. The corridor went a little distance past the two doors and then turned to its left and continued out of sight around the bend.

Jim headed down past the two doors. The first one he came to was secured by an iron bar, the unhinged end of which fitted into an enormous square dark iron lock. Locks, also, were not unknown in the fourteenth century, Jim knew from his medieval studies.

When Jim got close, it was a typical example of the Nuremberg type of lock he had read about. The heavy iron bar was bolted at its fixed end to what was obviously a heavy wooden door; and was hinged to swing upward from between the two fingers of a piece of ironmongery that was part of the lock.

The lock itself was, as Jim had expected, beautifully designed, ornate and artistically decorated. Also, as he had read in his studies, it should have a keyhole that even he could pick open with his dagger point. Locks of that time had depended for their security mainly on the warding, and not in the subtlety of the lock mechanism itself.

The trick would be to find the keyhole among the layers of artificial iron leaves and flowers on the lock's face. It would be hidden under one or more of them.

Even as he was standing there he thought he heard a sound on the other side of the door. He knocked on it cautiously. There was a moment's pause and then a knock came back and a voice called from within.

"Brian? James? Giles?" The voice filtered thinly through the obviously thick woodwork. "It's me, Dafydd ap Hywel! I've been locked up in here!"

Jim did a quick search of the face of the lock. He had no time to find it now. One of the inn staff could come along at any moment. He searched for a moment in his mind and put together an incantation.

ALL LOCKS⟶ OPEN

There was a small grating sound from in front of him. Jim made an attempt to lift the bar; and it came up quite easily. He pushed the door open, and Dafydd stumbled out.

"Quick," said Jim in a low voice, "back up to our room."

But at that moment men armed with clubs, knives, and even a few swords erupted from both the kitchen entrance and the opened door of the room just beyond them in the corridor.

CHAPTER 19

Jim reached in under his shirt, pulled out the extra sword from his hose, and shoved it into the hand of Dafydd. The two bodies of men from either side suddenly found themselves confronted, not by one startled and possibly unarmed—except possibly with a knife—individual; but instead by two men with broadswords and a servant of some sort with a table leg held as a club, ready for them. As a result, they did the instinctive thing.

They paused—and that was their mistake.

What they did not know, and what Jim himself had forgotten, was that Secoh was still really not a man. He was simply a dragon, temporarily enchanted into man-shape. He had once seemed to have an excessive amount of dragon caution; which is the same type of caution all wild animals and young children instinctively have. He had seemed, in fact, a complete craven; until he took part with the rest of them in the fight at the Loathly Tower.

But since his share in the victory there against the Loathly Tower creatures, he had lost all caution. Consequently he had been left only with the other side of the instinctive coin of his species, the "*dragon instinct,*" which caused his kind to go completely berserk when he did get into a fight.

Ever since then he had been known as the most feisty dragon for miles around. Much larger dragons tiptoed around him. He carried a chip on his shoulder that a breath of air could knock off; he was ready at any time to attack any opponent, regardless of size. He clearly believed he had nothing to lose; and those who did saw no profit in combat with him.

Consequently, now, when the people of the inn hesitated, Secoh did not. He flung himself at the men from the farther door, a couple of them carrying swords—and laid into them with his club.

It is one thing for a swordsman to face a club-wielding opponent who has a decent respect for the sword one holds. It is quite another to face a completely wild, red-eyed, apparent madman with a club. Secoh was not the least concerned about what those swords might do. Like many of the medieval knights, his thoughts were not on what they could do to him; but what he could do to them.

The result was that the better armed body of about six men found themselves on the defensive, instead of the attack, and backing away from this madman.

Jim and Dafydd, by mutual agreement, saw their moment and took advantage of it. They charged the people from the kitchen who, in addition to the two swords, were armed with such things as carving knives and cleavers, plus a few long daggers.

Jim, as he had freely admitted not once but many times—and as Brian had heartily agreed—was a very ordinary swordsman. But he at least knew what he was supposed to do with the weapon. Dafydd had had less training than Jim, but he had picked sword-work up as if he had a natural talent for the weapon.

The result was that when they charged, they came at the kitchen crew as men who knew their business.

The crew did not even back up. They turned and fled, back through the door through which they had come.

"Back up to my room," panted Jim. Dafydd turned to the stairs with him; and Secoh followed. Once in the room, with the door shut behind them, Jim and Dafydd collapsed panting; Jim on his bedroll, Dafydd on the pile of their other luggage. Secoh, who was not out of breath at all, looked at them with a mild amazement.

"M'Lord?" he asked, hesitatingly, after a moment. "Did I do right?"

"You did—just fine—Secoh," gasped Jim. "Now give Dafydd and me a chance to catch our breath."

"Yes, M'Lord," said Secoh, almost primly, grounding his now—sad to say—somewhat bloody table leg. Its far end was splintered and broken. Secoh stood waiting for them. Dafydd was the first to recover. Of course, thought Jim with a tinge of that same jealousy he had felt when he had asked Angie if she had ever been attracted to the bowman, Dafydd would be first. In spite of all Jim's exercising, and the active, physical fourteenth-century life he now led.

"Do you think they'll come after us?'" said Secoh hopefully, as they started to stir and sit up and move over to the seats at the table.

"Sooner or later," said Jim. "What do you think, Dafydd?"

Dafydd had poured himself a full glass of wine and he now emptied it down his throat thirstily; something he almost never did. Jim's attitude turned to one of concern.

"There was nothing to drink or eat down in the cellar?" he asked.

"There was food," answered Dafydd, pouring some more wine into his glass, but this time only sipping from it, "but the only drink was in kegs that had not yet been unsealed. I had no bung starter. Their bottled wine must have been stored elsewhere."

"But," began Jim, "how—"

"It was my own fault, look you," said Dafydd. "I should've been more ware and gone out with the lad and seen him safely on his way. But one of the servants had, it seems, been set to watch me; and followed the lad out to question him on what we spoke of. So the inn people found all out. Therefore, at a moment when the common-room was empty they fell on me, four or five of them, haled me to the cellar and locked me in. That was early last evening—"

He interrupted himself, stopping and shaking his head.

"But I tell this all wrong end to," he went on to Jim. "James, I have sad news. Brian and Giles are prisoned at the King's court, since about the middle of yesterday."

"They're prisoners?" echoed Jim. "How did you find out?"

"You may remember I said to you that sometimes more is to be learned by sitting still and waiting for news to come to you?" said Dafydd. "I sat and drank and kept my hands busy with little things such as shaping an arrow; and in a while, among those with whom I said a word or two, came this lad, an apprentice, though somewhat old for his 'prenticeship, and possibly in his last year of indenture."

"What's a 'prentice?" asked Secoh, wide-eyed. Neither Jim nor Dafydd answered him.

"Now, the 'prentices talk among themselves and know all that happens in the town. I bought him drink and he talked to me; so that I learned from him about two Englishmen, just lately come to the city, who had been found and taken by men-at-arms of the French King's court. They had been carried off to the court—there to be imprisoned. Whether they are in dungeons or some other place, I could not discover. But there they are."

He stopped speaking, his eyes steady on Jim.

"We can rescue them, can't we, m'Lord?" asked Secoh.

"We can try," said Jim grimly. "In any case, we can't waste much more time here. Those people down there will be getting some actual men-at-arms to come after us; and we won't be able to drive those off as easily as we did inn servants."

He got to his feet and they began hastily gathering what they would need. This consisted mainly of extra weapons and light armor for Brian and Giles. The full suit of war armor would be too cumbersome to wear.

"Now," he told the other two, "I'm going to make us invisible."

It had not been advisable to do this before. Ever since Carolinus had argued with the Accounting Office on his behalf, he had been allowed to draw on a certain amount of extra magic. But he did not know how much; and lately he had begun to worry he was close to exceeding even this extra limit.

But there was little choice now, if they were going to enter the French King's court safely.

The magic he chose to use was some he had come up with before on the eve of a battle between the French and English armies, at which Sir Giles had been killed. Giles would have been dead for good, then, if he had not been a silkie; and if they had not been able to return his body to the sea, where it had come back to life as a seal.

There was a tree just outside the room's window. Reaching out, Jim broke off three twigs to put in their headgear. On second thought he broke off and took two more. The incantation did not consist of words that made them actually invisible, physically. It simply, magically, induced a form of hypnotic trance in all people who saw the twigs, so that those people would refuse to believe what their eyes showed them.

It was as in the case of a person who had been hypnotized, who is told that someone in the same room is not there. The hypnotized person sees the person mentioned; but his conscious mind refuses to acknowledge the fact.

"Now," Jim said, once this was done, "you carry the extra arms and armor, would you, Secoh? Knights aren't supposed to be walking around carrying burdens; and I want Dafydd free to use his bow and arrows."

He glanced at Dafydd, who had lost no time in getting those items back hung about his person, the bow over his shoulder and the quiver full of arrows at his hip.

"Now," he said, "come outside with me. Secoh, have you got weapons, chain shirts and helms for both Giles and Brian?"

Secoh nodded, a large cloth-wrapped bundle in his arms.

Jim led them out into the corridor and closed the door behind him. Using the same warding spell he had used around the broken sapling and red cloth that had been a signal to Aargh, earlier, he set up a ward around the room. Then on second thought he thought of an addition of his own to this. He mentally wrote on the inside of his forehead:

REINFORCE WARD WITH EVER-
INCREASING—→ FEAR

Since he had been doing all this in his head, his companions had been staring at him, wondering what he was about. He stopped now to explain to them.

"I've put a ward—that is, I've set a protection—about this room, so no one can get into it," he told them. "Also, I added a little extra flourish. I've got it fixed now so anyone trying to get in is going to be very frightened."

"Frightened?" said Dafydd curiously. "May I try?"

"Certainly," said Jim. "Go ahead. You'll find the door will open and let you in a little ways. But I don't think you'll go any farther."

Dafydd took hold of the latch of the door and pushed it inward until it was only partly open and then attempted to put a foot through the entrance. He backed away hurriedly, closing the door behind him.

When he turned to Jim, his face was pale and there was a

faint sheen of sweat on his forehead.

"I'm not a man prey to many fears, look you," he said, "but what you have there is something I believe no one could face."

Secoh opened his mouth, as if he would offer to try himself; but at a frown from Jim closed it again. They went back down the stairs. At the bottom, the common-room looked as usual. There were no more than three customers. Whatever preparations were being made for storming the room belonging to Jim and the others had to be going on behind closed doors, someplace else.

The customers in the common-room looked right through them, so clearly the invisibility element was working well enough. They got out into the street.

"Hold on a second," said Jim, catching Dafydd by the arm, so that the other turned to face him. "We don't even know where the court is."

"I know," said Dafydd. "It was one of the things I felt we would need, so I got from the 'prentice as much as he knew of the court and where Giles and Brian might be. I can lead us to the chateau which holds the court itself; but I am less sure that I can easily find the entrance within to where the dungeons would be. But since we're invisible, we should be able to search and find them for ourselves. Think you not so, James?"

"Yes. Absolutely," said Jim.

The Royal Chateau, it turned out, was some distance away. It was a somewhat long hike, consequently, clear across Brest to its east side and away from the harbor near which the inn was set. Also, this was now an embarkation port; the streets swarmed with horses and men, knights, crossbowmen, men-at-arms and servants—all of whom could not see them and whom they had to avoid. But they came at last to the chateau. The main entrance had guards; but it was a simple matter to wait until these stood aside for someone recognized to enter, and follow closely behind him. Once inside they spoke in whispers.

Jim had thought, but too late, of also making their voices unhearable. Now, he did not want to take the chance of making fresh magic in the building holding the court, itself. It was reasonable that his magic would not be likely to trigger off whatever warnings Ecotti had set up. But this close, the danger was too great.

Accordingly, he waited until they were in the building and could find a corner where they could stand invisibly without being walked into by the inhabitants. Once there, he pulled Secoh and Dafydd close to him; and they discussed in whispers which direction in the building they should take next.

It was in fact, a long, rambling structure, but stoutly built, like a one-storied castle with an occasional tower or section of second story interrupting it. Plainly it had not been built to any plan, but more or less grown, as successive owners had added what they wanted to its architecture.

"The 'prentice seemed to think," whispered Dafydd, "that the quarters of King Jean and his immediate attendants were at the very end of the west wing."

"All right," said Jim, "we'll try there first. Dungeons should be close, but underground. Keep your eyes open, though, for any stairs that lead down. Dafydd, since you know more about the place than either Secoh or myself, why don't you lead?"

"I will that," whispered Dafydd.

He glided off. Aside from his invisibility, his skill as a woodsman to move silently made him an excellent leader here. His gaze was alert for anything which might be an intersection, or a place where they might be confronted by a gathering of people it would be difficult to go either around or through.

It was probably an illusion, thought Jim; but the distances within the building seemed almost as long to him as their walk through the streets to get here. But at last they reached an area where the furnishings became more luxurious and Dafydd drew them aside into the niche of a window alcove. Bright sunlight lanced through the glass beside them, for all the windows here had been paned.

"From here," said Dafydd, "the corridor splits to two corridors. From this point I've no more idea of which way we might take than anyone else. James, what do you think?"

Jim considered the situation.

"The right corridor," he said at last slowly, "has windows. The left corridor doesn't. I'd bet the left-hand corridor leads more directly to King Jean's apartments; since his rooms would have windows looking out the other side of the building."

He thought a moment.

"So, let's try the left corridor. We might even do better than just trying it. We might wait until a servant comes along to go down that corridor and follow him. Then, see if what he does, or the door he opens, can show us anything. We might learn something, that way."

"That is well thought out, James, and like you," said Dafydd.

"Just the toss of a coin," said Jim. "But it seems it might give us a slightly better chance. If we can make sure that the left corridor has entrances to the King's private quarters, then we know for certain that the right-hand corridor doesn't."

"My 'prentice told me," went on Dafydd, in the same whisper in which they had been talking all along, "that Ecotti's room is right next to the royal privy chambers, with a door from it to them, so that the King may summon him on an instant at any hour of the day or night."

"That's good to know—if true," said Jim. "We'll keep it in mind. Now, to wait for a servant going in the right direction."

They waited. It was a good quarter of an hour before a servant came by, and he went down the right-hand corridor where they did not intend to follow. However, almost on his heels was another, who turned down the left corridor.

This servant, like the one who had preceded him, was carrying a tray on which were a couple of wine bottles and two well-formed, clear glass wine cups. All those at the inn had been thick, clumsy utensils.

They followed the second servant. He looked right past them as he went by. The floor here was carpeted, and their feet made no sound. The servant stopped outside a door; and, balancing his tray on one hand, scratched at the door with his fingernails.

It was a common way for a servant to announce that he was there. Otherwise, and much more often than Jim had expected when he at first settled in the fourteenth century, a servant would just walk right in.

Servants ignored—or seemed to—whatever was going on inside the room; and certainly those inside the room of superior rank ignored them. In fact, as far as the occupants were concerned in a situation like this, the tray would waft itself in on invisible hands and place itself on a table. But now as Jim, Dafydd and Secoh waited close behind him, after a moment the servant shrugged, lifted the latch of the door himself and went in, leaving the door half open behind him.

They were about to follow him, when Jim held out an arm to stop the other two.

Without a word he pointed to the door and Dafydd and Secoh's eyes swung onto it. What Jim had noticed were a series of meaningless symbols painted on the door. Jim stepped back from the doorway and whispered to the others.

"Ecotti's room, I think."

Dafydd nodded. Secoh simply looked bright-eyed and interested. Jim turned back to the doorway and the others with him.

Within, the servant was now placing his tray on a small table by the side of a bed. In the bed a man lay asleep on his back. And as they watched his open mouth opened even wider and a loud snore issued from between the lips. It was a narrow face of the kind normally described as foxy. But the receding hairline just barely peeping from under the nightcap that was askew on the head of the man there showed sparse, wiry, black hair.

The servant, having delivered his tray-load, turned and came back out the door. Jim pushed the others back behind him and stepped forward to confront the man as he turned from closing the door behind him. Standing directly in front of him and looking directly into his eyes he said two words, which had been already keyed for use by his spell earlier. They had their effect hypnotically, not magically.

"*Still!*"

The man froze in mid-step beyond the door.

"You can't speak," Jim said to him in a low voice, "and you will still not be able to see or hear me. You will forget all about our conversation. You understand? Nod your head if you do, then be still again."

The servant's head nodded like the head of a mechanical figure.

"Then you may answer my questions with a nod or shake of the head," said Jim. "Is this the room of Ecotti the necromancer?"

The servant nodded.

"Is there a further door in the necromancer's room that leads to the King's quarters?" Jim asked.

Once again the servant nodded.

"Where are the dungeons, or any other place where the two Englishmen just arrested—Neville-Smythe and de Mer—are presently held? You may speak in a whisper."

"A room below the King's apartments," whispered the servant.

"Which room?"

"I don't know," whispered the servant.

"Good. Now, you will forget all about our conversation. You will remember only that you simply walked out the door and went straight back up the corridor the way you would ordinarily," said Jim. "Now!"

The servant turned from him and went away up the corridor without a word. He turned to the other two.

"I risked that," he said, "because the man on the bed was asleep and I was betting he was Ecotti. Those marks on the door are cabalistic marks, or I miss my guess."

"What's cabalistic, m'Lord?" asked Secoh interestedly.

"I haven't time to tell you now," said Jim. "The point is, with Ecotti asleep he's less likely to take alarm from magic being used in his vicinity. Now you heard the servant say there was a door inside his room that led to the King's quarters. But I'm hesitant to use it. Because Ecotti will undoubtedly have his room warded. And the wards will wake him, without a doubt, if we try to pass through the way the servant did."

He looked at the other two, hoping for a suggestion from either one of them. But they merely looked back at him.

"Well," he said, "our first duty is to rescue our friends, in any case. We'll wait until another servant comes. I'll deal with him the way I dealt with the one who brought the wine to Ecotti; and get him to show us the way down to the dungeons. Do you think this wisest, Dafydd?"

"Without a doubt," said Dafydd.

"Then," said Jim, "we'll simply have him show us the way to the dungeons, and I'll magically take over whoever's in charge down there. Then we'll see if our friends are there. If not we'll look elsewhere. It should be even safer if I have to use magic down there, since Ecotti wasn't woken when I used it up near his room."

"Should there be any need," Dafydd asked, "to use magic at all?"

"Maybe," answered Jim. "I'll try to use it to make the jailer think they have to be taken to the King and Ecotti. I'll make them invisible too. Then we'll all go up together, invisibly, into the King's presence—I'll fix things so Giles and Brian can see us. Then we'll have the four of us together; and, hopefully, the King and perhaps even Ecotti to ourselves."

He stopped and thought a moment.

"No," he said. "I'll have to do it all by hypnosis. If we show up with the other two with any kind of magic about us, and Ecotti's there, he'll smell it and know immediately what's going on."

"Why can he smell magic and you can't?" asked Secoh interestedly.

"Well," said Jim, "it's because I'm not a very good magician, yet. I haven't learned enough so that I can smell the presence of magic. But of course he—"

He broke off, suddenly thoughtful.

"Wait a minute," he said. "Carolinus said that the sorcerer's magic couldn't compare to that of a magician's. But I'm sure that he was thinking of a magician of his level or at least fairly near it."

He paused, still thinking hard.

"But maybe," he said, "it could be looked at the other way . . ."

He stopped and smiled at Secoh.

"Secoh," he said, "you just may have given me an idea. Damn this brain of mine that misses what's most obvious!"

CHAPTER 20

The other two were staring at him. He grinned.

"M'Lord," said Dafydd—and his use of the formal address for Jim was a signal that the matter had suddenly become very important—"what idea is this, now?"

His grin widened.

"You know, Dafydd, Secoh," he said, "in some ways I'm an idiot."

The other two protested at once that he wasn't.

"Oh, yes," said Jim. "I never thought of turning the thing around and looking at it from the other side. I'm not much of a magician; but maybe that's not the point. Maybe the point is how much of a sorcerer is Ecotti? Now, with any magician I would have expected him to come awake the minute we were outside his door; even before the servant opened it and we were able to look in and see him sleeping. He should have woken immediately and taken action—magical action—against us. But he's not a magician."

"But you just said he worked magic—" Secoh said puzzledly.

"That alone doesn't make him a magician," Jim answered. "He's a sorcerer, as Carolinus says. It could be that sorcerers are nowhere near as good at sensing the presence of magic around them as magicians. Or maybe just Ecotti himself isn't very good at that. Now, if that's the case—"

"Perhaps we can walk right up to him and he'll never even see us," said Secoh brightly.

Dafydd frowned at the dragon in human shape, and Secoh looked crestfallen.

"Sorry," he said in a small voice. "I know I shouldn't talk, just listen. But I get carried away."

"That's all right, Secoh," said Jim. "It just might be, if I'm right, that we can do exactly what you just said. The point is, though, it'd be a gamble. It could be that once awake he can sense magic as well as any—well, at least as well as a low-level magician like me. Or it could be that—while he can't sense magic well—when it's right under his nose, so to speak, he'll sense it. But at least we've got a good chance of having the four of us, armed, alone with the King of France and Ecotti himself."

"Ah!" said Secoh, all but rubbing his hands together in anticipation.

"If," Jim went on, "I can somehow use magic to tie Ecotti's hands, then we've got a couple of valuable prisoners that can tell us things, instead of them making Brian and Giles tell them things."

"We might," put in Dafydd thoughtfully, "even have hostages, James, who could help us get out of this city."

Jim thought for a moment.

"Maybe," he said, "but come to think of it, we don't want to attract that much attention to ourselves. It would be better all around if we can simply have the King and Ecotti forget all about seeing us; and then get away as quietly and invisibly as we can, taking whatever we've learned to England and Sir John Chandos—"

He broke off.

"Here comes a servant now," he hissed, dropping his voice to a whisper.

He waved the other two back into the window niche, and himself, still invisible, stepped out to stand directly in the way of the incoming servant. True to what he had expected, the fact that the man was essentially under hypnosis rather than under a magic spell alone, caused him to unconsciously be aware that Jim was in his way, even if his mind refused to credit the fact, and he tried to go around Jim.

Jim abruptly made himself visible, by hiding the twig with his hand.

"*Stop*," said Jim, meeting the servant's eye, as he hastily wrote on his forehead:

YOU ARE→ HYPNOTIZED

The man stopped.

"Now listen to me," said Jim. "You can't see me or hear me, but you will obey what I tell you. The King has charged me with a new order for you, that is more important than whatever else you were told to do. You are to show me the way down to the dungeons. Do you know where they are? Nod your head, if you do."

This servant also nodded his head.

"All right, then," said Jim. He made himself invisible again. "Turn around, and lead off. We'll be right behind you."

He glanced back to see if Secoh and Dafydd were with him, as he began to follow the servant back down the hall up which he'd come. They were right behind him.

He led them for some little distance back down the corridor, up another corridor, down a third and so by various ways to a door, which he opened on a flight of stairs going down. He led the way down, and the smell that came up to them told them that they were headed in the right direction.

Still invisible, Jim spoke in the servant's ear.

"Before you can be seen by anyone down there, stop, and give me a chance to look ahead of you. Do you understand? Nod if you do."

The man nodded.

The stair steps were planks of rough wood, without paint or carpeting, and open, with no riser behind them.

"Go quietly," hissed Jim in the servant's ear. "Tiptoe down."

The servant obeyed.

Jim, Dafydd and Secoh tiptoed behind him. The stairs would have been absolutely lightless if it had not been for meager illumination of the stone-walled and floored corridor at the bottom of the stairs. The light from this was enough to reflect up the stairs. Sufficiently, at any rate, to show them where to place their feet.

Three steps from the bottom, the servant stopped. Jim eased around him and stepped close to the left wall of the stairway.

It was not until he actually brushed against it that he realized the wall was plain earth. These dungeons, like many medieval dungeons, must simply be holes in the ground. The corridor below would be reinforced with stone above, below and on its sides, simply to keep it from falling in.

Keeping his hand brushing the earth very lightly, he went down as close to that wall as he could and gradually peered around its corner into the passage that led off also to his left. Then he remembered the twig that made him unseeable; and looked out boldly.

The illumination that had been guiding their feet was simply a tall and thick tallow candle standing in a mound of congealed wax on a table. He found he welcomed its greasy smell against the stench of the dungeons.

At the table sat a heavy, middle-aged man with several days' growth of gray beard. On its surface rested a couple of wine bottles and a metal cup, probably of pewter. Jim, peering around the corner into the corridor with one eye, leveled the tip of a finger at the warder of this dungeon, seated with his back to Jim, an arm's length away.

Jim said one word.

"*Still.*"

The man froze in the act of reaching for the cup. Jim took the twig from his helmet and, turning so Dafydd and Secoh could see him, signed to them to do the same. They did.

"All right," said Jim in the ear of the servant and no longer whispering, "go to the bottom of the stairs and stand there, until I come and give you further orders."

The servant went down. They followed behind him, passing by him once they had reached the floor of the corridor and going up to where the warder still sat immobile. Jim spoke to him.

"Listen to me, now," he said. "In a moment I'm going to say the word '*stop.*' When I say that, you will cease to be under the magic command of *still*. Instead, you won't be able to move or talk, and you stay that way until I give you further orders. If you understand me, you're now free to nod your head."

The warder nodded.

"Good!" said Jim.

"Now," he said to the others, "let's look—"

"James!" called Brian's voice. "James, is that you? James, if that's you, we're down here in the last dungeon. Giles and I!"

Together, they hurried down past the two doors on the left and the two doors on the right, which stood yawning open on darkness, to the one door on the left at the end of the corridor that was closed and bolted.

"Call out again, Brian!" said Jim, knocking on the door. "Is this the one you're in?"

"Yes!" chorused two voices, not only Brian's but Giles's as well.

"We'll have you out in a minute," called Jim, turning to the door.

The door was locked by a simple, rusty, iron bar about two inches wide that slid into an equally rusty iron bar holder on the other side. Jim tugged on it. It was rusted enough so that it resisted him for a moment, but then it slid back. Jim pulled the door open and was about to step inside, when he realized that if he did he would have taken a tumble. The dungeon within was a further hole in the earth at least four feet below him and maybe more. Brian and Giles were pressed against the earth wall of their prison, their heads on a level with his ankles. If the stench had been bad in the corridor, it was choking here.

"How'll we get you out of there?" asked Jim, almost choking on the fetid air.

"The warder just reaches down a hand and hauls us up, one by one. Of course, we're supposed to help, and anybody would want to get out of here, so we do." It was Brian's voice answering out of the darkness of the hole.

Jim glanced at the back of the still immobile warder, with a new sense of respect. Middle-aged the man might be, but he must have extraordinary muscles to lift men up out of a dungeon like the one below, all by himself.

"Dafydd," said Jim, "help me here. I'll take one hand and you take the other, and we'll lift."

Dafydd came up beside him; and with the bowman's added strength, which was—as Jim knew—considerable for all his slim build, they lifted out both Brian and Giles. As they came to their feet on the corridor above, they both clanked. Both had leg irons around their ankles connected by a short length of chain. Both men's ankles had dried blood around and about where the iron encircled their ankles.

Jim gazed at them in the light. Their faces were a little drawn and they stank, but other than the blood on their ankles, they seemed unchanged. Jim felt a sense of awe. Half an hour in that dungeon and he would have gone mad.

He looked down at their ankles again and felt a sudden fury, seeing those irons and the blood beneath them. He strode back to the warder.

"You!" he said, facing him. "Get up, go back and unlock those leg irons from those two prisoners! Wait! Are there any other prisoners in here?"

When the man did not answer, Jim remembered he was under hypnosis and needed to be commanded.

"Nod or shake your head to answer that question of mine. Are there any people in the other dungeons?"

The warder shook his head.

"All right! Come on, then!" Jim said. "Stand up, turn around, go back and unlock the leg irons."

The warder obeyed. The leg irons squeaked open between his hands, once he had unlocked them. Jim had been full of the intent of throwing the warder down into the same dungeon Brian and Giles had come out of; but thought better of it. It was not unreasonable to give the warder a taste of what he handed out all the time; but a sense of humanity held Jim back. It would not help any of those who had been confined in the dungeons before if the warder was shoved into one now. Besides, he was only a servant, after all, probably told to do this job simply because his arms were strong.

He had just finished thinking this as Brian and Giles had kicked their legs free of the irons, when he saw that Dafydd and Secoh were about to do what he himself had just thought of.

"No! Wait!" said Jim. "We don't want him in the dungeon, as much as he deserves it, maybe. We want him sitting here, forgetting we were ever here, and with a false memory of their being taken away on somebody's orders."

He spoke just in time to save the warder from going head first into the mixed dirt and ordure that carpeted the dungeon below.

"Go back to your table and sit down there again," Jim ordered the man.

He obeyed.

It took a few moments to bring Giles and Brian up to date on what was going on. This was slowed down a little bit, because the two had, immediately they were free, made a dash for the table where the warder was; and Brian snatched up one of the bottles of wine, Giles snatched up the other.

Unfortunately, the one Giles had snatched up turned out to be empty. Seeing this, Brian, with obvious regret pulled the—originally—nearly full bottle he himself was holding from his lips. He handed it, with what was still left in it now, to Giles. Giles poured it down his throat.

"By Saint Dunstan, I have a thirst that could drain a keg!" said Brian.

It was only now that Brian spoke again that Jim realized both men had very hoarse voices, clearly from the dryness of their throats.

"Put the bottles back where you found them, if you will," said Jim. "I'm going to replace everything the way it was and leave the warder with a false memory of you being taken out at somebody's orders."

He went back to the servant, still standing waiting at the foot of the stairs.

"Listen to me now," he said to the servant, "nod your head if you understand me."

The servant nodded.

"You're to go up to the warder and tell him you have the King's orders to bring the two prisoners immediately to his royal majesty."

The servant walked forward to the warder and spoke the words Jim had given him to the other hypnotized man.

"Now," said Jim to the warder, "you have just gone and gotten the prisoners out of their dungeon and taken off their leg irons because you were told they were to be taken to the King, and he does not want them recognized as prisoners."

To himself, Jim made a mental note to do something about the smell that Giles and Brian now carried with them. They stank almost as badly as the dungeons from which they had come.

"You'll continue to sit at this table," Jim went on to the warder. "You will not move, you will not send or signal for more wine. You will remember nothing but the servant coming, telling you, and taking away the prisoners. You will forget me, and anyone else you saw with me. After we leave, you will do nothing until whoever is due to relieve you comes down to take charge here. Do you understand? Nod if you do."

The warder nodded.

Jim turned away from the man.

"Brian and Giles," he said, "stand still a moment. I've got to do something about the way you smell."

He struggled a little bit with the form of the incantation he wanted and then came out with it, writing it on the inside of his forehead, silently.

DUNGEON'S ODORS ON BRIAN
AND GILES→ GONE

"All right," he said.

"They don't stink anymore!" said Secoh wonderingly.

None of the others bothered to comment on the fact.

Jim handed Brian and Giles each one of the two extra twigs he carried.

"Here," he said, "fasten these to you so anyone can see them. You're going to be invisible as we were when we attacked the French King last year."

Giles and Brian, who had been busy putting on the chain mail shirts, helms and weapons Secoh had been carrying for them, winked out of sight also.

"Good," said Jim, putting his twig back in view. "Dafydd, Secoh, put your twigs back."

"Now," he went on to the servant, "conduct us to the royal quarters. If there's a secret entrance to the King's private chamber, and you know about it, take us in that way."

Not merely kings, but people of any rank enough to own a large enough establishment to have private entrances and secret passages, had a tendency to find a use for such secret ways to their own private quarters. Jim was fairly certain that King Jean of France would be no different.

"Now," went on Jim to the servant, when they reached the corridor above, "lead the way to the King's private quarters."

They went along the upper halls again. Jim was feeling remarkably elated over the success of his use of hypnotism. Whether it was supplemented by magic or not, the sorcerer should not be able to sense it being used close to him. On the other hand, it was turning out almost too successful. He was a very amateur hypnotist, after all, having learned it second hand from an unsavory character named Grottwold, whom Angie had worked for in the twentieth century. He crossed his fingers against it backfiring, somehow.

He wished he knew how much the magic he controlled was helping it out.

But there was no way of measuring that, that he could think of. But even worrying about it had given him a further idea. There was one other thing he had been shown about hypnotism by Grottwold, that he had almost forgotten.

"Stop," he said to the servant.

The servant stopped. Jim walked around to face him. "Do you know where I can find parchment, pen and ink?" he asked. "Close by, if possible. The King must have need for a secretary to write his letters for him occasionally."

The servant neither spoke nor moved.

"Nod your head if you understand," repeated Jim for what seemed the thousandth time, impatiently.

The servant nodded.

"All right, lead us to that, first," said Jim.

The servant turned and led them back down the corridor they had come. Almost immediately they were at a door, which he opened and walked into. Too late, it occurred to Jim that there might well be other people in there; scribes, busily writing. Then, with relief, he realized that the room was empty. There was a high desk, at which the writer stood. It had a slanting top with a flat ledge along its top side. On the ledge was an ink well, a quill pen, and some carefully stacked sheets of parchment.

"Stay here, until I need you again," said Jim to the servant and walked hastily to the desk.

"I'm just going to try something," he said to Brian, Giles and Secoh, who had followed him to the desk and were peering over his shoulder at what he was doing. "I'm going to draw something that hypnotizes some people, but not all. It's impossible to tell who'll be affected and who won't. We could at least try it out on Ecotti, if we can manage to get him to look at it without suspicion."

He glanced up from the desk to see that both Brian and Giles had quickly averted their gaze from the piece of paper. Dafydd was still watching, as was Secoh, his eyes alight with curiosity.

Jim continued. He traced a large spiral in smaller and smaller circles at the top of a sheet of parchment. He did not lift the point of his pen from the paper except to re-ink it, continuing the diminishing spiral until it was less than half as wide across as its top and there was a good deal of the parchment left untouched.

Then he stopped, and started drawing another spiral inside the lower loops of the first one he had drawn, the line running between two of the lines of the larger upper spiral until he went beyond the end of the original helix and continued on down until he once more broke off at about half the width at which the second spiral had begun. Carefully re-inking his pen, he began a third spiral within the last lines of the second, and continued in this manner down to nearly the bottom of the page; where, by that time, the spiral had shrunk to a dot. He then went back and added a few other strange lines and swirls to the drawing.

He put the pen back where he'd found it and turned to his friends. Brian and Giles were still determinedly keeping their eyes averted from the paper. Dafydd was still looking at it, as was Secoh. Jim gazed at them for a second before he realized that both Dafydd and Secoh were still staring; not at where he now was, but where he had stood at the desk.

"Dafydd," he said softly to the tall bowman, and then turned his head a little to speak to Secoh. "Secoh! Secoh, Dafydd— wake up."

The eyes of both shifted from the table to him.

"What did you say, m'Lord?" asked Secoh. "I was so busy watching you draw that I wasn't listening."

"I said, wake up," said Jim. He smiled at both of them. After a second, Dafydd smiled back. Secoh looked bewildered.

"Indeed, I have learned a thing," said Dafydd, looking meaningfully at Jim. "I will not lightly listen to your warnings in the future, James."

"It's just random," said Jim. "As I say, some people it affects, others it doesn't. It doesn't mean anything that you were affected. The reason I made it for Ecotti to look at is that I want to get his attention fixed on something. Until I can move in on him with my own magic, that is; before he can use his."

Carrying the paper, he led the way back to the servant who had been standing by the door all this time.

"All right, now," he told the man, "take us first to Ecotti's room."

It took only a few moments before they were there. Outside the door the servant stopped and Jim whispered further orders in his ear.

"Take this," he said, handing the servant the parchment on which the helixes were drawn. "If the sorcerer is still asleep, you have my permission to wake him. When he wakes, hand him this parchment and say it was sent by the King's order for him to look at immediately. Nod if you understand."

The servant nodded, turned and went in through the door. He was starting to close it behind him, but Jim stuck the toe of a shoe in the way, so that they were able to see what went on within.

Ecotti was still asleep, his covers pulled up tight under his chin, and his snoring steady.

"M'Lord . . . m'Lord . . ." The servant repeated himself several times, speaking at first softly close to Ecotti's ear, and when he got no answer he ventured to touch the sorcerer through the coverlets on his nearest shoulder with fingertips only, and prod him gently.

Ecotti's snoring choked off, tried to start again, broke once more and his eyes opened blearily.

"Wha-what?" he said thickly.

"By the King's orders," said the servant, holding the parchment out for him, "you are asked to look at this immediately, m'Lord. Forgive me for waking you."

"Wha's—" Ecotti struggled upward in the bed so he was sitting against the headboard. He produced a hand from under the covers and took the parchment. "Look at this, you say?"

The servant, still under hypnosis, said nothing, but merely stood there. Ecotti seemed not to notice. He was trying to focus on what Jim had drawn on the paper. His eyes were becoming brighter and more awake all the time.

"What is this?" exclaimed Ecotti, finally, in a thoroughly awake voice. He threw back the covers with his other hand and swung his legs out—rather ugly, thin legs covered with black hair as far as they were exposed, with bare feet dangling at the end of them.

He was uncovered almost from the knee down; and it seemed to Jim most likely that while Ecotti might wear a nightcap like Carolinus, he tended more toward the fourteenth-century custom of sleeping naked. Ecotti glanced at the servant.

"Go on!" he exploded. "Get out of here! I'll take this up with the King myself!"

The servant obediently turned, went to the door, passed through it and closed it behind him.

Failure, thought Jim. It would have to be that Ecotti was one of those who were not fixated by the drawing.

"He'll probably go direct to the King," Jim said to his three friends. "We'd better go as quickly as we can to the King ourselves—but by another route.

"You!"

He was once more addressing the servant.

"Take us by that secret route to the King's private quarters, as quickly and quietly as you can."

The servant turned and led off. He took them only a small distance farther down the corridor that had led to Ecotti's room, and into a little alcove with a couple of chairs. There seemed to be nothing else there. But he touched one of the panels at the back of the alcove and slid it aside. He stood aside to let them enter, then followed after them. The panel closed behind them and they were in pitch darkness.

Jim heard the servant coming up past him, and caught hold of his livery as he went by.

"Hold on to me, hold on to each other," he said to the other four. He felt a hand take hold of his belt behind, and then they were all proceeding down the lightless passage with the servant leading.

Whether the servant knew his way so well he did not need light, or whether he was finding his way by touch on the walls that kept close on either side of them, Jim did not know. At any rate, it could not have been more than fifteen or twenty feet before he stopped. Another panel slid open before them and they stepped into a room beautifully and ornately furnished, but unoccupied.

It was clearly a sort of sitting room. The servant made no move to go farther. There were two further doors in the room.

"Where do we go from here to find the King?" asked Jim of him.

The servant did not answer.

"Point, if you can't describe it," said Jim.

The servant pointed at one of two doors in the room. The one he indicated was on his left.

Jim headed over to it, feeling the hand of whoever had held him letting go, but never doubting that the other four were following. He reached the door and pressed his ear against it. Vaguely, he heard a couple of male voices in conversation beyond it.

He reached down to the latch of the door and made an effort to ease it open, without noise. It turned quite easily and silently—possibly it was even designed and lubricated to do so. He opened the door a crack and peered through to see the furniture of what was evidently a bedroom. He opened it a little more and saw not only Ecotti, but King Jean himself. It was indeed the French King Jim had seen at the battle between the French and English forces that he had been able to stop by blackmailing the French dragons into flying in false threat above the battlefield.

It was not likely that Jim would forget this short, rather stout, but pleasant-looking man, who now stood with his short, gray hair tousled and a robe of green hastily pulled over him, listening to Ecotti now dressed in hose and short robe, who was talking and waving his hands—one of which held the paper Jim had drawn on firmly in its grip.

Jim hastily drew back from the door. Brian, Dafydd and Secoh, who had been peering through the crack with him, surrounded him.

"They are but two to our four, James," whispered Brian in Jim's ear. "The King of France is a gentleman, and therefore a man of weapons, though I doubt of great skill. The other is nothing in the matter of weapons; and if he is a sorcerer and versed in magic, why, you are a magician and versed in magic, also. Moreover, we must go in, in any case, must we not?"

"I'm afraid we must," Jim whispered back. "But it's not that simple. When we go in, whatever happens will be decided not by strength or skill or arms but by magic. And the trouble is, Ecotti's magic is not like mine, as Carolinus pointed out to me. His is built for attack. Mine is built for defense only. For defense to overwhelm attack, we need special conditions."

"I could put an arrow through Ecotti through that sliver of open door there from here," said Dafydd.

Jim felt uncomfortable at the thought. It was good, pragmatic fourteenth-century thinking to shoot down an unarmed enemy without warning, if that was the safest way of dealing with him. But it was something that all his particular twentieth-century training was against.

"We don't want to kill Ecotti, until we find out what he can tell us. Remember what Carolinus told us?" asked Jim.

"True," said Brian. "Dafydd, you remember. There is someone of great power, whom it is our first duty to find; and it may be that this Ecotti knows who he is and where we may find him."

"You are right, Sir Brian," said Dafydd. He turned to Jim. "Then, m'Lord, what is your counsel?"

He looked at Jim. Jim shook his head.

"Let me think a moment," he said.

His mind was still racing along with the idea of somehow distracting Ecotti's attention so that he could not bring his magic into play until Jim had brought his. The drawing had been a failure. For Jim to try to use his magic from out here was too risky. Surely, this close and with Ecotti wide awake, he would be likely to sense any use of magic in an adjoining room; even if the door was not slightly ajar between the rooms. And one kind of hypnosis didn't work on him.

He frowned thoughtfully.

" . . . *de l'audace,*" he murmured, "*encore de l'audace, toujours de l'audace . . .*"

He did not know what had brought up his memory of the words of Georges-Jacques Danton, one of the makers of the eighteenth-century French Revolution; unless it was that they were all at the moment in France, even if a much different and earlier France of the fourteenth century.

"Pardon me," said Secoh timidly, "but are you making another spell, m'Lord?"

Of course, thought Jim. The words he had just said would be so much nonsense to his friends—here where everybody, including some animals and sea life, spoke the same language—which was certainly not Jim's French.

Of course, they didn't speak English, either. At least not the English he and Angie knew, even if they spoke this world's language as easily as their native tongue, from the moment of their arrival here.

In any case, there was no point in translating to the four with him. In words they would understand, the French he knew translated to " . . . *we must dare, and continue daring, and keep on daring . . .*"

But let the rest of them think it was a magical incantation. It would make them more certain that he knew what he was doing. His mind was suddenly made up to gamble.

"I think," he told the others, "what we should do now is just stroll on in to the other room, as if we were the King and Ecotti's best friends."

CHAPTER 21

"First," said Jim, "hide your twigs—as I hide mine."
They did.

"Now," whispered Jim to Dafydd, who was on his left. "Remember, when I stop in front of the King and Ecotti, you make a break—I mean, you run for the corner of the room there. What I want you to do is attract Ecotti's attention for just a second, to take it off me. Brian, Giles, Secoh, you follow me."

Dafydd nodded.

"All right, then," said Jim. "Here we go—at a walk, everybody."

They went through the door.

"I'm happy to see your Royal Highness again!" said Jim confidently and cheerfully as they marched in. "You probably don't remember me—"

The King and Ecotti turned swiftly to stare at them.

"—but I had the great honor of meeting your Majesty once before. I'm Sir James Eckert, the Dragon Knight, who summoned the dragons to aid our attempts to stop the second battle of Poitiers, if you may remember. These two knights with me—"

He was proceeding with the introductions of Brian and Giles, as he came to a halt almost within arm's length of the King and the sorcerer. He did not bow to the King, although

Brian and Giles did so, instinctively.

In the moment in which they halted, Dafydd sprinted from behind Jim toward a far corner of the room. Ecotti immediately whirled to look after him and opened his mouth; but before any spell, incantation or command could come out of it, Jim had stepped forward and driven a fist firmly into the sorcerer's small but protuberant stomach.

Ecotti folded up on the floor, choking for breath.

"WHAT MEANS THIS!" thundered the King. Suddenly, he seemed to have grown six inches in height; and was no longer a pleasant-looking, rather middling-sized man, but someone very commanding and regal. Jim, however, had no time to spare him at the moment. Jim was too busy writing on the inside of his forehead.

> DAFYDD BACK WHERE HE WAS→ NOW
> —AND INVOKE HIGHWAYMAN POEM
> TOWARD BRIAN, DAFYDD, GILES, SECOH,
> ME AGAINST ALL→ FORCES

Dafydd was suddenly back at his side. They were all together; and they were all now protected. Jim had not progressed to the point where he could sense magic being made, where he could not see it being done, even if it was very close at hand. But he was beginning to feel his own magic when he used it. Accordingly, he could feel the ward that now protected them, as if it was an impenetrable glass box around them.

"I'm sorry, your Majesty," he was beginning, when the King interrupted him.

"Do you think that an apology is going to excuse this behavior, sirrah?" roared King Jean. "I'll have you taken care of—all of you! I—"

He broke off to bend down and help Ecotti back onto his feet. The sorcerer was looking very sour and rubbing his stomach and still struggling in his effort to breathe somewhat.

"Are you all right, Julio?" he asked concernedly.

"I'll be all right, sire," wheezed Ecotti. He glanced malevolently at Jim and the others. "But these won't!"

Instantly, the four were surrounded by raging flames. They did not burn the King and Ecotti, or anything else in the room; but Jim knew they would have burnt Jim and those with him to a crisp, if the flames had been able to get at them.

But Ecotti had lost the initiative. Jim had been able to get his magic working, before the other could get his started. It had undoubtedly been some time, if at all, since Ecotti had traded incantational blows with a real magician; and, as Jim was glad to discover, Carolinus had been right in saying that the real magic was stronger than anything a sorcerer could draw on from the Dark Powers.

It was true the real magic was limited by being only defensive; where Ecotti's sorcery was all built for attack. But where the odds were even, the real magic was the stronger. Jim and the other four with him, safe behind the ward he had just set up, looked out at the flames, as if they were indeed enclosed by the equivalent of a wall of glass that would not let anything inimical pass, solid or immaterial.

"*Still!*" said Jim, pointing a finger through the flames at Ecotti.

Ecotti froze where he was. For a moment he stayed that way, then Jim could see him struggling back into control over himself and throwing off the effect of Jim's magical order.

He must be using a command of his attack magic to bypass it, Jim thought; since the fact the ward was keeping them safe from his fire meant he could not directly overcome one of Jim's.

Ecotti had evidently also not tried to set up wards around himself; perhaps he could not establish wards, after all.

Clearly, however, he could find ways around the effects of at least some of Jim's magic; if that had not been established before he was ready to combat it. He recovered from the *still* command, able at first only to move slowly; but, shortly, he was back to normal movement.

Abruptly, Jim began to realize that keeping the ward around them was putting some kind of a drain on his own strength. He could not explain to himself what kind of drain it was: mental, emotional, or physical. But he felt it; and he realized that there was a limit to how long he could maintain this, if Ecotti kept attacking. But that meant there was also a limit to how long Ecotti could keep up his attack. It might get down to a test of strength between them.

Through the flames, now, Jim could see that the King was smiling approvingly at what Ecotti had done. Clearly, he was expecting to see Jim and his friends reduced to cinders.

Something had to be done to break the present pattern of their magical combat.

. . . *Toujours de l'audace* . . . thought Jim again.

The thing was to keep Ecotti off balance, and find defensive weapons that would do it. An inspiration came to Jim.

He wrote on the inside of his forehead:

TEMPERATURE OF FLAMES
30 DEGREES FAHRENHEIT → NOW

Then, gingerly, writing another incantation to protect himself, he pushed his arm out through the ward, unprotected, until his hand was in the flames. What he felt was actually something like a cold breeze blowing upward against the hand. He brought his hand back and smiled. He could see that this action had shaken both the King and Ecotti—though Ecotti was quick to hide his reaction.

Ecotti glared at Jim. For a moment Jim felt smug; then he remembered that his job here was not merely to defend himself against Ecotti's enchantments, but to discover information from the sorcerer or the King as to who was behind the sea serpents' invasion of England.

Hastily, he wrote a further brief incantation, making the ward soundproof as well as resistant to anything Ecotti might magically throw at him and his Companions.

That done, he spoke quietly out of the corner of his mouth to those with him.

"In a moment," he said, "I'm going to give a signal and I want us all to drop down and play dead. Half-close your eyes. Don't close them completely, leave them open enough so that you can see what's going on immediately near you. Everybody got it?"

Accustomed to Jim's occasional lapse into twentieth-century expressions, the other three men understood the general gist of his words and nodded. Secoh frowned, but seemed to understand.

"I want you each to say a word apiece, in turn, starting with Dafydd, next to me here, and then continuing with you Brian, then you Giles, and then you Secoh," Jim went on. "Dafydd, your word is '*you.*' When I nudge you with my finger after we're both on the ground, you say that word. Wait a minute after Dafydd has said it, Brian. Then you say your word; and your word is '*are.*' Giles, you wait another moment and then say '*both.*' Secoh, you wait a moment more and then say '*under.*' Then everybody just lie still. I'll take care of things from there. Everybody ready?"

Four voices murmured soft agreement.

"Everybody know his word?"

Once more, the murmur of agreement.

"Then down we drop," said Jim, "*now.*"

They all dropped.

For a moment, from under his half-closed lids, Jim watched the King and Ecotti staring through the flames at them and doing nothing. Then, Ecotti made a pass with his hand and the flames disappeared. Both men stepped forward to examine the fallen bodies.

"How clever of you, Julio," said King Jean. "They're all still alive. Just unconscious. That's fine. Now, we can question them at our leisure. Also, they will pay for the effrontery of entering my quarters as if it was part of some common inn!"

The King paused.

"Why are you paying so much attention to that little one there?"

"I'm not sure," muttered Ecotti, who was closely examining Secoh. "But he seems different from the others, somehow. I wish I could put my finger on it—"

Jim nudged Dafydd.

"*You.*"

The word rang out clearly in Dafydd's voice on the air of the room.

Both Ecotti and the King spun about and went back to prod and examine Dafydd.

"*Are.*"

Equally clearly Brian spoke.

The King and Ecotti abandoned Dafydd hastily and turned toward the three others.

"Which one spoke that time?" asked the King.

"I believe it was this one—" said Ecotti, kicking Brian roughly in the ribs. Brian, schooled in that hard educational establishment called knighthood, gave no sign of feeling that he had even been touched.

"Are you sure—" the King was beginning, when Giles, whose head was turned a little away from them, so that his mouth was not visible, spoke.

"*Both*."

"*Under*," said Secoh, rushing things a little bit. But— thought Jim—at this point it didn't matter.

By this time the King and the sorcerer were both completely befuddled. Jim envisioned the arrow on his inner forehead, waited for one dramatic moment, then uttered the one word beyond the arrow he had been keeping back for himself.

"—*HYPNOSIS*. You cannot move."

King Jean and Ecotti stopped moving and stood where they were, bent over in speculation above Giles.

Jim hauled himself to his feet.

"You can get up now," he said to the others.

The rest pulled themselves to their feet.

"What happened?" asked Secoh. "What did we do?"

"Well," said Jim, "you all helped me in making some magic."

Dafydd, Brian and Giles stared at him. Secoh also stared, but then his face was split by a wide grin of glee.

"I?" he said, whirling around on one foot in glee. "I made magic! I helped make magic, I mean! But I did, didn't I? I actually made some of the magic?"

"You most assuredly did," said Jim. "Just as the rest of you did."

Brian and Giles crossed themselves. The kind of magic that Carolinus did and Jim did was known as white magic; and was not supposed to be unchristian. But these two were taking no chances. They had been warned all their lives that the devil sets traps for unwary feet. Though both would have indignantly denied thinking for a moment that Jim was the devil, or in league with him.

But it cost nothing, the two of them clearly thought, to play safe.

"Why did you want them—what was it you said?" Dafydd asked.

" '*Hypnotized*,' " answered Jim. "You see, I needed to catch them unawares in order to—"

"One moment!"

It was the bass voice of the Accounting Office, speaking as usual with awful authority from a point about three feet above the ground next to Jim.

"We have just received a complaint from a certain Son Won Phon, B class magician, to the effect that you are using eastern magic; without having properly studied the same under accredited masters."

"But—" said Jim. "I thought hypnotism wouldn't be in the realm of magic at all. You see, where I come from—"

He was cut off by the voice of Carolinus, also out of thin air and sounding very irritable indeed.

"I thought we settled this some time since!" he said. "Where my apprentice comes from, these words and this practice are known worldwide and understood. His education was proper under those circumstances under which he learned about it."

"That has been accepted." The announcement came in the voice of the Accounting Office, which was undoubtedly also being heard right now by Son Won Phon, B class.

"Besides," Carolinus's voice snapped, "if license be required, let it be remembered that I am AAA+ rated. If I'm not fully qualified to teach eastern magic, I don't know who is! Have you anything to say to that, Son Won Phon?"

There was a fragment of speech that was cut off into silence before it could really become intelligible. The Accounting Office started to speak.

"I believe this should—"

—The voice of the Accounting Office suddenly also stopped and was heard no more.

Nor was the voice of Carolinus.

Jim was puzzled for a moment; and then a slow anger began to burn inside him. They had deliberately made the talk between them private and unhearable even by Jim, himself. He could see the others looking at him, wonderingly. He felt a sudden anger. He was the subject the Accounting Office and the others were talking about, wasn't he?

"I have a right to hear!" he snapped, out loud.

There was a short further silence, and then Carolinus's voice broke it.

"No matter, Jim," he said. "I think the matter has been settled. You're free to go ahead as you want. And I mean in any direction you want. Am I not correct, Accounting Office?"

"You are right, Mage Carolinus," boomed the almost always unexpected voice of the Accounting Office from its usual position in mid-air.

Dead silence followed. The others had turned away. This was more magic to avoid.

"Now, what do we do?" asked Brian, examining the motionless, stooped-over bodies of King Jean and Ecotti.

"We find out from these two as much as we can of what we need to know," said Jim. "Then we get out of here and get away with our information to England. First, however, I'd better make both more comfortable."

"King Jean. Julio Ecotti!" he said to the two hypnotized men. "You can straighten up. Go now and sit down in the nearest chair. Ecotti, pull your chair up beside that of King Jean, so I can speak to the two of you at once. Go!"

Hypnotized as he was, Ecotti made the mistake of heading for the closest chair, which happened to be the same one King Jean was heading toward. The King unceremoniously bumped him out of the way and took the chair himself. Ecotti turned about, found another chair, not too far away, pulled it up next to the King's and sat down.

Seated, the two looked back at Jim with no particular expressions.

"I'm going to ask you some questions," said Jim. "If you know the answers, to them or to anything connected with them, you will tell me. King Jean, when is the invasion of England to be?"

"In five days," the King said in an unemotional voice, "weather permitting."

Jim continued with his questioning. From both men he got fairly ready answers; and he was helped out by his friends too, when he inadvertently overlooked certain things. For example, it was Brian who thought to ask about the numbers and kind of the King's forces. It was Giles who thought to ask for a description of the ships that would be acting as troop ships. Altogether they found out a great deal. But there was one thing they did not find out.

They did not find out who it was who had sent Essessili to get in touch with Ecotti. They learned only that Ecotti had found a message by his bedside one morning telling him to go down to a particularly deserted section of the seashore, where he was unlikely to be seen by anyone else or overlooked by any buildings.

He had gone; and Essessili had come out of the surf to talk to him; and tell him that the sea serpents had their own vendetta against the dragons of England. They would be happy to join the King. They would even help him get his own troops over there to fight whatever humans might attempt to oppose them on the British island.

But nothing the sea serpent had said brought them any closer to an answer to that question of who was engineering the help of the serpents—apart and solitary creatures as they were normally.

It was past belief that it was Essessili. Carolinus had been sure of a hidden, powerful, magically trained identity behind it all.

Jim tried vainly, by phrasing his questions in different ways, to see if he could not discover some more information from Ecotti; but Giles eventually interrupted.

"If we are to cross the Channel," he said with a meaning glance at the two hypnotized men, evidently not too sure but what they might be able to hear and remember what he was saying, "it would be well to be elsewhere before the light is gone. After dark it will be difficult to find what we want."

"That's all right," said Jim. "You can talk freely in front of them. I'm going to make sure they forget everything before we leave. You mean we need to find a ship to take us over, and once it becomes dark, this is going to be difficult if not impossible? Right?"

"That is it, James," said Giles.

"You're right, Giles," said Jim. "I'll give up here, then; and as I say, I'll make sure they forget everything before we leave."

He turned to the two seated men.

"You'll sit exactly as you are until you can count to yourselves slowly up to five hundred. At the end of that time you will wake up, but not remember anything that happened after the moment just before we walked into the room. You understand? Nod if you do."

Both men nodded.

Jim turned away and led them all back out the door, picking up the servant as he went, and remaking their invisibility.

Once out in the corridor, Jim had the servant lead them back to the front door through which they had entered; and then just short of the door, they all stopped and Jim reminded the servant to forget everything that had happened from the first moment Jim had spoken to him. He too was supposed to start back toward the King's quarters, counting to a hundred slowly as he went, before he also woke from his hypnosis.

With him out of the way, they made their way invisibly past the guards at the outer door, safely into the streets of Brest.

"It'll take us too long to get down to the harbor on foot," said Jim. "I'll transport us there by magic."

"Our horses!" Brian cried, before he could form the incantation. "I'll not leave Blanchard behind!"

"Very well," said Jim, "our horses can meet us down there, transported from their stables by the same magic."

He wrote the incantations and all of a sudden they were there; with the rough timbers of a wharf sounding hollowly under the hooves of the horses as they stamped their feet uncertainly, finding themselves suddenly shifted from the semidarkness of the stable to the still bright, but rapidly declining, day. A pile of baggage, made up of possessions they had left behind in the inn room, was also beside them.

CHAPTER 22

❦

Jim glanced at the sun. In the two years he had been on this world, he had picked up the medieval habit of estimating time from the position of the sun, almost as if he had been born here.

"Counting twilight," he said, "it looks like we've got about two hours to find our ship and get away. I'm not used to bargaining, and I imagine Brian may have more experience than I do."

He glanced at Brian, who looked uncomfortable at being reminded of his poverty and his straits in keeping his Castle Smythe going, with only his tourney winnings and what little the estate provided in the way of self support; but, Brian nodded.

"And Dafydd. Dafydd," said Jim, "you're probably the best of us at driving a bargain. I'll hope it's you that comes up with the ship. But Brian and I'll do what we can, working as a team. Secoh, you stay here and guard the horses and the goods."

He glanced at the mere-dragon in his human form and noticed that aside from the eating knife at his belt, which the inn servant had bought him as part of his clothes, and which everybody carried, he was unarmed.

"Here," he said to Secoh, "you can take my sword and poignard; that will keep them from thinking you're an easy mark to rob."

He began to unbuckle the heavy belt around his waist that carried both weapons. Brian and Giles exclaimed immediately in protest.

"What are you thinking of, James!" said Brian. "A commoner to wear a knight's belt? Someone who is not a gentleman masquerading as one?"

He dived at their possessions.

"Here!" he said, pulling out a spare sword and dagger. "We have extra arms. Here, Secoh, you can have these. But a knight's belt—never!"

"Indeed, Sir," stammered Secoh, "I had no thought to—perhaps even these—"

"Go on, take what Brian's handing you, Secoh," said Jim. "He and Giles are quite right. I wasn't thinking."

"Yes, m'Lord," said Secoh, accepting the sword and dagger from Brian. Jim watched him with commiseration. He had forgotten one of the cardinal points of conduct in this medieval era. In fact, Secoh, with his own intense dragon-pride, had probably understood the reaction of Giles and Brian better than Jim himself had.

"Sorry, gentlemen," said Jim to Brian and Giles.

"It is no light matter, James," said Giles, who evidently had also been shocked to the core by what Jim had proposed. "If common men started to wear the marks of gentlemen, let alone a knight's belt, which is not earned lightly or easily, where would we be? An ordinary man could just as well be taken for one of coat armor!"

"Yes, I know," said Jim, with absolute sincerity. He had been playing the part of a knight now, long enough to begin to understand how much had to be learned to become one. He glanced again at Secoh, who, in his human body, and holding the two weapons, still did not look very dangerous. He thought for a moment and wrote a quick incantation on his forehead, then beckoned Secoh aside and spoke to him in a low voice.

"Secoh," he said, "just to play safe, in case sword and dagger won't do the job for you, drop them, and clap your hands together."

He demonstrated, meanwhile writing the necessary spell in his head.

"If you do that, I guarantee you'll be back in your dragon body. Then fight like a dragon will!"

Secoh's eyes lit up.

"I'll tear them to flinders!" he muttered between his teeth.

"But remember," murmured Jim, "only if you have to!"

He went back to rejoin Dafydd, Brian and Giles; who, with good medieval manners, had not taken it amiss that he had gone off to speak with Secoh privately. They had it firmly in mind that the rank of Baron, which Jim had thoughtlessly claimed when he had first landed in this world, entitled him to be their superior and therefore have the right to do what he wished without offense to them, his inferiors.

"Now, Dafydd," said Jim, "why don't you go down the wharves along the left line of ships; and Brian and I'll go to the right."

He hesitated, still looking at Secoh. It would not be good to have him turn back into a dragon if it could possibly be avoided.

"Giles, could I ask you to stay with Secoh?" Jim asked. "He may well be able to defend our horses and gear by himself. But the trick is really going to be to keep people from attacking in the first place. The sight of the two of you, and you obviously a knight, should be enough to deter even a gang of would-be thieves."

"If you wish it, James," said Giles. He gave the right-hand tip of his mustache a twirl. "They will be deterred if they are wise. Ruffians of that sort I should be glad to take care of by myself, without help."

"Thank you, Giles," said Jim. He turned to the others. "Now, as I said, Dafydd, you go left and Brian and I had better stay together and go to the right. We two can act as a team. These people will try to drive a hard bargain, undoubtedly, with the invasion this close. Even if they don't know the date, they know it's close. But I've got no worries about you; and Brian and I will do the best we can. Now, for your information I have—"

He fished under his shirt and pulled out the purse that was fastened to his belt—actually, a leather bag with a stout drawstring that circled the belt itself, and allowed the bag to be tucked inside the shirt out of sight. He opened it, reached inside, and came out with a handful of coins.

"I'd estimate," he said, "that I've got perhaps forty to fifty silver shillings' worth of coin. We must try to cross the Channel for no more than half of that, because we'll have expenses on the other side."

He knew only too well that the others had no money to speak

of and they knew it too; but as long as nobody mentioned the matter none of them had his feelings hurt.

They went off, accordingly, leaving Giles and Secoh behind; Dafydd along the wharves down to their left and Jim and Brian along those to their right.

But as they investigated, they found to their surprise, that though it was still nearly two hours to darkness all the boats they investigated seemed empty. Tentatively, Jim and Brian stepped off the wharf onto a number of the craft—they were really not much bigger than the good-sized, offshore, sport-fisher boats of Jim's twentieth-century world, the kind that would go out to sea ten or fifteen miles to fish for tarpon and sailfish. But in every case, the boats they tried had no one aboard. The sail on each single mast was furled; and matters about the deck as well as in the one smelly cabin up forward were relatively in order; although, by and large, the boats were both dirty and disorderly in the extreme, viewed with the twentieth-century eye.

They were heavy, round-bodied—almost tub-shaped—craft. Jim knew from his previous voyage to Brest and home again, however, that they were remarkably able to face the chop and cross currents of the Channel waters, although they sailed slowly and required at least two men—usually three—to sail them.

In fact, on both Jim's earlier trips, there had been six to eight sailors aboard each craft; one being the master, who mainly gave orders, but a fair share of the time also lent a hand doing whatever required extra muscle.

They had investigated their twelfth empty boat before they were aware of a small crowd of what looked remarkably like sailors headed down toward them from what seemed to be a line of inns or drinking places set back a little distance from the shore. The members of the crowd did not appear too happy.

Jim had been wondering slightly at the trusting nature of French mariners, that caused them to leave their ships so unguarded and unobserved. Apparently he had been wrong about the unobserved part.

He and Brian, of course, stood and waited for them, their hands on their belts, not far from their swords. It would have been unthinkable for two knights to do otherwise, regardless of the number of people descending on them.

"Well, sir knights!" said the short, broad man in the lead as the crowd halted before them. He had a dark, pockmarked face, very tanned from the sun and weather; also something of a paunch on what was evidently otherwise a fairly heavily muscled body. He had his hand on the long knife in his own belt. "And what do you want aboard our ships without our leaves, sir knights?"

He had stopped about five feet away, with the rest behind him. Those farther back were openly scowling and looking fierce.

"And what is that to you, sirrah?" snapped Brian.

He did not move his hand to the hilt of his sword; but this was plainly a gesture of contempt, rather than one of fear that a hostile move would provoke a reaction from the crowd. Brian had taken fire immediately in his usual fashion; and was not, as Jim knew, pretending in the least. He was quite ready to take on the lot of them, single-handed if necessary, unless they were respectful and agreeable.

Jim had a sudden inspiration.

"Yes, indeed!" he said, pitching his voice to Brian's tone as best he could. "We are on secret service to the King. If we choose to burn your boats where they stand, that is no business of yours, if it is by Royal Order!"

The crowd did not exactly fall back before this speech; but Brian's words and Jim's alike clearly gave them pause. There was a moment's silence among them. Then the man who had spoken first and was in the forefront opened his mouth again. But this time his tone had become conciliatory.

"Those boats are our lives, sir knights," he said. "If you speak of burning them, you might as well speak of burning us as well. For then, we shall starve, together with our wives and children."

"Then keep a civil tongue in your head, fellow!" snapped Brian, still not mollified and obviously itching for a fight.

"It's not that we don't understand," said Jim, picking this opportunity to pour oil on the troubled waters of the present conversation, "but we must think of France first!"

A muttering broke out among the crowd behind the foremost man. Jim thought he heard some comments on the order of: "Huh! France! What did France ever do for us?"

The pockmarked man squared his shoulders; but took his hand from his belt and its close proximity to his knife.

"Were you searching for someone?" he asked.

"Certainly," said Brian, before Jim could speak. "An honest English master and ship to take us to England."

"English!" Now it was an angry response from most of those in the crowd.

"There is no English mariner to be found!" said their leader stiffly. "We are all Frenchmen here, sir knights!"

Then he abruptly looked at them almost slyly.

"Or is it that you are really English yourselves?"

"Scottish *and* English!" said Jim before Brian could speak again. "We are gentlemen who honor King Jean, and have just finished speaking with him. Now, we must follow our honor and duty to him back to England—such is our intent. But it is private matters that move us, not to be discussed with you."

The pockmarked mariner was not offended by Jim's words, as Jim had known he would not be. It was simply commonplace for a knight to stick his nose in the air and tell a common man that he didn't understand, or wouldn't be given an explanation because he had no right to one. It seemed to satisfy the mariner completely.

"Nonetheless, sirs," said the pockmarked man in what was now quite a polite tone of voice, "as I said, there are no English among us. And you will not find a Frenchman to carry you across the Channel this day—or tomorrow for that matter. The word is that the King plans to invade any day now. I know not how you will get there, consequently, but you had best get there in a hurry. We will go back to our drinking."

"I wondered," said Jim, "why you French shipmasters were so willing to let your ships stand open and unprotected. What if someone should steal one of them?"

The pockmarked man stared for a second. This was a most unlikely question for a knight to ask. In fact, the idea of a knight, or most commoners saying they had "wondered" about anything was all but unthinkable. Then the man laughed.

"This is Brest, sir knight. And to reach the open waters you must pass through the Rade of Brest. No one not knowing the Rade is likely to be able to take a ship out there, without either going aground, or getting caught on a rock. As for those who do know how to get out safely, French and the occasional English, they are all well known to us. Not only would whoever tried it be caught on his ship in mid-water, and unable to flee; but we would know who he was the minute the ship was gone.

"We give you good eve, sir knights," he added, and turning on his heels followed the rest of his companions, who had already started back up the slope toward the inns, and the wine or whatever else they had left behind them.

"Hmm," said Jim to Brian. "Brian, you know that's something I forgot. Remember how we got hung up on the rock coming into Brest on our last trip—even with a shipmaster who knew his way, or was supposed to?"

"I well remember," said Brian. "Nonetheless, Giles is still with us, and still capable of turning himself into a silkie if we ran into trouble; could he not get us from it again?"

"You forget," said Jim, "we were just very lightly caught on that rock. If we had been run firmly upon it, it would have taken another ship to tow us off, if we could be towed off at all; and our ship would have sunk under us, the minute it was off the rock and the hole in its side let water in to pull it down under the sea."

"Hah!" replied Brian. "I understand."

"Well," said Jim, "in spite of what that man just said, it wouldn't do us any harm to look at the rest of the ships here and make sure that there isn't an English mariner on one of them. If not, we'd best get back to Secoh and Giles as quickly as we can and make other plans."

"James," said Brian, as they began to move down the line of boats again, "forgive me if I venture into areas where you should not be questioned; but could you not move us all by magic back to England?"

"Possibly," answered Jim, "but there's two things. I don't know if I could transport us all that far. Secondly, I don't know how much magical ability I have left."

"Now, I don't understand, James," Brian frowned. "I have been transported by Carolinus—"

"Carolinus could do it," interrupted Jim, "but you and the rest have to understand how much greater his magic is than mine. That's a long way."

"I don't understand," said Brian. "Magic is magic, is it not?"

"Then let it go at this," said Jim. "I've been allowed to use more of it than I had a right to. I'm afraid I may already have reached my limit, if not gone beyond it, just getting us down to these docks in a hurry. In fact, I was planning to avoid using any more until we're back in our own castles. Then I'll ask Carolinus how much I have."

Brian nodded. Spending more than one could afford was something he well understood.

They completed their search but found no boat with a fellow Englishman. There were other boats moored to buoys farther out. But Jim saw no way of getting to them, or any signs of life on them. They turned back to join Giles and Secoh.

"Any trouble?" asked Jim, as they got back within speaking distance of these two.

"None!" said Giles. "And damned boring it's been, too! Furthermore, James, did you know that this man-dragon here doesn't know the first thing about holding a sword or dagger, let alone using one? Not that I expected him to be of any value if we had marauders."

Secoh did not look other than normally ashamed at this statement.

"You can't blame him, Giles," said Jim. "After all, he's never held weapons in his hands before."

"And a good thing too!" grunted Giles. "Did you find a ship?"

"None for us," Brian answered before Jim could speak. "Dafydd is still not back?"

"No," said Giles. "And the sun is close to the horizon."

"Yes," said Jim, "he'll need to come soon. And if he doesn't—"

"There he is now!" cried Secoh, interrupting. "And somebody with him. We couldn't see them before because they were behind those big square things that are piled up down there."

"Bales of goods, probably," said Jim, squinting at them with the late sun in his eyes. "At any rate, he'll be here in a minute. Meanwhile, Giles, you must understand about Secoh. Suppose, for example, you were turned into a dragon suddenly—"

"James!" cried Giles, stricken.

"Oh, I wouldn't do it," said Jim. "I'd never turn any of my friends into anything they weren't, except to save their lives or something like that. That was the reason I turned Secoh; and I'm going to turn him back as soon as it's safe to do so. He doesn't like being a human any more than you'd like being a dragon. But stop and think. If you were turned into a dragon, wouldn't you be at something of a loss as to how to use your claws and teeth? Now think about that."

"Don't see why I should," muttered Giles, "but in any case, I don't want to be a dragon—even to save my life."

By this time Dafydd and the man with him, who was a head shorter, though also slim and wiry-looking, had reached them. However, Dafydd's new acquaintance had the weathered face and hands, and the slightly rolling seaman's gait; and was already close enough so that Jim could politely ignore Giles.

"Dafydd!" he called, while the other was still a dozen feet distant. "So you found us an Englishman!"

"He did not, sir knight!" snapped the man with Dafydd, in a loud voice. "There are no English here! I am a man of France!"

By the time he had finished this he was close enough to Giles, Brian, Jim and Secoh to lower his voice. He and Dafydd came to a halt.

"Sir knight," he said softly, "will you get me killed? Aside from losing me my boat and whatever else may happen to me?"

"Oh," said Jim, lowering his own voice. "Sorry."

"I was born here of an English father and grew up in England. But I know this town as well as I know the Cinque Ports of our own land. I have always gone back and forth between them and Brest, and the local people here know me as one of them. It is a double identity that makes itself well worthwhile, on occasion. But do not raise your voice and call me Englishman, again, m'lord, if you value my life at any price at all. And if you want to get back to England, you'd best value my life. For you could not get there in my ship alone, I tell you this."

Jim had sense enough to accept this. However, Giles's quick temper was still not back at rest.

"And why not, master mariner?" snapped Giles.

"Even if you could get out past the underwater rocks of Brest safely, sir," said the man, "the Channel winds and waters would keep you from reaching the other side. You know nothing about ships, or about weather. You know not when to furl or let fly, when to turn and run before the wind or use it. That and more other things than you can count. But, let us not argue. I am with you because you are Englishmen; and because I'm told by this Welshman here that it is to England's great service that you be gotten back there as quickly as possible. My name, sirs, is Giles Haverford—"

"Hah!" interrupted Giles again, scowling fiercely. "Giles is *my* name!"

"I cannot help that, sir," said the shipman. "It is mine as well, as well as the name of many in England, and France as well. I am known in this port as Edouard Brion."

"Then I shall call you Edouard. Hah!" said Giles. He looked around at his Companions. "And my friends will also, possibly?"

"Be glad to," said Jim. "Anything to keep peace in the family."

Everyone but Dafydd, who was not ordinarily given to facial expressions that showed what he was feeling, blinked at Jim.

"Er—just a saying where I come from," said Jim, "it simply means I think it's a very good idea if we do all call the master, here, Edouard."

The others all made noises of agreement.

"Now, sirs," said Edouard somewhat rapidly, "if we were away it would be best to make it now, without further delay, on the outgoing tide which is now just past its full. Come with me as quickly as you can, then. We will board and up sail."

Secoh loaded himself with their baggage. Dafydd led the horses; and they followed Edouard. They were led nearly to the end of the wharves in the opposite direction from which Jim and Brian had gone. At last they stopped by a boat that was one of the slightly larger ones docked there; though it was built in the usual pattern, with an open deck, except for the forecastle cabin up in the bows. Its deck lay perhaps six inches below the level of the wharf.

CHAPTER 23

Edouard Brion (or "Giles Haverford," when he was in England) turned away from the boat, looked up the slope at yet another line of what appeared to be drinking establishments; and stuck two fingers in his mouth.

He whistled shrilly. Then, without waiting for an answer, he turned again and jumped down onto the deck of his own ship.

"I'll throw a rope from the bow of the vessel," he called. "As you see, she's moored by her stern. One or two of you will have to catch it; and at least two of you will have to help pull her bow around to the deck. Meanwhile I'll be getting some planks to make a way to bring your horses down to the deck."

He did exactly what he said. Dafydd and Secoh caught the line and pulled the bow in; partly because neither Giles nor Brian made any move to do so and partly because the other two apparently took it for granted that they were supposed to do such things.

The bow came slowly around so that the port side of the boat bounced gently against the rough edges of the planking that made the surface of the wharf. Edouard arose from an open hatch midway in the boat, dragging two long, thick planks, each possibly a few inches more than a foot wide. He pulled these to the side of the boat and passed them up into the hands of Dafydd and Secoh; who by this time had, under Giles's direction, tied the rope from the bow about one of the blocks which for that purpose protruded upward from the face of the planks and were spaced regularly along the wharves.

The two loose planks were laid and the gear was carried aboard; while Edouard laid the steering oar in its chocks, ready to have its blade lowered into the water. Then the horses were both coaxed and pulled down the planks. The last aboard was Brian's magnificent war horse, Blanchard of Tours; to buy which he had spent all his inheritance, except the half-ruined Castle Smythe and the immediate ground around it, with a few poor farms and the serfs who worked them.

Blanchard had now been persuaded to get on the planks, but once on them, he had decided that he did not like them; and even less did he like the fact that they sloped downward ahead of him and felt slippery underhoof.

"Come on, Blanchard, damn you!" snapped Sir Brian, pulling hard on the horse's reins. But Blanchard, who was afraid of nothing in battle, had a horse's instinctive dislike for insecure footing. He neighed and refused to move.

"Look! Look!" cried Secoh, suddenly from the wharves to the vessel. "More georges, in their shells, coming out on the wharves on horses and getting down from them!"

Edouard swore.

"I'll have a fine time talking myself back into the good graces of the shipmen here in Brest after this!" he said. "However, in for a penny, in for a pound."

The men-at-arms were indeed coming in their direction.

"Blast and damn you to hell, Blanchard!" roared Brian. "You *will* come!"

Bending down swiftly, he pulled the golden knight's spur from his left heel and jabbed it into the nearest side of Blanchard's hindquarters.

"Charge, Blanchard!" he shouted.

Training broke through instinct, just long enough to get Blanchard moving. He half galloped, half slid down the planks and headed at speed up toward the front of the vessel. If it had not been for Brian and Giles both grabbing at his reins and stiffening their heels against the deck boards to hold him back, he would have tried to gallop down the steps of the forecastle, and undoubtedly broken both front legs.

He came to a trembling halt, panting and wild-eyed.

"Swef, swef, Blanchard," said Brian in a soothing voice, "now, now, calm, great horse . . ."

He patted and stroked the neck of the sweating and still terrified animal; and Blanchard began to calm.

"Will you leave the beast be, sir knight?" shouted Edouard, hauling with all his strength to get the planks back on board. "Better he go overboard than let those men-at-arms catch us and we all be put to death right here."

Jim was staring at the oncoming troop. The only thing he could imagine was that after counting themselves back to ordinary consciousness, Ecotti could have used some of his sorcerer's magic—not possibly to make himself remember what had happened while he was under hypnosis or the King to remember consciously—but to make the King tell him what he had told Jim.

If that had happened, Jim's questions and the King's answers would have been known. These men-at-arms would have been dispatched immediately. On horseback, the residence of King Jean was only minutes away. Now, what Edouard said was only too obvious. Either the boat got underway immediately; or the men-at-arms would overwhelm them. Forty or fifty enemies all at once were too many.

Though that number was already being reduced. Dafydd, with his usual coolness, had laid out his quiver of arrows where it was convenient to reach; and one by one he was knocking off their horses individuals among those who were charging at them.

The men-at-arms were identically dressed in chain mail; but all wore steel breastplates over this, with the royal French arms graven upon their surfaces, and now shining red in the light of the setting sun. Possibly that was why Dafydd's arrows were taking them in the throat or some other less protected spot on their bodies. However, in any case, any of those he hit were out of the fight that was coming. But there were too many of them for the loss of these to make an important difference in the odds.

"Cut the bow and stern ropes!" Edouard was shouting.

But, while the men-at-arms were still some little distance up the wharf, approaching at the trot to which the weight of their arms and armor reduced them, three barefoot young men in ragged shirts and trousers had now appeared on the wharf above the boat. They had come at a run; and now they leaped down lithely to its deck. They went instantly to casting loose the ropes with which the boat was tied to the wharf fore and aft.

As the last rope came free, the boat began to drift away from the dock.

Unfortunately, at that moment, an errant wave obstinately chose to push them back against the dock again. Their return was just in time for the leading members among the men-at-arms to reach the wharf above the vessel and begin jumping aboard.

Meanwhile, one among them had thrown a rope with a grapnel on the end and caught hold of the bow; and several of them together pulled the boat back alongside the wharf.

The rest of the men-at-arms swarmed aboard. The sheer weight of their numbers drove Giles, Jim and Brian back across the deck. None of the three had had time to put on more than their chain mail shirts. Jim had donned his before leaving the inn; and Brian and Giles had put theirs on the minute Jim had got them out of the dungeon.

They were otherwise without armor, and, except for Jim, without helmets. For weapons, they had only the swords and poignards hanging from their knight's belts, plus Dafydd's bow.

So weaponed, and lightly protected, the three of them met the rush of their heavily half-armored opponents; who by weight and numbers alone, threatened to overwhelm them.

There was no doubt that Brian and Giles, at least—and probably Dafydd, who had now laid aside his bow and was fighting alongside them with the long knife he always wore in a scabbard down along his leg—were man-for-man more than a match for any of their attackers. But faced with so many, it was only a matter of time before they were slain or captured.

Secoh clapped his hands.

The human clothes that Jim had caused to have bought for him flew apart in rags and tatters. He was once more a dragon.

With one powerful pump of his wings he rose above the heads of everybody there, to about a dozen feet of height; and kept himself there with an occasional downbeat, opening to the full his massively toothed jaws and spreading the scimitar-shaped claws that tipped his forelimbs. He roared.

The royal French men-at-arms were brave men. Probably, unusually brave men. Else they would not have been wearing the Leopards and Lilies, which were France's coat of arms, engraved on their breastplates.

In dragon terms Secoh was a shrimp. But, hovering now just a few feet above their heads, with more than twenty feet of leathery wing outstretched, the setting sun behind him casting his shadow for yards along and up the slope toward the drinking houses beyond the wharf, he was too much like some creature out of a nether world for them to stand and face.

He had, as far as they could tell, appeared from nowhere; and that he was hell-born was all too likely. The English, as everyone knew, would use any abomination (witness the fact that His Holiness, Pope Innocent the Second, at the Second Lateran Council in 1139, had banned bowmen, like the one here, as unfit for Christians to make use of—except, naturally, against infidels).

The men-at-arms could not get away from the boat and wharf fast enough.

One of the crew—those three who had leaped aboard just before the men-at-arms got there—cut the grapnel-ended rope. The other two had already been busy setting the sail; and Edouard was now putting the blade of the steering oar in the water. In a moment they were moving—slowly, it was true, but moving—away from the wharf, gaining speed as they went and heading toward a part of the bay where no land showed, the mouth of the Rade of Brest to the open sea. Secoh landed back on the deck, looking pleased with himself.

"Well done, Secoh," said Jim.

Secoh ducked his head bashfully. "It was nothing, m'Lord," he said.

Behind them, up on the hill, the drinking houses from which the pockmarked man's group of mariners had come were now fronted by a silent throng of human bodies, who stood and stared after them.

"I will have to think up a fine tale, indeed," said Edouard between his teeth, "before I risk myself in Brest again. I shall expect you to keep that in mind when you pay me, messires; aside from the lean price the Welshman drove with me. That price did not include cutting off access to the port that is my main source of income."

The words registered strongly on Jim. Whatever pockmarked and his friends might have believed about Jim's story before, the sight of King Jean's men-at-arms striving to take them would have pretty well given it the lie. He and the rest indeed owed Edouard more than had been bargained for originally.

"So far as it is in my power," said Jim to the shipmaster, "I'll see that you don't lose by this."

No sail tried to follow them; and it was not long before they had left the Rade of Brest behind them and were on the open sea.

The sunset still gave them light and the open sea, insofar as they were moving into it, was evidently in a good temper. There was no more than a usual chop; of the sort that the kind of ship Jim thought of as a *ship*, in contrast to this little boat, would hardly have felt.

In this small ship, however—and Jim made a mental note to remember to call it a ship, since the shipmaster and his crew clearly thought of it in those terms—the motion was definitely noticeable. However, Jim had always been fairly immune to ocean sickness; and his friends also seemed equally free of any problem that way, while Edouard and his crew were quite at home upon the waters.

"A fine day to be returning to England!" said Brian, voicing what Jim thought must be the thoughts of all of them.

But Edouard frowned.

"I would rather be in darkness, or rain," he said. "Our sail can still be seen from a large distance."

"That's not good?" asked Jim.

"We might find an enemy upon the waters who considers us fruit ripe for plucking," said Edouard. "We'll shortly be on the high seas; and prey to any other ship which can take us. Ah, well, we can do nothing but wait for trouble and meet it as it comes."

He turned back to his duties. Jim was becoming confirmed in an earlier opinion that shipmasters were all born pessimists.

They sailed northwest toward England. Night descended and dawn came. From time to time in the moonlight, they had glimpsed other sails at a distance. But none came close, and it was not long before they saw a dark line on the watery horizon ahead. They had seen similar lines on their right most of the trip so far, evidence of the western seashore of France. These ships, Jim reminded himself, liked to stay in touch with the land in their sailing, since they were restricted to navigating by sun and stars once out of sight of any shore.

Abruptly, Secoh spoke.

"M'Lord! M'Lord!" he cried. "There is a dragon up there, staying with us."

He pointed up and seaward, and Jim looked. In his human body he did not have Secoh's dragon-sight. But there was a flier up there, and he was soaring very like a dragon.

"Shall I fly up and challenge him?" asked Secoh eagerly.

"Maybe you'd better," answered Jim slowly. "Don't get into a fight if you can help it."

"I won't!" said Secoh, and took off, with an explosion of wings.

Jim watched. The other dragon let Secoh approach, and for a while they flew so close together they seemed to touch. Secoh left the other, who turned away. In moments, Secoh had thumped back down on the deck making an awkward, one-foot landing. With the other foot he clutched something half-hidden under his body.

"M'Lord!" he cried. Jim hurried to him and felt a heavy bag thrust into his hands. "It was Iren—one of those French dragons. They'll join us against the serpents! Here's their surety."

Jim barely opened the bag and looked inside. He saw gems— many more of them than had ever been in any dragon passport he had carried. The bag held more than an Emperor's ransom— its worth would have made ransom for a dozen Emperors. Hastily, he passed it back to Secoh.

"You keep it, and guard it," he said in a near whisper.

"Yes, m'Lord," said Secoh softly, but with pride. He took the bag.

Jim turned away with what he hoped was an indifferent expression. He would tell Brian and the others later.

But now there was no doubt that the line ahead of them was the southern-facing shore of England. They were at first too far away to see anything but that streak of low-lying darkness. But with remarkable quickness, it began to grow and resolve itself into the hills and low points of a shoreline, although it was still too soon to make out harbors or towns.

However, there was another sign that they were getting close to whatever harbor had been picked as their goal; for the number of sails to be seen on the waters about them as the day brightened had increased.

The eyes of the crew, and of the shipmaster himself, were now directed at these other sails; apparently to find which, if any, were headed in their own direction.

Edouard himself stood in the prow of the vessel, where its deck raised to become the roof of the forecastle underfoot.

The three other members of the crew stood on the ship's railing, holding to vertical ropes, shading their eyes against the sun and peering both right and left.

The dark line of land ahead was now taking on some shape. Without warning, one of the crew swung himself outside the rope he held to and began to swarm up it. Reaching the top of the mast, he held on to it with one hand, leaning out to gaze under his palm at a ship in the near distance.

The other crew members were now watching him. For a moment there was silence. Then his voice rang out.

"Master! It's Bloody Boots!" he cried. "Fine on the larboard bow, sailing to meet with us!"

Edouard himself, now balanced up on the prow railing itself, where the two sides of the boat converged, held to one of the lines of the mast and peered in the direction indicated.

"I can't make out the sail clearly!" he shouted back up to the man on the mast. "Can you see the patching?"

"I'm all but certain sure, master!" the lookout shouted back. "Two large overlapping patches low on the starboard side of the sail. And the ship is as Bloody Boots' ship has always been told of, with fighting castles high in bow and stern."

Jim had located the ship they were talking about now. But he, no more than anyone else aboard—for all were looking now—could make out anything special about the sail. He had a sudden idea. There was a bit of magic he had used before at least once. Dragons had vision very like that of hawks; they were able to make out relatively small objects on the ground from as high as two thousand feet above. What it required was a dragon's vision, plus a certain amount of focusing, so that the eyes literally shifted from a close-up view to a distant one. He wrote the necessary spell on the inside of his forehead.

ME TO HAVE DRAGON→ DISTANTVISION

Instantly, the ship he was looking at seemed to leap to half the distance from them that it had appeared before. It was as the lookout on the mast had described it, a larger vessel than their own, with two walled platforms, high in the bow and stern. These platforms were filled with men; and, after a second, Jim made out the fact that they were holding some dark objects that looked very much like crossbows. In the waist of the ship there were more men.

He wrote the counterspell to return his vision to normal; and found himself staring almost directly into the face of the nearest seaman, who was staring back at him with features as white as paper. Jim was puzzled for a second; then he remembered that in order to focus his eyes for distance vision, a dragon altered their shape and moved them forward. In the deep eyesockets of a dragon's face, this change was not so apparent. In the human face it must have seemed as if his eyeballs had been bulging clear out of his head.

But there was no time to explain now.

"Edouard!" shouted Jim. "I can see distance very well. I've just looked at the ship. It does have a patch on the sail, and it does have the fighting castles fore and aft, with men on them who seem to be bearing crossbows. There are more in the waist!"

Edouard dropped back onto the deck near the prow, his boots thudding heavily on impact. He dropped down to the lower portion of the deck to face Jim and his other passengers.

"Messires, we are done for!" he said grimly. "I cannot outsail him in these light airs, and he carries men and weapons aboard that will surely finish us off; for no one is ever left alive on the losing side in these encounters on the narrow seas!"

"What's this?" snapped Brian. "What matter if they outnumber us? Unless they have armored knights aboard, we are the equal of any men they might be carrying!"

"Who is this Bloody Boots?" asked Giles.

"A damned Scotch pirate!" replied Edouard. "He slips down from Scotland, takes a prey, and is away again before any force can be brought against him greater than his own. As you see, he is carrying far more men than he needs merely to crew his ship. They will be weaponed and ready to kill those aboard any ship they take. We carry no valuable cargo—but he cannot know that. There is this ship, of course; which, if he can take it undamaged, he can crew with his extra men and sail back up north to sell."

Jim thought of the Emperor's ransom in jewels that they were secretly carrying; and which belonged to the French dragons. At the same time, he himself did not see how this Bloody Boots could have heard about that. Unless word had been somehow passed to him by magical means that among their baggage there was wealth beyond imagining.

"How many men would you say he has aboard?" Brian was asking Edouard.

"Twenty, at least," answered Edouard. "If not twenty, at least so many as we cannot stand against."

"Speak for yourself and your crewmen, Master shipman!" said Brian. "I tell you again that unless he has knights armed and armored with him, if he had thirty men we need not fear him."

"He is a knight himself, I think," said Edouard. "But I cannot think that he will have any others of his rank with him. But his men may well be in half armor, or light armor, or however you landsmen say such things."

"As I say," said Brian, "we are their match and more. You have three knights, who can be in full armor by the time they are next to us. And of them, I, at least, am no babe with weapons; and I venture to say the good Sir Giles is not either, and Sir James—"

There was a slight hesitation in his voice but then he went on boldly enough.

"—He is the very man I would like to have at my side in such small bicker as this will be. Do you sail on, as if you had not seen him, or care not whether he is there or not; and meanwhile I and my two friends will dress for battle."

"Sir knight, sir knight," said Edouard almost wearily. "Did you not hear messire here"—he nodded at Jim—"say that there were crossbowmen in their fighting castles? Even your armor will not be proof against their bolts at very short range. I tell you, we are helpless before them, as sheep before the butcher."

"Nay, Master shipman," interposed the quiet voice of Dafydd, "it seems you have forgotten I am one of your passengers. I am a bowman, look you, a bowman of Wales. As such I can outshoot, for distance and for proper aim, any crossbowman that puts stock to shoulder. If you will but find me a place in which I am at least partly protected, with a clear view of the other ship, I will promise you that many if not all of their crossbowmen will not get within twenty ship-lengths of our craft."

Edouard turned to stare at him. Dafydd smiled down to him, comfortingly.

"By all the saints!" said Edouard. "You are one of those devil English archers who have wrought such havoc among the French armies in near times!"

The comforting smile vanished from Dafydd's lips.

"Wales, '*of Wales*,' I said, Master shipman!" His voice was not raised, but had a whiplash in it that his friends had never heard before. "Did I not say 'of Wales' clearly enough for you to hear?"

"Why . . ." Edouard literally stammered, "is it not almost the same thing? I meant—"

"Of Wales," said Dafydd, still softly but implacably. "I am a Welsh archer, one of that breed who were putting arrows where they were aimed while those of Britain still fumbled with string and sticks in their attempts to shoot a short bow. Of Wales! I am a master of my trade and a greater master at it than you are at yours, shipman. *Of Wales!*"

Dafydd was tall already, but now he seemed to tower over all of them; and, most of all, over Edouard, who was short by comparison even with Giles and Brian, though broad-shouldered and able-looking.

"Of Wales," agreed Edouard meekly. "I crave your pardon, Master bowman. If what you say is true, then indeed there is hope this day for all of us. But it is a slim hope, even at best; for we have no fighting castle on either bow or stern from which you can loose your bolts. Yet, we will do our best to build you some sort of shelter in the time that remains before we are caught by Bloody Boots."

He turned to Jim and the other two knights.

"As for you, messires," he said, "I will suggest that you do your armoring and whatsoever else is involved down in the forecastle out of sight. There is no need to let them know our strength before they are upon us."

"Stay!" said Sir Brian, frowning. "It is not done that belted knights should shelter behind a bowman; even such a bowman as Dafydd. We'll do our changing on deck."

Edouard looked savage.

"Do you that, sir knight," he said, "and we throw away half the advantage there is to be gained by you, your armor and your skill with weapons."

"Nonetheless—" Brian was beginning; when Jim decided that he had better lose no time in interfering.

"Brian, Giles," he interrupted, "perhaps we should have a private word by ourselves; and perhaps the forecastle is not a bad place to do it. For one thing, there is a matter with Secoh. Meanwhile, you, Master shipman, must think of some way of hiding our horses from the sight of the other ship. Perhaps you have odds and ends you can pile around them. So that if they do not neigh, they will not be suspected until the other ship is so close it will make no difference."

It was a little, thought Jim to himself in the wake of his own words, rather like the lion tamer's trick of presenting a lion with the four legs of a chair. Whether it was true or not he did not know; but he had been told that the reason the chair legs baffled the lion was because they created a conundrum in the animal mind. The question was which one of the four legs menacing him should be batted down first; and while he hesitated, the tendency to flee rather than fight—or at least, back up, was likely to take control of him.

Jim himself had just now confronted Brian and the others around him, not with merely one but three things to be done; and while they sorted out their objections to find the one with which they should argue, he was already walking toward the entrance of the forecastle, all but herding the other two knights and Secoh before him.

CHAPTER 24

Getting Secoh down the stairs proved to be the largest problem. Even with his wings folded, the doorway was a very tight fit for him; and although, being a dragon, he was perfectly at home in darkness and enclosed spaces, the fact that he had to head down the stairs to get to it in this case caused him to hesitate.

However, Secoh had long since given up any self-acknowledgment that he could be frightened by anything. So, even though it was somewhat gingerly, he wedged himself through the doorway and made his way down the steps.

No more was said by Brian or Giles until they were all in the forecastle; but with all of them there, including Secoh, the space which might have held as many as six or eight men was definitely crowded—particularly for three men who would be trying to get into armor and helping each other in the process. It was apparent to all of them.

"Would you like to turn me back into a . . . human?" asked Secoh of Jim.

Jim felt a twinge of emotion. He knew now how little Secoh had liked losing his dragon form for a human one.

"No, Secoh," he said, "I'm going to send you for help. All of you wait a moment, would you please? I want to ask our shipmaster something more. I'll be right back."

He turned to the ladder leading back up to the deck.

"James?" said Brian. "You called us aside to have a privy word with us; and now instead of that you are off to talk to the shipmaster. This is strange behavior, indeed. I should think—"

"Bear with me, please, Brian," said Jim. "It's only a word I want. I'll just go to the top of the ladder and call him. Then I'll be right back down. The rest of you can listen if you like."

Without waiting for any agreement from Brian—and in fact, he got none—Jim went on up the ladder and stuck his head out the opening to the forecastle with its sliding door, which could be closed to keep out sea water that came aboard, but which now was slid completely back to let some much-needed fresh air into the rather smelly space below.

"Shipmaster!" Jim called. "Would you come here a minute? It's important!"

With his head out of the forecastle he was able to hear a sort of grumble among the mixture of voices up toward the front of the boat beyond the forecastle and out of his sight. Then, after a moment the sound of footsteps thumped overhead and Edouard jumped lightly down opposite the forecastle door, crouching over to look at Jim.

"What is it, sir knight?" he said. "If we are to build a protection for the bowman, every moment counts—"

"I know that. And I want Dafydd protected as much as anyone else—possibly more," said Jim. "But I've got a quick question for you. You're carrying no cargo, are you?"

"Hmm," Edouard looked at him shrewdly for a moment, "you know something of the sea, messire. No, we have no cargo. How could we when we had to take off so swiftly with you?"

"That means we're riding high in the water, doesn't it?" said Jim. "And our riding high in the water has got to be visible to this Bloody Boots or whoever he is? By the way, why is he called Bloody Boots?"

"He's supposed to pour the blood of captives into his boots before he boards another ship, so that it will leak out of the boots and leave his bloody footprints everywhere," said Edouard. "My own thought is that it is probably cattle or sheep blood that he uses to begin with, at least; though I would not put it past him to slit the throat of a captive just to get blood for his boots. No, you're right. We have no cargo. I have been puzzled myself why he should choose us to attack, when there must be richer-looking ships around that would be equally easy prey."

"And you came up with no answer?" asked Jim.

"No answer, messire. You are correct," said Edouard.

"Ah. Thank you," said Jim. "That's all, then. I was simply wondering about that myself. You can go back to whatever you were doing now and we'll get busy dressing."

"An idle question to use up such good time!" grumbled Edouard, even as he was getting to his feet. He leaped upward the short distance to the upper deck that was also roof to the forecastle; and they heard the thump of his sea boots moving toward the prow.

Jim returned down the ladder.

"What is this, then, James?" asked Brian, when Jim once more faced them on the forecastle floor. "What matters it if our ship has cargo or no cargo, or why this Scotch pirate chooses to attack us?"

"I just wanted to confirm a suspicion that magic's involved in this," said Jim. "I still don't have solid proof; but as far as I'm concerned, I'm now sure. Secoh?"

"Yes m'Lord," offered Secoh once more. "As I said, m'Lord, if you'd really like to change me back into a george to give you more room here—"

"Not at all, Secoh," said Jim. "In fact, I've got a real need for you to remain a dragon. I want to send you on a mission for help."

"Help?" said Brian and Giles in the same voice. Secoh merely stared at him with his round, dark dragon eyes.

"Yes," said Jim. "Didn't it strike the two of you those French royal men-at-arms caught up with us very quickly? As if they knew where to look for us."

"It is true," said Giles slowly. "They did come directly to the wharves without wasting any time elsewhere, plainly. On the other hand, would they not have taken for granted the fact that we would try to get back to England?"

"That'd certainly have been a possibility in the mind of the King and Ecotti," said Jim, "but to send them on horseback, as if there was no time to lose, directly to that destination alone, made it almost too good a guess. I suspect magic was involved in their knowing where to find us."

"But you said," Giles protested, "Ecotti's was a different kind of magic than yours. If you couldn't find out from the King what you wanted to find out, how could he find out something like where we were headed?"

"That's exactly a question to which I can think of only one answer," said Jim. "I'm beginning to believe that one of them, either the King or Ecotti, is directly in contact with the greater and stronger magical mind who's behind all this, but doesn't know it, himself. It could be that even as we were talking to the King and Ecotti, this greater magical mind was learning all about what we were doing. If it was Ecotti that the hidden magician was in contact with, then it could be that the minute we had left, he had Ecotti discover from the King all that the King had told me."

"And if it was King Jean?" asked Brian.

There was skepticism in his voice. Jean was an anointed King; as such, he should not be capable of being part of any magical agreement.

"I don't think it was the King," said Jim. "Ecotti's more likely."

"Then?" asked Giles.

"Well," said Jim, "I don't believe Ecotti could use the type of magic I used to find what happened when they were both under hypnosis. Also, they'd both certainly have had to stay under the spell until they had counted numbers I gave them. But after that, Ecotti, or the Mastermind using magic through Ecotti, could have used his powers to find out exactly what went on while we were there."

"M'Lord," said Secoh, somewhat bashfully, "I don't understand."

"If I'm right," said Jim, "the Mastermind could guess we were headed for the seashore and a ship for England; and made sure the King ordered the men-at-arms after us without delay."

"But even if this is all true," said Brian, "what has it to do with sending off Secoh for help—and what kind of help can he bring us in time, in any case?"

"Well," said Jim, "if magic was used in what I said, it may have been used in another way. I haven't told you, but the Mastermind—that unknown magician behind Ecotti and the sea serpents—may have somehow gotten information to Bloody Boots that we've now got a greater fortune in jewels with us than any human is likely to see in his lifetime. That explains his choosing us as a ship to attack. Forgive me if I cannot tell you why we have these jewels."

"You need no forgiveness from us, James," said Brian. "But you do think Bloody Boots may know this?"

"I have to consider it a real possibility, Brian," said Jim.

"And how, then," said the other knight, "can Secoh help us? Surely within an hour, or a little more, that other ship will be alongside, for all Dafydd's arrows and his skill as a bowman."

"We're very close to the south shore of England," said Jim, "Malencontri and Cliffside are only about thirty miles from here; and a dragon can fly very swiftly, particularly with the wind behind him—and we seem to have an onshore wind. With this type of day I would expect onshore winds at a higher altitude too."

He stopped talking to Brian and turned to Secoh.

"Secoh," he said, "I want you to do two things. First, go back up on deck and fly away from this ship, keeping low above the waves and keeping this ship between you and the other ship of Bloody Boots. By the time our vessel can hide you no longer, you should be distant enough not to attract the pirates' attention. As soon as you think so, immediately climb to some distance in the air, so that you seem only a speck to those of us here on the sea's surface. You can do that?"

"Oh, certainly, m'Lord," said Secoh, "but how will this help?"

"Once aloft, you will turn and head toward the shore of England and Malencontri. If Carolinus is there, tell him what we've learned. The French invade in five days' time if the weather holds. If he isn't there, don't waste time hunting for him."

"But then . . ." Secoh broke down and stammered a little, "m'Lord, I shall be at least half an hour's flight from you at a time when I could help you in this battle against these george pirates. Are you sure you want me to go?"

"Yes," said Jim, "because then you can see about getting help for us. I want you to go immediately to the caves of the Cliffside dragons and gather at least half a dozen, if not more, of the dragons there to come back and help out."

"They aren't likely to come just because I ask it," said Secoh doubtfully. "You know those fat cave-dwellers as well as I do, m'Lord. They will not fight, except to save their own lives. If this invasion of sea serpents comes, they will fight, of course; but anything less than that . . ."

"Ah," said Jim, "but I want you to get together your recruits from your friends among the young dragons. And I don't expect them to fight!"

Secoh, as Jim knew, had become very much a favorite of the younger dragons of the Cliffside. A dragon was considered a child until he had lived at least fifty years; and a wet-eared youngster after that, until he was a hundred or more. Younger dragons were consequently used to being shouldered aside and ordered about by their seniors, who treated them as if they were not only useless, but in the way most of the time.

Secoh, because of his mere-dragon ancestry, under the original blight that had come out from the Loathly Tower, and the lack of food in the meres while he was growing up, even at the age of two hundred and ten years was scarcely bigger than most of the fifty-year-old dragons and smaller than some of the slightly older, young Cliffsiders. Moreover, he was exciting to the young dragons.

Not only was he brave enough to face up to any of the other dragons, no matter their size, in the Cliffside community; but was apparently unafraid of anything. Moreover, he knew stories, particularly the one about the fight at the Loathly Tower, where he had been one with Jim, Brian, Dafydd and Smrgol, the grand-uncle of Gorbash—the dragon whose body Jim was inadvertently occupying at the time.

It was, in fact, together with Smrgol—already partly crippled by a stroke and his great age—that he had fought and eventually helped slay the renegade dragon Bryagh, who had abandoned all else to enlist in the services of the Dark Powers that controlled the Loathly Tower.

Second, Secoh had had further adventures, as well as learning, word-for-word, some of the tales that Smrgol had been able to tell. When Smrgol had been alive, even though the older dragons always groaned in mock protest when he started to tell one of these they were the ones who tucked a keg of wine under one of their forelimbs and took all the choice spots right next to Smrgol, crowding the youngsters to the outskirts. With Secoh, the youngsters had their own tale-teller. Also, they were more adventurous than their elders; and might be tempted by Secoh into engaging in a real-life sort of adventure such as they had heard about.

"Get me half a dozen or more of the young ones, particularly the eager young ones, who've done a lot of flying because they haven't put on a great deal of extra weight yet."

"I suppose . . ." said Secoh doubtfully. "But—"

"You needn't get them into the actual fight at all," said Jim. "You know how hawks like the peregrine falcon dive on their prey? They close their wings and simply fall like a stone; then spread their wings at the last moment to check themselves just before they hit whatever it is they're after on the ground?"

"Oh, yes, m'Lord. Any dragon knows that," said Secoh.

"Well, you get your youngsters to do the same. Back where I come from there was a time when it was called dive-bombing. The only difference is, you tell these young dragons to stop a good fifteen or twenty feet above the masthead of the ship Bloody Boots is in."

Secoh's face lit up.

"Oh, yes," he said, "the young ones'll like that!"

"Meanwhile," Jim went on, "Brian, Giles and I will have done our best to put out of action any crossbowmen that Dafydd has left still able to fight; so your friends should be in no danger. I'm pretty sure that not one, but a whole wing, of dragons like that should scare Bloody Boots off completely. But, you mustn't waste time! Go right away. Now!"

Secoh crowded himself between the bodies of the men, found the ladder and climbed it. For a moment his body filled the entrance. Then he squeezed through out onto the deck; and a moment later with a noisy flap of wings he took off, just above the deck and through a gap between the lines that ran from the taffrail of the ship to its mast. Crowding together up the ladder, they had a faint glimpse of him flying away some thirty feet or so above the waves.

"I hope he stays low," said Jim. He turned back to putting on his armor.

Giles and Brian had been busy getting their own armor on, and were all but ready to go on deck. Now both of them lent Jim a hand in getting dressed and armed. Shortly, they all clumped up the ladder; and, crouching down below the roughly three-foot rise which was the front of the forecastle above the lower deck, they peered ahead at what was going on in the bow.

Up where the two sides of the vessel came together in a sharp point, Edouard and his three crewmen had built a sort of three-sided, half-roofed shed about six and a half feet tall. It was of double thicknesses of the same sort of rough planks the shipmaster had pulled out to make a runway by which the horses could be brought aboard.

The planks had been tied together rather than nailed; and Jim saw that the steering oar had been lashed in position, so that the ship sailed itself on course before the steady, following wind.

In the shelter they had built was room for Dafydd to stand, with his quiver of arrows hung on a nail in front of him. He could shoot out both ahead and to his sides, through eight long slits some three to five inches in width. He stood now, with an arrow fitted to his bow; but was not shooting as they approached.

The four shipmen turned as Jim, Brian and Giles clumped toward them; and Edouard started, then froze suddenly at the sight of the device on the shield hanging from Jim's left shoulder. His crewmen had turned also, at the sound of the noise; and at seeing him react so, they looked wonderingly at him and stood still in turn, gazing from him to the shield and back again, as if half in puzzlement and half in fear.

Jim had opened his mouth to speak to the shipmaster, but Edouard beat him to it.

"My Lord!" he said. "I did not know—are you indeed the Dragon Knight?"

"Yes," said Jim, "only I didn't expect you to recognize me."

"I am English more than French, m'Lord," replied Edouard. "But even if I were only French, word of your doings has reached at least this part of France. Your arms are as well known there as in England. You have been on French soil before, if I mistake it not?"

"I," said Jim, "and these gentlemen with me. Have you heard of them, too?"

Edouard looked at the shields of both Brian and Giles, swung his eyes back to stare at Dafydd—who, however, was paying no attention to him but concentrating on his view through the slit in his protective planks that was most directly ahead. Edouard looked back at Jim. There was a strange expression on his face.

"Mage," he said, "it is an honor for me, even at this moment, and once in a lifetime, to meet all of you. But mostly to meet a magic worker of your repute and rank."

"I shouldn't be addressed as Mage," said Jim wearily. How many times and to how many people had he tried to explain this? "As a magician I'm very low in rank. The term '*Mage*' should be only for those who have reached the highest possible rank. You would address Carolinus, my master in magic, as

'Mage' and be correct; or you would have so addressed Merlin if you had lived in his time. Call me simply m'Lord, as you've been doing."

"If you wish it," said Edouard. "Still, I am enheartened to have such knights of legend about me. It gives me some hope that we may win through after all."

"Don't expect too much," said Jim. "We're only men, after all, and can't do the impossible. It may be this Bloody Boots will overwhelm us; the same way the men-at-arms would have done, if Secoh hadn't changed himself back into a dragon."

"It was that that first made me suspect you might be more than ordinary mortal man," said Edouard. "But do you mean that dragons can change themselves to humans and back again like werewolves? That is something I did not know."

"Not without help, they can't," said Jim. "Meanwhile, since the subject of Secoh's come up, I want to tell you that when you saw Secoh fly off right now, I sent him to see if he could get us some help from other dragons. Without that help, I don't know what chance we have."

"It's true I had no hope at all at first—" began Edouard; and was interrupted by a heavy thud that seemed almost beside them.

"They have crossbow bolts to spare, evidently," commented Dafydd, still with his eyes fixed on the view beyond his slit. "I have less than thirty shafts, and each one must take out its man, because once they are all shot, I am no longer a bowman; but only one more man with a knife."

"Why do you not shoot, then?" asked Edouard.

Without a word, Dafydd pointed upward into the half-ceiling that roofed his enclosure. The sharp metal end of a shaft protruded perhaps an inch and a half through the wood. Edouard swore softly.

"And that through two thicknesses of plank!" he said. "At close range they will come right through. But why do you not shoot back, bowman?"

"Do you not see that the bolt struck downward upon us?" answered Dafydd. "It was fired as high as the crossbowman dared aim it, and still not have it fall short of this ship. It came as far through the wood as it did, as much from its falling as from its original force. But since what comes down once went up, it is true that at close range these crossbow bolts may not merely pierce the planks, but come through. It is a powerful weapon, the crossbow, if a slow and clumsy one. As for why I do not shoot back, look you through this slit, shipman."

He stood back a little and Edouard took a step forward to peer out through the aperture.

"By all the saints," he swore, "it is still at some distance from us."

"Just so," said Dafydd. "Now, from here, with my bow and my skill I could hit any man of them; but I could not be sure of killing whoever I aim at. So, since I have less than thirty shafts, as I said, I will hold them until each one will do its task. Stick to your ship, Master shipman, and leave the bow-work to me."

Edouard stepped back.

"I will so," he said. "I crave your pardon for seeming overeager, Master bowman."

"Granted," said Dafydd, once more with his eye on the slit. "I will shoot when I am ready."

Edouard turned back to the others.

"Best we all stay hidden until we're closer," he said. "In these light airs my ship can sail no faster; and in any case, even if we could go faster, he can sail faster yet. It is a bigger boat, with a larger sail and a faster hull for speed through the water than mine."

The sense of this was so plain that no one else said anything. Jim, Brian and Giles, as well as Edouard and his three crew members, went back to the edge of the forecastle and dropped down to the lower deck level, settling with their backs on the three-foot-high forecastle wall; and so becoming invisible to the crossbowmen.

Brian lifted off his helmet. Jim and Giles followed suit. Their visors had been open all this time; but there was considerable difference in comfort between a helmet with an open visor and no helmet at all.

"Now, Master shipman," said Brian, "it is time you began to tell us what you now believe the numbers to be of the foe we shall encounter in the ship approaching us, what manner of arms and armor they will have, and how they will attempt to board us—unless we board them first."

CHAPTER 25

E douard stared at him for a second.

"For a moment, sir knight," he said, "I had forgotten who you were. Surely no one but paladins would speak of boarding a ship such as that, in the face of the numbers aboard her."

"Come, man!" said Brian, somewhat sharply. "You are about to give us your best estimate of those numbers and the other things I asked you."

"I may have made the guess earlier," said Edouard, "but if so I now repeat it. I suspect he has between twenty and thirty men aboard, mostly Scots like himself. He will be the only knight among them, but the rest will be mostly armored in all sorts and fashions, and carrying all sorts of weapons, from daggers to spears. He, himself, it is said, carries a heavy, long, two-handed sword called by some outlandish Scots name—cly . . . clid . . ."

"*Claihea mor,*" said Giles, harshly, "in ordinary speech, you would say 'great sword.'"

"Exactly. 'Claymore,'" went on Edouard. "He is a giant among men and it is said no man can stand against him when he uses that weapon."

"Hah!" said Brian. "There are ways of shield and ordinary broadsword to deal with such an oversize blade. It may be I shall show you and him some of them today."

223

Their talk had been interrupted by several more thuds of crossbow bolts hitting the shelter around Dafydd. Jim, who had now been listening, had also three times heard the twang of his bow. But now Giles twisted about from where he was sitting with his back against the forecastle wall, and lifted his head above it enough to look toward the bow.

"Dafydd is scratched," he said.

They all looked. The latest crossbow bolts to come in were coming clear through the wood at least half their length if not more. One of these had angled down and come through far enough so that its tip had cut Dafydd's thigh. As they looked now, he leaned against the protruding crossbow shaft with his knee to break it off. It snapped close to where it emerged from the plank. The movement of the leg seemed to indicate he had not been seriously hurt, but the hose of his left leg was now dark with blood for most of its length, so that the wound was bleeding freely.

Brian swore.

"It is not right," he said, "that knights should hide behind a naked man with only a bow."

Edouard risked standing and peering beneath his hand at the approaching pirate ship. He sat down again quickly as a crossbow bolt hummed past him, clear across the width of the vessel and over into the sea beyond.

"It is close," he said.

"How long?" snapped Brian.

"Not long," said Edouard. "We have time to say our prayers, perhaps, provided our sins are not too great."

Somewhat to Jim's startlement—although he told himself almost in the same instant that he should have known it—everyone there except himself proceeded to do exactly what Edouard had said; crossing themselves, joining their hands, in some cases closing their eyes and beginning to mumble to themselves.

After a moment's indecision, Jim decided to join them. As a magician, perhaps it might not be expected of him. On the other hand, solidarity was always a cheering thing. He closed his eyes, joined his hands and tilted his head downward. He could not bring himself to pretend to pray, since it was not a natural act for him; and he felt that falsity at this moment could be carried too far. At any rate, he composed himself to wait until the others should stop.

One by one, they did. Giles and Brian were first to lower their hands and lift their heads. But after them came Edouard, then two of the crew. Surprisingly, it was the youngest who prayed the longest and most earnestly. For the first time it struck Jim what it must be like to be young and in a situation like this where death was being almost accepted by his captain and crewmates.

Jim wondered that he himself was not more fearful at the moment. The odds against them seemed insurmountable. Also, it was anyone's guess whether the dragons would arrive in time; or would have any effect in saving their lives even if they did appear.

But he found himself strangely unmoved; and now that he thought back on it, except for the moments when he had been in an actual fight, such as at the Loathly Tower or against the Hollow Men on the border of Scotland, or at tight moments on their previous visit to France, he had not really felt any great deal of fear—except perhaps for a few moments just as combat was joined. Then once into the fight, he was apparently too busy to think of it.

He found himself wondering. Perhaps his knowledge that he was a magician gave him a false sense of security? Or perhaps the reason was even more far-fetched. That somehow to him, even now, this world did not seem as real as his original twentieth-century world; and consequently it did not seem as if he could really die here—in the essential meaning of that word. Unobtrusively, he pinched the skin of his left wrist with the fingers of his right hand.

He almost jumped at the bolt of pain that shot up his arm. He had forgotten he was wearing metal gauntlets. This world was real enough. But there was no time to think more about that now.

The thudding of the crossbow bolts upon Dafydd's shelter had become almost steady; and other bolts were zipping across the deck at a height that would endanger any of them who stood up. Some of these also thudded into the sides of Edouard's vessel.

"The poor lad bleeds heavily, now," said Giles. He had turned around once more to look at Dafydd.

They all turned to look. What he had said was no less than true. A number of bolts had come most of the way through the woodwork around Dafydd, and others were now coming clear through, although they usually fell to the deck, spent, once they had penetrated. But Dafydd, while he had taken none into his upper body or arms, had been cut by several of them; and it seemed that there was no part of his clothes, except that part of his body protected by his hauberk, that did not seem soaked with blood. The quiver in front of him now held only two or three arrows.

He was supporting himself now with a knee on one of the crossbow bolt shafts that had penetrated. Apparently that first leg to be hit had been hit again, and he found it either too painful or too unsteady to rest his weight on it. As they watched he took another arrow, fitted it to his bow, drew it to its head and let it go out through the side slit to which he was now devoting his full attention.

The impact of the bolts had now lessened in number; but almost at regular periods one struck the shelter.

"I have all but their last crossbowman," Dafydd said over his shoulder. His voice was calm, but weak. "There are others loading and cranking extra crossbows for him, which is why his bolts come so steadily. And others stand in front of him, so that I cannot get a clear shot at him. But I will get him yet."

His face was pale. He turned his attention back to the slit.

"I fear me he will faint from the loss of all that blood," said Giles.

"That does it!" roared Brian, jumping to his feet. He would have been exposed to the enemy now, except that the shelter built for Dafydd blocked their sight of him. "By Saint Edmond, Saint Richard and Saint Oswald, shipmaster! Lay me alongside that vessel—or your own life be on it!"

He had drawn his sword and dressed his shield.

"Sir knight," said Edouard, still crouching below the protection of the forecastle, "be sensible, I pray you! The oar is lashed, and it would take a seaman to undo it. But if I or any of my lads tried to reach that oar, that crossbowman would have us dead within feet, if he has crossbows readied to his hand. Get down again, I beg you, and wait. They will bring themselves alongside soon enough!"

"Tied!" shouted Brian. "Then I will cut it loose and steer for the enemy myself!"

He turned and ran to the oar in the bow of the ship. Almost within seconds Giles was following him. A crossbow bolt struck Brian, but he was running with his shield held over as cover for his right side; and the bolt only partially penetrated the shield, then dropped. As Brian reached the steering oar and swung around, he swung the shield with him. Giles reached him then, also with his shield up, and placed himself between Brian and the enemy's ship.

Beyond Giles they could see Brian's blade flash overhead briefly in the sunlight and then there was a chopping sound as if an ax was hitting wood. A moment later the ship yawed; and as Brian and Giles stood back from the steering oar, it could be seen that Brian had half cut, half broken in half the oar itself, so that it now no longer guided the ship.

"I knew it!" cried Edouard. Half bent over, to stay as far as possible below the bulwarks, he ran toward the stern of the ship himself. But, strangely, no crossbow bolts flew at him. Jim was about to follow him, then realizing there was little he could do there, he swung back to look at Dafydd.

Dafydd was lying on the deck within his enclosure. Jim leaped onto the upper deck as the ship began to swing around, giving a view of the other vessel almost upon them coming prow foremost. Ignoring this, Jim ran to Dafydd, who looked up at him with a pale smile.

"I got him—the last one," whispered Dafydd. "All of them are down that can use the crossbow. Forgive me, James. I would help you now, but . . ." His eyes closed.

Ignoring everything else that was happening around him, Jim dropped on his armored knees beside the bowman and rapidly began to tear Dafydd's clothes into strips to make bandages and tourniquets around the wounds that were leaking Dafydd's life out on to the deck.

He cast one desperate glance at the skies over the land ahead, to see if there was any sight of the dragons coming. He was sure that if Secoh could get no one to help him, the mere-dragon would come back himself; but the danger was that he would get involved in too much time-consuming argument in collecting the other dragons to get them here in time.

Jim thought he saw some specks in the sky, but could not be sure. With his dragon sight he could have made sure, but there was no time for magic now. There was time only to finish bandaging Dafydd. He tied the last piece of torn cloth about the other's left leg, which had taken several cuts, then pushed himself to his feet, drew his sword and ran to help the others.

He was a little too late for the moment in which the two ships ground their sides together. The shock of it threw him and everyone else off their feet; and probably did the same to those on the other boat. By the time he was up again Brian was leading not only Giles, but Edouard and his three crewmen, over the joined bulwarks, now held together by grapnels and ropes thrown from the larger vessel.

Edouard and his seamen were armed with what looked like very long-handled axes, having also a metal point fixed to the thick part of the top of the blade. Such a weapon, swung over some distance, would be as devastating to armor as any knight's weapon could be. Also, whether it was Brian's example or not, the seamen were wielding them like madmen.

As for Brian, he seemed completely demented with the urge to do battle; and Giles appeared to have caught fire with him. They were literally carving their way through most of the men before them; and Brian was shouting at the top of his voice. For a moment Jim could not understand what he said, so many other voices were shouting at the same time. But his familiarity with the timbre of Brian's voice and a notion of what he was trying to call out allowed Jim to finally piece together the words he was using.

"To me, Sir Bloody Boots!" Brian was crying. "To me!"

If Brian and Giles had been literally carving their way through the mass of more lightly armed and weaponed opponents before him, so, to his surprise, was Jim himself. He realized suddenly that, dressed in full armor as they three were, and showing their knighthood by the arms upon their shield, they represented opponents too threatening for anyone but perhaps the pirate captain to willingly take on in combat.

Jim had had enough experience with mêlées like this, few as they had been, to spin around every third step, each time turning in an opposite direction; and so he was able twice to catch individuals who were trying to slip up beside him with a long dagger and find a joint in his armor into which they could plunge its point. But largely, he was occupied by pushing his way through the crowd of their opponents, and striking down or aside only those who had the hardiness enough to stand before him.

At this moment, a new factor entered the situation. A bull-like voice could be heard roaring, even over all the tumult.

"Out of my way, damn you all!" the voice roared. "Out of my way and let me to him!"

It was the voice of Bloody Boots. For the first time, Jim caught sight of him. He was not a giant in the same terms as the Ogre had been at the Loathly Tower—Jim had estimated the Ogre to be at least a dozen feet tall. Still less was he a giant in the sense that the Sea Devil Rrrnlf was. But he was well over six feet and powerfully built. As he and Brian came together, it looked like a man face-to-face with a half-grown boy; for Brian, stretch as he might, could barely lay claim to five feet seven inches of height.

So as those around them were swept away, not merely by Brian's blade but that of Bloody Boots, who evidently did not scruple to use his weapon even on his own crew, to clear himself fighting space; the general combat slackened, so that everyone, from both ships could watch the encounter.

Bloody Boots swung his great sword over his head and brought it whistling downward. Surely, it seemed, nothing could stop that sharpened iron from literally cutting Brian in two. But when it struck Brian's shield, instead of carving it apart, it glanced off; still with almost the same force behind it, so that it struck its point deeply into the wood of the deck and stuck there.

Brian had just demonstrated one of the tricks at which he was such an expert, and which he had striven so hard to teach Jim— the art of slanting his shield to make a blow against it glance off as Bloody Boots' had just done. The giant swore and tore with all his strength at his sword handle, to get his blade loose.

He succeeded, but there was a moment in which Brian could strike at him. And if it had not been for the fact that the pirate captain was armored from the knees upward as well as Brian was in steel mail—a woven shirt of metal links, reinforced with plates and with pieces of armor on his legs and arms—Brian might even have ended the fight there.

Certainly he tried, for his own broadsword swung not at the armored part but at the giant's legs, where they were unprotected above his wet and sloshing calf-high leather boots and below the metal protection just above it.

But Bloody Boots, apparently, was as skilled in the matter of protecting his unarmored area as Brian was in angling his shield to deflect blows. His shield had already gone down to intercept Brian's blow, even as he cursed and tugged at his sword. The result was that Brian's blade dented and drove the shield cruelly back against the big man's knee, but did no large damage. Meanwhile, Bloody Boots had gotten his own blade free. He swung it up and returned to the attack.

CHAPTER 26

Little by little, the other battling members from the two ships had become a ring of spectators that followed Brian and the pirate leader as they moved backward and forward across the upper deck of the larger ship, striving to both get at each other and at the same time protect themselves.

Brian's advantages lay not only in his ability to angle his shield but in his ability to start to seem to swing his sword at the other's upper body, only to have that swing change into another blow at the unprotected legs. Also, he was much more agile than the big man, and could literally leap out from under a blow of Bloody Boots' sword; and be attacking almost from the side of the larger man before the other could get his shield and himself around to face Brian.

On the other hand, Bloody Boots' advantage was still that tremendously heavy and long weapon he swung. He had swung it first as lightly as a slim stick of wood. But, the grunts that followed his misplaced blows, that ended against the deck, the mast, or some other place than Brian's armored body, bore witness to the effort he was putting into his swings. Now Jim saw the perspiration starting to stand out on that part of his face that was visible—for he wore his visor up, even in the heat of battle. Jim found Giles standing beside him, and murmured to the other knight out of the corner of his mouth.

"If Brian can just keep him working like that for a while longer," Jim said, "he may outlast the man. Big as he is, he can't swing that large a sword forever."

"I am of the same mind," murmured Giles.

They watched.

It became clear to Jim—and he was sure it must have become clear to Giles also, if not to the others around them—that Brian in his leaping around was essentially forcing the big man to follow, which meant also forcing him to carry the weight of his armor and his sword more than perhaps he might have liked in such a one-on-one battle. From what Jim could best judge of Bloody Boots, he seemed to be the sort who liked to plant himself with a wide-legged stance and simply clear the space around him with unstoppable swings of his sword.

In fact the same idea seemed to have occurred to Bloody Boots too, because now he roared out at Brian.

"Stand still, sir flea!" he thundered. "Are you a knight, or a mountebank dancer? Stand to it and fight, if you have a heart within you!"

Brian made no answer. Nor did he change his tactics. By this time they had covered most of the upper deck, that was the roof of the forecastle on this larger vessel.

Also, because it was a larger ship, the vertical drop from that upper deck was closer to five feet than the three feet that it was on Edouard's ship. It was not the kind of a drop that any man dressed in armor might like to take in a jump.

Aside from the fact that the impact would come with between forty and sixty extra pounds of weight from the weight of the metal they wore and carried, there was the fact that an armored man jumping down, and clumsy in his protective covering, was almost certain to lose his feet. In that case, the one who was slower to regain an upright stance would be almost at the mercy of his opponent.

Consequently, the upper deck had become something like a cockpit, which neither man dared leave, even if the circle of spectators around them had parted to let them through.

On his part, Bloody Boots was clearly trying to drive Brian either backward against either side of the ship, or back against the mast which rose directly against the forecastle. Pinning Brian in either way would curtail his movement to a certain extent.

Then, with Brian so hampered, perhaps that great sword could manage to overcome the effect of the slanted shield, particularly since the shield itself was becoming beaten into dents and hollows, so that there were now places that the big blade might catch.

Brian had so far managed to dodge being cornered against either bulwarks or mast. But now a sudden lumbering run from the giant, who so far had contented himself with long strides to corner Brian, forced him to dodge toward the edge of the drop-off from the forecastle.

As Bloody Boots swung to follow him, the pirate was panting heavily; but Brian was also breathing hard within his helmet; and both men could be heard clearly in the silence of the watching crowd. If Bloody Boots was showing a slowness with which he now heaved up his heavy sword to bring it down, so Brian also appeared to be more ready to dodge to avoid the impact of the blade than to take it cleverly on his shield and shunt it aside.

"A good big man against a good little man," said somebody in the crowd not far from Jim, "who can doubt, then, which way the fight will go?"

A murmur of agreement ran through those others nearby—a murmur of agreement which Giles and Jim met with an obstinate silence.

But it was undeniable that Brian was being backed toward the edge of the drop-off. If he was first to go over, the other man might lower himself more cautiously, and so be sure of landing on his feet. Brian dodged sideways along the edge now, and within a few steps found himself backed against the mast.

"Hah! Now!" grunted Bloody Boots' deep voice breathlessly; and then he swung upward his blade for a down-blow that would catch Brian between a sharpened steel edge and the mast itself.

In that moment, Brian moved with a speed that gave the lie to the slowness he had been showing for some little time now. He jammed his shield upward in Bloody Boots' face, dropped his sword with his gauntleted right hand and reached across to snatch the long poignard from the other side of his sword belt. Drawing it in one swift movement, he thrust it home, in the moment in which the pirate's arm was upheld, revealing the unarmored space at his armpit. The blade buried itself in that unarmored space, deep into the other's body and lungs.

Bloody Boots seemed to soar upward, then crash down, delivering the blow he had already begun. But it was now unaimed and a reflex rather than a planned action. Its edge bounced off the lower edge of Brian's shield and the point of the weapon buried itself for a last time in the wood of the deck. Bloody Boots fell.

He collapsed like a stone statue that has been struck by a sledgehammer behind its knees, breaking the sculptured legs. He went down to a kneeling position, dropping the hilt of his sword, rocked there a moment and then fell on to his side, rolling over onto his back. Brian stood above him and placed a foot on his breastplate to hold him where he lay.

"Yield you!" panted Brian.

"I . . . yield . . ." gasped the man on the deck, "but I am slain. Come down to me. Let me at least make what confession I can to you before I go. Or are you . . . no Christian?"

For answer Brian let his sword fall from his hand and dropped upon his metal-clad knees beside the fallen man.

"My worst . . . sin," panted the giant as a twisted smile crossed his lips, "is that . . . I've always planned . . . that I would never . . . *die alone!*"

With that, he thrust upward, with his own poignard, on the hilt of which his former shield-hand had been lying. The weapon was a ballock-dagger, its hilt connecting to a needle-pointed triangular sliver of blade, designed specially to pierce chain armor. He drove it with all his remaining giant strength into the chain mail between two of the plates that guarded Brian's breast.

The force of the blow was such that it half pushed Brian to his feet, and his legs drove him the rest of the way, as he tried to avoid the blade. But the point went into him a good handsbreath.

"Recreant!" he shouted. "False knight—to strike a blow after yielding!"

He scooped up his sword in one swift movement and, throwing all his weight behind it, drove its point in between the top of Bloody Boots' breastplate and the bottom of his helmet, where a pale strip of flesh showed, nailing the larger man to the deck and all but decapitating him.

He straightened up, and stood over his late opponent, swaying, breathless. Giles spoke for him.

"So dies your master!" Giles shouted to the crowd around him. "So will you die also, if you continue the fight against us! Are you ready for another storm of arrows, from our bowman behind his security on our ship, even as the rest of us work our will on you?"

His words, however, instead of making the pirate crew drop their weapons, seemed to bring them out of their trance. Also, just at that moment, after standing for a few seconds, Brian fell and lay still. His fall seemed to put new life into the pirate crew. Rather than drop their weapons, they clutched them and turned on Jim, Giles, Edouard and his men.

"Guard yourself, James!" Giles just had time to shout, before the first wave of attackers hit them.

At that moment, however, came an interruption that nobody there expected, but Jim should have; except that he had been so caught up in watching with fascination the battle between Brian and the pirate captain.

There was a crack like thunder over their head. They all looked up to see the shape of a dragon, which Jim recognized as Secoh, checking himself on his wings just above their mast, the long, leathery spread of them casting a shadow over all below. In the same moment he had begun to fly again; and was moving away from the vessel. But almost in the same second there was a second thunder-crack; and another dragon, obviously a young dragon from his size, appeared next above them for a moment, then fled.

For a moment, as even the second dragon was followed by a third and, looking up, Jim saw other specks falling swiftly toward the vessel they were on; his heart rose and he thought the day was won. But at that moment a voice from somewhere in the crowd shouted over all their heads.

"It is the devil himself loose among us!" the voice cried. "Fight for your lives, for there is no safety for us otherwise. If we kill and clear these from our decks, perhaps the dragons will leave us alone!"

The body of pirate seamen wavered. There was muttering among them; and for a moment it seemed that they swayed back and forth between action and inaction. Then as another dragon opened his wings with a clap above them, they gripped their weapons more tightly and began to move toward the upper deck, where Bloody Boots lay dead and Brian lay fallen beside him.

"Serpents!" screamed another voice suddenly.

For a moment it seemed the word was not understandable, the scream had been so primitive and plainly a shriek of fright. But it brought instant silence. The words that followed it echoed clearly over all the ship. "Heaven and all angels preserve us! The great serpents! The great serpents, I say!"

The pirates froze.

Jim looked out beyond that side of the pirate ship that was not blocked by Edouard's vessel and stared at what he saw. For several hundred yards around them the sea seemed to be boiling.

Just then, another of the young dragons opened his wings, checking his flight just above them; and instantly half a dozen great heads, and massive, snakelike bodies, broke the stirred-up sea surface, shooting ten to fifteen feet into the air toward the dragon—which, happily, was still well above them. The serpent heads were massive, shaped rather like a bulldog's, but with incredible jaws that now gaped twice the width of any dragon's, and showed teeth half again as large—greenish teeth, streaked with black.

The dragon which had just appeared saw them, and let out a bellow, which failed only by the fact that it was three octaves too low to be recognizable as the shriek of fear Jim knew it to be.

The young dragon took off as if a rocket had been attached to his tail—not in level flight across the sea into the distance, as Secoh and the others had done, but straight upward for as much altitude as he could reach.

The serpents fell back into the sea. Jim himself was shaken as he had never been shaken before.

Were these the creatures that Rrrnlf, Granfer and Smrgol had spoken of?

From what Jim had just seen, it seemed impossible. These things outweighed, and undoubtedly outreached, a dragon in every way. Before he could think further on the subject a clamor from the pirate crew distracted him.

"Let them go! Let them go! They've brought the serpents on us, too!" A third voice was raised above the pirates. Jim woke suddenly to the changed situation. He jogged a still-paralyzed Giles with his elbow.

"Quick," he said to Giles, "let's carry Brian and get Edouard's crew back on their own ship. Then we can cut loose from this one—before these people here change their minds again!"

Giles started. Without a word, together they managed to lift Brian from the deck. He was unconscious. Edouard and his crewmen pushed through the crowd to help them, and together they went back over to their own ship. The pirates did not try to stop them.

Jim had planned to cut the grapnels loose, but when he turned from laying Brian down on their own vessel, he found that the pirate crew had already cut them and were drifting away. The stirring of the waters that had signaled the presence of the sea serpents was calming, now that no more dragons came down. Soon there was nothing but the waves. Meanwhile Jim and Giles were busy getting the armor off Sir Brian to reach his wounds.

It turned out only one was serious; the stab from Bloody Boots' dagger that had pierced his armor and into his chest. But it had not gone deeply; and Jim's main worry was that it might have carried some bits of Brian's clothing—which were not too clean, though perfectly acceptable by fourteenth-century standards—deep into the body, where they could become sources of infection.

Happily, the wound had bled heavily. It was this, more than Brian's exhaustion—for indeed he had fought himself to a standstill against the larger man—that had him unconscious now. As soon as Brian was bandaged, Jim turned to Dafydd.

The bowman was also still unconscious. There was no doubt about his loss of blood. He had bled until he was dangerously white.

Jim cursed himself in his own mind for not knowing more magic; particularly, the magic that Carolinus used to heal wounds. He had planned to use no more magic than he had used already out of the extra supply Carolinus had gotten him. Carolinus had succeeded in that only after an acrimonious debate with the Accounting Office. Jim had been planning to save whatever was left for an emergency.

However, if this wasn't an emergency, what was? He turned to Giles.

"I'm going to have to get Carolinus to heal them," he panted. "You sail into the nearest port with Edouard; and have both Brian and Dafydd carried to a comfortable inn. Don't—repeat *don't*—let anyone bleed them! They've both lost more blood than they can spare already. In fact, don't let anyone who says he's a leech, a doctor or anything like that touch them. That sort will only help them to their deaths. Carolinus can save them."

He turned to Edouard.

"Name me an inn where Sir Giles and the others can be put up," he said, "in the closest English port!"

"Plymouth," said Edouard, "and the Inn of the Boar and Bear, there."

"Good," said Jim. "I'll bring Carolinus there or to you on this ship; or see if he won't move them to wherever he is. If Giles, Brian and Dafydd should suddenly disappear, Master shipman, don't be alarmed. They'll have been transported magically to help. What do we owe you? I need to pay you now."

Edouard smiled crookedly.

"And I could name any price, indeed," he said, "seeing the one of you who struck the bargain for the trip with me is now unable to tell you what that price was. But I think you have saved the lives of me and my lads here twice over; once from Bloody Boots and once from the serpents. There will be no charge by me for this voyage, sir knight. It's been an honor to carry you and your friends. I'll never forget the Dragon Knight and those with him."

"You're good, Master shipman," said Jim. "Nonetheless, I'd like to see you paid, anyway. For if we've saved you, your seamanship has saved us. But I'll see you paid eventually—"

"I will not accept it!" snapped Edouard. "I am neither knight nor noble. But I am a man of the sea; and I have said that this voyage is free to you and those with you. That word stands. You would insult me to offer me payment after that!"

Jim realized he had touched a fourteenth-century nerve.

"In that case, my thanks," he said. "Now I'll go."

Hastily, he wrote the necessary spell on the inside of his forehead:

MOVE ME TO WHERE IS → CAROLINUS

The boat and the seascape around him winked out.

He found himself occupying a seat in a large amphitheater; an amphitheater filled with some hundreds of men and women each wearing a robe of some dark, rich color, such as the robe of a magician-red that Carolinus favored, and most of them wearing tall caps that came to a point at the top.

In the center of the amphitheater was an oval of smooth, white sand, brilliant under a hot sun in a cloudless sky; and down on the sand stood three individuals. One was a tall, oriental-looking man with a smooth middle-aged face and wearing a purple robe.

At right angles to this man was a lady, almost as tall, but thin and cadaverous-looking. She wore an intensely dark green robe and a sort of skullcap of the same color. Her face was bony and long and her expression was stern. She stood between the other two like a referee at a boxing match, with the oriental-looking gentleman on her left.

To her right, with a tall, red cap on his head that looked as if it had seldom been worn, but otherwise dressed in his usual worn, red robe, was Carolinus.

CHAPTER 27

This was all wrong. Jim's magic should have brought him out almost beside the older magician. He felt a sudden panic. Automatically, he tried to stand up and shout to Carolinus. But he could do neither. He could move as much as he wanted while seated, but he could not leave his seat; and when he tried to shout he found he could speak, but only at conversational volume.

"Youngster, aren't you?" said a voice to his right.

He turned, desperately, to look into the face of a stocky, possibly middle-aged—it was impossible to tell because he had one of those faces that is absolutely timeless—magician occupying the seat at his right. The other could have been any age from twenty years to sixty. He was not oriental, but he was not exactly western in appearance, either. His robe was a midnight blue; and instead of a peaked cap he wore a flat one rather like a beret, of the same color. His eyes were a bright brown and his mouth was smiling.

It looked like the kind of mouth that smiled readily.

"I've got to get to Carolinus!" said Jim. "Right away. It's an emergency!"

"An emergency, or anything else, will have to wait," said his neighbor, "until the duel is over. What's the problem?"

"Two of my friends—two of Carolinus's closest friends— are nearly dead. I need Carolinus to save them," said Jim. "I'm

240

his apprentice. I know him. I know he'd drop whatever he's doing now, and go help them, if he knew; but I can't seem to get down there and I can't seem to call and get his attention."

"You won't be able to, either," said his neighbor sympathetically, "until the duel's over. Never mind. Where are these friends of his?"

"They're just a few miles short of the south shore of England in a boat," said Jim. "Their boat was attacked by pirates. That's why the two of them are in such bad shape."

"South shore of England," said the man beside him, frowning. "Let me see, now. South shore, you said . . ."

He half closed his eyes, which had the effect of making him look slightly more oriental, while still remaining overall very definitely not so.

"Yes, I think I see them now. A small boat. Six men aboard, one of them with a heavy loss of blood, another's taken a dagger thrust in the chest. Am I right?"

"Yes!" cried Jim. "Why? Can you see them? Can *you* heal them? They're battle wounds; and Carolinus said that it was possible to heal battle wounds, though not cure sickness with magic. I'm only a C in rank, so I can't help them, but maybe you—"

"Martti Lahti, youngster," answered his seatmate. "B+ in rank, myself. No, I can't cure them. It takes a magician like your master for that. But I'll tell you what I can do. That's suspend time on them for—say—half an hour or so. What it means is that during that half-hour they won't be conscious of time going by, their wounds won't bleed, and any damage that's done won't get any worse. In half an hour the duel will be over. Just hope it's your master who wins."

Jim felt an unsuspected coldness all through him.

"You don't think he'll lose?" he asked.

"Lose?" said Lahti. "Well, of course there's always the chance, youngster. Not saying anything against your master, you understand. He's a great magician and a great man. People half the world away know his name and talk of him as they talk of Merlin."

He paused and looked at Jim as if gauging how much to tell him.

"But there's a feeling going around," he went on. "It's only fair to say, there's the matter of his getting along in years. The thought that he might be getting just a little past it, you know.

Oh, I don't mean anything drastic, but losing his grip a bit. It wouldn't matter ordinarily—but in a contest like this when he's up against a very strong B who's worked at eastern magic ever since he was a child, there's just the possibility . . ."

He let his voice trail off.

"I see," said Jim slowly. He was hollow inside. A sudden fear gripped him. "What'll happen if he loses?"

"If he loses?" said Lahti. "He'll be fined most of his magic, down to a C level; and the fine will be equally divided among the rest of us—it makes merely a token amount, apiece, you understand, but it's the principle of the thing. Of course he'll still have that knowledge and skill he has now. No one can take those from him. But he'll have to build up magic enough to qualify himself to work again at the AAA+ level—if he ever can—before he's raised to that rank."

Jim felt coldness all through him. If Carolinus suddenly had no more magic than Jim, how could he transport Dafydd and Brian to Malencontri, which was the only place where they could be nursed properly; and also, would Carolinus have enough magic to heal them?

"Don't look so worried, youngster," said Lahti. "It may be Son Won Phon who loses."

"Son Won Phon?" the name exploded from Jim's lips.

"You know him?" said Lahti. "Yes, it seems he challenged Carolinus over his knowledge of eastern magic and his right to teach it. Were you involved in that?"

"Yes!" said Jim between his teeth.

So all this was his fault, for using hypnosis on Ecotti and the King of France. If Brian and Dafydd died now from their wounds because Carolinus couldn't help them, it would be because Jim had used twentieth-century knowledge.

Meanwhile, he had to sit here and simply watch the duel. And hope. Meanwhile—the thought suddenly occurred to him, Lahti, here beside him, had offered to help.

"Did you suspend time on them?" he asked, turning to Lahti.

"Not yet," said the other magician. "I was waiting for you to say definitely whether you wanted me to or not."

"Yes. Yes, I do. Right away!" said Jim.

"Then—it's done," said Lahti. He had not stirred a muscle.

Jim suddenly felt very humble and grateful.

"Thank you—er—" Jim fumbled over what to call the other. He knew enough about the ranking of magicians by this time to know that a B+ would not be addressed as "Mage" by anyone knowledgeable in the magical field. On the other hand the other was his superior. Jim's instinctive urge to simply put the title "Mr." before the name of the other as he would have back in the twentieth century, would not work here. Metaphorically, he closed his eyes and dived in. "Thank you, Marty Lockty."

"That's spelled M-a-r-t-t-i L-a-h-t-i," explained the other, kindly. He paused on the double "t" and pronounced the "h" in an odd, breathy way.

"Oh," said Jim. He considered making another effort to say it more correctly; then wisely decided not to.

"Well then," said Lahti, "now that that's taken care of you can sit back and we'll watch the rest of the duel. They've been dead even up until this part, your master and Son Won Phon."

"What's going on?" asked Jim, staring down at the sandy floor of the arena. "None of them seem to be doing anything."

"They're dueling right now on the third astral plane," Lahti explained. "That means of course none of us can see what's going on. Only the two combatants and the referee there can. But you can feel the flow of magic forces back and forth, can't you?"

"I—" Jim was about to confess that he could not, when he began to realize that indeed there did seem to be a sort of electricity in the air, darting back and forth between Carolinus and Son Won Phon. It felt a little as if there were invisible lightnings flashing out either from one or the other.

Suddenly this ceased. Son Won Phon walked over to the woman who apparently was refereeing.

"What's going on now?" asked Jim, leaning forward in his seat anxiously.

"Can't you hear—oh, that's right, you're only a C," said Lahti. "You probably won't be able to manage far-hearing until you're at least a B. Son Won Phon is consulting with the Observer. Your master has passed all the tests Son Won Phon has thrown at him so far, in the exercise of eastern magic. Now, Son Won Phon wants to skip the rest of the preliminary tests and jump right to the hardest one of all, the deciding test."

"What's the Observer got to do with it?" asked Jim.

Lahti stared at him for a second.

"Are you sure you're a C?" Lahti said.

"Yes," confessed Jim, "but it's an unusual situation. Even though I'm a C, I don't know all the things a C ought to know. I'm sort of a special case."

"Evidently," said Lahti, his brown eyes curious. "Well, the Observer is the one who makes the duel legal. Essentially she speaks for all the rest of us in the seats here. Normally it should be a superior to both the contending magicians who acts as observer. But as you know, there's nothing higher than a AAA+ rank. So it has to be one of the only two others in the world who've got a rank equivalent to Carolinus's. Her name is KinetetE."

"Kinetee . . . yuh?" Jim tried to echo Lahti.

"No," Lahti said. "Kin-eh-tet-E. Accent on the end. She has to give permission for the intervening tests to be skipped."

Evidently, KinetetE had; because Jim now saw Son Won Phon backing away from her to his original position; with what, even from his seat in the stands, Jim felt was a satisfied smile.

Abruptly, there was an elephant in the amphitheater, down on the sand with the three people. Jim had not seen it appear; but he was not surprised. If elephants were wanted in situations like this, undoubtedly this was the way they would be produced.

"What—" Jim began.

"Just watch," Lahti told him.

Son Won Phon had now produced out of thin air what at first glance looked like a tall, thick staff. But it proved not to be that but a roll of material. Setting it up on one end, he began to unwind a long piece of opaque fabric, a sort of dull green in color, around the elephant.

The fabric stood up by itself as he unrolled it; so that it eventually formed a screen which completely hid the elephant, not only from the gaze of Carolinus and the Observer, but from those in the seats around them.

Possibly, thought Jim, the magicians in the highest row of the amphitheater might be able to look over the edge, but he rather doubted it. The screen was probably designed so that no one could see over its top edge.

"Now," said Lahti, "Carolinus will have to see if he can make the elephant disappear."

Jim stared at him in some surprise.

"I wouldn't think Carolinus would have any trouble with that," he said.

"Ah," said Lahti, "but you see, it isn't just making an elephant disappear from inside an ordinary screen. The screen is locked around the elephant by a very cunning lock using the highest form of eastern magic. Carolinus will have to discover the combination to that lock, in order to undo it. He will be given one full minute after the screen is completed."

As he spoke, Son Won Phon did indeed bring the end of the screening material back around to touch the beginning of it. The two ends joined as if they had been woven together. Son Won Phon stood back, the Observer pointed skyward, and the face of a very large clock—at least several yards in diameter— appeared in mid-air over the sand of the amphitheater.

A hand started to move around the clock face, past a number of marked divisions that were too numerous for Jim to count. But from the speed with which the hand moved, Jim was sure that it was counting off less than the equivalent of seconds. Already the hand was a third of the way around the circle and sweeping onward toward its starting point in upright position.

Jim held his breath.

The hand made its complete circle to the vertical position and stopped. Son Won Phon stepped forward and began to unroll the screen. There was a confident air about him as he began, but this disappeared as the widening gap in the screen showed more and more empty space within.

By the time he was a third of the way around, Jim could see there was no elephant within.

Son Won Phon suddenly threw up both arms in what seemed to Jim to be a gesture of both despair and anger. The screen vanished. There was no elephant there. The Observer vanished. Carolinus and Son Won Phon were left facing each other on the sand.

All about Jim, seats began to empty as magicians also vanished; evidently leaving for their own places in typical magicians' manner. Jim felt suddenly free of the restraint that had held him in the seat. He tried to get up, and discovered the feeling had been correct.

"Thanks for everything!" he said hastily to Lahti. "Got to go now!"

He turned and began to run down the nearest aisle toward the bottom of the amphitheater and the open sand. Son Won Phon was ceremoniously bowing to Carolinus.

Carolinus bowed back.

Jim reached the bottom of the amphitheater and a stone barrier there, about waist high, that barred off the ranked seats from the sand below. He put a hand on the barrier and vaulted it neatly. Son Won Phon was once more bowing to Carolinus. Jim started toward them just as Carolinus returned the bow. Son Won Phon bowed a third time, Carolinus completed his return bow just as Jim reached him. Son Won Phon disappeared.

Jim reached Carolinus's side, panting.

"Carolinus—" he gasped, "Dafydd and Brian may be dying, right now. We need you right away—"

"All right, all right," said Carolinus, still gazing with a smile at the empty patch of sand where the elephant had stood. "You can tell me all about it once we're back at Malencontri."

"But they're not at Malencontri!" said Jim. "They're on a boat in the English Channel—"

"Well, I'll simply bring them to Malencontri, then," said Carolinus, with an undertone of unusual savagery. "We'll deal with that in a moment. Did you notice how neatly I handled that? Accuse a AAA+ magician of not being able to handle eastern magic, will he? This taught him a lesson he'll never forget."

"Never mind that! Brian and Dafydd—" Jim suddenly broke off, remembering that this duel had been all his fault for using hypnosis; and that Carolinus had been putting at risk essentially the greater part of what he owned, as well as the rank that went with it. It might have taken him—Jim really had no idea—years, possibly, to win back enough magical credit to regain his original rank of AAA+ magician—"if he could . . ." Lahti had said.

Instead of blaming, Jim should be apologizing. Even better, instead of apologizing, he should be trying to get Carolinus on his side.

A touch of congratulations might help.

"Carolinus," he said, "that was magnificent, the way you made that elephant disappear. The magician sitting next to me didn't really believe, I think, that you'd be able to find the key to doing it in the time they gave you. So, you were an expert in eastern magic all the time!"

"Was?" said Carolinus. "I was not at all. But as I keep telling you, magic is creative. Theoretically, if you knew all languages, you would find newer ones easier and easier to learn until you could pick up one more in no time at all. You'd get to the point where you'd only have to hear just a few words in an unknown language, to understand how it was put together and how to speak it."

"Just that?" said Jim. "I can't believe anyone ever—"

"Of course there's been!" snapped Carolinus. "There was a linguist who did just that, either in the fairly near future or the fairly recent past—I forget which. He was employed—by the King of Prussia, I think—because of his great knowledge of languages; and the first time the King met him, one morning, the king spoke to him in a tongue he didn't know. One the King himself knew it because it was the tongue of a very small area where he'd grown up; but it was unknown elsewhere. To the King's surprise, at dinner time the linguist spoke to *him* in the same tongue."

"He did?" said Jim.

"Of course!" said Carolinus. "Knowledge and creativity. Once you've mastered a certain amount of both, the rest of it has to lie inside boundaries you know. Now that's your trouble, as I keep telling you. You have to learn to think magic. You have to think directly in magic—as if it was another language. Eventually, you ought to be able to translate from one magic to another, with no trouble whatsoever. Oh, yes, I know everybody around here and all the animals, nowadays, speak the same language. But this world has known different tongues and will know different tongues again in the future. The principle still holds."

"I see," said Jim humbly. He hurried to back up his agreement. "I know what you're talking about, I think. Back in the world I come from, in the mathematics department, there were people who could literally think in mathematics—"

"Mathematics?" Carolinus stared at him.

"Well, it's a sort of advanced arithmetic," explained Jim. "You see—"

"No, no!" said Carolinus. There was suddenly that unusual sour, almost angry, note in his voice that had started to appear there since his illness. "Don't try explaining it to me. I've got too many things to think about already, without lumbering my brain with information I'll never use, anyway. If you understand, that's the main thing. Think magic. Knowledge and creativity. Knowledge and creativity. Drum those things into your brain and you can do anything in an area you've started to explore—after you've reached a certain level of knowledge and experience, of course. Again, I doubt that you, Jim, ever will."

"You're probably right," said Jim wistfully.

"Well, what are we standing around for?" said Carolinus. About them the amphitheater was empty, except for a handful of figures that were vanishing even as he spoke. They were vanishing in all sorts of ways. Some winked out, some faded out, some went transparent for a while, then suddenly disappeared. But all were going; and in a second Jim and Carolinus would be alone here.

"That's what I say!" said Jim. "Let's go. I was sitting next to a magician named Lahti—"

"Ah, yes, the Finnish lad," said Carolinus.

"—And he was able to stop time for half an hour for both Dafydd and Brian. But that time is going to run out before you—"

Jim never finished. For the very good reason that they were no longer in the amphitheater. They were now standing on the catwalk just inside the top of the curtain wall that encircled Castle Malencontri, just inside its moat. The curtain wall that would be the first line of defense against sea serpents if they came.

CHAPTER 28

Possibly because of having made two shifts close together by magic, to distant destinations, on arrival at Malencontri Jim experienced a moment's disorientation at finding himself back home. It took a few seconds to adjust to his familiar, but changed, surroundings.

In this case, if anything, the disorientation was made worse because with him on the battlements were a couple of people, one of which, at least, he had not expected to find there.

The other, the one he was not astonished to find there, was Angie; and at the moment he was so glad to see her that if she had been at all within arm's reach he would have hugged her, in spite of the fact that she probably would have screamed and struggled at suddenly being seized by someone appearing where there had been no one before.

But, as luck would have it, she was the farther from him, perhaps twenty feet away. In between her and him was the unexpected visitor on the battlements. He was Sir John Chandos; and he was talking animatedly to Angie.

In fact, he continued talking for a few moments, before the fact that Angie was staring, transfixed, at Jim, past the older knight's shoulder, caused Chandos to turn, catch sight of Jim and Carolinus himself, and break off abruptly.

What Jim had just heard him say was:

"—the levies have been ordered from all of south England. These will raise quickly; but it'll still be a matter of at least a week for them to gather into an army. Luckily, we probably have another week or two before King Jean of France makes any move across the Channel—"

It was at this point that Angie left him with a rush.

"Not two weeks. Five days, Sir John—" began Jim, and then Angie was in his arms. After a long moment he was able, without letting her go, to speak over her shoulder to Carolinus.

"Carolinus," he said. "Dafydd and Brian! Remember? They're both badly wounded, and probably dying, on a ship in the English Channel. I didn't know how to bring them here magically, or else—"

"I'll bring them!" said Carolinus. He whirled on Angie. "Do you have a chamber ready to take them?"

"They can go in our room for now—in the solar—" said Angie, letting go of Jim. "Bring them quickly, Carolinus. I'll get some men to carry them up to the room." She turned and headed toward the stairs from the platform above the main gates.

"If I may say a word or two to you, Mage Carolinus—" Chandos was beginning, when Carolinus interrupted him without even looking at him.

"You may not!" he said sharply. "No time. Never mind getting men to carry them, Angela—"

He was interrupted in his turn by a massive shadow that fell over all of them. Jim turned to look behind him, and realized that at his back all this time, making one of the group, was Rrrnlf. His height was such that he could simply stand on the ground inside the battlements and look out over them. Now he reached out and took hold of Angie, who was already starting to run down the stairs from the battlements, picked her up gently in one hand as wide as a pair of double barn doors, and bent to place her on the ground below by his feet.

Angie shrieked as her skirt billowed out about her during her descent. He set her gently on the ground, but her face was furious.

"Don't do that!" she shouted up at Rrrnlf. "Do you hear me? Never do that!"

She emphasized her words by kicking Rrrnlf's big toe, which stuck out from the sandals he wore. Rrrnlf's great face looked confused.

"I only thought to save you time, wee Lady," he said.

"Well, just don't!" cried Angie.

She turned her back on him to head toward the entrance of the Great Hall, that would lead her into the castle proper; but suddenly she was back on the catwalk. She gasped, reached for the stones of the battlement that were nearest, to steady herself; and now she glared at Carolinus.

"And don't *you* do *that*!" she shouted at him.

"I started to tell you," said Carolinus, completely undismayed by her tone or words, "that there was no need for you to fetch men to carry Brian and Dafydd. They are already in your solar."

Now he glared at Angie.

"Oh," said Angie.

"I'll go there immediately," went on Carolinus, "and see what I can do about their wounds. Do you intend to come with me?"

"Of course!" said Angie, recovering the indignation she had lost for a moment. "Of course I want to go with you!"

They both disappeared.

John Chandos looked across the empty space between himself and Jim. The knight's face, for the first time in any of their meetings that Jim could remember, was bewildered.

"I don't really understand all this . . ." he said, somewhat unsteadily.

"I'm sorry, Sir John," said Jim. "But Sir Brian and Dafydd are in dire need; and Carolinus is the only person who can possibly help them. There wasn't any time to waste."

Seeing that Chandos still stared at him without understanding, Jim added.

"I mean," he said, "that's why it all happened—what just happened."

"Oh," said the unbelievably deep bass voice of Rrrnlf behind him. "Now I understand. They were in need of aid from the wee Mage."

Jim glanced over his shoulder at the giant Sea Devil.

"That's right, Rrrnlf," he said, and turned back to Chandos, who looked at him, still with some traces of the bewilderment on his face.

"Did you say the invasion was planned for five days from now, Sir James?"

"Yes, Sir John," said Jim. "We were just coming back to tell you when we were attacked by pirates in the Channel waters."

Sir John was clearly not interested in pirates, attacking or otherwise.

"Where did you learn this?" demanded Chandos.

"From King Jean himself," said Jim. "I won't bother you with the whole story, but it ended up with my using a little—er—magic on both him and his sorcerer Ecotti to see if I couldn't get them to talk. Ecotti really knew nothing. But King Jean told me, under magic, that his invasion was to begin in five days, weather permitting."

"Why, it's impossible!" said Chandos with what—for him—was almost a note of irritation in his voice. "It would take him a week and a half to two weeks to embark his troops. Did you see any signs of his troops embarking while you were in France? Where were you in France?"

"At Brest," answered Jim. "No, there were no signs of troops embarking, although the town was full of them and the ships were there—all sorts of ships; since I suppose he is simply pulling together every merchant ship he can find to carry troops."

"I tell you, it makes no sense!" Chandos took a turn up and down the walkway, almost stamping his feet as he went. "But of course, he must have been lying to you."

"He couldn't," said Jim. "As I told you, I had him under magic compulsion. He had no choice to tell me anything but the truth."

"What under heaven can he have meant?" fumed Chandos.

"He has the sea serpents as allies," said Jim. "Has there been any activity on their part? Perhaps he was simply answering my question as simply and directly as possible and considering them part of the invasion."

"Well, there's no doubt they've been around here—they, or something like them!" said Chandos, stopping right in front of him and looking fiercely at him. "Certainly there have been cattle, and even men, women and children, eaten; or so the stories run. No one will leave a place of safety. I believe your Lady has nearly every tenant and serf on your land within these walls at present, since that's the only place they feel safe. But why would the fact they were here . . . ?"

Chandos's anger collapsed.

"I don't understand," he said helplessly.

"People may have been eaten, and cattle and so forth," said Jim, "but I would think that was only because the serpents simply eat anything they run across."

He turned to Rrrnlf.

"Am I right, Rrrnlf?"

"Of course," said Rrrnlf. "I mean, anyone has to eat; and in the sea you eat whenever you get a chance. You saw it in Granfer. He spends all his time eating. I told you that."

"Who's Granfer?" demanded Chandos.

"A—you'd call him a sea monster I think, Sir John," said Jim, deciding that the word "squid," or even "kraken," would only start the knight to asking all sorts of questions. "He's so old and experienced he acts as sort of an advisor to other creatures in the sea—the ones he doesn't eat, I mean. With his long tentacles he drags fish to him and swallows them whole. Some of them are very big fish, too. I think he stays on the sea bottom all the time."

"He used to come up on the surface sometimes, when he was younger and smaller," put in Rrrnlf. "But I think he thinks it's too much trouble now."

"He told us he advised one of the sea serpents—I think probably the sea serpent who's leading all this attack on our island," said Jim, "against doing it. But the sea serpent—Essessili—didn't listen to him."

"Yes," growled Rrrnlf dangerously behind and above Jim, "he's the one who has my Lady, I know it!"

"But you see, Sir John," said Jim, "the sea serpents really aren't after us humans. They want to find and kill off all the dragons in England and anywhere they can find them. Because we're an island we're easier for them to come ashore on."

"Don't like being dry, the serpents don't," said Rrrnlf. "Don't like fresh water either. Now, we Sea Devils don't care whether it's salt or fresh; and we can go anywhere on land we like—except there's no point to it. Not very interesting, this dry land of yours; and just wee little fish in the lakes and rivers if you want a bite."

A thought had just occurred to Jim. He looked at Rrrnlf curiously.

"What brought you here—I mean to the castle?" he asked.

"Essessili wants the dragons," said Rrrnlf, deep in his throat. "You're the link to the dragons. He's got my Lady; and if he comes he has to come to you, sooner or later. When he does, I'll—"

He made twisting motions, his two great hands turning in opposite directions. Jim winced at the image of the serpent caught in them.

"Take my Lady, will he . . ." Rrrnlf was trailing off into a grumble, when a flapping noise made them suddenly all look up, and see a dragon descending toward them at an angle. He landed on the (for him) narrow catwalk, teetered for a moment flapping his wings in alarm to keep his balance, then found it and folded them. It was Secoh.

"Secoh!" said Jim. "How'd you get here so fast?"

"Fast, m'Lord?" said Secoh, panting slightly. "Well, yes. It was far past noon when I left the ship last, and the sun is more than halfway toward the horizon now. Look!"

Jim looked.

In truth, the sun was already past its afternoon mid-point. Jim guessed that it was at least four o'clock. Perhaps, counting the longer summer days they had here in the British Isles, which was north of the latitude at which Riveroak had been back on his own world, it might even be five o'clock. If so, where had the time gone to? He had instantly translated himself here—

A sudden thought stopped the direction in which his mind was going.

"Secoh," he said, "how did you know I was here?"

"I chased after the young dragons; but they were too deep in fear of the serpents to come back. So I gave up," answered Secoh. "Of course I came here next. But if you don't mind, m'Lord, there are urgent matters—"

He broke off and looked over Jim's shoulder at Chandos.

"If you don't mind, sir knight," he said, in a somewhat lofty tone, "what I must say to m'Lord involves dragon matters, not to be overheard by everyone."

Jim turned quickly about. Chandos was standing just where he had left him. There was no startlement to be seen on his face and no look of surprise. But Jim got the immediate feeling that the other was just about to explode. He, Sir John Chandos, who was used to sending lesser humans than himself from the room while he talked about things they should not hear, had just been invited to take himself off. Not merely by a lesser knight, not merely by a common man, but by an animal. *A dragon!*

As the realization of this sunk into Jim, he suddenly understood what it was that had made it do so. Chandos's face had not changed expression, except in one strange way. It had no expression at all. Absolutely no expression. Jim realized suddenly that this utterly unreadable face was the most terrifying visage he had ever gazed upon in another human. He began to understand why Chandos was so feared in battle and in tourney.

"If you don't mind, Sir John," he said quickly and placatingly. "If you'll excuse us, Secoh and I will just step off down the platform a little distance. I'll be back in just a moment. Your pardon for this, if you will."

The terrifying expressionlessness was suddenly gone from Chandos's face.

"Why, of course, Sir James," he said in his ordinary voice—but his eyes were very direct and their glance was steely. Jim turned and hurried Secoh ahead of him, waddling down the walk until they were out of easy earshot of Chandos.

"Secoh," he said, reproachfully in a low voice, once they had stopped in front of each other again, "you really should watch how you talk to Sir John Chandos. He hasn't any high rank, although it's been offered to him many times; but he's one of England's most important leaders and someone to be polite to."

"I thought I was polite," said Secoh.

"Well, try a little harder next time," said Jim. "Now, what was this you wanted to talk to me about?"

"Well . . ." said Secoh.

Jim sighed internally. Dragon style, Secoh was going to go back to the very beginning of the story and tell it step by step the way it had happened, instead of coming immediately to the important part.

"You see," said Secoh, "the young dragons were very frightened when the sea serpents started jumping up out of the sea toward them. They all headed back for Cliffside. I flew along with them a while, trying to talk some sense into them and get them to turn back. But they wouldn't do it. So I went back myself. By the time I got there, you'd already disappeared and Sir Brian and Dafydd were still unconscious on the deck. Then they disappeared; and I knew that you must have found Carolinus and gotten him to move them, since you didn't want to do it yourself, the main george on the ship told me. So, you were gone and they were gone, but you know—you left something behind you. All your things you carry around with you."

"Oh, my God!" said Jim, suddenly realizing in what direction this account of Secoh's was heading.

"That means—" he began.

"Well, of course," Secoh was going on, as if Jim had never interrupted, "that's why I wasn't here sooner. When I gave up on the young dragons and went back to the ship, to give what help I might, I realized at all costs what must be taken away by me—"

He looked meaningfully at Jim.

"And you did?" said Jim impatiently.

"I had the ship georges tie the sack around the base of my wings, so that it rested nicely on my back and didn't unbalance me for flying," said Secoh. "Then I came back this way. But I went to Cliffside first. I took the bag of gems the French dragons had given you as surety to show our English dragons that the French ones would be here to help you fight the sea serpents, and let them look at the gems in it. Then I took it away and hid it in the Meres—taking my own gem out first, of course."

This time Secoh interrupted himself long enough to open his mouth and extend his long red tongue with the enormous pearl that was the single item in his hoard and a treasured heirloom in his family.

The tongue withdrew, the pearl vanished; and Secoh went on, with the pearl, as Jim knew from past experience, tucked safely into the pouch of one of his cheeks.

"I told the Cliffside dragons to spread the word the French dragons would help. They were very impressed," he said. "After that, I came here."

"Well done," said Jim, "and thank you, Secoh. You have more wisdom than I have when it comes to saving what's worthwhile."

"Oh, thank you, m'Lord," said Secoh. Dragons could not blush, but judging from the way Secoh ducked his head, if he could have blushed, he would have. "I know it's not true, but it's very good of you to say it, m'Lord. Very good!"

"Nonsense," said Jim grimly. "I meant every word of it. Now we've got to get back to Sir John; and hope we didn't make him too angry."

"I don't understand why he's so important?" asked Secoh, as they went back. Happily, the dragon still kept his voice down so that Chandos would not have overheard him.

"It's a george thing," said Jim, shortly, with no time to explain fully.

" '*Thing*'?" echoed Secoh puzzledly, behind him; but they were already back with Chandos. He looked at them both and smiled agreeably. He had either got over his temper, or decided to lie back and see what might come, like the old fox Jim knew him to be.

"I take it we can finish our talk now, Sir James?" he asked.

"Absolutely, Sir John," said Jim, "and again my apologies."

Chandos made a dismissing gesture with his right hand.

"Not necessary," he said, "but it will be something of a change for me, Sir James. Some day, perhaps I can even finish that conversation I started with Carolinus just before he vanished."

"I'm sorry about that too—" Jim was beginning; but once more Chandos waved his words away.

"Not at all. Pay no attention to what I just said," said Chandos. "I seem not to be in my best manners. I will strive to amend that. Now, we were considering the puzzle of how King Jean intended to invade in five days, when he hadn't even started to embark his men. I believe you said something about the sea serpents."

"Oh, yes," said Jim. "I was mentioning that he had the sea serpents to help him. They can be useful helping to tow his boats out of difficulties or help him across the Channel, if necessary; they're so large and powerful. But it occurred to me that he also might think that sending them in first might be considered the beginning of the invasion. I thought I heard you or Carolinus say something about the fact that there were some already roaming this part of the countryside, and I can see for myself how people have taken refuge in this castle of mine because of it."

Chandos frowned.

"I don't like to think of our levies having to fight these enormous sea serpents, from what I understand of them," he said. "We'll have enough trouble with the French, alone, if they manage their landing."

"I think that's just it," said Jim. "They won't have any trouble landing if they land unopposed. And they may well land unopposed if they have a screen of sea serpents out in front of them clearing the way. Those who've been prowling around here so far may be just the first ones to come. Scouts, to spy out the land, as it were."

Chandos looked thoughtful.

"I suppose," he said. "Yes, Sir James, you could well be right. But if that's the plan, we need to know it in advance. And how could we possibly find out? I don't suppose we could ask one of these sea serpents and have him tell us?"

"Why not?" boomed the voice of Rrrnlf above them. "Stay here. I'll go get you one."

As they both turned to look at him, he placed one hand on a solid portion of the wall. Without warning, he vaulted over it, landing on the far side of the moat with so much of his massive weight upon his relatively small feet that his sandals sank deeply into the dry earth beyond.

The wall was too stoutly built to crumble, as Jim had immediately feared that it would do. But it shuddered; and a quiver ran through the wooden walkway under the feet of both Jim and Chandos; so that they both had to grab at the stone of the wall itself, to keep from falling over—or even falling off.

He woke to the fact Chandos was speaking to him.

"—And so, perhaps, Sir James," the older knight was saying, "perhaps at last, now you might tell me all of your experiences and discoveries, since you last chose to vanish from my sight— just as I was about to send you to France."

CHAPTER 29

By the time Jim had finished telling Chandos the whole of their adventures, the sun was out of sight behind the trees, and could only be just above the horizon. Fantastically, still maintaining his balance on the walkway, Secoh had tucked his dragon head under one wing and gone to sleep while Jim was talking.

Jim had only noticed this after he had been talking for a while; and at first it had puzzled him. Then he had realized that Secoh must be very, very tired indeed after flying in to gather the young dragons, flying out to the boat with them, then flying back to land again, visiting the Cliffsiders and then coming here, very probably with only the slight pause at the Cliffsider cave while he showed them the jewels and talked with them. It would have been impossible not to talk with them for a while. The dragon way forbade that impoliteness. But their conversation could not have been long.

Meanwhile, Chandos had been listening without a word. His face was as calm and undisturbed as usual, except for one moment where he evidently could not help lifting his eyebrows, at Jim's description of the size of Granfer.

Jim had been surprised that Chandos had not reacted earlier when he had first mentioned a monster. But he had seemed to take that individual completely in stride. Everybody in the fourteenth century knew that there were monsters in the sea.

But the idea that the monsters could be any larger than the sea serpents he had heard of, or the Sea Devil he had seen, stretched the limits of Chandos's imagination beyond reasonable limits.

Nonetheless, he listened until Jim was through.

"And this Granfer, too," he asked, then, "believed that—what was it you called him—Essessili, is the leader of the sea serpents, in their move onto English soil?"

"That's right," said Jim.

"And yet," said Chandos, "Carolinus also seems to doubt that a sea serpent could have the magic that he feels is at work behind the situation?"

"That's right, too," said Jim.

Chandos shook his head, baffledly. He looked out over the battlements toward the redness behind the trees that was the setting sun.

"Our large friend is not back yet," he said, "with or without the sea serpent. If the sea serpent is as large and dangerous as you say, I'm a little surprised that he thinks he can bring one back for our inspection so easily. Nonetheless, Sir James, is there any reason why we should not await him in more comfort in the Great Hall? I find my throat somewhat dry."

"No reason at all," answered Jim.

Secoh woke up instantly; almost as if he had had one ear cocked. The Great Hall meant the high table for georges like the knights and the long, low table where lesser persons could sit. But it also meant wine—and a dragon's love for wine was only second to his love for gold and jewels.

He started to follow them, accordingly, down the stone steps built on the inside of the wall from the catwalk to the ground, found them somewhat narrow for his liking, and ended up taking to his wings, flying over Jim's and Chandos's heads to land at the big double doors of the Great Hall and enter ahead of them.

Jim and Chandos made their own way at a more normal pace, entered the hall and seated themselves at the high table. There was only a slight wait before a servant put plates with bread, cold meat, and cheese before them, and pitchers of wine with cups close by.

Secoh had already politely settled himself at the lower table, right next to the dais upon which the high table was set. He was not sitting on a bench, because nature had not built him so he could. He was squatting on the floor.

Even so, squatting, his head was high enough to be almost on a level with theirs. It was also close enough so that Sir John gave some mild evidence of being a little disturbed at the way the dragon had assumed he would be part of their conversation.

The fact was, Jim noted, their heads were now only about four feet from his, so that even speaking in a low voice they would be overheard. Chandos also seemed to note with some astonishment the fact that Secoh already had two large pitchers of wine—and no cup. As they watched, he drank directly from the pitcher, a pint or so at a swallow.

"I got here just in time, Sir John," said Jim, filling both their cups from the wine pitcher in front of him to take the knight's attention from Secoh, "to hear you telling Angie that the levies had been raised; but it would take about a week to draw the army together. Is a week the fastest time this can be done?"

"It is a miracle of speed," said Chandos seriously. "Incidentally, Sir James, by law you should be bringing your own levy to the field, now that you're back from France."

Jim had forgotten this. Being directly in fief to the King had its responsibilities.

"Would you actually like me to raise fighting men now, and join the army, Sir John?" he asked.

"As a matter of fact," said Chandos, "no. Your greatest value lies in staying with me, because of your knowledge of magic and these sea creatures. I but mentioned your duty. However, I'm sure that my word will excuse you from it."

"Thank you, Sir John," said Jim, with some relief. He had no great desire to be part of the disorder and downright filth of a medieval army; with or without his men-at-arms and whatever tenants could be also armed and brought to the war. Also, just as Chandos had said, he would be far more valuable here, doing the other things that were needed. He had been a little afraid that he might have to defy both his feudal responsibilities and the elder knight by flatly refusing to do his baronial duty in this respect.

But now that matter was settled. Jim was relieved. He wanted nothing to do with the difficulties of gathering and using a medieval army. The feudal system only seemed simple, as each vassal reported to his feudal superior with as many armed men as he could bring.

But the duty of these vassals was only for ninety days; at the end of which time, such an army was likely to fall apart—

particularly if it had lost a battle, its leaders were arguing with each other, or experiencing any one of the possible troubles that could happen to it.

"The important fact," Jim said, "is, the sea serpents are interested only in exterminating England's dragons. To meet this, for once I believe the dragons will fight as a group. They'll gather themselves. They have a code of their own, Sir John, not like ours but nonetheless effective when the time comes. Aren't I right, Secoh?"

"Yes indeed, m'Lord," said Secoh from the lower table. "We would go and exterminate the sea serpents ourselves, if we were able to find them in the sea and do so. It is an ancient enmity. Also, pardon me, m'Lord, but we would look to see you among us if we were able to do that."

Jim was reminded once more that his ability to be a dragon at will, like his direct vassalage for Malencontri to England's King, carried with it obligations. He felt slightly uncomfortable.

"I would be, Secoh," he said, "provided I was not needed more elsewhere. You mustn't forget I'm also a magician."

The words were hardly out of his mouth before he suddenly realized that he had just mentioned a third obligation. He was, in effect, torn three ways, condemned to play three roles, Lord, dragon and magician. So far they had not conflicted. But, with a sudden shiver, he realized that the time must inevitably come when at least two would conflict, if not all three.

A voice spoke suddenly out of thin air just above the table before them. It was Carolinus's voice.

"Jim!" it said. "I need you in the solar."

Jim pushed his bench back from the table and got to his feet immediately.

"Forgive me, Sir John," he said hastily. "There must be some sudden crisis with either Dafydd or Sir Brian. Will you be all right here, until I get back?"

"Indeed, yes," said Chandos. "Take care of your friends, Sir James. They are well worth that care."

Jim turned and headed back through the kitchen and up the stone stairway toward the top of the tower. He did not realize that he was not alone until he became aware of a loud panting behind him.

Stopping to turn, he discovered that Secoh was laboring up the stairs after him. These particular stairs were quite wide enough for Secoh's feet; but, as Jim had discovered for himself when he had tried to cover ground in a dragon body, that body was not built for walking—particularly for walking swiftly; and dragons seldom did walk swiftly. If any need for speed came up, they normally flew.

"Pardon me, m'Lord," gasped Secoh. "There was something else I needed to tell you. I was a bit worn out, and forgot about it, in telling you about what happened with the young dragons."

"Yes, yes, make it short," said Jim, poised on one foot.

"Yes, m'Lord," Secoh said. "But when I was with the Cliffside dragons, I learned that representatives of all the dragon communities in England, and even up into Scotland, had gathered there; just to talk to you, before they made a united front against the sea serpents. They want you at Cliffside tonight!"

Jim's mind spun. Two of his three obligations were evidently determined to conflict right now. For a moment he thought about the impossibility of being counselor to the dragons; and its possible clashing with his being counselor to Chandos. Then he remembered he was on his way to Brian and Dafydd; and that Carolinus had called him to come with every evidence of necessary haste.

"I'll be there," he said to Secoh hastily. Turning, he stole a torch from one of the ones already alight in their holders and hurried on up the stairs. Secoh did not follow.

When he got to the solar, only one of the two invalids was in bed. That one was Dafydd, who lay covered with blankets, in spite of the fact that a fire was blazing in the wallside fireplace, with its new-fangled chimney that Jim had caused to be built. Four torches added illumination to the firelight.

Brian was sitting up in one of the chairs at a table, drinking a cup of wine.

"Brian!" said Jim happily. "Carolinus was able to take care of your wounds all right, then. But should you be drinking?"

Brian stared at him.

"Why not?" he said.

"He's all right!" said Carolinus from across the room by Dafydd's bedside, which was essentially Jim and Angie's bed, as opposed to the temporary one of piled-up furs that had been made up for Brian. "He's lost a little blood and the wine will help replace it. But come here to Dafydd!"

Jim went. Carolinus twitched back some of the covers. Dafydd's face, neck and what could be seen of one hand appeared completely bloodless.

"I am helpless to aid," said Carolinus, replacing the covers. "He has lost too much blood. About that, I can do nothing. I can heal the wounds of battle and accident; since these were damages that should not have happened in the first place. But magic cannot cure disease, nor make anything live that did not live before; and the blood in a man's veins, or a woman's, is a living thing."

Jim reached under the covers, found Dafydd's wrist, and felt for his pulse. It was very light and rapid.

"He needs a transfusion," said Jim, almost to himself.

"Oh, Jim," said Angie, standing on the other side of Carolinus by Dafydd's head, "how can you? We don't even know his blood type; and we don't have any glass tubes or needles to inject the blood into his veins . . . or anything."

"Wait a minute, though," said Jim thoughtfully, holding up a hand. "Maybe we can get around that. I seem to remember reading . . ."

He stood for a moment in silence, trying to remember.

"That's right!" he said at last. "The early way of comparing blood types was to put a smear of a person's blood on a glass slide and look at it through a microscope, then mix it with the blood from another person and see if the red blood corpuscles clumped."

"And how are you going to do that?" said Angie. "We don't have microscopes. We don't even have slides."

"Wait," said Jim, holding up his hand again, "let me think. There have to be ways around this lack of what we'd normally use. We do have magic."

"Well, I can see you transferring some pints of blood from one of us into the veins of Dafydd, magically," said Angie, "but if it's the wrong type, it'll kill him!"

"I know that, I know that," said Jim. "As I say, let me think. Now, first for a microscope . . ."

He turned on Carolinus.

"I need a microscope—" he began.

"A what?" demanded Carolinus.

"Now, now," said Jim, "I know you haven't got one. I know you don't even know what one is. That doesn't matter. What you can get me probably is a magnifying glass. Am I right?"

"A magnifying glass?" Carolinus echoed. His own faded old blue eyes became abstract. "I believe there are such things. Yes. This is what you mean, isn't it?"

Jim discovered that something that looked rather like an oversized monocle had appeared in his right hand. It was simply a circle of glass with, of all things, a carefully made and fitted, square wooden frame around it. The frame was wide enough so that someone could handle the glass without getting fingerprints on the transparent surface.

He used it now to examine the cloth on his sleeve. The glass did not have a great deal of magnifying power. He judged that it might magnify somewhere between two or three times—about as much as a cheap pair of child's binoculars might do. In addition, the lens part was not an excellent job of grinding. Things seen through it seemed to waver or bend in spots that they did not in real life.

"I'll need another one of these," said Jim, holding up the magnifying glass for Carolinus to see. "Also, perhaps you and I should step outside into the corridor. We're going to have to talk about magic and I would guess you wouldn't want anyone else to hear."

Carolinus's white eyebrows raised. But he followed Jim without a word across the room and out the door. Once the door had closed behind them, Jim turned to face him, holding the two framed pieces of glass.

"Let me give you the whole problem in as few words as I can," said Jim. "The only way of saving Dafydd is to fill his veins with more blood. Further, the only way to get that blood is from one of us and transfer it by magic from the veins of one of us into Dafydd's veins. Do you follow me so far?"

"I should be a child or an idiot if I did not!" said Carolinus. "This is a piece of magic I've never done but there's no reason why I can't do it."

He started to turn back into the room.

"Wait a minute," said Jim. "That's the last thing we do, and the easiest. First we have to make sure that the blood we give him won't kill him."

"Kill him?" demanded Carolinus. "Blood is blood. How could that kill him?"

"That's just where, if you'll forgive me, Mage, you're not correct," said Jim, as diplomatically as he could. Carolinus whirled about to face him.

"I? Not correct?"

"Where I come from," said Jim, as gently and as clearly as he could, "we've discovered in my time and world that human beings have different kinds of blood. There are only a few different types of this blood. But if you mix the wrong two together you kill the person in whom the mixing is done. Please, Mage, take my word for that."

Carolinus stood glaring for a second. Then his face relaxed.

"Well, well," he said, suddenly weary. "I'm getting old. I'll listen, Jim. You talk."

"Thank you," said Jim gratefully. "Now, what we've found out is that there are four main types. There are actually more than this, but there's no way we would be able to distinguish between those. Just possibly, you and I, here and now, using this instrument called a microscope, may find someone whose blood can safely be put into the veins of Dafydd. That's if we can bring the microscope into being, and some pieces of glass on which to put a drop of blood from everyone in the room and you and I as well. The different types of blood are called A, B, AB and O. Someone with AB can take anyone's blood. Dafydd may have AB. If he has, we're lucky—but there's no way I know of that we can be sure that that's what he has. Anyone who has type O can give his blood to anyone else."

"I see," said Carolinus. "But to find out whose blood is safe you need this—what did you call it—'microscope.' And there's no way I can give you such a thing. I'm sure I explained to you—but if I didn't, I should have—that magic is creative. That's what makes you so useful, even disgracefully ignorant of ordinary magic as you are. Because you've come from an—er—different world, you can imagine things even I can't. I can't imagine a microscope. So I can't make one for you, for all I know of magic."

"I understand," answered Jim, "but if we work together and I tell you what I want, part by part—"

Carolinus's face lit up.

"Of course!" he said. "Jim, my boy, you've had an idea, a magical idea of worth! Just describe what you want, and I'll produce it for you."

"Well, first," said Jim, "I need another magnifying glass just like this one. Oh, thank you. Now, I need the glass taken out of these wooden frames and put them at opposite ends of a black metal tube. Better put them in the very ends of the tube so they'll stay there. Thanks."

Jim took the rather clumsy steel cylinder that now had two oversized magnifying glasses in it and took another look at the sleeve of his left forearm.

"I must have one of these in backward, or something," he said. "All I get is a blur. Let's try reversing the bottom lens. No, that doesn't do any good. Try reversing the top one now. No, that doesn't seem to help either . . ."

They worked together for the better part of half an hour, by the light of a torch in the wall nearby, and at the end of that time they had an apparatus; but one that seemed completely useless.

"I guess we'll have to give up, Carolinus," said Jim finally. "I'm sorry to have put you through this. I really thought we might be able to do it. But come to think of it, I don't think those glasses magnify enough for me to see the clumping of the corpuscles anyway."

"Pack of nonsense," said Carolinus grumpily. "There ought to be a way of doing it directly by magic."

CHAPTER 30

Jim lit up.

"Of course!" he said. "Look, this is an easy one, Mage. Will you do this for me? Just give me some rectangular pieces of glass about two inches long and one-half inch wide and about, oh, an eighth of an inch thick. Give me six of them."

"That," said Carolinus acidly, "is something you ought to be able to do for yourself, magically. However, to save time, here you are."

Jim found himself with a stack of the glass pieces he had requested in his hand. They were not as clear or as nicely formed as the microscopic slides he had been thinking of. They were also too thick. But that didn't matter. They had surfaces that would work for him.

"Now that you've got them," said Carolinus, "what do you propose to do with them, pray?"

"Let me try out a spell," said Jim. "I'll say it out loud as I write it on the inside of my forehead and you can stop me if I'm doing something wrong. Ready?"

"Of course I'm ready!" snapped Carolinus.

"All right, then," said Jim. He spoke the following lines of a spell as he formed them inside his head.

A BLOOD WILL REFUSE TO MIX WITH *B* BLOOD IF
PUT TOGETHER ON THE PLATE→ NOW

BOTH *A* AND *B* WILL EACH MIX
WITH *O* AND *AB* → NOW

IF BLOOD WILL MIX WITH ANYONE ELSE'S BLOOD
THEN THAT OTHER PERSON'S BLOOD CAN BE USED
TO TRANSFUSE INTO DAFYDD → NOW

Jim paused, looking at the senior magician.

"All right?" he asked.

"It'll do," said Carolinus. "Clumsy, but it will cause what you want to happen. Let's go back into the room again."

They went back in and back up to the bedside of Dafydd. Dafydd was as white as ever and had appeared not to have moved. Suddenly alarmed, Jim hastily felt for his pulse again, and breathed easily only when he felt it. He turned to Carolinus.

"Now I can probably get a drop of blood from one of Dafydd's wounds," he said, "by pressing the flesh around it. But wouldn't it be easier on him to get the blood by magic—and for that matter, from the rest of us by magic?"

"You want me to do this, of course," said Carolinus.

"If you don't mind," said Jim. "I know it's—"

"An imposition!" snapped Carolinus. "And you know it. Nonetheless, for the sake of Dafydd, we'll do it that way. Where do you want this drop of blood?"

"On one end of one of these pieces of glass," said Jim. He took the top one from the pile and held it up. "If you'd put it toward the left end, I can remember it's Dafydd's. It's his left arm that controls his bow. And then when we take a drop of blood from someone else we can always put it at the right end. Then I'll try to mix them and see if they will."

He had hardly finished saying this when a single drop of red blood appeared at the left end of the single piece of glass he was holding.

"Good!" said Jim. He turned around to see the rest of the room. "Now, we want a sample drop of blood from—"

"Me!" said Brian, starting up. "We fought together, and now we must share what blood is left."

"No, Brian," said Jim. "You may not have lost as much as Dafydd, but you have lost more than you should have. We'll use another donor. Now, sit down—if you won't lie down!"

Indeed, Brian was wobbling a little as he stood and was forced to support himself with his fingertips on top of the table beside him. Reluctantly, he dropped back heavily into his seat.

"Try me," said Jim.

"No," said Angie. "Try me first, Carolinus. Jim, I think I remember that I'm O type. And O type is universal donor. I asked them what type I was, the first time I donated to the Red Cross; and they told me. I'm sure it was O type."

"If your blood mixes, then you're about to lose a pint of it," said Jim. "Think of that, Angie."

"It's not going to kill me!" retorted Angie. "Besides I've done it plenty of times when I donated blood. They always took that much."

A second drop appeared at the far end of the piece of glass Jim was holding. He took the knife from his belt sheath and used the point to try to mix the two drops together. But the reaction of the two drops was that of a couple of blobs of mercury. The two bits of blood would have nothing to do with each other.

"Sorry, Angie," said Jim, "you must be wrong about that O type."

"I could have sworn!" said Angie. "I'm sure they told me O type!"

"Well, if it was O type, then Dafydd's blood should be willing to mix with it. I'm sorry, Angie," said Jim. "Carolinus, clean off that drop of Angie's blood and try one from me. I'm rather afraid, though, that I'm A type. So, if Dafydd's anything but A type, then my blood won't work either."

He felt nothing, but another drop of blood appeared where Angie's had been after the glass had for a moment been clear of anything at that end. Once more Jim used the point of his knife to try to mix the two together.

"It works!" cried Angie. She ran to Jim and hugged him. "Jim, your blood works! It mixes beautifully!"

"Good!" said Jim, enthusiastically hugging her back. "Well, Carolinus, all you have to do now is transfer a pint of my blood into Dafydd's veins. Even an imperial pint shouldn't be too much for Dafydd the way he is now; and if it should be too little, we can tell by his color and give him another quarter-pint, or some such—wait a minute, though!"

He had suddenly remembered something.

The transfer of blood that he had experienced, like Angie, when donating blood in their original world, had been a slow process with the blood flowing slowly out of a blood vessel in his arm into the waiting bottle that collected it. That slowness might well have been because the blood came only as fast as it could be pumped by his heart. On the other hand . . .

"I think," he said, "we'd better play it safe. Perhaps a pint of blood dumped all at once into Dafydd's veins, partly collapsed as they are now, might be dangerous. Carolinus, can you magically make the blood be transferred from me at about the rate my heart would pump it from its source in me into Dafydd's veins and arteries?"

"Of course!" said Carolinus. "There, I've made it so."

"You mean you've begun pumping already?" asked Jim, curiously.

"Why," demanded Carolinus, "do you keep asking me to do something; then ask me immediately if I've done it? Did you want me to wait? If so, you should have said so."

"It's just that I don't feel anything."

"What makes you think you should?" asked the magician.

There was, of course, no reason. What Jim actually had felt during the times he had donated blood back on his own world, he realized now, had been the needle in his arm that led the tube carrying the blood to the collecting bottle.

"I really should be getting back downstairs," said Jim uneasily. He had been carrying in the back of his head for quite some time an image of Chandos left alone with no one to talk to but Secoh. This would be all right if Secoh did not venture to say anything. But Secoh just might. Also, a snub by the knight might shut Secoh up again—but then again it might not. The knight had endured enough interruptions and slights for one day. Jim felt that it was time for an apology. "How far can I go and still have the transfer of blood from me to Dafydd keep up?"

"Go?" said Carolinus. "You can go anywhere. You can go to the other end of the world, if you want. It doesn't make any difference where you are. Magic is magic."

He looked upward at the ceiling.

"—And they want me to make magicians out of the kind of apprentices that come along nowadays!" he said.

"You might want to stay," said Angie to Jim, a little sharply, "and see if Dafydd needs any more blood. He just might, you know."

"Yes," said Jim. "But I'll only be downstairs; and if Carolinus calls me the way he did a little earlier when I was at the high table—and that's where I'll be again—I can be back up in seconds. Meanwhile, Dafydd will still have the first pint inside him. I just want to soothe any rough feathers that Sir John has, from being left alone this way, particularly with Secoh."

"Secoh?" asked Angie.

"Yes," said Jim hastily, already on his way out the door. "He's seated at the near end of the low table. Close enough to talk to and be talked to by Sir John. I don't think it's the best of ideas for them to have a conversation. Also, Sir John is owed an apology or two. Call me and I'll be right back up."

As he said the last few words, he was already closing the solar door behind him. He started to run along the corridor; but Angie's voice stopped him.

"Jim!" said Angie. Her voice was pitched low, but imperative. He checked himself and whirled about.

She was standing outside the door to the room they had been in, which door she was now closing behind her; she beckoned him back to her.

He returned.

"I thought I'd tell you," she said in low tones, "I signaled Aargh to come in. He's in one of the other rooms here—he doesn't like it, by the way, waiting there by himself, but I had to keep him hidden until I had a chance to speak to you. I'm going to have him look at Carolinus and see what he thinks about this difference in him."

Jim nodded.

"That's a good idea," he said. "After all, he's known Carolinus longer than any of us—and his senses are not human senses. He may notice something, or understand things better than we do."

"That's what I thought you'd say—or something like it," said Angie. "But I wanted you to know. It hurts me to see him trying to cover up whatever's bothering him by being grumpy in ways that he usually isn't. It must be something really bad that's preying on him."

"Yes, I think so too," said Jim. "Well, maybe Aargh can tell us something."

"I hope so," said Angie. "Now you go on downstairs, and I'll take Aargh in, and we'll pretend he's just come to see how the others are doing."

"Good," said Jim and took off.

This time she did not stop him.

He ran along the corridor and down the stairs; and so made his way to the Great Hall, where Sir John was still seated with the dragon.

To his relief, as he got close, he saw that the two were evidently very cheerfully and amicably in conversation. Evidently, he should not have worried. They had talked after all; but Sir John seemed to be, if anything, enjoying it.

"Ah, Sir John," said Jim, interrupting and sitting down breathlessly beside the knight at the high table, "sorry to have left you alone like this—"

"He wasn't alone," said Secoh. "I was with him. How are Dafydd and Brian?"

Jim suddenly remembered that the bond that existed between himself, Brian and Dafydd also included Secoh. He felt a sharp twinge of conscience.

"Brian is sitting up and drinking wine, in spite of all we can say. Carolinus healed his wounds; and you know Brian. Now he thinks he's as good as ever," answered Jim. "Dafydd needed blood; and magically we've been able to give him some of mine. If he needs more from me, Carolinus's voice will speak, the way it did the time before when I left you both; and I'll go back upstairs. But for the moment, I can sit here and relax."

"And have a cup of wine," said Chandos, filling one and pushing it in front of him. "I'm glad to hear that the two good men are doing well. As for me, I've been quite enjoying my talk with Secoh. First dragon I ever spoke to. Most of my life I've made a practice of talking to anyone I had a chance to speak with; and I've always said that every time I do, I learn something. Now, Secoh's just been telling me about how he and this other older dragon conquered that rogue dragon, Bryagh, in your famous fight at the Loathly Tower. I had no idea that their wings were so useful to dragons in a fight."

"Yes indeed," put in Secoh, "I am not a large dragon, but with one wing—"

He suddenly extended one of his wings across the lower table, stretching it out in the hall. Inside here, it seemed to stretch a remarkable distance.

"With that wing," Secoh went on, "I could knock over five to ten of your georges; and few of them would get up again. With that wing alone I could break the back of a cow—er, that is to say I could break the back of a deer, no matter how large it was. I could knock over a bear, or send a boar tumbling. Most georges don't realize it, but what a dragon uses most in taking a prey or in fighting are his strong wing muscles. In fact, in fights between two dragons, both will be trying to break the wing or wings of the other dragon."

"Eagles have very powerful wings," put in Chandos.

"Ours are powerfuller," said Secoh. "Now, when we fought Bryagh, he was so big he would have broken both my wings quickly if I'd been fighting him alone. But Smrgol, in spite of being old and crippled by that illness, whatever it was, had wing-bones as strong as Bryagh's—though the wing on the side of him that had gotten sick was a little weaker than it should have been. At any rate, because he was fighting both of us, Bryagh couldn't devote all his attention to breaking my wings, so we just sort of bit and clawed and pounded on each other, all three of us—"

He broke off. There had been a sudden uproar of noise in the courtyard, just outside and beyond the entrance door to the Great Hall. It was a mixture, Jim suddenly realized, of screams of human beings, the booming tones of Rrrnlf, and the high shrill sounds of a voice that was not too different from the tones in which Granfer had spoken when Jim, Brian and Giles had made their excursion with the Sea Devil down to see the huge and ancient squid.

"He's got one!" shouted Secoh gleefully, pulling in his wing and jumping up from the table. "The Sea Devil's got a sea serpent!"

A sea serpent. Of course! Mentally, Jim kicked himself for not making the association between the sound of Granfer's voice and the shrill one he was hearing now—although hearing it was not quite the right word, since Secoh's voice was practically drowning out the sounds that were coming in from the courtyard.

Secoh had already started toward the front door.

"We'd best go too, Sir James—think you not so?" said Chandos.

Even as he said it, he was rising from the table and starting toward the front door himself. Jim accordingly followed him.

Secoh was through the door in front of them, in spite of the fact that they were hurrying. They burst out afterward to find the courtyard all but deserted of its usual workmen and other servants who would be passing to and fro. In the center of the courtyard Rrrnlf was standing in the light of the torches around the walls that lit up the whole courtyard. The refugees there had all backed off to a safe distance.

In his two great hands spaced fifteen or sixteen feet apart, he held an enormous green serpent with four short, stubby little feet. One of Rrrnlf's feet was on the serpent near its tail, immobilizing the twitching of that part of its body. His right hand grasped it almost at its middle and his left hand held it just behind its head. The serpent's jaws, which seemed capable of gaping wide enough to take in a whole horse, were snapping at empty air, while its voice shrilled in anger and protest.

CHAPTER 31

"Ah, wee knights!" said Rrrnlf. "Is the wee mage also about? Perhaps he might like to see the serpent too. This one's name is Iinnenii. He got away from me but I ran him down and carried him back here. Had to drag him over that wall of yours, though—be quiet, the two of you there!"

His last words were a roar directed not only at the serpent, who was squeaking so loudly that what he said was not understandable; but also Secoh, who was standing just out of reach of the other's wide gaping jaws, with his own neck outthrust, shouting insults at the serpent.

Secoh stopped. The serpent lowered his voice but kept up his complaining. Now he was understandable.

" . . . All dragons and Sea Devils, and clean them off the bottom of the sea, or anywhere else they try to hide!"

Calling the serpent's vocal efforts "squeaking" was probably the wrong word for it, thought Jim; but if that was not what it was, it was something very like it, a high-volume squeak.

"I said, be quiet!" roared Rrrnlf, taking his hand off the middle of the serpent's body in order to ball it into a fist and bring it down on the top of the serpent's head. Jim winced. A steel wrecking-ball dropped from a height of two stories onto a highway surface of concrete would have made much the same noise. The serpent went suddenly quiet, and stopped snapping its jaws. It hung in Rrrnlf's grasp as if it was dazed.

"Foolish creatures," said Rrrnlf in an ordinary tone, as an aside to Jim and Chandos. "The lot of them wouldn't stand a chance against a few dozen of my people—if you could ever get two dozen of my people together in one place. But, never mind that now. Here he is, that sea serpent you wanted to ask questions of. I may have hit him a wee bit hard, but he should be able to talk in a moment or two."

"While we're waiting," said Chandos, "you mentioned the problem of getting several dozen of your people in one place. They don't get together, then?"

"Well, no," said Rrrnlf, "not ordinarily—except in mating season."

"And how often is that?" asked Chandos.

"Let me see." Rrrnlf became thoughtful. "I'm pretty sure there was one in the last hundred years. Maybe, though, it was two hundred. No, I'm pretty sure that there was one in the last hundred years."

"A hundred years between mating seasons?" said Jim. "Isn't that rather a long time?"

"Well, you know how it is," said Rrrnlf. "Someone like myself—"

He looked down at himself complacently.

"—Isn't ready to fend for himself, the way a Sea Devil should, until he's at least eighty. Also, he doesn't really become what you might call full-grown for about five hundred," he said. "So those first eighty years his mother has to look after and protect him."

His eyes became misty.

"I had a wonderful mother," he said. "I wish I could see her again—if I could only remember what she looked like. I think she looked something like my stolen Lady."

He shook the unconscious sea serpent roughly.

"Wake up, you!" he growled. "You've got some questions to answer."

The serpent stirred slightly in his hands and blinked its eyes.

"What happened?" the serpent squeaked.

"I hit you one," said Rrrnlf grimly. "And I'll do it again, if you don't start giving us the right answers right away. Where is Essessili? He's got my Lady!"

"Lady? Lady?" said the sea serpent, still dazedly. "What Lady?"

"My Lady!" said Rrrnlf. "Don't tell me he hasn't got her, because I know he has. Where is he?"

"I don't know!" shrieked the serpent, as Rrrnlf let go of its body with one hand and balled that hand into a fist again. "I really don't! He's out in the Channel waters someplace, or maybe back at the shore of the other place, what do they call it, France. He didn't come ashore with the rest of us. I don't know if he has your Lady. I've never seen him with anything like a Lady. What does a Lady look like?"

"She looks beautiful!" snarled Rrrnlf. He seemed just about to thump the sea serpent on the head again with his fist, then apparently he remembered that there were reasons for keeping it conscious. He turned to Jim and Chandos.

"Did you two wee knights have questions?" he asked.

"You know we do, Rrrnlf," said Jim reprovingly. He had been startled, and not a little scared, by the tremendous power that Rrrnlf seemed to contain in that huge body of his. Even allowing for the enormous size of his hands, it seemed a little unbelievable. Then Jim remembered that the Sea Devil was wedge-shaped; and above those big hands must be even more outsize wrists, forearms, upper arms and shoulders, all with muscles appropriate to their size.

No wonder the curtain wall of the castle had quivered, when he had used it as a pivot to vault over onto the other side. But since that first reaction, Jim had remembered that his magic had been good enough to make Granfer go *still* when he gave it as a spell. Rrrnlf, too, must be susceptible to his magic and to that command, in particular, if necessary.

"How many of you came ashore in England?" snapped Chandos, walking around to stand in front of the sea serpent's head so that they could look each other in the eye. The serpent was probably more than thirty feet long, but its body was nowhere thicker than about four feet, with stubby little legs; and its neck and head were its smallest body-parts. So Chandos could be eye-to-eye with it.

"I don't know," said the sea serpent. "I don't know anything. I was just told to come here. So I came. I've eaten a few little land creatures, but anyone would do that. I just came and haven't bothered anyone—"

Rrrnlf growled.

"I'll ask you again," said Chandos, "and this is for the last time. If you don't answer then, I'll let Rrrnlf see if he can't get the truth out of you. How many of you are ashore in England right now?"

"I really don't—" the serpent was beginning, when Rrrnlf, who had both hands back on the serpentine body, began to rotate the grip of each hand in a different direction. The serpent broke off in a scream.

Jim winced internally. He had come to accept the fact that in this world it was simply standard practice, if you wanted information from a captured enemy, to make life as painful as possible for him until he either told you what you wanted, or died from the process of being made to talk. But Jim had never become accustomed to it; and he knew he never would.

"Let him try to answer again," Jim said to Rrrnlf. The Sea Devil relaxed his grip.

"I don't, I really don't—I could only guess—" gabbled the sea serpent in its high voice. "But I will guess, if you want. I'll guess. There's about fifty or sixty of us. That's all, just fifty or sixty."

"Two hundred and thirty more like," snarled a harsh voice behind Jim and Chandos.

They turned swiftly, Chandos instinctively putting his hand to the sword at his side as he found himself confronted by a wolf the size of a small pony. Then he recognized the wolf as Aargh, with Angie standing beside him, and let go of his sword.

"Good. Leave it where it is, sir knight," the wolf said, "or it'll be the last thing you ever touch."

Such words were a fighting challenge to any knight of courage—and few knights lacked that quality. Certainly, Chandos was not one of them. Jim interposed quickly to avert trouble.

"Sir John," he said quickly, "you remember this one of our Companions at the Loathly Tower and since. Also, a good friend; and one who knows more about the countryside than anyone else, including this serpent Rrrnlf is holding."

"Ah," commented Rrrnlf, "a wee wolf."

"Not so wee, sir giant or devil, or whatever you are!" snapped Aargh. "And you're not so big that my teeth can't cut your heel-strings through and leave you flopping on the ground."

"No, no, Rrrnlf!" shouted Jim, as Rrrnlf let go of the serpent with his right hand. "He didn't mean it the way it may sound to you. Let me explain to him."

He turned to Aargh.

"Aargh," he said, "this is Rrrnlf, a Sea Devil. A friend. He doesn't mean anything by calling you wee. He calls everyone who isn't his size or bigger 'wee.' "

"That's as it may be," said Aargh, looking directly and speaking directly to Rrrnlf. "But I am an English wolf, sir Sea Devil, and whoever you may be, or however large you may be, makes no difference to me. You stand on my land, by my sufferance. If James and Angie didn't vouch for you, you might find me more difficult to handle than you think, for all your muscle and height!"

Rrrnlf hesitated, then took hold of the sea serpent again.

"I don't understand you land people," he said. "Have I offended, someway? I did not mean to offend. On the other hand, being what I am, I'm naturally not afraid of anything."

"That's as it should be," said Aargh, in a tone that was strangely almost satisfied. "Neither am I. Nor should anyone be."

Jim was not quite sure why; but the two, the Sea Devil and Aargh, seemed to be looking at each other now with a kind of mutual approval. Any nonviolent solution was a good solution, he told himself. He took advantage of the opportunity to have a moment's low-voiced conversation with Angie.

"What did Aargh say about Carolinus?" he asked.

"He said Carolinus smelled differently," Angie spoke equally low-voiced. "He said Carolinus had a sort of sick odor to his normal smell. That was all he could tell me."

"Well, at least he agrees with us," said Jim. The thought reminded him of what they had been talking about before Aargh had spoken up. He turned to the wolf.

"To a more important point," he said hastily, "how do you know the number of sea serpents that have already come ashore in England, Aargh?"

"It is my land, James," said Aargh. "How should I not know? I would have guessed at that number anyway; but it happens I heard two of these long, green creatures talking, and they mentioned that number. The rest are to come later—some three or four thousand of them."

"Three or four thousand!" said Chandos in a voice that for once betrayed an emotion of astonishment. "There are that many of them in the sea?"

"There are many, many more of us than that!" cried the sea serpent Rrrnlf was holding. "We will sweep through this island of yours, leaving nothing left alive!"

"Maybe," said Aargh, "and maybe not. There are those who'll fight you."

"And the dragons will fight you," roared Secoh, who had been obediently silent up until this moment. "And if you count your numbers in thousands, we count ours in thousands too. And one dragon is more than a match for one of you, any day."

The sea serpent gave a high-pitched cackle of laughter.

"A match for one of us. Indeed!"

It laughed again.

"You find it funny?" demanded Secoh, sticking his nose almost within reach of the jaws of the serpent. "What of Gleingul, the dragon who slew his sea serpent on the Gray Sands, not twenty miles from here?"

The serpent stared at him for a second.

"No dragon ever slew a sea serpent by himself," he said.

"Either they never told you; or you know it and won't admit it!" roared Secoh. "But Gleingul slew one of you; and all of our dragons can slay sea serpents. You hide down there in the deep water and tell yourself that a dragon is not better than you are. But you're wrong! Wrong!"

"Secoh . . ." said Jim, moving over to the dragon and putting a hand on the tight neck of him, for Secoh was working himself into the type of instinctual dragon fury that Jim knew, from his own experience in a dragon body, could lead the mere-dragon into trouble. "Secoh, for the sake of all of us, let the serpent be. We've got things to learn from him yet."

"Yes," said Rrrnlf, "when does Essessili get here? If he's not here now he'll be coming in with all these others you mentioned. When do they come? Because I will have my Lady back from him if I personally have to slay every serpent on land and sea!"

"I don't know," said the serpent, almost mockingly.

"Do you not!" said Rrrnlf. He turned to Jim. "That swamp water around your castle," he said to Jim, "it's mainly fresh water, isn't it?"

"Well . . . yes," said Jim. He had tried very hard, he and Angie both, to clean up the open sewer that was the moat around Malencontri; in common with just about all moats around all medieval castles. But it was far from being the kind of water he would like to take a swim in himself, particularly now, with all the refugees in the vicinity.

He and Angie ruled this castle and the area around it, but the habits of their servants and the people who lived there were hard to change.

"Mainly fresh," he said.

"Good!" said Rrrnlf. He began to carry the serpent toward the curtain wall, beyond which was the moat. A gentle, nearly full moon gilded the teeth in the jaws of the serpent Iinnenii, as he was lifted up, ready to be carried over the wall. "We'll just dip this long, green fellow in it and see how he likes it."

"Not fresh water!" cried the serpent. "No! No! Not that. I don't know anything; but I'll tell you anything I know, anything at all. Listen—Essessili will come in on the third wave, tomorrow, probably in the morning; and then we'll carry everything before us, routing out the dragons and slaying them as we find them. That's all I know. I tell you that's every bit of the things I know! After us will come the people in their things called ships and find we've cleared the land before them!"

Rrrnlf took hold of the curtain wall, ready to vault it, after which, presumably, he would drag the serpent over.

"Stop, I tell you!" wailed Iinnenii. "Stop. I'll tell you everything, then. He's coming here, Essessili is—he's out to get the one they call the Dragon Knight, first; and I was one of those sent to keep an eye on this place until Essessili got here with our main forces!"

CHAPTER 32

Jim felt a jolt of adrenaline all the way through him.

Of course, the sea serpents, and especially Essessili, would consider him as one of the dragons—and possibly the most dangerous of them all, since he was at the same time also a magician. Why Essessili should want to risk himself against a magician, and the powers that a magician must have, was still a question; but it was obviously a question to which their sea serpent prisoner did not have the answer.

Rrrnlf was still standing by the curtain wall, holding the serpent by the neck with one hand, with the other on the wall, ready to vault over.

"Shall I dip the serpent in your castle's swamp, after all?" he asked.

"No, no . . ." muttered Jim. He raised his voice. "No, just tie him up someplace. We may have a use for him later on. I've got to make some plans. We've all got to make some plans . . ."

Carolinus had appeared beside him, evidently by magic from the solar. But that was not what occupied Jim's attention at the moment. For some strange reason the courtyard and the castle and even the ground underneath him was both rocking under him and beginning to rotate slowly in a very strange sort of way. He found it hard to keep his balance. He staggered.

Angie caught hold of his left upper arm, and someone else caught hold of his right arm, holding him upright.

"You're out on your feet!" said Angie. "Forget about making plans or anything else. Right now bed is what you need. Bed and sleep."

"But the solar . . . Dafydd . . ." It was even difficult for him to talk.

"Dafydd and Brian are both out of the solar now," said Angie. "Brian is up on his feet and going to be down here in a moment or two. We can't stop him. Dafydd was sensible enough to let us talk him into lying down on a bed in one of the smaller rooms. I think Brian's going to fold up just the way you're doing, shortly. Then we'll get him to bed too. But for right now, you come along with us and we'll help you to our bed in the solar."

"But . . ." began Jim.

He never finished. A wave of darkness seemed to close in on him and the ground threatened to come up at him. Then the darkness enclosed him and that was all he remembered.

Some later time, it was impossible to say how long it had been since he had blacked out in the courtyard, Jim woke up to discover himself lying happily naked, cocooned by the bedding and furs of their bed in the solar, with the rays of an early morning sun striking through the glass in the window slits and into his eyes. He was supremely comfortable. He yawned, ducked his head away from the light and snuggled down into the bed, ready to go back to sleep again.

Perhaps he did, because when he opened his eyes again Angie was standing over him.

"How do you feel?" asked Angie anxiously.

"Comfortable. Sleepy," he said. "This is really a very good bed, you know?" He stretched out an arm to her. "Why don't you join me in it?"

Angie, however, resisted when he tried to pull her down into the bed.

"What about the serpents?" she said.

"Serpents?" he echoed. "What serpents? *Serpents!*"

He sat up suddenly in the bed and began throwing off the covers.

"Where are my clothes?" he said. "Where's my armor? What day is this?"

"You can have your clothes and armor when I'm sure that you're all right," said Angie, without moving. "You don't need your armor right away, anyhow. Everybody else is gathered down in the Great Hall, trying to put some plans together. If you're up to it, they need you down there with them."

"I'm fine. I tell you, I'm fine!" shouted Jim, bounding out of bed and feeling the sudden chilliness of standing naked in the room. "I'll go down right away. Where did you hide my clothes?"

Angie folded her arms and stared at him.

"On the other side of the bed," she said.

Jim went hastily around it and found a neat pile of clothing: fresh underwear, shirt, hose and cote-hardie—or jacket—such as he would normally wear, all neatly folded and piled there for him. He began scrambling into them.

"You said everybody was downstairs," he said to Angie, even while he was occupied with this. "Who did you mean by everybody?"

"Carolinus, Sir John, Brian, Giles, Dafydd, Aargh, Secoh . . . and to answer your earlier question, you've slept for about thirty-four hours."

"Slept?" raved Jim, putting on his hose under his shirt, and shrugging himself into his cote-hardie. "Do you realize I was supposed to see the leaders of all the dragons that same night that I fell asleep—or whatever I did?"

"You collapsed, that's what you did," said Angie, standing still. "As for your meeting with the leaders of the dragons, Secoh took them a message that you'd had no sleep for several days, and simply couldn't come right now; but you'd see them as soon as you were able to."

"You let Secoh go with a message like that?" raved Jim. "They'd tear him to bits—"

He checked himself suddenly not only in what he was saying but in dressing. He stared at her.

"But you said he was downstairs?"

"Yes," said Angie. "Carolinus took me and we showed up at the Cliffside dragons' cave at the same time as Secoh got there. They *were* inclined to be a little upset with Secoh but Carolinus made it clear to them they were just going to have to wait. They listened to Carolinus."

"What did he do?" asked Jim, finishing his dressing. "Turn them all into beetles for a minute or two, before he started explaining things to them?"

"Not exactly that," said Angie. "He merely convinced them. At any rate, they're expecting you as soon as you wake up. But what you're going to have to do is make some plans of your own, first. The dragons don't have any—except to sail into the sea serpents and get themselves torn to pieces, even if they do manage to kill off a good share of the sea serpents first."

"True," said Jim. "I'm going to have to come up with some kind of workable plan. That's no way to deal with an enemy like this. Come to think of it—it must be all the sleep I had—I've just got a notion of something from what you said, right now."

In fact, it was true. Sleep had acted on him like a tonic; and his mind was racing. What he had just had was only an idea. It might turn out to be nothing. On the other hand, it might be worth elaborating.

"These other dragon leaders are over at Cliffside cave right now, aren't they?" he asked Angie, as they started down the stairs of the tower together.

"As a matter of fact, no," said Angie. "Brace yourself. They're going to have to get back to their own communities in time to carry out whatever decision you've all come to. So they decided—well, Secoh helped talk them into it—that they'd come here and wait for you to wake up. That way, as soon as something's planned, they can take off for home right away, each one of them."

"Couldn't be better!" said Jim, all but rubbing his hands together in satisfaction at the way the idea was growing and maturing in his mind. He was half tempted to mention it, just as it was now, to Angie; if only to try it out. Then he thought better of it. Better to get the whole thing in shape, first.

They reached the bottom of the stairs and went out into the Great Hall, emerging just behind the high table.

They stepped up to the high table and took seats at the far end, where the stool there and the one right next to it had been left empty—undoubtedly deliberately, in expectation of their arrival.

Jim took the seat at the end of the table where he could see everybody, including the dragons that were now at the lower table with Secoh. Angie sat down behind the table next to him. Next to her was Chandos followed in order by Carolinus, Brian, Giles and Dafydd. All the humans sat behind the table overlooking the dragons below.

The dragons, on their part, not being restricted to benches at the lower table, had simply squatted down facing the men above them. Whether it had been part of Secoh's enticement or not, the long table next to them was loaded with pitchers, both empty and full of wine; and the five dragon visitors seemed to be thoroughly a part of the lively conversation going on.

And it was, indeed, a lively conversation. Not merely Chandos and Carolinus, whom Jim would have expected to have entered into a conversation with anyone, including dragons, but Dafydd and Brian and Giles were all involved in the debate, as were the dragons. A certain amount of order was evidently being observed, however, in that once one had really begun speaking, the rest fell silent and listened to him.

But still, so lively was the verbal exchange that for a moment or two it continued, ignoring the arrival of Jim and Angie. Then, one by one, Chandos and the other knights fell silent, and the dragons did also.

There were five of the dragon representatives, and the least of them dwarfed Secoh, who was squatted closest to the wine on the table, on its left-hand side and more or less in front of the others. Jim wondered for a moment if he should have turned into a dragon before he came.

But it would have been awkward, as a dragon, squatting at the high table with the other knights; and on second thought, since the dragons all knew he was a george part of the time, if not most of the time, the other dragons would simply accept the fact that he was being a george at the moment.

He opened his mouth to speak, but Secoh was before him.

"M'Lord James!" cried Secoh. "It's wonderful to see you up and around again. May I introduce the representative dragons from other parts of our island?"

"By all means," said Jim. "I'm surprised, though, to see only five of them. I thought there were more communities than that between here and the end of Scotland."

"There are," said Secoh; and the other, larger dragons all nodded their heads to show their agreement. "We could have had several hundred dragons here as representatives; but it was thought wisest to send as few as possible. So each of these here speaks for a large section of the island. Nearest to you, Jim, is Egnoth, of the Lower West Dragons. I will give all places the names you georges give them; so you'll be clear about where each of these representatives comes from."

"Thank you," said Jim. The knights looked surprised. So did Secoh.

"What did I do, m'Lord?" he asked, flustered.

"You were being helpful," said Jim. "Go on talking."

"Well—Egnoth, at my furthest right, speaks for the Lower West Dragons from the Mersey River to the mouth of the Severn to its South; and inland some sixty or eighty miles. Next to him is Marnagh of the East Dragons. He speaks for all dragons from the Humber River in the north down the coast to the bight of land beyond the East Anglican Heights, and again in toward the island's center perhaps fifty to seventy of your miles."

Jim's mind scrambled with his mental picture of England, Wales and Scotland, and his knowledge of place and topographical names. He got a mental picture, though it was not a sure one, of the areas Secoh was talking about.

"In and below these two," the mere-dragon was continuing, "is the area of the third dragon you see before you, and next to me. She is Artalleg, who speaks for the land between the other two you were just introduced to. First on my left is Chorak, the fourth dragon before you, who speaks for all dragons north of the Cheviot Hills. Finally, beyond him is the fifth dragon to which I have the honor to introduce you, who represents all the land in the south to the sea, from the Channel waters to the Irish sea. His name is Lanchorech."

Secoh stopped speaking. There was a moment of silence, while Jim hesitated over a proper phrase with which to acknowledge the introductions.

"My greetings to all you dragons," he said finally. "You honor the place where I live by coming here."

The five dragons nodded again, apparently not ill pleased by what he had just said.

"As we were saying just before you got here—" Brian broke in. Brian, in his usual impatience with anything that was not action, had been tapping the tabletop with his fingers while the diplomatic introductions were going on. "We and these good dragons have been considering—"

"I heard what you were considering as I came in," Jim said. Far from being insulted by this, Brian actually looked relieved. "You were trying to decide where the best place would be for both the george army and the dragons to join and fight the sea serpents that must be even now coming ashore, if they aren't here already. Well, I've been considering another possibility. A way to get rid of the sea serpents, possibly without fighting them at all; and a way to get rid of the French without fighting them, either."

These words were greeted with a moment of silence, broken by Chandos's cultured tones.

"You speak most interestingly, m'Lord," he said. "Pray tell us more."

Alerted by the fact that Chandos had chosen to emphasize his feudal rank by calling him "m'Lord," instead of simply "Sir James"; even though he, Chandos, was not only the senior knight but had a greater reputation as a war-captain, Jim decided to use the authority of that rank to play for time while he got his plan in order.

The idea still had a lot of holes in it that could give rise to questions by the others. He wanted to put it into the kind of form that would be attractive both to the knights, who would just as soon have a battle; and the dragons, who probably preferred not to fight, but were ready to, if they had to.

Happily, he had a powerful argument in the French dragons' promise of aid.

But that should be saved for the proper moment.

"First," he said, "I want to know more about the situation as it now stands. You all know I've been asleep nearly two days; and things must have been happening. My apologies, but I simply didn't arrange to have myself wakened the way I should."

"He need not apologize, gentlemen and dragons," said Angie, firmly beside him. She was sitting with her arms folded and looking as much like the rock of Gibraltar as a rather small, attractive, black-haired woman could. "It was my decision to let him sleep. And now that he's slept, why waste any more time, since I gather time is precious, in talking about it?"

Artalleg opened her mouth, but closed it again on being nudged by the dragon on her right.

"Well, to go on, then—" Jim suddenly broke off. "Come to think of it, where is Rrrnlf? I know he probably couldn't get into this hall, but—"

"Rrrnlf," Angie's clear voice cut in again, "is not interested. As soon as he heard that Essessili was coming here and that all he had to do was wait for him, he left anything else up to the rest of us. He simply curled up next to his sea serpent, who's tied up so that he can't move, and went to sleep. Outside of the fact they're both taking up a lot of space in the courtyard, Rrrnlf might as well not be here."

"I see," said Jim, and coughed a little self-consciously. "Well, then some of the rest of you can tell me. What's the situation with the sea serpents now? Are we starting to have more around the castle? Do we have any idea whether a lot more have come ashore yet—"

"*I* can answer that," said Secoh. "I've flown out three times now to take a look at the nearest shoreline, not far from the Loathly Tower. I stayed always high up in the air, so that I wouldn't be recognized as a dragon. Anybody looking up could see something, but he would probably think it was a bird. Of course, sea serpents don't seem to look up, anyhow."

"Did you find out about more sea serpents coming ashore?" Jim asked.

"They're not coming, they've come," said Secoh. "Thousands of them. They landed all up and down the shore, a ways down below the Meres and the Loathly Tower. Then some of them started to move this way, but not all of them. The last time I looked, most seemed to be still just getting into groups."

Jim turned to Carolinus.

"What do you think?" he said. "It's still your opinion the Dark Powers aren't behind all this?"

"Curiously enough," said Carolinus, "this once, the Dark Powers don't seem to be having anything to do with it. It's merely Chance and History colliding. Also, the unknown magician Mastermind. I've still no idea who he or she could be."

"That," Jim said, "we can worry about later. The important point right now seems to be what to do about the sea serpents."

He looked at the five dragons.

"How soon could you bring your dragons down here?"

Lanchorech spoke up.

"We talked that over among ourselves, back at the Cliffside cave," he said. "From the time we leave here to pass them the word to come, until they're overhead of your castle here, is going to take at least six hours, even if all are ready and waiting to fly."

"You may have some assistance," Jim said, "from the French dragons. You know that?"

"*If* they come," said Lanchorech gloomily.

"They will," said Jim as confidently as he could. "Remember, I have their surety in gems. At least, that is to say, I had it—"

Secoh broke in unexpectedly.

"You do still have it, m'Lord!" he said. "I was careful to collect it from where I'd hidden it, when these dragon representatives here left Cliffside for your castle. In fact I have it with me, under the table here. After all, it was you who was given it to hold!"

"In that case," said Jim, "perhaps you'd just pass it up to me."

Secoh's head dipped under the table for a moment and he came up clutching a certain large and bulging sack. He passed it up to Jim at the high table. Jim took it, undid the leather thong that held the mouth of it shut, and spilled some of its contents on the table in front of him. The effect on the five representative dragons was automatic; even though they must have seen these before.

"Jewels—such jewels!" said Egnoth. "Never have I seen such jewels!"

This was the moment to play that ace.

"They are precious to the French dragons," said Jim. "Now, they didn't commit themselves to fight. But they said they would come; and you have some idea of the numbers of how many dragons they can bring. If you can fill half the sky over the head of the sea serpents, they can fill the other half. Together, you could seem an endless host."

"If they won't fight, they're not going to be much use," growled Egnoth. "Just what you'd expect of Continental dragons!"

"If neither you nor they have to fight," said Jim, "then no harm's done. And, as I say, I think I have a plan that may save anyone from having to actually fight the serpents. But first—"

He turned to Chandos, just beyond Angie at the high table.

"What of the English army, Sir John?" he asked. "Was its gathering point close enough to the place where the serpents are coming ashore, so that they might have encountered serpents by now?"

"I doubt it," said Chandos. "The gathering place was to be some distance north of here, perhaps a day and a half's march once the army's assembled. In fact, I'd asked Carolinus before you joined us whether perhaps individual serpents might not have surprised the levies already. He gave me his opinion that he did not think the serpents, any of them, would have penetrated that far north yet."

"They haven't!" said Carolinus. "Check with Rrrnlf when he wakes up, if you want. But I've lived long enough, and had enough to do with those in the sea, to know that the sea serpents, particularly when they're alone, are not all that brave where it means going into strange territory. Which is what all 'high land' is to them."

"Second question, then, Sir John," said Jim. "Do you think the full army is gathered by now?"

"It should be," said Chandos, "except for those who come from Northumberland, or from some of the deeper parts of Wales."

"And you think what is formed right now would take about a day and a half or two, to get here?"

"Yes," said Chandos, a slight frown between his eyes. "What's the importance of having them here? Aside from the fact that if this serpent—this Essess-something—is going to come here, so I take it you mean that other serpents will come along with him? I'm not so sure his Highness, the Crown Prince, and the captains of the army, will be so eager to put their fighting men against the serpents here at this spot, merely to save your castle."

"No," said Jim, "I don't think so either. But that wasn't what I had in mind. What I'd like them to do would be to march down and around, and get behind the serpents; who, a day and a half from now, should certainly be surrounding the castle. The serpents may be great in numbers, but they're built low to the ground, and they haven't any war engines to assault walls like ours. Also, I wouldn't judge they're built to climb the walls, smooth as those are, with just those small, stubby legs of theirs. We could last for some time, even with thousands of serpents camped around us."

"But you said you wanted the army to march around and get behind the serpents. Why?" demanded Chandos.

"Because," said Jim, "they'll then be between the serpents and the sea. We'll have to wait until Rrrnlf wakes up to get a firm answer to this; but I believe the sea serpents, being sea creatures, may well be inclined to panic if they think their escape to the sea is threatened."

"What's all this to do with us dragons?" demanded Egnoth.

"Well, picture it for yourself," said Jim. "The sea serpents come ashore on dry land, which is not their usual home; and then they discover all of a sudden an army of georges is behind them, between them and their escape to the sea. At the same time—imagine this from the north—the sky begins to fill with wave after wave of dragons on wing; and at the same time, from the south and east, the sky there also begins to fill with wave on wave of dragons on wing from France. Until the two waves meet overhead; and they find themselves with an army blocking their way of escape and more dragons overhead than they ever knew existed."

Jim finished speaking on a note of triumph. To his intense surprise, what he had just said was greeted merely with a complete silence on the part of everyone, knights and dragons alike.

CHAPTER 33

Jim chilled. He was afraid he knew exactly what he had done wrong. Countless times he had told himself that when dealing with fourteenth-century inhabitants on this world he should never spring anything on them.

These people had good reason not to want things sprung on them. In this place and time, mistakes in decision could kill you. Even apparently harmless wrong decisions could kill you. Like planting the wrong crop, planting a little too early or a little too late. Taking the wrong way home could kill you; because it might lead you either past a robber—and robbers of this world routinely killed their victims first, as the simplest way of making sure that those victims didn't put up a fuss while being robbed—or some large and dangerous animal that could end your life.

This world, in short, was full of pitfalls. No one leaped without looking first. Even children knew that what appeared to be good luck should be looked over cautiously and examined from every angle before being accepted for what it seemed.

Jim winced at the faces around him; then felt his heart suddenly bound upward with relief, as he saw Chandos looking back at him from the other side of Angie. The senior knight had little wrinkles at the corners of his eyes and a hint of a smile at the corners of his lips.

"An excellent plan of battle, m'Lord," he said. "But I see only one minor problem. How is it to be told to the captains of the army, who are no small distance from us, over land which may be filled with sea serpents?"

Jim had literally not thought about this. Or rather, he had thought of it, but assumed that there would be an easy way of getting around it.

"And, furthermore," went on Chandos, "even when the message is carried to them, can you be sure that the captains will agree to move the army as you suggest?"

This was something Jim had not thought of at all.

He had forgotten medieval commanders all had minds of their own; and it was seldom any two of them agreed. Each leader was used to being the only leader. If only the young Crown Prince of England was old and experienced enough to dominate his captains, Jim was fairly sure he would agree to a plan coming from Jim; since it was Jim and the others who had rescued him from the rogue French magician, Malvinne. But the Prince was not old enough yet.

Jim decided to take the easiest question first.

"Well," he said, "to answer you, Sir John, I don't myself have the magical ability to send someone to where the army is now. But I was hoping—" He looked at Carolinus, who stared back at him with a determinedly set face.

"Jim," he said, "you must learn something, once and for all. You cannot be a spendthrift with magic. Now, compared to yourself, I must look like a wealthy noble compared to some serf toiling at his meager strips of personal earth; but—"

He broke off suddenly; and Jim realized that his alarm was showing in his face.

"Don't worry about the others," Carolinus said. "They see our lips moving, but they can't hear me nor you, until I let them."

"I—I don't understand," said Jim awkwardly.

"I mean simply you've had one problem from the very beginning, when it became apparent you had a magical balance with the Accounting Office," answered Carolinus.

"But—" began Jim. Carolinus's voice overrode his.

"Listen to me," said the senior magician. "You gained that balance by sheer accident; by coming from another place, not of this world, and leading your Companions to a defeat of the Dark Powers. You'll remember that when you allowed that balance to lie, unused, it began changing you into a dragon, whether you wanted it to or not. So, you had to come to me, become my apprentice, and start to learn something of magic in order to control what you had."

"True," acknowledged Jim, humbly.

"However," said Carolinus, lifting a stern finger and holding it upright as in warning, "once you began to have some control over your magical account, you immediately used it all up, and I had to come to your rescue. The upshot of that, you'll remember, was that I managed to get you promoted to a C level magician, with a special extra drawing account. I'd remind you now there are reasons for not allowing low-ranking, inexperienced magicians to have access to a great deal of magic. One of them is that an inexperienced magician could misuse a great deal of power to make a great deal of harm. You haven't done that; but you've already exhausted your extra credit, or nearly so."

"But you—" began Jim.

"As I say," Carolinus interrupted, "you look on me as the serf looks on the noble. You know I have vast amounts of magic at my disposal, compared to yours. But a thing can be large without being unlimited. A dragon's hoard may be fabulous, but it is not all the wealth in the world. It could all be spent. Ask your friend Secoh about that after he and his kind were blighted by the Dark Powers in the Loathly Tower."

Jim glanced at Secoh involuntarily. The mere-dragon, like all the rest there, was watching their silently moving lips puzzledly.

"So," Carolinus said, "in short, I must save what I have left; so that I've adequate reserves with which to do battle with this other, unknown magician. While I easily could use some to transport your messenger to the army, I must refuse. You'll have to find some other way of doing it."

Jim sat, stunned. Then he became aware that the others were all looking at the two of them and talking; and that the others had been allowed by Carolinus to hear his last two sentences.

"If the Mage won't send someone," Secoh was saying, "how are we going to get a message to them? True, one of us dragons could fly to the army, for its gathering place is no secret to us. But would they listen to a dragon, of all people, who asked them to move their whole george army?"

"You're quite right, of course, Secoh," said Jim soothingly.

"I wouldn't ask one of you dragons to go. Of the rest of us, all but one are georges of some reputation, but not such that the leaders of the English army would listen to us."

He looked at Chandos.

"Sir John," he said, "the only one of us who stands a chance of persuading the English captains to move the army around behind the serpents is yourself. You must know that."

"In fact, I do," answered Chandos, "and it will be no easy task, even for a gentleman with some little repute, like myself. But while I am not without skill with weapons, I'm not sure whether I could pass safely through the land between this castle and the army, if I encounter one of the sea serpents. Nor am I sure that I could win through, even with as many men-at-arms as you could lend me for escort. Then again, there is a matter of the time involved in getting there."

Jim found himself checked once more.

"It's very simple," Angie's voice broke in decisively. "Rrrnlf will have to take him. Not only can Rrrnlf take him safely past any sea serpents that are in the way, Rrrnlf can carry him; and so cover the distance in very little time. Besides, their seeing Rrrnlf will back up Sir John's arguments."

Jim stared at her in mingled awe and admiration. He had become used to her excellent management of the castle, to say nothing of the Malencontri estate as a whole, in times when he had been gone; but when she had joined them for this council of war he had not really thought of her as taking a decisive part in it. He was suddenly ashamed of himself.

"It's an ideal solution, Angie!" he said. "Perfect!"

Then, he thought of something else.

"But will Rrrnlf do it?" he asked. "Remember, he doesn't want to leave here, because he's waiting for Essessili to show up, and he doesn't want to miss a chance at getting his Lady back."

Help came from an unexpected quarter.

"In that, since it is a small thing," said Carolinus, twisting the right wing of his mustache, "I believe I can aid."

They adjourned to the courtyard.

The sleeping Rrrnlf and the trussed-up sea serpent beside him—who seemed also to be sleeping, surprisingly enough— were an awesome sight. The two enormous bodies were such as to make Jim feel that he, and those with him, were just as "wee" as Rrrnlf was fond of calling them.

"Wake up!" said Brian, kicking the nearest part of the huge Sea Devil's body, which happened to be the calf of his leg. Apparently, he could have just as well kicked a mountain. The toe of his dark blue, slipperlike footwear, that was considered to be shoes for those of gentle blood when they were not in armor or in some activity requiring boots, did not even dent the Sea Devil's flesh; and Rrrnlf went on sleeping.

"I think I can wake him," said Angie. She pulled a pin from the back of her hair, so that the hair fell loose, and she shook it free for a second; then she walked around to Rrrnlf's feet and, bending over, drove the point of the pin into the tip of the big toe protruding from one of Rrrnlf's sandals.

"Whup! What?" roared Rrrnlf, waking immediately and leaping to his feet, into a posture of defense, with both big hands ready to take action.

There was a moment of bewildered silence all around. Rrrnlf had just awakened and did not know why. The humans at his feet were regaining their balance, after the ground shock caused by someone Rrrnlf's size suddenly going briefly up in the air and coming down with a thump on his feet next to them. Angie was the first to recover.

"I woke you," she told Rrrnlf. "I had to stick a pin into your right big toe to do it. Isn't it sore?"

"I don't think so," said Rrrnlf bewilderedly, reaching down to feel his right big toe. "Yes . . . maybe."

He straightened up and looked down at them all.

"Why?" he asked.

"Because we need you," Angie said. "Jim, you tell him."

"Never mind," said Carolinus decisively. "I'll take care of this. Rrrnlf, you are to carry Sir John Chandos across country to where the army is gathering. You are not to let anyone harm him on the way, particularly sea serpents."

"Ha!" said Rrrnlf. "As if they could—with me carrying him. But, just a minute, wee Mage. I can't take your Sir John anywhere. Essessili is coming here. I have to wait for him."

"Nonetheless," said Carolinus, "it is necessary that you take Sir John as I say. If Essessili comes while you're gone, we'll make sure he stays here until you get back. I shouldn't expect it to take you more than a day to go and come."

"It wouldn't," said Rrrnlf. "But—all the same, wee Mage— I'm sorry, but I'm not going to do any such thing. I'm not going to take the chance of somehow missing my Lady; just because you asked me to carry someone someplace and so I was gone when that sea snake got here with her."

"Rrrnlf!" said Carolinus; and, while he did not suddenly grow in stature to Rrrnlf's size, his voice suddenly resonated on the air as clearly and penetratingly as Rrrnlf's itself. "I will not say it again. I do not ask you, I *command* you to take Sir John to the army, by virtue of my rank as Master Magician."

"I've already said, 'No'—"

Rrrnlf disappeared; and his words were cut off in midsentence. Everyone there stared blankly at the empty space where he had been a moment before.

"Where'd he go?" said Brian, turning around. "I don't see him—"

"Don't move!" snapped Carolinus. "Don't any of you move your feet."

He was now pointing at the ground almost at his own toes.

They all looked, including Brian, who had to crane his head back over his shoulder to do so. What they saw in line with the pointing finger of Carolinus was a large black beetle—large, but not extraordinarily so. It was standing upright on its two hind legs, its middle two arms merely hanging, but its upper two arms extended and crooked as if they were powerful engines of bone and muscle with hands bigger than barn doors at the end of each of them.

"Don't take that tone with me, sir!" said Carolinus, speaking to the beetle. "Mind your manners! You're a beetle; and you'll stay a beetle until I change you back to your original shape again. Do you hear me? Then say so!"

There was a slight pause.

"No, I will not have mercy!" said Carolinus. "A beetle you are and a beetle you'll stay until you are prepared to take Sir John to the army!"

The next second Rrrnlf was back with them in all his thirty-odd feet of height, staring down in anguish at Carolinus.

"Wee Mage!" he said, in anguished tones. "You will lose me my Lady—that is absolutely sure. I feel it."

"Nonsense!" said Carolinus. "I give you my word, the word of a Mage, that you will have your Lady back from Essessili the moment he turns up with it. Now, let us decide how you are going to carry Sir John."

It took a bit of discussion, and a bit of engineering on Jim's part, plus some work by the castle carpenters and blacksmith (during which Brian went back with Chandos into the castle to arm and armor the senior knight). But eventually they had built an arrangement that fitted over Rrrnlf's right shoulder and was not only firmly fastened there, but padded against any possible jolts and jars of travel. Attached to it was Sir John's saddle, facing forward.

Rrrnlf lay down on the ground to have the apparatus attached to him; then got back to his feet, vaulted the courtyard wall and lay down again beyond the moat outside the castle.

Chandos reappeared, ready to travel, said his polite farewells and strolled out the now-open main gates to the Sea Devil. He climbed aboard the saddle with absolute coolness, as if he was going for a canter on some familiar horse. Rrrnlf rose once more to his feet and strode off in a northeasterly direction, until he disappeared among the trees.

"Well, m'Lord," said Brian, "perhaps best you give the order for the great gate in the curtain wall to be closed again, the drawbridge pulled up, and the portcullis let down. Then the rest of us can adjourn to the Great Hall and the wine cups for a further discussion of what we may do by way of defense, if and when the sea serpents reach us here."

"If m'Lord doesn't mind," said Dafydd—and the fact he used the word "Lord" to Jim was effective notice that he intended to do what he was just about to announce, whatever Jim might think about it—"I think I'll stay on the wall in hope a stray serpent may show up. I have a mind to try some arrows on such if it appears; to see if I cannot find the more vulnerable parts of it that an arrow might reach. There are the eyes, of course; and I suspect that a war arrow driven deep into its throat should have some effect; but there may be other possibilities."

"Fine," said Jim. "Brian, I'm afraid you and Carolinus may have those wine cups to yourself. I think I'd like to go back up to the solar, take off my clothes and change into a dragon. Then I'll take off from the tower roof and fly east and south to have a look at the numbers of the sea serpents that Secoh had reported. Perhaps Secoh will go with me?"

"Oh, yes!" said Secoh. "I mean, of course, m'Lord."

"As for you other dragons," said Jim, turning to them, "you will no doubt want to take word of our plans back to your people."

"Indeed we do," said Egnoth. "And as quickly as possible." He looked at the other dragons.

"Unless I am mistaken about one of the other representatives? Perhaps one of them still has a question, or wishes to wait for a while for some reason?"

The other dragons all murmured negatives. As the humans watched, they took off from the courtyard with a tremendous explosion of multiple wings, and disappeared into the sky in various directions.

Jim picked up the sack of gems and, followed by Angie and Secoh, followed Brian into the Great Hall; but continued on up to the solar alone, to make his preparations for overflying the seashore and the sea serpents.

CHAPTER 34

From a much lower height than he had earlier thought might be safe, Jim studied the invading sea serpents.

Secoh had been right; they did not look up. It was evidently not easy for them to do so without rolling on one side, so that they could turn their heads left or right, rather than lift them on their thick necks, which were less thick than their bodies, but not much.

He was therefore still more than a thousand feet up; but any one of those below that did look up would have been able to tell quite plainly that he was a dragon, not a bird. But none looked.

On the other hand, he was looking a great deal.

There was no doubt that the serpents were now ashore in enormous numbers and some were still coming. Below him they covered the shoreline for two miles to his right and left, making a four-mile front in all. From there, their numbers stretched inland, still thickly packed together, for perhaps half a mile.

They avoided any streams, he noticed. The ground was rocky here; and lifted rather quickly away from sea level. But it was not steep enough to make it difficult for them to climb.

From the air, their green bodies looked small, and relatively harmless. It was difficult to remind himself that each one of those he could see below him was longer than Rrrnlf was tall, if you measured them from nose-tip to tail. They did not, of course, have the Sea Devil's massive upper body bulk and strength. But, compared to a human being, each one of them was an unstoppable engine of flesh and blood.

For a moment Jim felt queasy over the message he had sent with Chandos, that the human army should wait until they had moved inland and then get into position behind them. It was hard to imagine how humans could stand for any time at all against these creatures.

Packed as closely as they were, and moving all together, they reminded Jim of an invasion of green worms that, one bright fall season, had attacked the trees at Riveroak College, where he and Angie had taught in their original world. The worms had seemed uncountable in number, then, as the sea serpents did now.

But his first impression, that they had been moving mindlessly together as the tree-worms had done, was wrong. Now, as he studied them, he began to see that they formed large groups. He found himself thinking of these groups as battalions; because they were roughly rectangular in shape and each possibly held around fifteen hundred of the sea creatures, traveling as a unit.

He noticed that as soon as one of these units was formed, it started inland. Meanwhile, the number of new arrivals still coming from the sea was becoming less and less.

Still, at a rough estimate it looked like at least ten thousand serpents had come ashore. For a moment he felt the hollow touch of despair. There was enough strength below him in those battalions to overwhelm both the human army and all the dragons of England, if they ventured to come to grips with the serpents directly. Somehow, some way, his plan to avoid an actual clash must be made to work. The dragons would most certainly be destroyed by sheer numbers. Ideas tumbled about in his mind, but as yet, none of the details were solid. All were only hopes.

It was just then that he became aware of another speck, circling possibly as much as a thousand feet above Secoh and himself. He focused on it with his dragon telescopic vision; and his immediate suspicions were confirmed. It was another dragon.

"Secoh!" he called to the mere-dragon soaring not far off from him. "We'll go talk to that dragon upstairs."

Having said this, without looking to see if Secoh followed, he began to mount toward the speck. He found himself apparently climbing very rapidly; then realized the speck was descending toward him at the same time. A moment later, he and the other dragon were soaring wing to wing, and in seconds Secoh appeared on the other side of the unknown dragon.

"M'Lord! M'Lord!" called Secoh. "You recognize Iren? You remember he was one of the three representatives from the French dragons who talked to you at the inn in Brest?"

"Oh? Oh!" said Jim, for the fact was he had not recognized the French dragon; and would not have known him at all if Secoh had not identified him. Jim had got to the point where he was able to recognize most of the Cliffside dragons; but he was not as good at remembering and identifying dragons he knew less well.

"Iren!" he said. "I didn't expect to see you here."

"And why not?" answered Iren fiercely. "We are French dragons; and you have both our word and our gems. One or another of us has been keeping watch here on those creatures below, since they started coming out of the sea. They are all on land now—all that matter—now that their leader is here."

"Their leader? You mean Essessili?"

"Whatever he's called," said Iren, as if to even speak of the sea serpent left a bad taste in his mouth. "He got here a short while back; and from the time he arrived, they began forming groups and starting northward, inland."

"Did you see—" Jim broke off, unsure how to describe it and still keep the importance of Rrrnlf's Lady a secret. "Did you notice if Essessili was carrying anything; say, something like the figurehead of a ship?"

"He carried nothing," said Iren. "How could he, and why? What difference if he did?"

"Oh, probably none," said Jim hurriedly. "I just wondered. Since you've been keeping watch here, you've probably also been watching Brest; or wherever else the French georges are getting ready to sail to England."

Iren nodded.

"Do you know if your georges are close to sailing?" Jim asked.

"They have begun already," said Iren.

The three dragons were all soaring together now in large, lazy circles above the shore and the departing sea serpents. The peacefulness of their effortless floating through the air was at odds with the turmoil inside Jim.

"Our georges," Iren went on, "also have some more of those unmentionables, below, with them; in case some of their boats need assistance. So those boats should be reaching this part of the coast—for it is here, I understand, they are headed—in the next two days."

"Just about the time it should take Essessili and the serpents with him to reach Malencontri," said Jim grimly. "Secoh, can our dragons gather there as well, by that time?"

"It is certain they can," said Secoh.

"Also," put Iren, "our French dragons are in waiting, close here, but out of sight of the serpents. They can be at your castle in one hour . . . or a little more."

"Good," said Jim, hoping that would not be too far.

"I was going to fly to Brest to see the French ships for myself; but now I don't need to," he added. "I think, instead, Secoh and I will swing east and north to the place where the army of our English georges has gathered. They too should be moving soon, I hope, in this direction."

"Good!" said Iren. "I'll come. The more we know of matters here, the better. Just let me send a signal to the next watcher."

Immediately, Iren started to mount, leaving them below him. After he had gone a couple of hundred feet he turned, went into a dive for half the distance back down to them, braked abruptly in mid-air, made one small, tight circle, then dived again and checked himself beside them.

"What was all that?" asked Jim. "Was that the signal you said you were sending to another watcher?"

"Have you so poor faith in us not to guess that?" said Iren. "I told you. We've been keeping watch on the southern coast of your island for some days now."

"It's a long flight here from Brest," said Jim. "Not that you couldn't do it, of course—"

"You underestimate us," said Iren. "I am only one of five French dragons on wing at all times. The next in the air, watching from farther out at sea, and south of us, can see me and he'll have seen my signal just now. It told him all watchers should move up one position. In short, that watcher who got the message will repeat the signal to the next in line, then move here to take up my position, so that he can replace me, and even be ready to follow the march of the sea serpents inland, if needed."

"But still—" Jim was saying doubtfully. Iren cut in on him.

"You did not let me finish," he said. "I said there were five watchers. When the farthest off of them moves out from where our dragons are gathered, a new one takes wing, to begin the chain. So there are always five aloft. Our watch periods are two hours, unless a dragon feels that he should leave his post for some reason. Then all the rest move up one. You understand?"

"Yes," answered Jim, "it's a very good arrangement."

"So," went on Iren. "Each dragon in line sees the other; and so messages such as I gave just now can be sent. Just before you got here, I had sent a signal that the sea serpents were beginning to move on from the coast. Now, I am free to go with you, to find this English george army of yours."

"It'll be something of a flight to the north," said Jim. "Nothing for Secoh and myself, of course, since we're close to home. But it'll make your own flight back to France a long one."

"You have our word, and you have our gems," said Iren. "Do you think so little of French dragons as to imagine one of us would not extend himself to the utmost in this case? True, it may be a long flight. But as you know yourself, we dragons are capable of soaring for days, if need be, and covering great distances; though it may not be easy."

Jim felt a small, unexpected, bump of pride and warmth on finding himself included by Iren among the other dragons. It was something like the feeling he had had when Smrgol, the grand-uncle of Gorbash in whose body Jim had first appeared in this world, had taken time out before the battle with the Ogre at the Loathly Tower to give him advice.

For a moment the memory came clearly back to him. It had only been seconds before the very old dragon had locked himself in personal conflict with the young and powerful Bryagh; and it was at a time when Smrgol himself was half-crippled from a stroke. Still, Smrgol had taken time out, both to encourage Jim, and advise him on how to fight the Ogre, since Smrgol had fought one once himself.

The warm feeling spread all through him. It was strange, this business of wanting to feel kinship with two entirely different species. It was confusing; but there was no doubt that deep within him, he wanted to belong to both.

"Well," he said, to get his mind off the subject, "here we go, then."

He led, hunting from updraft to updraft in a northern direction that diverged from the movement of the sea serpents below.

There was no doubt at all now, he noted, that the long, massive, green creatures were headed for Malencontri. Recognition of the fact did not make him feel happy.

He forced his mind back to present matters.

He had been both impressed and touched by what Iren had told him about the actions of the French dragons. He had under-estimated them. Possibly he had been influenced too much by the fact that the English dragons, like the English georges—he corrected that thought in his mind: the English people—considered all others to be somewhat less than themselves. He had fallen into the easy trap of assuming they were right and the French dragons were more fearful, less ready to honor their obligations, and in every way inferior to the dragons he knew. They were clearly no such things. But then, the French dragons held similar opinions about the English ones.

For that matter, his thoughts ran on, he was continually both intrigued by and dismayed with all of this world around him—with its people and animals, its dirt and refuse, its tempers and manners.

Possibly that was what had made Angie and him decide to stay here in the first place; after the victory at the Loathly Tower. Even at the cost of giving up their one chance to return to the world they knew.

It took the three of them a couple of hours of alternately flying and soaring to reach the location of the English army. Happily, Secoh, with his natural dragon instinct for location, was able to take them directly to it; even though they came by a way the mere-dragon had not used before.

Now, the day around them had moved into mid-afternoon. The weather was still fair, evidently, over all of southern England; with only a few scattered clouds in the sky, so that they were clearly able to see what was below.

Humans, unlike dragons, did look up. But clearly, no one in the English army was expecting dragons; and hopefully, they would jump to the conclusion it was a bird if they did look up. What Jim saw, when at last they looked down on that army, was a good-sized host. His own best estimate was it held roughly the same number of humans as there were sea serpents—possibly more.

Unlike the serpents, however, the humans were clearly divid-ed and grouped according to the part they would play in battle. The knights occupied tents clustered around one large tent, which must be the Prince's, apart from the rougher shelters of the heavily armed footmen, the scanty ones of the more lightly armed footmen—and the near-shelterless area of whatever levies had been brought from farms with only a pretense of armor and an occasional scythe or other homely weapon.

Last of all, and a little apart, were the shelters of the longbowmen and crossbowmen.

Nowhere among all these could he see any sign of Chandos, or—one who would have been much more visible—Rrrnlf. On the other hand, probably Rrrnlf had already got there, left the senior knight, and headed back to Malencontri. The Sea Devil could already be halfway back, considering his anxieties over his Lady, which Jim had just unhappily found out Essessili was not carrying after all. Another potential cause of trouble at the castle.

"What are the georges doing here?" asked Iren suddenly. "Shouldn't they be moving to the seashore to fight our georges when they land?"

"Actually," Jim answered him, "they're supposed to move, soon. But the place I want them to move to isn't the seashore; but to a point between the sea serpents and it. So they'll seem to be blocking the serpents' escape back to the sea."

"Escape?" demanded Iren sharply. "What makes you think the sea crawlers want to escape? The last we saw of them they looked like doing anything but escaping."

"That's true," said Jim. "But I'm hoping to change their attitude."

Iren looked at him strangely.

"Magic, you know," said Jim lamely, giving his all-purpose excuse. But Iren, unlike many other dragons—and most humans—did not seem impressed.

All the way on the flight from the seashore Jim had been considering taking Iren and the other French dragons into his confidence. Now, he decided to do so.

"At the moment, our most important georges in the army are arguing," he told Iren, "about what to do. But we've got one very important george speaking for us. His name is Sir John Chandos. If he succeeds, he'll get the army to where I just told you of."

"But you aren't telling me why they should do that," said Iren.

"My hope," said Jim, "is that the serpents can't either climb over or break down the walls of Castle Malencontri. If they fail in that, they've got to begin doubting their ability to capture me, who they evidently think is leader of all the English dragons."

"Well, you are!" put in Secoh, unexpectedly and strongly.

"Thanks, Secoh," said Jim, looking fondly at the mere-dragon, "but I think they're seeing me as more capable and powerful than I am. At any rate——"

He turned back to Iren, who was soaring on the other side of him from Secoh.

"At any rate," Jim said, "if the serpents start doubting they can catch hold of me, we want to reinforce that doubt. If most of the sea serpents are at Malencontri, we'll then call in the English dragons, who will take the air over them at about half our present height, so they seem to fill the north part of the sky. Happily, the serpents won't be able to see very far beyond the tree-tops, because they're built so low to the ground. Then, if you and your fellow French dragons, who've been waiting in position but out of sight, move in when I ask, to fill the southern part of the sky; then the sea serpents will find themselves completely closed in overhead by dragons, and faced by a castle they can't take."

He paused, but Iren was silent. Presumably the French dragon was thinking it over.

"My hope," said Jim, "is to get them to turn away, without actually having to fight them. Our advantage is, with you French dragons joining ours we'll seem to outnumber them. Also, whether they'll admit it or not, most of them know that one of them was slain in single combat by a dragon named Gleingul, a hundred years or so ago, at a place called the Gray Sands. So most of them must know that there's at least the chance that, one-on-one, our dragons can destroy them. Now, I haven't asked you French dragons to do any more than show up and help us try to frighten the serpents; but——"

"If dragons fight serpents, and there are French dragons where the fighting is going on," said Iren, "French dragons will be fighting too!"

The unexpectedly savage tone of Iren's voice sparked a sudden jolt of conviction in Jim. For the first time, direct combat between the dragons and the serpents—just like his combat with the Ogre when he had first come to this world—became a reality to him. Along with it came the realization that

if the dragons were fighting sea serpents, he would be fighting
one, too.

He felt a cold savagery building inside him. He had forgotten for the moment that, as always, in magically taking on a
dragon's body, he invariably took on a full measure of dragon
instincts; one of which was the dragon-rage which the dead
Smrgol had warned him against in his fight with the Ogre—
cautioning him not to let it cause him to lose his head, but to
fight a thinking battle.

Smrgol had reminded Jim he was faster than an Ogre. Ten to
one, Jim thought now, he should be faster than a sea serpent—
particularly on land where the pull of gravity would be slowing
them down; gravity ordinarily balanced out in the sea.

Also, as a dragon he was used to fighting on the land and they
were not. True, certain things would be unaltered, but many of
their battle reflexes would be based upon that weightlessness
they were used to under the waves . . .

He woke up suddenly to the fact that Iren was no longer with
him and Secoh. The French dragon evidently had peeled off to
begin his long flight back to France.

"You know, Secoh," said Jim, his dragon's voice carrying
easily across the forty feet of air that separated him from Secoh,
"we ought to have our own dragons aloft, keeping track of the
serpents, and the george army's movements. But, come to think
of it, I suppose as things stand now you wouldn't be able to get
any of the Cliffsiders—"

"The young dragons'll jump at the chance!" cried Secoh.
"I'll get them taking turns, and relieving each other every so
often, just the way the French dragons are doing it."

"But I thought—"

"Oh, they'll want to!" said Secoh. "They're very much
ashamed of themselves, after getting frightened and flying
off, leaving the Dragon Knight to face those sea serpents alone.
They'll do anything to make up for it. I'll probably have more
wanting to do it than we have jobs for."

"I see. Well," said Jim, slightly embarrassed, "then, maybe
we'll have enough so we can use some as liaisons between us
and the rest of the English dragons as they gather and move in."

"Liaison?" asked Secoh.

"Carriers of messages," explained Jim.

"Oh," said Secoh. "Yes, they'll make very good liaison-uh-
ers. And there'll be lots wanting to do it. Just leave it to me."

"All right," said Jim. He was startled to see Secoh start to turn away from him in mid-air and soar in the direction of what must be another thermal. "Where are you going?"

"To Cliffside!" Secoh called back. "We're practically there now, anyway."

"We are?" said Jim. The time had gone faster than he had thought since they had left the English army. Clearly his thoughts had gone on too long. "Wait a minute—"

Now he really had to shout. Secoh was some distance off. But Jim's voice evidently was equal to the task.

"Am I headed back toward Malencontri?" Jim roared. His dragon senses told him he was; but he wanted to make sure.

"Just fly straight ahead!" Secoh's voice floated back to him.

"All right," said Jim to himself, but with a touch of foreboding.

He looked at the landscape ahead for some point to line himself up on; and saw a dark section of forest, of the same color as that around Malencontri. He flew toward it.

He went on for some three miles, dropping altitude as he went, and was pleasantly surprised to make out first a clearing amongst the tree-tops, then an actual clearing that held the castle itself. He thumped down in the castle courtyard beside Rrrnlf, who was seated with his elbow on his knee and his chin in his hand, looking despondent.

"Don't worry, Rrrnlf," he said to the Sea Devil. "We'll get your Lady back all right—oh, by the way, I'm Sir James Eckert, but wearing my dragon body."

"Ah, a wee dragon, now, are you?" Rrrnlf nodded sadly. "That's the way the world goes. A wee knight one moment. Then a wee Mage. Then a wee dragon. Why not? Nothing matters, anyway."

"Cheer up!" said Jim. "Carolinus promised you back your Lady; and he's a magician who keeps his word."

"That's what they all say," said Rrrnlf, still sadly.

Jim gave up trying to lift the Sea Devil's spirits. With a flurry of wings that raised an explosion of dust in the courtyard, he half jumped, half flew to the top of the castle's tower. Folding his wings there, he was about to start downstairs to the solar when a thunderous sound shook the air of the courtyard.

For a moment he froze; then realized it was simply Rrrnlf sneezing in the dustcloud. He went on down the stairs, and into the solar, gratefully shutting the door behind him.

He realized suddenly he could use some sleep, himself, after all the flying he had done; in spite of his long rest before he had left Malencontri. Maybe in sleep the back of his mind would come up with some better ideas. If the serpents were going to be at the walls of Malencontri in their thousands, in just a couple of days, he would need to think of some way of making sure of stopping them from overcoming the walls.

Scuttling along on the ground on their short legs, it was hard to imagine how they could get over even the curtain wall; but there might be ways he did not expect. He needed to let the question soak in the back of his head while he slept. With luck, he would wake up with an answer.

He changed out of his dragon body into his human one and tumbled naked into his bed, pulling a huge pile of blankets and furs over him. There was a chill of foreboding deep inside him. Never mind, he told himself sternly, as he drifted off to sleep; ideas often come during slumber.

But when the next day dawned, no ideas had come to him.

Nor did the second day's dawn bring any. But it brought the serpents.

CHAPTER 35

Jim's first warning that their attackers were there in full numbers came from Angie, who woke him and told him that the castle was surrounded.

"My God!" said Jim, rolling out of bed and beginning to scramble into his clothes. "We've had individual ones moving back and forth across the open between us and the trees for the last two days, but when did they show up in large numbers?"

"During the night, evidently," said Angie. "Everyone else is on that new observation platform. You know—the one we built just inside the curtain wall by enlarging the platform for the big pot on swings that was there to pour hot oil on anyone trying to break through the front gate? You'd better get there right away."

"Just as fast as I can!" said Jim.

"You know, Jim," said Angie as he dressed hastily, "I'm really worried about Carolinus. He's not at all like himself. He's refusing to help; and it seems almost as if he wants the sea serpents to kill us all. As if he can hardly wait to be killed by them himself. It's almost as if he's looking forward to having everything over with."

"Will you help me with my armor?" interrupted Jim. "Everybody else is in armor, aren't they?"

"The knights, yes."

"Well, give me a hand then, will you?" said Jim. "Thanks. Angie, I'm sorry about Carolinus. I'll try to do what I can if there's a chance to find out what's troubling him. But right now there's no time for that. This is a matter of staying alive. Now, the greaves, if you don't mind. Tie the leather thongs tight above the bulge of my calf muscles. Otherwise, just walking stretches them loose and they're likely to work around my legs. I need them to protect the front of my legs . . . that's right . . ."

They both fell silent, as they struggled to get Jim into his armor and weaponed. Dressed, Jim headed off down the stairs of the tower, with Angie beside him, through the Great Hall and out into the courtyard. It was far different from the courtyard he was used to. Nearly every foot of space was taken up with people or domestic animals; for all the people living on Malencontri lands, and some simply close to them, had come for sanctuary inside the castle.

Makeshift tentlike shelters had been put up around the walls for the privacy of those who had the material and could afford it. Temporary latrines had been dug in a courtyard corner that gave a little privacy. Meanwhile the moat was smelling worse than ever, from the human waste and garbage dumped in it, through various chutes and over the curtain wall.

Angie had long ago set up garbage holes and disposal areas outside the castle walls; and the moat had become almost clean. Now it was back to smelling like the moats around most castles. Jim had been a little surprised at how quickly he had begun to ignore the stink. You simply lived with it; and that was that.

With Angie close behind him now, he ran up the steps to the catwalk around the curtain walls; and looked over them to see the open land around the castle now one carpet of long green bodies. It was a beautiful morning. He half ran along the catwalk to the enlarged platform above the gates, where not only Brian, Giles and Dafydd were waiting for him, but also Carolinus, Secoh and—to his surprise—John Chandos.

"When did you get back here, Sir John?" panted Jim, as he came at last to a halt on the platform. The senior knight smiled at him in his usual calm manner.

"Eight of your dragons flew me in from where the army was placed," he said. "The lift off the ground and the return to earth were a bit bumpy, but the rest, quite pleasant. M'Lady had made and sent with the dragons a sort of long net bag in which I could lie, padded with soft cloths and eight lines each harnessed to each of the eight dragons—"

Chandos made a slight, involuntary-seeming gesture of his right hand toward his upper lip before checking it. It was exactly the sort of a motion Giles would have used if he had been about to twirl the end of one of his magnificently long, blond mustachios in satisfaction.

"—If any other Englishman," Chandos went on, "with, I suppose, the exception of yourself, Sir Dragon, has ever so flown through the air, I do not know of it. I shall long remember the faces of those nearby as eight dragons landed to carry me off!"

There was a slight tone of condescension in Chandos's voice as he mentioned Jim that gave Jim a twinge of a faint unhappiness. It was the other side of the coin, he told himself, of the pride he had felt at being included by Iren among the family of dragons.

To Chandos, even to Brian and Giles, he would never really be an Englishman, never completely one of them. Not that they would remind him of it, for the world; and, being his friends, they would draw their swords at the very intimation by anyone else that he was less English than those around him. But deep within, they were aware he really was not; and could never be. They knew it, and he knew it. Just as he knew that he really was not a dragon and could never really be one.

He shook off the touch of emotion, and looked at Chandos with relief.

"But why did you come back?" he asked.

"The Prince had other captains," said Chandos. "I got them to agree to move as you said; and then felt I could be of best use back with you here."

"Well, I'm very happy to see you here," said Jim. "Since you are, certainly you'll do me the great kindness of taking command."

"Well, Sir James," said Chandos thoughtfully, "you do me honor. Nonetheless I think it best you lead. I find the Lady Angela is at least as well trained to siege defense as I am; and in fact, no doubt, much better. She has evidently been taking instruction from a neighbor of hers. M'Lady Geronde Isabel de Chaney."

He glanced at Brian.

"Whose favor Sir Brian, here—ah—wears."

"The Lady and I are betrothed, Sir John," said Brian, with some emphasis on the word "betrothed."

"Oh? I was not aware," said Chandos. "My apologies and felicitations, Sir Brian."

"I am honored by them, Sir John," said Brian. They did not exactly bow to each other; but they somehow reminded Jim of Son Won Phon and Carolinus, after their duel in the amphitheater had been won by Carolinus.

"At any rate, Sir James, the Lady Angela is much better at internal command of a siege than I," went on Chandos, "who, in fact, has had more experience attacking castles than defending them. Moreover, it is your castle and you have abilities that I would not try to match. You are therefore the very man to command."

"Well, I . . ." Jim turned, almost in desperation, to Carolinus. "Carolinus—"

"Don't look at me!" snapped Carolinus. "I'm a magician, not a knight; and I've never had a castle in my life. Besides, as John says, you have what I might call special . . . abilities, to handle this situation."

"I'm glad you think so," said Jim unhappily. He turned to Angie. "How are we fixed for stores and supplies and things like that, m'Lady?"

"We have enough to last us for several months," answered Angie crisply. "Possibly even to feed everyone within our walls, including those who've just come in the last few days, until cold weather. I can't imagine the sea serpents sticking it out that long if they can't get at us."

"Neither can I," said Jim. But he was staring at her in some amazement. "How did we happen to accumulate that much in the way of stored food?"

"*We* didn't," said Angie. "I did; during the times when you were off on some trip or other. I stored all our own harvesting, and bought extra grain and root vegetables to increase what we had. Primarily, I was interested in lasting through the winter without some of our people starving to death. But also, from what Geronde told me, I wanted to be well stocked up in case of something like what's happening now."

"You bought extra?" asked Jim. "Then how are we fixed for—" He quickly searched his mind for words that would convey his meaning to her without betraying it to the fourteenth-century people around him. "—financial reserves?"

"Effectively," said Angie cheerfully, "we don't have any."

"Don't have any!"

"No," said Angie slowly and deliberately, "but we've got what's necessary to feed our people, put a roof over their heads and keep them warm, until next spring. There's other currencies than money. You've got the wherewithal to keep alive a large number of fellow humans, until spring brings fresh crops and fresh food. You're rich, my dear Lord."

"I see," said Jim feebly. "Well, it was wonderfully done, Angie. You always amaze me."

"Somebody has to!" said Angie, but the tartness in her voice faded toward the end; and looking at her, Jim could tell by familiar small signs that she was really not feeling as sharp with him as her words had indicated.

He turned back to the curtain wall and looked over it.

"Well, it's a great relief to know we're that well fixed," he said. "Though I don't know what kind of weapons we can use against attackers like this."

"With luck, look you," said Dafydd unexpectedly, "a clothyard shaft with a broadhead point will kill one; if only it can be fired into its open mouth at the right angle so as to reach back to whatever they have for a brain. I have had some small success that way. But it is a chancy business, particularly firing from above. They must look up, first, or the shaft will not strike home. I doubt if many of our own archers or crossbowmen can do any great damage that way. Aside from that—"

He broke off, looking past Jim out in the field. Jim followed the direction of his eyes. A relatively small-looking, gray, four-legged figure was dodging in and out among the great, green bodies, sometimes leaping up and running right along the back of one of them and jumping to another. Massive jaws snapped viciously at him, but were always a few seconds too late. As the figure approached the castle, it was plain to see that it was a wolf; and that the wolf was Aargh.

As he got closer to the castle, Aargh leaped from one back to another, no longer touching the ground at all; and ended up by running along the back of a serpent at the very edge of the moat opposite the updrawn drawbridge. He leaped from the very tip of the serpent's opened upper jaw into the moat.

He swam across to the few inches of earth at the foot of the curtain wall and called up to Jim and the rest. His speaking voice was not equipped for shouting words; effectively, he howled his request up at them.

"A rope!"

Jim looked around frantically; and was astonished and happy to find a coil of rope not more than two steps from him. He started toward it, but Dafydd already had picked it up, and was letting one end of it down as fast as he could to Aargh.

Aargh seized the end of the rope in his jaws as it reached him; and Dafydd began to haul him up the side of the cliff. Jim and Brian quickly grabbed hold also, lending their strength to the task. Aargh rose rapidly, and a moment later was pulled over the edge of the curtain wall, dropped the rope and leaped down to stand before them, soaked and smelling very badly indeed.

"Aargh!" cried Angie, hugging him, indifferent to the wetness of him and the odor. He licked briefly at her face, wagging his tail.

"Aargh!" echoed Jim. "I didn't think . . . I mean, it didn't occur to me—"

"What you mean is," growled Aargh, "you hadn't taken time to worry about the wolf."

Jim felt ashamed.

"Yes," he said.

"Well, why should you?" said Aargh. "Aargh looks after himself. Then, if he has time, he looks after his friends, too. Right now you're busy looking after yourself. No—"

He licked out at Angie's face again.

"But it's nice to be made much of by your female."

Angie hugged him once more and then let him go.

"I forgive you for that 'female'!" she said to him. "The main thing is that you're in here, now; and safe."

"Am I safe?" asked Aargh.

He looked around at the rest of them, ending with his gaze fixed on Jim.

"I don't know if any of us are," said Jim. "What's it like out there?"

"I stayed out as long as I could," said Aargh. He started to shake himself; then snorted and grinned wickedly at the rest of them. Turning, he walked away along the catwalk for half a dozen feet and shook. Fetid moisture sprayed in every direction, but fell short of the others. Then he stalked back to them.

"What's it like?" he echoed. "What it's like, is that these invaders have cleared out everything living; from the sea to

here and east and west as well. Anything eatable's been eaten—
for as far as I searched. Those green monsters will feed on
anything. I saw one push a tree over so it could reach and eat
a squirrel's nest with the squirrels in it. I saw another seeming
to eat earth; until I realized he was after a mole, underground
there—which he got."

"But you," said Angie. "How did you survive?"

"I?" said Aargh. "By being fast. There were too many of
them to hide from—even for me to hide from. And I cannot
kill them quickly. Their vital parts are too deep in those thick
bodies for my teeth to reach. The only way I can slay one is
by bleeding him to death. And that I'll be able to do best in the
narrow corridors and rooms of this self-made cave of yours you
call a castle. They'll kill me, but I'll take some with me; even
though they do their dying after I'm already dead."

"Did you see anyone who seemed to be their leader among
them?" asked Jim anxiously.

"Leader?" Aargh was interestedly sniffing at his own right
flank. "—All sorts of interesting things in that waterway of
yours down there—"

"We know," snapped Carolinus.

"No," said Aargh, "I didn't see any leader."

"If they're all here because they're concentrating on me,"
said Jim, "Essessili must be among them someplace—"

Rrrnlf's head came up.

"Essessili?" he said. "Where?"

He was on his feet before any of the rest of them could
respond.

"Still!" cried Jim, jabbing his finger at him.

But Rrrnlf already had his hand on the curtain wall, preparatory to leaping over it.

"Carolinus!" cried Jim, turning to the older magician.

But Carolinus already had his finger extended; and his voice
was echoing Jim's.

"*Still!*" he said.

Rrrnlf froze in position, his body turned toward the curtain
wall, his head looking out over the open area with the green
bodies and his hand on the curtain wall.

"Rrrnlf, wait!" shouted Jim. Rrrnlf did not move, and Jim
turned to Carolinus.

"Let him turn his head and speak, at least."

Carolinus gave a small twitch of his fingers. Rrrnlf turned his head on an otherwise motionless body to glare down at Jim and the others.

"Essessili's out there!" he snarled. "What do you hold me for?"

"Are you sure he's out there?" asked Jim. "Can you recognize him among all these others?"

Rrrnlf turned his head to look out over the curtain wall again. The sight of him had caused the shrill voices of the serpents to raise in volume. The Sea Devil stared for a long moment, then cried out on a note of exaltation.

"There he is!" he said. "And—"

He broke off, his head suddenly as still as his body. Then he threw it back in what was an ear-numbing howl of pain and despair.

"HE HAS NOT GOT HER!" he roared, like some enormous lion in deep torment.

So powerful and unexpected was that great, agonized cry that suddenly there was silence everywhere; silence within the castle and silence among all the serpents without. So quiet was it that a breeze could be heard faintly moving the branches of the trees beyond the open space.

Rrrnlf's head sagged. Then he turned it back suddenly to Jim.

"He's hidden her somewhere. Let me go! Let me go so I can make him tell me where he hid her!"

"*Still!*" snapped Carolinus once more, and Rrrnlf remained unmoving, his mouth opened as if he was still speaking. "He never had her. If he did I'd know it; but there's no trace on him. He has never touched your Lady!"

"Let him speak, Carolinus!" begged Angie.

Carolinus twiddled his fingers again, and once more Rrrnlf's face turned toward the humans on the platform, his eyes seeking out Carolinus.

"I don't believe it! He must have!" he said brokenly. "How can you be sure?"

"I feel it!" said Carolinus. "And if I feel it, Sea Devil, you had best listen to me!"

"Rrrnlf," said Jim, in calmer tones, "if we release you from the command that holds you from moving, will you sit down again? You see what's out there. Even if he had your Lady, the chances are you couldn't reach Essessili. Not even you can take on thousands of these sea serpents at once. Stay with us and you may get her back. Go after Essessili now and you'll be the one torn apart; and you'll lose all chance of ever seeing her again."

He waited a moment for this message to sink in, then Rrrnlf slowly nodded his head.

"All right . . . for a while," the giant said. "I'll wait. But I'd better get her in the long run or else anything that stands in my way is going to be slain, until I'm dead myself."

Jim looked at Carolinus; who nodded, twiddled his fingers and Rrrnlf's body moved as a whole. Slowly he sat down again, his head bent and his face staring at the ground between his knees. It was almost as if he had never moved.

"There are many questions we have to answer here," Jim said, still trying to console the giant. "But I think we'll answer them in the end, and one of them will give your Lady back to you—"

"But not immediately!" Dafydd's voice cut in on him. "Now it seems that those serpents have finally decided on a way to attack us. The moat has been holding them back because of being fresh water. But now they move about; and some of them have gone off into the woods. Nor is it that I think they are giving up their attempt to get at us, look you."

Jim looked and Dafydd was right.

"I wonder what it is about fresh water—" He broke off and turned to Angie. "Angie, you had a salt water aquarium in your apartment at Riveroak before we were married. Do you know why salt water creatures don't like fresh water?"

"It's not a matter of liking," said Angie. "It's an actual physiological reaction that can be very uncomfortable for them. In fact, it can kill them. Their body cells are loaded with salt, not like ours, and haven't the ability to keep out fresh water that comes flooding into the cells, as ours can. The result is, cells keep getting filled with fresh water until they actually burst. If you lived in the sea originally, it'd be a rather horrible end for you to be put in fresh water; and even a brief plunge into it, like into our moat or a stream, would be very uncomfortable."

"Hmm," said Jim. He remembered how the serpents coming ashore had avoided the fresh water streams running into the sea along the shore front. "Well, so the moat's been holding them off until now. But do any of you have any idea of what they'd have gone for in the woods?"

"If they were men and soldiers—like us," said Chandos, "they'd have gone to build a portable bridge, or, more likely, fascines to fill the moat."

Fascines, Jim knew, were bundles of sticks used to fill any ditch that stood in the way of an invading army.

"Indeed!" said Brian. "We would do that. But since they are sea serpents only, would they think of fascines? Surely not."

"Portable bridges, certainly," said Jim. "Fascines, now—that might just occur to them. Something, anyway, to fill up the moat so that they can get at the gate. They must know that, even barred, with its portcullis down and the drawbridge up, it's still the weakest part of our defense."

"Here comes one now," put in Dafydd, "dragging something large. I can still not see what it is, though."

Jim found himself wishing for his dragon-sight. He wheeled on the mere-dragon.

"Secoh," he said, "what do you see? What's that serpent dragging?"

"Why, it seems to be a whole tree, m'Lord," said Secoh. "He is dragging it by the roots, and the stem and the branches are trailing behind. Also, here comes another one with another tree. The trees are not very large."

"Large enough, probably," said Jim grimly, "if they keep bringing them. Let's see if they do what we expect and try filling the moat before the gate."

Down in the open area, the other serpents were opening up lanes in their numbers, through which serpents emerging from the forest could drag their trees. Sure enough, they headed directly for the moat in front of the castle gates.

Dafydd put several arrows into the first one to get close. But he failed to make the vital shot through the mouth into the brain, in spite of the superb archer and marksman he was.

The serpents' eyes were hooded by the ridges of a bony skull that could evidently deflect an arrow. One arrow did stick in the skull of a serpent, but the serpent ignored it. It reached the edge of the moat; and with the help of other serpents pushed the tree, top first, into the moat.

Close behind it was the second serpent and behind it, a long line of other serpents dragging trees.

The moat was not more than eight feet deep, anywhere. Clearly, it would not take them long to fill up the space before it. Then they would be able to reach the underside of the portcullis. Even if they did not go on building until they could get to the top of it, and use their great strength to snap the chains that held it, and battle their way through the portcullis to the gate itself.

CHAPTER 36

Jim leaned over the top of the curtain wall just above the archway containing the two great wings of the main gate, with its portcullis and drawbridge. There was a cold, crawling sensation in the region of his stomach.

"There's got to be an answer to this," he said. "It seems to me I remember—"

"There is," said Chandos, "but I'm sure your Lady-wife can tell it to you as well as I can."

"Certainly!" said Angie crisply. "Let them fill it up until they're well up on the drawbridge; but not high enough to reach the top of it and use their weight to pull it loose from its chains or break the chains. They'll want it high, anyway, to make sure they don't get their feet wet. Also, they won't feel secure in that until they've got enough wood piled up and pounded down into the mud until it doesn't float; and does stick up at least half a dozen feet above any water."

"And then what?" asked Jim.

"And then we use this," said Angie, slapping the round metallic side of the deep, iron pot on its pivot beside them, which clearly had the capacity for at least a barrel of liquid. It was suspended from two points high on the rack that supported it above a wide fire-pot; so it could be tilted to empty its contents downward. "I've been saving my rancid oil for some emergency like this. We'll start putting it in the pot right now, and heat it up as fast as we can."

She pointed to the firepit underneath the pot, placed there for that exact purpose of heating.

"Then," she went on, "when they've built as high as it's safe for us to let them, we pour it over on them. Then we toss blazing torches down."

"What if the oil doesn't catch fire?" Jim asked uneasily.

"If it's heated sufficiently," said Chandos, "it will start fire—and very suddenly. Colder, it will still probably catch fire; and the trees, catching fire beneath it, will help; but it will not blaze up so quickly."

"And it should end with several of those serpents nicely singed," said Angie, with a bloodthirsty relish of which Jim would not have thought her capable. "But, mainly, we'll have destroyed their causeway."

"Excellent!" said Jim. The cold feeling had left him to a small degree. Then a worrying thought occurred to him. "But how much oil have you? If they fill the moat and try it again, and keep that up—"

"They won't try twice," said Carolinus. "At least, in all likelihood they won't try twice. How are they to know you don't have an ocean of oil; and can keep pouring it, and setting fire to it, indefinitely?"

"I hope you're right," said Jim.

He wheeled about and shouted down into the crowded courtyard below.

"Ho! A man-at-arms or a servant here, immediately!"

It was only seconds until a gasping man-at-arms had reached the top of the steps and was standing before them. Jim was about to speak, but Angie was faster.

"Fetch enough men," she ordered him, "then go to the castle cook and have her point you out the barrel of rancid oil we've been saving. Take as many men as you need to bring it here. Then start filling it into this pot beside me. You understand?"

The man-at-arms nodded, too breathless to speak. He turned about, ran down the steps again and was lost in the crowd.

Within ten minutes the barrel was being rolled up the stone steps to the walkway by four men pulling on a rope that had been tied and rolled around the barrel before its ascent started. Another half-dozen pushed from below. The lower group gazed fearfully at the rope, in case it should break and let the barrel roll over them on its way toward the ground. But it did not. Another fifteen minutes saw the pot filled and the fire blazing merrily beneath it.

By that time the serpents had got a number of trees into the water. At first, these tried to float away; but the following ones, piling so rapidly on top of them, forced down the earlier ones until at last they were mounded up well above the level of liquid. The water that had formerly occupied the space where they now were was now pushed off to the right and left in the moat itself, and some of the serpents were gingerly trying their weight on the causeway.

Their great weights pushed the trees down farther to the soft silt and mud at the moat's bottom; and compacted them into a mass, until they had become a thoroughly firm platform, still several feet above the level of the moat; and wide enough so that three or four of the sea creatures could be on it at the same time, without any danger from the unsalted water.

Above them, Jim was in a fever of impatience. The fire had been blazing away merrily, but the oil had been stored in a cool part of the interior of the castle; and it was even now not too hot for his testing fingers to endure, when he stuck them into it.

Meanwhile, the fire below had the pot itself almost red-hot on the bottom.

Jim abandoned the pot to its heating and looked again over the edge of the curtain wall. There were three serpents on the causeway they had built; and, as he watched, one of them tried to stand up against the underside of the drawbridge, using the soles of his front feet against its surface to support him.

But he was only able to achieve an angle of about twenty degrees. The tips of his great jaws were still eight to ten feet below the edge of the drawbridge itself. He dropped down on all four feet again; and, with his two companions, retreated to let the line of serpents still dragging in trees add more height to the causeway.

Shortly, the oil in the pot was so warm that Jim did not want to risk putting his fingers any farther than close to its surface.

"Hot enough, Sir John?" he asked, turning to Chandos.

Chandos also held his hand out over the oil, standing as far away from the pot as he could because both the fire in the fire-pot and the pot itself radiated a fierce heat.

"I think so," said Chandos. "In any case, it would be unwise to wait much longer. The new trees are adding all their bulk to the height of the causeway. Also, at any moment, the serpents may think of climbing on top of each other to get closer to the edge of the drawbridge. If one of them can take hold of the edge of the drawbridge with his jaws and hang all his weight on it, I fear me both your chains keeping it upright at short draw, as they now do, will break."

"But we don't want to take any chances on the trees not catching fire," said Jim anxiously.

"I do not fear that," said Chandos. "I've seen oil cooler than that take flame, if the torches are well afire, well coated with pitch and tightly bound. The smaller branches will catch quickly."

Jim glanced at Angie, who nodded. He swung back to the servants who had been keeping the fire going. There were six of them on the platform, and room for a few more if necessary.

"All right," said Jim. "Dump the oil on them!"

The men looked at him and hesitated. One or two made tentative movements toward the heated metal of the pot, but most stood still.

"You idiots!" snarled Jim. "Use poles! What do you suppose those ears there, with the sockets in them, are for?"

The "ears" he referred to were a couple of metal extensions from the top rim of the pot on either side. They had holes in them to a depth of perhaps four inches, which was perhaps half the thickness of the extensions themselves. Jim almost never lost his temper with the servants. His doing so now, as the result of the pent-up nervousness in him, made the men glance fearfully at him, then hurry down the steps. He might forget, but they never did, that he had the legal right to hang them, or worse, if he simply took the whim to do so.

They were back in moments, with a pair of quarterstaff staves.

There was a further delay while Jim fumed and the ends of the quarterstaves were whittled down to fit in the holes. To Jim, the men working with their knives seemed to take half an hour to do it. In all probability it was less than another five minutes.

Meanwhile, he had looked over the curtain wall again. The serpent currently trying to reach the top edge of the pulled-up drawbridge was now bringing his jaws to only four feet below it.

"Ready!" Angie sang out behind him. Jim spun about just in time to see the poles inserted and the men throw their weight on them.

For a moment it seemed that the pot would not tilt. It had probably not been moved out of the vertical position for some years; during which it had sat in the rain and air, rusting in position. Then the top creaked. It canted forward a little, then a little more—then, with a sudden movement that had the first two men on the poles falling forward almost into the still-blazing fire-pot, it went full over. The heated oil cascaded on to the causeway and those serpents currently on it.

Brian let out a shout of delight.

"They like that little!" he shouted. "They're tangled all together, trying to turn fast and leave the causeway without falling into the moat!"

"The torches!" shouted Jim. "Haven't you men got them lit yet? Light them, then!"

"Yes, by all means light them," said Chandos, in an unruffled voice. "But do not throw them down until all those now leaving have either been replaced by others on the causeway, or come back themselves. They will soon find out that the oil alone, though unpleasant to them, does them no real harm. The aim is to teach them a real lesson; and the way to do that is to set the causeway and several of them alight at the same time."

"The oil may have all drained down by the time they come back," said Jim doubtfully.

"Fear not," said Chandos. "There will be enough still coating the dry wood on top to cause it to flame up immediately and that will set fire to the rest. Wait and see."

They did wait. And, true to Chandos's prediction, after about fifteen more minutes, the serpents ventured back onto the causeway, finding it a little slippery underfoot, but not otherwise altered.

They began to cross over tentatively, then finished with a rush; and others crowded behind them until there were a good six serpents on the causeway—which was really too many. Jim, and everyone else now up there watching with him over the wall, saw one of the serpents in front trying to climb on the one who had put himself against the base of the drawbridge.

Having the other serpent's back to stand on lifted the climbing serpent by a good four feet. But this time, as he opened his jaws, he was at the proper angle for Dafydd's bow. There was the twang of a bowstring, the flash of an arrow disappearing between his jaws; and this time, clearly, the arrow went to the killing spot it was aimed at.

Jim had expected the serpent to thrash around to a certain extent before dying. Instead, he simply fell back from the wall like a tree just chopped down, landed with a thump on the serpents below, and lay still.

There was a certain amount of consternation amongst the others. They pushed the dead body off into the moat, where it floated.

A couple more of the serpents rushed forward over the backs of those already on the causeway and began to try climbing the underside of the drawbridge, this time prudently keeping their jaws shut.

Dafydd drove several arrows into both of them, but he might as well have been throwing darts into a piece of wood, for all the reaction he produced.

"All right!" shouted Jim, seeing the torches were blazing strongly by this time. "Throw the fire down at them!"

The men holding the torches lobbed them over the edge of the curtain wall. Jim stood where he was, at a reasonable distance from the hot pot. With Brian, Giles, Dafydd, Sir John and Angie, he peered over the wall to see the results.

Jim had been wrong in the case of the serpent who had been slain by Dafydd's arrow. He found himself equally wrong in what he had expected would happen when the torches hit the oil-covered wood. He had expected a slow catching of fire, during which time the serpents on the causeway would have time to withdraw.

No such thing happened. There was a sudden explosion of flame and smoke, as apparently a certain amount of vapor from the hot oil caught fire first; and a second later Jim had hastily turned his back on the wall, with everyone else—as not only the causeway, but the serpents upon it, were suddenly encased in flames.

Shrill screams came from beyond the wall. Jim and Angie deliberately tried to shut them out. Jim found Angie's hand going into his. He held and squeezed it. Everybody else on the catwalk and on the platform had happily run to a section of the wall well away from the heat; and was eagerly leaning over to watch the spectacle.

"By the Seven Saints!" Chandos's voice came. "Will you see that one fellow! He's rolling over and over on the dirt beyond the moat, as if to put out his fire. He looks like a log come to life in a fireplace!"

The others cheerfully chimed in with comments.

"I feel sick," said Angie in a low voice to Jim. She had let go of his hand, stuck her fingers in her ears, and closed her eyes. "Jim, lead me down the stairs and away from here."

Jim led her by the elbow and they were halfway down the stairs before she suddenly stopped, took her fingers out of her ears and opened her eyes.

"What am I doing?" she said. "Is this the way the fourteenth-century chatelaine of a castle would act because she repelled attackers on her castle with fire? Let me go, Jim."

Jim let her go. She turned around and went back up the stairs. He followed her. To tell the truth, he had been rather glad of an excuse to leave the wall himself, at that moment. But now that Angie was returning he felt under an obligation not unlike hers.

If she felt she had to go back and face what was happening to the serpents who had been caught in the fire he, a knight, could hardly do less. In fact, by turning his back to the wall, even with Angie for an excuse, he had probably lowered himself in the opinion of his friends and companions. He and she went back up; and both of them deliberately looked over the wall, rejoining the others there.

What was left of two of the serpents was still on the causeway. Three more lay black and unmoving beyond the moat. The other serpents on the far side had pulled back from the terrific heat; just as the humans and Secoh, on the wall above, were already moved off to right and left along the catwalk. They all watched the fire burn down. There was a sudden thunderous crash as the half-burned drawbridge fell on top of the dead serpents.

"Usually lose a drawbridge when you use fire," commented Chandos, so philosophically that Jim glared at the senior knight—a glare that Chandos happily did not see.

"Well, well," said Brian with equal philosophy, to Jim. "You've still the portcullis; and the gates are only singed a bit."

He raised his eyebrows inquiringly.

"Actually," Brian went on, "right now would be a moment to sally, wouldn't it?"

"Go out against several thousand sea serpents?" said Jim. He knew Brian loved fighting, but this was ridiculous.

"Yes. Not the usual enemy, here," said Chandos judiciously. "I think wiser not, gentlemen."

"Ah, well, just a thought," said Brian. "I'd been thinking—a quick sally to slash a few throats, then back through the gates and close them behind us. But—as you think, Sir John, and you, m'Lord."

"Yes," said Jim.

Below them, the flames had now dropped to a flickering above the black mass. It had now burned down enough that water from the moat had been able to flood in over it to the depth of perhaps six inches. The moat water had not completely taken the place of the causeway, because there was a sufficiency of unburned lumber a little below the surface, packed so tightly with mud and the weight of the serpents upon it earlier that it still remained a potential causeway between land and castle.

"The only question," said Jim, "is what they can try now."

"It's important that the portcullis survived; though those iron bars of it must still be pretty hot," said Angie.

Jim moved closer to the wall, to a point where he could stand and look directly down. Even now, leaning over the wall, Jim felt a fierce heat striking up into his face from below.

"The important question is," he said to himself, but also out loud to the rest, "whether they're going to try to rebuild that causeway."

The others had come to join him where he stood above the gateway, looking over the edge of the wall briefly, and then backing away from the heat that was still coming up. Curiously, before anyone else could speak, he was conscious of something very large looming over him.

Looking up, he saw Rrrnlf was on his feet and beside them. The Sea Devil had probably been there, for some time, watching the burning serpents, with the same amount of interest as the medieval humans on either side of him.

Jim felt a pulse of encouragement at the giant's sudden awakening of interest in the siege.

"What do you think, Rrrnlf?" he asked, looking up at the Sea Devil. "Will they try to rebuild it?"

"Perhaps. Perhaps not," answered Rrrnlf. "How can they know but what you can burn as many trees as they can put in the water there to build a way to your gate? But I tell you,

wee Mage, wee knight—or whatever you are at the moment—
I know no more than you what they are likely to do next."

"This is not rocky country," put in Brian, "but there are
boulders, here and there, even if part-buried in the soil. I think
they would have little trouble prying them out. They could try
building up the causeway again, this time with stones, which
will not burn."

"Oil would coat them and burn; and it would coat on the
water beneath and burn," said Chandos.

"Still, I was thinking we might have a chance to discourage
them," said Brian. "When they first approach with the stones,
which they would probably have difficulty ferrying on their
heads or their backs or in their mouths or however, we could
make that sally I suggested earlier and see if we could not kill
a few of them, thereby discouraging the rest. Think you not?"

"The question's moot," said Angie's crisp voice. "There's
not enough oil left to begin to make a worthwhile amount to
dump. We used it nearly all up in that first pour."

It seemed to Jim the time had come to play their last card.
If the serpents had been able to think of building a causeway
with trees, they certainly—almost inevitably—would think of
rebuilding it with other stuff that would not burn. They might
well believe it was the trees that caused such a fierce fire, rather
than the oil that had poured down on them earlier; and which
had seemed to have no particularly real deterrent effect.

He turned to Secoh.

"Secoh," he said.

"Yes, m'Lord?"

"Get one of your messengers down here, right away. I want
to start moving the English dragons into the northern half of
the sky as quickly as possible. Oh—and, come to think of it,
you better have another messenger standing by you, ready to
leave the moment I want to give the word to the French also to
move in."

"They draw off," said Brian, looking out at the serpents.
"Now, why is that?"

None of the others around him had any kind of an answer.
They all stood and watched as the serpents pulled back toward
the edge of the woods, where they packed very tightly almost
directly in line with the gate and only a few yards out from the
woods itself. Then a space appeared at a point in the midst of
them, and one serpent was seen alone. He was held on the backs

of three other serpents, crossways, so that he was above the rest
and they could all see him clearly.

He was talking to them. At the curtain wall, they could hear
his voice; but now he was far enough off so what with his
shrillness of tone and the distance it was impossible to make
out his words.

"That's Essessili," growled Rrrnlf, pointing out in the general direction of the one serpent that was standing on the others.

"You mean, the one who's talking?" said Jim.

"Yes," said Rrrnlf. "He is speaking to all of them."

"What's he saying?"

Rrrnlf shook his head. "I can't hear."

"He's saying," offered Secoh, "they must all assault the castle together, regardless of losses."

He broke off and began reciting what was evidently word-
for-word what Essessili was saying right now.

" '*You might not want to push a brother serpent ahead of you
into the fresh water of that moat,*' " he repeated, " '*but if it is
for the good of all, you must remember that some have to be
sacrificed and shoved in.*' "

"That's Essessili!" muttered Rrrnlf. "None of them want to
be shoved in, but none would hesitate to shove in another. A
clever way to put it, and just like him!"

After a brief pause, he added a few more words.

"It still makes me to wonder, though," the Sea Devil went
on. "The serpents are not usually to be talked into anything at
all by another serpent. Rather, their way is to deny and dispute
whatever another serpent says. It is a marvel they listen so."

"No marvel," muttered Carolinus. "Magic. Whatever magic's been behind this all the way through is helping your
Essessili right now."

"My Essessili. Yes," said Rrrnlf, flexing his huge fingers.
"My Essessili. I shall yet get him in these two hands."

Jim continued to listen to what was evidently a rabble-
rousing speech by Essessili, as repeated and reported by
Secoh, and looked anxiously skyward. He was worried that
a messenger had not shown up before this, one he could send
to ask the English dragons to move into sky position overhead.
He interrupted Secoh.

"Where's the messenger we're going to send to the English
dragons?" he demanded. "Whoever he or she is ought to be here
by this time!"

"Oh, I didn't need to call in someone to send that message," Secoh said. "I had a messenger overhead simply waiting for me to extend my wings like this."

His spread his wings while still on the ground, then put them back at his side.

"As soon as he saw that he took off with the prearranged message, m'Lord." Secoh looked appeasingly at Jim. "That was all right, wasn't it?"

"That was excellent," said Jim.

Nonetheless, he continued to scan the sky. He was afraid Essessili would not continue talking long; and it would take time for all those English dragons to move into position in the sky above them.

CHAPTER 37

I t took some fifteen minutes, during which Essessili continued with his speech to his fellow serpents and Jim waited impatiently; but by then the first few mature dragons had begun to show themselves at some altitude overhead, soaring in tight circles. They were quickly joined by others, some at different altitudes as airspace around the first arrivals became crowded. But gradually the northern sky filled; and, as Essessili talked on, they increased until their presence overhead was considerable.

Jim was beginning to relax, but only slightly. The appearance of the first dragons had already begun to make him feel more certain that nearly the full complement of British ones, at least, would be showing up—something he had been by no means sure of until now.

Meanwhile, however, even the enlarged platform around the hot oil pot was becoming definitely crowded. This, even though most of the servants had prudently retreated at least partway down the stairs or along the catwalk, with their eyes warily upon the—not one, but two—young dragons, who had joined Secoh on the platform and were now the prime cause of the crowding.

Secoh had evidently decided he needed an extra messenger for unexpected orders; and, on second thought, Jim was glad the mere-dragon had. Anything could happen. He should have thought of that extra messenger, himself.

Meanwhile, the young dragons were staring with wide and fascinated eyes at Jim and the others. They had never been this close to georges in their life. This one experience would be enough to give them stories to tell the other dragons, once they got back to their Cliffside home. Dragons nowadays had very little to do with georges. Once upon a time, in the past, of course, they had preyed upon humans as on any other eatable animal.

But then it began to turn out that georges could be dangerous prey to go after; and when, eventually, some georges began coating themselves completely in armor it became clear that the largest and stoutest-hearted dragon was taking his life in his hands by attacking one.

So the dragons had come to leave georges severely alone; and to keeping out of their sight as much as possible.

So the young dragons' presence here was exciting to them, as well as reassuring to Jim. Just as the increasing number of British dragons filling the north sky was also reassuring. Jim had been afraid Essessili would finish his speech before the dragons were all gathered. But the leader of the serpents talked on; perhaps he liked the sound of his own voice. The rest of them seemed content to listen, also entirely unobservant of the dragons gathering over their heads.

Still, when a fair amount of time had gone by and the British dragons had increased to the point where they cast a shadow over the castle and the north part of the cleared area—though Essessili with his serpents were still in sunshine—Jim decided that there was no point in taking further chances. He turned to Secoh.

"Secoh," he said, "what's Essessili been saying now—I mean for the last half-dozen minutes or so?"

"He just keeps saying the same thing over and over again," said Secoh. "He says they've all got to throw themselves at the castle wall here until some part of it goes down and they can get inside. He says it different ways, each time, but it's all the same thing, over and over again. That's all, m'Lord."

"I think we better call in the French dragons. He may stop talking any minute," Jim said, "and then we'll only have the time it takes the serpents to charge across the open space at us here. Oh-oh—"

He had still been in the process of saying this, when Essessili had suddenly broken off.

"Call in the French dragons, quick!" shouted Jim to Secoh. But then, Essessili began speaking again.

"I already have, m'Lord," said Secoh, and indeed, there was only one of the young dragon messengers left on the platform.

"I may have waited too long!" said Jim, between his teeth. "If Essessili stops and they attack, we'll just have to do the best we can to hold them off until they get here."

He turned to Dafydd.

"Dafydd!" he called. "Have you told the other archers and crossbowmen how to shoot down into the serpents' throats?"

"I have," said Dafydd.

He waved a hand right and left; and Jim saw that indeed all the bowmen and crossbowmen of the castle were now stationed on the catwalk around the wall, as far as he could see. Either way, before his view was cut off by the buildings of the castle itself, they were standing ready. Dafydd was only twenty feet from him on the catwalk, and holding a cow's horn that had been fitted with a sounding nipple.

"I'll give them a horn blast to tell them when to start shooting." Dafydd raised his voice to speak to Jim. "But I doubt they'll need it. When the serpents get close it'll be plain when to start shooting. Can you get some spearmen up here to help fill the empty spaces on the wall between them? It may be a spear shoved down the serpent's throat will also slay."

"Of course!" said Jim. "I should have thought of that, too."

"Too?" Dafydd raised his eyebrows.

But Jim ignored the question. He raised his voice.

"Theoluf!" he shouted to the courtyard below. "Somebody get my squire!"

"I'm right here, m'Lord," answered the voice of Theoluf.

Theoluf had evidently been waiting at the foot of the stairs. He was wearing most of a full suit of armor like the knights'. He should have been matching them exactly in this department, except that it took time to gather a full suit of armor from the various people who made or sold it; and also time to raise the money to buy it.

Jim had given him the strongest horse in their stable, after Gorp, and advanced him a certain amount of cash; but theoretically, the squire was supposed to supply his own armor and horse. Most squires had relatives or influential friends to help

bear the expense. But a former chief man-at-arms was unlikely
to be that lucky.

He was a man in his mid-thirties, of middling height and with
a face badly disfigured by scars of some form of pox. He was
wiry rather than solid, with short black hair; and he had dark
eyes in a v-shaped face. Now, he ran lightly up the stone
stairway to the catwalk and crossed to the platform, speaking
as soon as he arrived, without any apparent breathlessness
whatsoever.

"What do you wish, m'Lord?"

"Did you hear Dafydd just now?" Jim asked.

"Yes, m'Lord."

"Well, get the men-at-arms together with the longest spears
they can find; and have Dafydd tell them how to use them. You
take care of it. You understand?"

"Yes, m'Lord."

Theoluf turned and ran along the catwalk to Dafydd, spoke
for a few moments; then the two of them hurried down to the
courtyard.

Jim turned his attention back to the sky.

Surely, all or nearly all of the available British dragons must
be up there right now, although they were soaring in tight circles at different altitudes; for the airspace at any certain altitude
quickly got filled up, if they wanted to stay close to and above
the castle.

Jim looked out into the southern sky and saw a few forms that
must be their French dragons, messengers or possible allies,
appearing above the trees in that direction—just a few.

"They'll never get here in time!" he told himself, feeling
empty inside.

However, surprisingly, Essessili continued to talk; and slowly, but undeniably, more dragons appeared in the southern part
of the sky. They appeared in a more orderly fashion than
the British dragons; possibly because they had been waiting,
ready in formation, just out of sight beyond the tree-top
horizon.

Jim suddenly realized that he was no longer hearing
Essessili. He looked quickly out toward the serpents, and
saw them swarming toward the castle. The thunder of their
heavy feet, at first inaudible, was building.

"Ah!" said Brian beside him, happily. "They come!"

But, surprisingly, as they watched, the first ranks of the charging serpents began to slow. Swiftly, the charge was coming almost to a halt.

In fact, it had not halted. But it was moving forward only because of pressure from the serpents in the rear ranks. In front was a mound of serpents, three or four deep, who were desperately trying to crawl rearward over the backs of those behind them, but were being stopped in that attempt and pushed forward in spite of themselves.

"What's going on?" said Jim out loud, without thinking.

"What do you expect?" growled Rrrnlf, above his head. "I told you Essessili was being clever when he talked to them about pushing other serpents into the fresh water. Those in front don't want to be shoved in; and those behind don't want to let those in front get away from being there."

Jim sighed with relief. It was ridiculous; but the delay was welcome. He looked again into the southern sky and saw that the space was finally filling very nicely with dragons. He realized suddenly that he had not told either side how close they should approach each other in mid-air. He had just assumed they would come close enough so that they would appear to be a single covering group.

Mentally, he crossed his fingers now and prayed that, in spite of a certain amount of ancient antagonism between the dragons of the two countries, they might still approach each other close enough to seem a single force.

He looked again at the field. There was no doubt the serpents were approaching. But it was still at about the speed of a bull-dozer that had all its blade could push before it.

There were five or six ranks deep of serpents, now, fighting to get to the back; while all those behind them tried to push forward.

Now, as he watched, the shadow over the castle began to be matched by one forming over the struggling serpents; as the French dragons above them began to block out the sunlight.

It was an eerie sort of light that resulted. The French dragons were directly occulting the summer sun, and the twilight resulting was like that in a total solar eclipse. There were worried murmurings in the courtyard behind Jim. The serpents appeared not to notice.

"The people don't like this," said Angie, beside him.

"I know," snapped Jim, "but there's nothing I can tell them that would help now."

He looked back over the wall. The serpents were getting very close. They were probably only about thirty yards from the edge of the moat.

"What's wrong with them?" he said irritably. "Those serpents aren't paying any attention at all to the dragons overhead!"

"M'Lord," put in Secoh, almost timidly, "remember? They don't look up."

Jim suddenly felt like an idiot. Of course! It was not physically easy for serpents to raise their eyes, and in the sea they probably didn't, ordinarily.

He had a sudden inspiration; and turned to Secoh.

"Send your messengers up," he said, "to both our own dragons and the French ones. Tell them to roar!"

" '*Roar*,' m'Lord?" Secoh blinked at him.

"Shout! Bellow! All together. Any word you want to use for it! I want them to use their voices and make a lot of noise. Can you tell them that?"

A light of understanding woke in Secoh's eyes. A light of glee.

"Yes, m'Lord!"

He spun about to speak to the one young dragon next to him.

"You heard Sir Dragon! You tell our dragons and I'll go tell the French. Hurry!"

They both took off with a loud flapping of wings and separately rose swiftly toward the two gatherings of dragons above.

But, at the same time, Jim heard the shrill screams of the first of the serpents in front—those who were being forced into the fresh water of the moat.

Within minutes, all of those manning the wall had no time to think of anything but fighting, because the moat had been quickly filled with the bodies of the unfortunate serpents leading and those behind were piling on top of them, until the topmost were high enough to push their gaping, multitoothed mouths above the edge of the curtain wall—to be met by the spears and arrows of those humans that were there—as Dafydd's horn sounded unnecessarily, but clearly, through the tumult.

Then, drowning out all other sounds, the dragons above them—both British and French—began to roar.

CHAPTER 38

It built from a few individual voices to a thunder that shook the air and earth beneath it. Dragons had powerful voices; and these now drowned out the screaming of the serpents and all other sounds.

—More. For the first time, joined in that tremendous chorus, the dragons felt their united strength. Jim could see their dark numbers lowering like a blanket of promised death, above the green bodies below; and Jim himself felt the battle fury in them gathering like a solid increase in air pressure.

Oh, no, thought Jim. Not now, he prayed, not yet—let them not attack yet!

For a moment humans and serpents alike stood, motionless, staring upward. For the first time the serpents woke to the eerie twilight, the sky filled from horizon to horizon with their ancient enemies. For a moment no one moved, man or serpent.

Then, one serpent turned, then another—and after that, breaking away from their attack, the others followed. They tumbled over backward to get away from the castle. In moments, the whole green horde was running as fast as their short legs would take them, toward the distant tree line and the forest beyond.

As they retreated, the ones who had been farthest back, but now led the way, vanished among the trees. The rest were starting in after them, as the dragon voices, one by one began to cease; and the powerful chorus dwindled and stopped.

With it finally began to die the voices of those in the castle; who had also been shouting without realizing it.

Silence fell.

But the eerie half-light continued.

It illuminated one green individual, left behind by the other serpents halfway between castle and woods. He had reared up the front part of his body, lifting his front legs off the ground, and had his mouth open toward those running.

As silence came, his screaming could finally be heard at the curtain wall. He was close enough so that they should have been able to understand him, but Jim found he could not; partly because of the shrillness of the voice, but also because of words he seemed never to have heard before.

He turned to ask Secoh to tell him what was being said; then remembered he had left with the younger dragon, to carry the message for the dragons to roar.

"Ha!" said the voice of Rrrnlf unexpectedly in his ear. "It's Essessili. Now he says what he thinks of them!"

"I can't understand him," said Jim.

"He's using a lot of deep-sea terms," said Rrrnlf grimly. "But I agree with every one of them. If I had him in my hands now I'd let him live long enough to keep on saying them as long as he had wit to think of more to say!"

"But I mean," Jim said to the Sea Devil, "what's he telling them?"

"Telling?" echoed Rrrnlf, looking at him in some surprise. "He's simply trying to shame them into coming back and fighting. Of course, it won't work."

Rrrnlf should know. But at the same time Jim saw that Essessili was evidently having a certain amount of effect. At least the serpents had stopped their mad rush into the trees; and they were coming out again to form a circle around him. Shortly, he was mounted once more on the backs of three others, orating to them.

Now Rrrnlf was laughing. Jim stared at him.

"Now," said Rrrnlf, "he's asking them if they're serpents, or *starfish*."

"Starfish?" echoed Jim.

"Of course!" said Rrrnlf. "Would you want to be called a *starfish*?"

"Well . . ." Jim ran out of words; at a loss to explain how he himself saw nothing particularly insulting in being called a starfish.

"Of course," went on Rrrnlf, "it won't do any good. You can't shame serpents into anything. None of them have any sense of shame."

"No sense of shame?" said Brian incredulously, finally breaking off his own shouting. He had been yelling "*A sally! A sally!*" at the top of his voice. "None?"

"Of course not," said Rrrnlf. "What they're interested in is what's going to happen in their own lifetime and how they can have the best of it while they're alive. There's nothing they want to die for."

Brian looked shocked. Then his face became grim. He turned to his fellow knights, including Jim.

"Then let us thank God, gentlemen," he said, "that we have Him, England, and our arms, for any of which each of us would die, rather than bear one spot of shame on them!"

Jim found himself oddly moved. He did not doubt Brian for a minute. By "arms," he knew Brian was referring to the coat of arms each of them possessed; which also stood for their personal and family honor, and for all else that in Brian's and the others' minds made up their concept of a knight and gentleman.

Jim could not honestly join them in saying these were things that he also would die for. He wondered what, indeed, he would die for. He was—he did not know what—as far as belief in a God went. He was no real Englishman, not even a real knight.

But he felt instinctively that there *was* some part of him that would die for—something. Angie, of course. But what else? Nothing suggested itself, but still he felt a stubborn sense of something like faith in him.

But faith in what?

The thought nagged at him. He knew he was an idealist, an optimist as far as the human race was concerned. He believed in its future—far beyond the twentieth century from which he had come. Perhaps it was—he boggled a little at the idea—but perhaps it was that. At any rate, it was the only thing he could think of; a sort of faith in humankind as a whole, ridiculous as that sounded.

There was a sudden thump on the platform. Secoh was back.

In the claws of one forepaw, he held a bulging sack that could only be the French dragons' jewels.

"M'Lord," he said, "I stopped at your solar to pick up these. We may need them."

Jim forgot all about what had been on his mind a moment before. He whirled on the mere-dragon.

"There you are!" he said. "Secoh, signal in other messengers. Oh—and good thinking on the gems. You hold them. And, from now on, don't leave me, yourself. All right?"

"Certainly, m'Lord," said Secoh.

Jim turned to Rrrnlf.

"What's Essessili saying now?" he asked.

"He's—" Rrrnlf broke off to guffaw. "He keeps telling what they think they already know; that one-on-one they're a match for any dragon. He's offering to challenge you to a duel, to prove his point. He says if he can do it, then they ought to believe they can do it; and there's just as many of them as there are dragons up there."

Jim turned cold inside. He swung to face Carolinus.

"Carolinus," he said, "you have to be able to do something!"

Carolinus, who had been staring off into the distance over the heads of the serpents, as if he could see through the trees to the far side of the world, turned a face toward Jim that startled him. Carolinus's skin seemed pulled tight over his old bones. He looked unbearably weary, and older than Jim had ever seen him. Like someone who has been pushed to the limit of his endurance.

"No! What could I do?" he said emptily. "What business is it of yours anyway? Do you question your master, sirrah?"

Abruptly, he turned his back on Jim and went back to staring out at the trees and beyond.

Jim stood where he was, dazed and dumbfounded. He felt a touch on his elbow, and turned to see Angie.

Angie put her finger to her lips and led him a few steps aside.

"He's gone like that several times lately!" she whispered to Jim. "I think the best thing is just leave him alone; and see if he doesn't come out of it by himself."

"But we need him," Jim whispered back angrily.

"Well, he's no use to you as he is!" whispered Angie.

Jim turned back to Rrrnlf.

"Has Essessili already promised to make this—this challenge?" Jim asked.

Rrrnlf nodded.

Within Jim there was now a maelstrom of feeling. If such a challenge had indeed been made, then he could not avoid meeting it—not with the situation as it was, and particularly not with Brian, Giles and Chandos right beside him.

In fact, maybe it was the only way out of this situation. The dragons—the French ones at least—had not really promised to fight; and in spite of their roaring right now still might not.

Even the British dragons might not fight, though Jim now believed they probably would. Only, if that happened they would be outnumbered . . .

But if he had to fight Essessili—in his dragon body, of course—how could he hope to win? When he had fought the Ogre in the battle at the Loathly Tower he had had the advice of Smrgol to help him. But the only dragon known to have killed a sea serpent on his own had been dead a hundred years or more.

"Secoh!" he said, turning to the mere-dragon. "Did you hear what Rrrnlf just told me? Essessili wants to fight me, to prove whether a sea serpent should be afraid of being killed by a dragon."

"I heard, m'Lord." Secoh's eyes were shining. "And before all the dragons of Britain and France. What a happy chance!"

Well, that settled that. Secoh was taking Jim's winning for granted; and therefore all the other dragons would be. He, himself, had no such optimism. But if he did not accept, the dragons would abandon him in disgust, and the serpents would take the castle. He would die; but more to the point, Angie would die.

That last thought was unbearable. Somehow he must not only fight the sea serpent, but win.

He turned back to Rrrnlf.

"Well," he said, "if he really does challenge me—"

"No 'if' about it. Here he comes now, wee Dragon Knight!" Rrrnlf chuckled. He seemed to be getting an inordinate amount of fun out of the idea of Jim as a wee Dragon Knight. "Look!"

Jim looked.

A single long, green form was approaching the moat. Jim could still not tell Essessili from any of the others. But according to Rrrnlf, this was he.

Now he was hardly more than twenty yards from it; and in

a semicircle behind him the other serpents were moving up. Jim suspected this was more for the purpose of hearing the interchange between Jim and Essessili, than with a sense of backing up their leader.

Essessili halted. His shrill voice rose in the air.

"Dragon Knight! Dragon Knight!" he called. "Show yourself at the top of your wall!I challenge you—show yourself!"

The die was cast. Jim moved forward and stood with the upper part of his body revealed above the wall. Then he had an idea.

"Rrrnlf," he said, "why don't you move up with me? I'll talk to him in my ordinary voice. But then, you repeat what I've said, so they can all hear. Will you do that?"

Still chuckling, Rrrnlf moved forward.

"That I will," he said under his breath to Jim. "You speak. I'll repeat."

"Essessili," Jim began, deliberately speaking in his normal tones, knowing that most of the serpents, and Essessili himself, could not possibly hear it. He paused.

Rrrnlf boomed out the same word almost in his ear.

"You see me," went on Jim. "And I accept your challenge. As you see, I'm in my human form. It'll take me a few minutes to change out of my human body to dragon form. Stay where you are. I'll be down to meet you. But first we've got to agree on some conditions for the duel."

"What conditions?" shrilled Essessili. "I'm here to fight you, to show that no dragon can win against a sea serpent if he is alone. That's all there is to it."

"Not quite," said Jim and waited for Rrrnlf to repeat the words; which the Sea Devil did in a voice that must have carried well beyond the nearest fringe of woods. "The terms I have in mind are: if you win, you can assault this castle at your will. If I win, your serpents will give up the hopeless attempt to fight the dragons above you, and return to your proper place—which is the sea—like the sea creatures you are."

"Oh, we know about you!" shrilled Essessili, as soon as Rrrnlf had done his job with rebroadcasting Jim's words. "You are a two-legs, a man of magic and a dragon. None of this frightens me, Essessili. If I lose they will withdraw. You have my word—a sea serpent's word—on it. I do not fear you. But for the sake of those with me, I want to prove the weakness of dragons by defeating you when you fight with nothing but your dragon body and your dragon abilities. Are you willing to do that? No magic, now!"

"I am willing," replied Jim, with Rrrnlf backing him up.

"Very good, then," Essessili shrilled. "Then there's no good reason to delay. I'll be waiting here, impatiently. Oh, and let us hear no more from that Sea Devil beside you. From now on speak with your own voice if you speak at all!"

"How about you fighting *me* one-on-one?" roared Rrrnlf. "If you don't like the sound of my voice that much!"

Essessili turned his head away, as if he had not heard.

"*Still!*" said Jim, pointing a finger at Rrrnlf, who froze in position.

"Now listen, Rrrnlf," said Jim, in a low voice which he knew perfectly well that Rrrnlf could still hear, "you're to repeat my words, just that. Never mind getting into arguments on your own. Now, if you're agreeable to that, I'm going to release your neck and head so that you can nod. Not your voice but your neck and head. All right—released!"

He released Rrrnlf's neck and head. Rrrnlf nodded energetically.

"Tell Essessili then," said Jim in his normal voice, "that all he has to do is stay where he is and have the other sea serpents draw back to give us room to fight. They're entirely too close to him now for my liking. Tell him if the other serpents don't draw back I won't fight him."

Rrrnlf was still relaying this, as Jim turned away. Essessili grudgingly agreed. The other serpents pulled back about thirty yards.

Jim had finally worked up a combination spell—he was learning to make more and more complex spells—which combined the one which changed him into a dragon with one that magically took off all his clothes, armor and weapons first; and left them neatly piled ready to be resumed afterwards.

He used this spell now, and in a moment was his dragon self. Secoh, who had looked large beside him before, now looked small and insignificant.

Nonetheless, in spite of that insignificance, he had need of Secoh.

"Secoh," he said, in a low voice, "I need your help."

"Yes, m'Lord—m'Lord Dragon Knight," stammered Secoh.

"You remember the fight at the Loathly Tower?"

"Oh, yes, m'Lord."

"Do you remember Smrgol giving me advice on how to fight the Ogre?"

"I remember . . ." Secoh was hesitant. "Something about something Smrgol said to you because he'd fought an Ogre before. Something about their arms, their elbows, I—I think."

"That's right," said Jim. "Now, the only person who could tell me how to fight a sea serpent would be Gleingul, Smrgol's ancestor who slew a serpent by himself at a place called the Gray Sands. Now don't tell me there isn't a story about that fight that's told and retold in dragon circles. And don't tell me you don't know it practically by heart."

"Oh, yes, m'Lord Dragon Knight," said Secoh eagerly. "There is such a story, and a great story it is!"

"Good," said Jim. "Now, quickly—what can you remember from that story that would tell me how to fight Essessili?"

Secoh sat down on the platform and his eyes became abstract, almost dreamy.

"It was more than one hundred turnings of the sun ago," he began. "It was in a time when Agtval was already a very old dragon, and no longer left his cave to do the mighty things he had done earlier—"

"No!" shouted Jim. Secoh stopped abruptly.

"I don't want the whole story," said Jim. He knew only too well the dragon tendency to start a tale deep in the past, and make as long as possible a story out of anything worth telling. "I want you to think. I want you to tell me what you remember from that tale that would help me in fighting Essessili. In short, how did Gleingul do it? Just how did he attack the serpent? What did he do to the sea serpent to put him in a position to win? How did he finally kill the serpent?"

Secoh looked disappointed, but swallowed and thought hard for a long moment.

"Well, m'Lord," he said at last, slowly, "there's this business that Gleingul mentioned about using your wings. He said it was very important. Wings made the difference. Oh, I don't mean for flying, m'Lord—"

"What do you mean then?" Jim coaxed him.

"I mean for *hitting*, m'Lord! Of course," said Secoh, "you know our wings, how strong they are. Otherwise how could we take off and lift so quickly into the air as we do? Everything that flies has strong wings. It's said a goose can knock a george, a grown george, right off his feet if he hits the george right with one of his wings. You can imagine what we can do. Use your wings, was what Gleingul told us to do if we ever fought serpents."

"I see," said Jim.

And indeed he did. The first time he had ever tried flying as a dragon he had shut his eyes and pumped his wings wildly for fear of falling off the cliffside where he had launched himself into space. When he had opened his eyes he had found himself high up, very much higher than he had expected.

It had been his first experience with the tremendous power of the muscles that drove their great, long wings. Those wings might not be lovely to look at—in fact, they looked more like enormous bat wings than anything else—but he knew their power.

Now that he stopped to think about it, he could feel the heavy bands of muscles that crossed his chest above the breast bone. Yes, the wings would be the equivalent of heavy clubs—even when a sea serpent was on the receiving end.

"Good," he said hurriedly. "What else can you tell me? Think!"

Secoh squinted hard at the platform between his feet. He was giving every physical evidence of thinking just as hard as he could. After a moment though, he shook his head.

"That's all I can recall, m'Lord," he said.

"Thanks a lot," said Jim. A sarcastic note escaped into his voice. He hastened to make up for it. "Forgive me, Secoh. You've been a great help."

"Forgive you, m'Lord?" said Secoh, raising his eyes in wonder. "What for?"

"Never mind," said Jim. "I appreciated you helping me as much as you did."

"Oh, that!" said Secoh. "Any dragon could do you that much, m'Lord. I wish I could do more."

"No," said Jim. "It's up to me, now."

He looked for Angie. Gazing around, he saw her standing on the other side of him. Forgetting he was in his dragon body, he leaned forward to kiss her, suddenly realized, and instead licked out a long tongue that just touched briefly on her cheek.

"I love you, Angie," he said, in a very low voice.

She stepped forward and threw her arms around his dragon neck, burying her face against his rough scales.

"You know I love you, Jim," she said.

She stood back.

"You'll take care of him, Jim," she said in a strong voice. "I know you will!"

"Thanks, Angie," he said.

Reluctantly, he turned from her, spread his wings and went up in the air over the edge of the wall, swooping down to where Essessili waited for him.

At the last moment he changed his mind. An inspiration had just struck him. There was no reason why he shouldn't take a page from the method of peregrine falcons he had seen. He would rise to a great height, and then dive on Essessili with all possible speed, pulling out at the last minute to strike with, not his open claws, but those same claws gathered into heavy-boned fists.

Below him, the sea serpents burst out into shrill cries of condemnation, seeing him apparently turning to flee. Above him, the waiting dragons of two nations were ominously silent. He knew what they must be thinking. After accepting the challenge, he had suddenly turned fearful; and was running from the fight.

"M'Lord! M'Lord!"

Jim paused in his climbing for altitude, to see Secoh laboring to catch up with him in mid-air. He held his position, going into a tight, soaring circle as Secoh finally joined him.

"I thought of something else, m'Lord!" panted Secoh, as he began to soar alongside Jim. "The tale definitely says that Gleingul killed the serpent by driving his claws deep, deep into the base of the serpent's throat. But he did it from behind. Clinging to the serpent's neck and reaching around it to drive his claws in!"

"His throat?" said Jim.

He remembered how Dafydd had been having success shooting arrows into the back of the open mouths of the serpents. His arrow undoubtedly passed into the roof of the throat, behind.

Clearly it must reach the serpent's brain, or some vital nerve center. It sounded as if Gleingul had killed his sea serpent by hitting the same spot with his claws.

"Thanks, Secoh!" he said. "I think maybe that's just what I needed to know. Now, stay clear. I want to climb a little more and then dive—I mean stoop. You might tell the dragons above that's what this whole maneuver is about. Will you do that?"

"Oh yes, m'Lord . . ." Secoh's answer floated back vaguely to Jim's ears as he mounted yet higher, the dragons above him moving sourly aside as he reached their altitudes.

At a height he thought would do, he turned about. Using his telescopic dragon-sight, he picked out Essessili far below. He turned down; and, pumping his wings strongly, dove.

It was strange. He could feel the pressure of the air against him as he picked up speed. At the same time, he seemed to be hanging in space with the ground below growing before him.

There was a last moment when it suddenly leaped at him; so suddenly he barely had time to clench his claws, come out of his dive and feel the terrific impact of the fists against the back and side of Essessili's head—before he beat upward for altitude again.

At a hundred or so feet above the ground he checked, turned and looked. Essessili, he saw, had been knocked over; and in fact was still rolling. But apparently he had not done any great damage to the serpent leader. Stopped rolling, Essessili got to his feet with only some slight evidence of grogginess, and turned to look up for Jim.

Nothing to it, Jim thought, with a sudden uprush of optimism. For the first time he began to feel some hope that he might be able to win this one-sided encounter.

But even as he thought this, he was busily climbing for altitude again. In his head was the idea that enough hits like that and he might make Essessili dizzy enough to become an easy prey. He reached sufficient altitude, turned and dived.

He whistled downward, still thinking that this was an excellent way of fighting, when he suddenly woke to the fact that Essessili was not in the same position as before.

Now Jim saw that the other had curled himself up, as any snake might. Being thicker and shorter in proportion to his thickness than any snake, he had not been able to coil as gracefully as a rattler or cobra might. But still, most of his body was now tucked below him. Above it, guarding it, and threatening Jim's attack at the same time, were his enormous, toothed jaws, yawning wide open.

It was directly into those jaws that Jim was now diving.

CHAPTER 39

Jim jinked aside at the last moment, icy with sudden fear. He slipped past the waiting jaws; but out of sheer clumsiness, nothing else, his right wing struck across Essessili's neck below the serpent's head as Jim turned.

Scrambling for altitude, and looking back down, once he had gained enough to feel safe, he was surprised to see Essessili rubbing the side of his neck against the earth, as if to take away the effects of Jim's blow. Secoh's words came back to him then, the advice from Gleingul's story of his fight with the sea serpent on the Gray Sands, about the power in a dragon's wings. A lesser creature than Essessili might have had his neck broken, if not torn right off.

For a moment the fear left him. Then it returned. He had been no more than lucky in avoiding Essessili's gaping maw on that last dive.

He had not climbed as far this time and he circled for a moment, quickly trying to think what advantages he and Essessili each had. Essessili was larger, more powerful, and had a much more dangerous set of jaws and teeth.

Also, he was able, at least partially, to move like a snake. He was not quite as agile as the ordinary snake. But he still had that ability, plus his teeth.

Jim himself, on one hand, was lighter. His own powerful jaws and teeth were still no match for Essessili's. On the other hand he had his claws, and had made good use of them as fists on that first dive.

He was probably quicker than Essessili; and he could fly; which gave him more mobility than the other.

Plainly, he was ahead darting in and out, trying to do as much damage as he could with his wings. The only drawback was that he could strike much harder if he was standing firmly on the ground. But on the ground, Essessili would be able to coil around him.

Still, he had to try being airborne around Essessili while he battered the serpent. Maybe he could get Essessili into a state where he was less dangerous. Jim decided to try.

He dived, swung aside just before he reached Essessili and tried to get behind the serpent's head. But Essessili was there to face him, no matter how quickly he jinked and dodged.

Jim went back to making quick dashes in, striking one blow and one blow only, then out again, hitting either with his right wing or his left at Essessili's neck.

This, he found, he could do. Occasionally, Essessili swayed aside in time so that the blow hardly grazed him. But usually, Jim hit hard.

But it began to dawn on Jim that Essessili was absorbing the punishment too well. Meanwhile Jim, himself, was getting wing-tired and out of breath.

As he had learned almost immediately on finding himself for the first time in his dragon body, a dragon was built not so much to fly as to soar. It was capable of some remarkable movement for a short length of time—rather like a lion in its charge. But it was limited in the amount of time it could keep up the effort. Normally a dragon flew for only a few minutes, then coasted in soaring position, with wings stiffly outstretched, until it was necessary to put in another spurt of effort.

Here, in this particular combat, he had been on-wing almost steadily; and it was beginning to tell.

In desperation, he landed facing Essessili, thumping down far enough back to be out of the serpent's immediate reach. He began to use his wings at full extension to batter Essessili's neck.

For a moment he saw a look of surprise in the serpent's eyes, on finding him suddenly a stationary target on the ground.

If that look was there, however, it was wiped out by Jim's first wing-blow with his right wing at Essessili's neck. The serpent's head went almost over to the ground, and he had barely recovered when Jim's left wing caught him from the other side.

Jim pounded away with his wings, as if he was a boxer with an opponent in a corner where he was trying to batter the other to the canvas.

Then suddenly Jim found himself knocked a good twenty feet backward. Even his powerfully muscle-protected dragon's chest felt smashed in. Instinct, and instinct alone, saved him. He had taken to his wings without thinking on being hit. He scrambled aloft to get space and a moment to breathe.

He climbed high enough to catch a thermal that would let him soar and catch his breath.

Essessili had suddenly uncoiled. The sea serpent had struck at him, serpent fashion. His jaws had missed their grab for Jim's own long dragon neck; but the force and weight of the head-blow against Jim's chest had almost won the fight. All of Essessili's strength had been brought into play from his coiled position, which anchored him for that effort.

Circling, Jim looked down and saw the serpent, apparently unhurt and waiting for him.

This could not go on much longer. Once more he climbed and dived. Once more Essessili coiled himself and opened his jaws above his coiled body, both as protection for it and as threat to Jim.

Jim whistled downward. But while Essessili waited for him to come directly toward the jaws and jink aside as he had done before, Jim slanted off imperceptibly at an angle so that he actually approached the ground a good forty yards off, pulled out of his dive early and drove straight at the coiled serpent in a shallow swoop with much of the speed he had accumulated in his dive.

It worked. He had deliberately come down a little to one side of Essessili but in view. He shot forward and just before he got to the serpent jinked slightly away from the upheld head so that for a second he was behind the other. In that second, he hooked his right claws into the side of Essessili's neck, let momentum swing him around so that he could hook the claws of his left fist in on the other side and held; at last behind the serpent's head and mouth, where Essessili's jaws could not reach back to get at him.

Essessili made one effort to tilt his head back far enough to bring his jaws into play against Jim; but Jim was pumping with his wings and holding his body out at arm's length. In fact, he was also holding Essessili's head off the ground—so that when Essessili tried to put it down a moment later so as to roll his whole body and get the weight of it on top of Jim, he was not able to do so.

The power of Jim's wings was not enough to lift an adult human being. Certainly it was nowhere near enough to lift even part of the sea serpent; but it was enough to keep the head, jaws and the somewhat narrower neck just behind it up off the ground. It was as he had hoped, and as he had more than half expected. The serpent had to put his head down in order to roll over. That had been obvious when he had seen how the serpents had all lowered their heads and rolled on their side when it became necessary for them to look up enough to see the dragons overhead.

It became a battle of wills, where strengths were almost equally matched: Jim's dragon strength against the strength of Essessili's neck. The neck was indeed narrower, but not so much so that his six-inch claws, and the ten-inch bony fingers to which they belonged, could dig deep enough into the neck to touch any vital spot. Plainly, thought Jim, he was not forward enough on the neck.

On a sudden inspiration he used his wings to cover Essessili's eyes so that the serpent was temporarily blinded; and in that moment in which Essessili stopped struggling to figure out what was going on, he moved one grip forward and was just about to move the other when Essessili woke up to what was going on and shook himself violently.

Jim clung desperately, so as not to be thrown from his hold. Essessili continued to shake for several minutes, but evidently he could not keep it up indefinitely. The shaking slowed, and Jim took a chance during a slight pause to move his left claws forward also. Now they were almost side by side at the front of Essessili's throat. He put all his strength behind them and tried to drive them in as far as he could.

Essessili went into a frenzy. No longer trying to roll over on Jim but merely thrashing himself around as if to shake Jim free by any means whatsoever. Jim felt his grip weakening in spite of himself. He closed his eyes and concentrated. *For Angie*, he thought; and put all he had into one last thrust to get the claws in even a little bit deeper.

Essessili's head suddenly thumped to earth and his body lay still.

For a moment Jim stayed as he was, claws still in the throat of the sea serpent, dazed by what he had been through and the sudden termination of the fight. Then he came back to himself enough to pull his claws loose. He stepped off the body and looked around.

He looked behind him—and saw the great wave of sea serpents all around coming at him and at the castle as fast as they could.

So much for a sea serpent's word—he could hear Rrrnlf's voice saying those words inside his head right now. He was worn out; but he mustered up enough strength to take to the air, at least to lift himself enough so that he would be out of reach of the oncoming serpents. Then, turning, he flapped slowly and painfully to the wall and clung to the top of it, like a swimmer who has crossed some great expanse of water and comes at last to the outcropping of a shore.

CHAPTER 40

He clung for a moment, and then two massive hands—Rrrnlf's hands, holding him delicately so as not to hurt him—lifted him over it to safety and deposited him on the platform.

Dimly aware, Jim collapsed on the rough but level surface of the platform. His senses swam. Dragons were not supposed to faint.

He fainted.

However, it felt as if he was out for only a second or so. He swam back to consciousness to be aware of a gabble of voices all around him, and piercing through them the single feminine one of Angie speaking to him desperately.

"Jim!" she was asking. "Are you all right?"

"Fine," he muttered . . . Although he was not sure whether he muttered it sufficiently out loud for anyone to hear. "Just worn out, that's all."

He managed to raise his voice a little.

"Just give me . . . a minute . . . to catch my breath."

In fact, his head was clearing; which was a tribute, not only to the fact that he was really nothing more than as he said, exhausted; but to the tremendous recuperative powers of which dragons were capable.

It occurred to him that possibly the most reassuring thing he could do would be to change back into his ordinary self.

His still somewhat clouded mind struggled to link the proper pair of spells together, to both change him back to human, and dress him once more in his clothes and armor. Then he wrote them on the inside of his forehead.

A second later he was standing upright on the platform. He swayed a little bit, but he was now upright, human and fully dressed. He smiled down into the face of Angie who was standing right in front of him, looking deeply concerned.

"See, Angie," he said. "I couldn't be better."

"Yes, you could!" snapped Angie. "For one thing, you're white as a sheet!"

She was very pale herself, Jim noticed; but he was enough in possession of himself now to realize that was probably not the right thing to mention to her at the moment.

"Well, I'll get my color back quickly. Wait and see," he said. "If you want to stand and watch, you can even watch it come back."

Angie laughed shakily.

"We don't have time for me to do that," she said. "While you were lying there unconscious, one of the young dragon watchers came in with a report."

She half turned away from him. Jim turned to look in the same direction as she was looking, and saw Secoh had one of the young dragons with him; one that was hardly larger than himself. As his gaze fell on them, both dragons shuffled forward, and the knights, surprisingly, made way for them.

"M'Lord!" said Secoh. "Listen to this! Tell him, Gnarjo."

Gnarjo bobbed his head several times before speaking—a sure sign of embarrassment in a dragon.

"M'Lord," he said in a bass voice that at the same time was almost squeaky, even for a young dragon, "I was over the coast, watching the sea in case more serpents should come."

"Well?" asked Jim. "Did you see more serpents coming?"

"Oh no, m'Lord," said Gnarjo. "But there's something big. Something terrible big, coming out of the ocean!"

"How big is it?" asked Jim.

"It's big—it's so big—" Words failed Gnarjo. "It's—it's two or three times as tall as this wall behind me!"

"That big?" said Jim. "What did it look like?"

"Well it was big and sort of—I don't know—" stammered Gnarjo, "sort of gray? No, sort of gray-blue? But there was a sort of flash of white about it—in the water around it, I mean—oh, m'Lord, I didn't really wait to see much after I saw how big it was. I just came straight back here to tell you!"

Gnarjo hung his head miserably.

"That's all right," said Jim. "You did exactly the right thing."

"I did?" said Gnarjo, his head coming up with a snap and his eyes brightening.

Jim looked at the serious faces of Angie, Brian, Giles, Dafydd and Chandos.

"I wonder what those flashes of white around it were?" he said, to himself as much as to them. "It sounded at first like one very large creature. But maybe those white flashes mean there're others with it, or something . . ."

"The wee dragon," rumbled Rrrnlf, above his head, "may have been too fearful to see clearly what he was looking at."

Gnarjo looked indignant, but neither Jim nor anybody else paid attention.

"I ought to look at it myself," said Jim.

He broke off, suddenly aware of the silence along the wall. Startled, he suddenly realized that, long since, the serpents that had been chasing him should have reached the wall and be attacking it. He took one step forward and looked out into the open space.

The canopy of dragons still darkened the skies above them. But the serpents had stopped, as if at a magic line, an invisible barrier running across the open space through the spot where the dead body of Essessili lay. As he looked closely at them, he saw that most of them had their heads down and were also canted to one side, so that they could look upward and see the dragons overhead; and at once understanding came to him.

If the Dragon Knight could kill Essessili, then perhaps there was no reason why each one of those dragons above could not kill one of them. For the moment it was stalemate.

But not for long, if this new intruder from the sea was a factor entering the situation. He thought again of changing back into a dragon, flying off himself to see what was coming; and then decided that there was no time for that. The stalemate could break at any moment, one way or another. The serpents might decide to attack after all. Or the dragons might decide to attack the serpents, or—

Anything was possible.

Desperately, he turned to Carolinus, who had his back to him. He walked around to stand before the older magician; and was shocked at what he saw. Even in the little time that had gone past since he had last looked at him, Carolinus's face had become even more haggard and unnatural. His body, which always before had been ramrod-straight, now stooped, with rounded shoulders. He had looked old always; but now, for the first time, he looked old and frail. Carolinus met his gaze with uninterested eyes.

"Carolinus!" said Jim. "You can do this much for us, anyway! Let me have a look at what's coming from the sea toward us. Do that, at least!"

"Leave me alone," said Carolinus, in a voice that seemed to come from a great distance. "I'm past it, I tell you. You'll have to do without me."

"*Carolinus—*"

Jim checked himself. Simply shouting at Carolinus would do no good. Whatever was destroying him was not something that could be shouted away.

But it was absolutely necessary that he be roused from the depths of the depression that now held him; and had been holding him for some days now, at least since his illness and his rescue from the two wise-women. He tried to think of words that would stir the older man. Words came to him. Perhaps they were not the right words; but they were the only ones Jim could think of that might work in this moment.

"Carolinus!" he said fiercely. "At least you can do this much. I can't, but you can—easily! Give us a sight of this new intruder!"

For a moment Carolinus's eyes cleared, briefly; and the dullness disappeared.

"Well," he muttered, "it alters nothing, now. But I can give you that. And I wish you joy of it!"

He turned to face outward over the wall and, with his arm outstretched, and his finger pointing, he drew a circle perhaps three feet in diameter in the air.

Suddenly, looking into the air within that circle, Jim and the rest saw—not the land, the serpents, the trees and the dragons beyond, but instead, something like a tremendous, living tower of light gray flesh, with two enormous eyes, crashing through a belt of woods, running lightly across an open space at the speed of an express train and crashing into a farther bit of forest.

"Granfer!" said Rrrnlf, staring.

"Yes," said Jim. "And headed this way."

For a second they all stood, gazing wordlessly at Granfer as he plowed through a stand of trees that went down before him like stalks of asparagus. His three-story body was upright; and he ran nimbly on several of his tentacles.

"How can he move that fast? How can he move at all," said Angie in a hushed voice, "when he's so large and so heavy? Those tentacles can't hold up all that weight, can they?"

"They aren't," put in the dull voice of Carolinus. "It's magic. He's traveling the way he would travel underwater. See what he carries."

None of them had looked closely before, but now Granfer brought into full view a tentacle which he had been holding half-hidden by his bulk; and what it held became visible in the lens.

"My Lady!" howled Rrrnlf. He had one hand on the wall and was about to go over it, when Jim pointed a finger at him and snapped out a single word.

"*Still!*"

Rrrnlf froze where he was.

"I'm sorry to stop you, Rrrnlf," went on Jim, more gently. "But stop and think. Maybe you can tear sea serpents apart with no trouble at all. But think; you know you're no match for Granfer. If you want your Lady back, stay here. Let's fight him all together. That way we've got a chance. I'll *unstill* you now. Think it over."

Carolinus gave an unpleasant grating laugh, of a sort that Jim had not only never heard from him before, but would not have been able to imagine him uttering. For now, however, Jim ignored it. He turned on Brian, who knew the area better than any of them.

"Where is Granfer right now?" he asked. "And Brian, can you make me a guess at how fast he's coming toward us; and how soon he should be here?"

Brian stared into the screen.

"He's going much, much faster than the fastest horse could gallop," Brian said slowly. "Indeed, I think he may be going as fast as some birds can fly. Carolinus must have been right when he said it was magic; for surely no living thing could move with that speed."

"And Brian," said Jim, "how soon do you think he'll be here? Where is he now?"

"He is coming in from the beach where the serpents landed," Brian answered, still staring into the telescopic window. "It's longer that way than from the fens; but at the speed he's coming, I'd say he'd be here in less than a quarter of an hour. Nay, less than that. In as much time as a man may say ten to fifteen Pater Nosters, he will be upon us. He is already entering on the Round Hills. Past that he will plunge into the woods that run for some six miles right to the edge of your cleared space around this castle."

Brian cast a longing glance at Carolinus's turned back; and Jim knew that the knight longed to ask the magician questions; but dared not, after his rebuff of Jim.

"Even under the sea," said Giles, in a tone of awe, "I did not think the monster was so large. Why, he overtops the trees. He'll go through this wall and the rest of your castle as a knife goes through a cook's pastry, on his weight, alone."

Giles's also pale but resolute face with its still-brave, blond mustachios, looked in troubled fashion at Jim.

"How may we fight him, do you think?" Giles asked. "If he were alone, perhaps all those dragons overhead could pull him down, do you not think it? Would they come if you called them? Of course, if Granfer and the serpents are of one mind against us—"

"They are muddled now," put in Chandos moodily. "But they will hear the noise of the shattered trees as he gets closer, very soon. Then they'll know who comes to their aid."

Jim looked out over the wall. The serpents were milling around, talking to each other and pausing to glance at the dragons overhead. They seemed undecided whether to stay where they were, attack the castle, or retreat. Their chittering voices, low-pitched for conversation with each other, made a sound almost like that of a host of crickets.

"Can you do nothing against them magical?" Chandos asked Jim.

Jim shook his head.

"And Carolinus—"

Chandos looked from Jim to the mage. Carolinus whirled about at his words, as if he had been pricked.

"And I?" he snarled at Chandos. "Do you think I can do anything? You are all fools. That out there is the one we have all been searching for from the beginning. The one behind it all."

"The magician we couldn't find?" demanded Jim.

"Yes, fool!" said Carolinus. "Double fool, because you come from a place and time where you should know more, not less, than the rest of us. You had no suspicion? Did you ever ask yourself why I, Carolinus, one of the world's great magicians, should be taken abed of some simple illness and be waited upon almost immediately by butchering midwives; who fed me draughts of poisonous liquors against my will, and might indeed have poisoned me—except that he—"

He pointed out into the telescopic area at the approaching Granfer.

"—was too clever for that. The Accounting Office might take note of the direct murder of a AAA+ magician!"

He went on, almost raving.

"How else could I be so incapacitated, made so helpless, except by magic I could not fend off? Did you have no suspicion when I told you that even the Accounting Office did not know who was behind Ecotti and the sea serpents—yet still they affected us?"

"Well—" began Jim. But he really had no defense; and his voice faltered.

"No, you did not. You did none of these things; because in spite of all you know, you are a fool. I knew from the beginning the danger that must be lying in wait for us. But I was a fool, too."

He paused and his voice grew even more bitter. "I thought the work of this magician must be all in favor of the French King's attempt to invade England. What a pitiful idiot I was! What a puling babe! That kraken you see there in the circle I drew cares nothing for France or England, or dragons or serpents or anything else. He only wants to rule the world. And to rule that, he must rule all magicians first. That was his aim—and he chose me as the first target for his campaign! Now, he comes to close that campaign with his first win."

"But there was no real evidence—" Jim protested, and was cut off by Carolinus.

"No real evidence, you say?" Carolinus snarled. "You came back to tell me about a kraken reading a book. Did you never stop to think—did you never once stop to think? Tell me, how can a book be read underwater?"

"Why—" began Jim; and then what Carolinus was driving at suddenly struck him like Rrrnlf's fist.

"You mean—the ink!" he said to Carolinus.

"Of course the ink, fool!" said Carolinus bitterly. "Any book taken under sea water for any length of time with any ink folk know how to make, will have that ink blur, run, and be unreadable within minutes at most. Even the parchment of the pages will at last turn to pulp, stick together and fall apart in chunks! So—what kind of book could this Granfer have been reading?"

"No book, surely!" burst out Brian; half in defense of Jim.

"No. One book," said Jim, for Carolinus's eyes were still hard upon him. "The *Encyclopedie Necromantick*. A book of magic is a magic book. A magic book could protect itself against sea water or anything else. But how would it get into the grasp of someone like Granfer?"

"Who knows?" said Carolinus, throwing his arms wide. "Perhaps a magician, traveling aboard a ship on the deep sea, died; and the superstitious louts that crewed it threw the book and him, and all else connected with him, overboard— for fear that some unearthly trouble might come upon them, now he was dead. What matters it? The point is that Granfer is probably thousands of years old. He would have had all those years for that book to come into his possession. He would have had hundreds of years to learn how to read it, to study it after he had learned what it told. To master the knowledge within it; and dream his dream of owning the world."

"But you've also mastered it," said Jim. "That's why none of us can see why you—"

"He taught *himself* magic!" cried Carolinus. "Don't you understand? He taught himself magic as he found it. It's his own magic, unlike any other magic in the world today!"

"How is it different?" demanded Jim.

"It is the most primitive form of magic," said Carolinus. "Long forgotten by the rest of us. It is the magic of men when they crouched in caves and tried to control the weather and the animals who preyed upon them and other things, by means beyond their own physical strength. Why do you think he took and carries that which was once the figurehead of a ship; and which Rrrnlf calls his Lady?"

"I don't understand," Jim said.

"Totemic magic!" Carolinus's voice rose and broke. He slumped. When he spoke again, he sounded very weary. "Forgive me, Jim. I should not have called you fool. I saw these evidences too and did not put them together. You might not have known, but I should have known. I did not—until it was too late. His magic makes use of a totem."

"Why do you say it's too late?" Jim said.

"Hush—" interrupted Chandos suddenly.

They looked at him and he was holding up one hand and listening. Outside in the field, the serpents had fallen silent.

Far off, there was a sound like sticks being broken—in the distance, far, far off. It was a steady crackling as of branches being trod upon, by someone heavy footed.

"He comes," said Carolinus, still in that weary voice. "And neither you, Jim, nor I, can stop him. He uses magic that uses as its totem Rrrnlf's Lady. We have no totems to combat it with. Nor is it possible even for me—to become in seconds a master at totemic magic."

His voice dropped to a mutter.

"Once, maybe," he said. "But I am old—old. I recognize that, now."

He stopped speaking. They stood silent. The noise of the trees being broken down by Granfer as he came closer now, was loud in that silence. Granfer himself, seen in the telescopic circle, was more enormous than ever. Now it seemed to Jim that he even recognized the falling tops of trees, whose height he knew, trees from woods he owned as Lord of Malencontri.

Abruptly his whole soul rebelled against giving up. Carolinus had shrunk back into his dullness of eye and bentness of shoulder.

"You told me," Jim cried, turning on him, "that a master in magic like you could watch another magician in action for only a short time and know all his secrets, be able to duplicate and surpass them. You told me that after your duel with Son Won Phon. Have you forgotten your own words?"

Carolinus did not answer. He hardly seemed to have heard.

"All you need is a totem!" Jim drove at him, trying desperately to rouse him from the withdrawal within him. "A totem; and then shake off this sense of defeat that's overtaken you! I can get you a totem. In fact you already have one! What about that kettle that came to call me to save you?"

Carolinus still did not respond in any way.

"That kettle's known you for years, maybe for centuries!" Jim said wildly. He hastily threw together a spell in his mind, wrote it on the inside of his forehead; and a moment later Carolinus's kettle, on the boil as usual, was dangling from his right fist.

"Here you are—ouch!" The yelp from Jim was involuntary. The kettle, swinging a little, had brushed its hot metal top against his knuckles.

"You don't understand," said Carolinus in a dead voice. "That which Granfer carries was the figurehead of a ship carved and painted to represent one of the waves. Aegir, the Norse sea god, and Ran, the giantess, had nine daughters, who were the waves. Last and greatest of these waves was the ninth, named Jarnsaxa—'*the Iron Sword.*' Even though pagan times must have been all but past, that figurehead was carved by pagans for pagans—"

"*Pagans!*" said Brian suddenly, putting his hand on his sword hilt and staring grimly at Rrrnlf, as if measuring him as someone to be challenged.

Carolinus raved on, as if he had not heard.

"—To them it was Jarnsaxa and had life to cleave the waves for them; for Jarnsaxa is the ninth wave, the one that goes farthest up on the beach, according to legend. When Rrrnlf found the sunken ship with that figurehead upon it, he took it off, replaced its missing paint, stripped it of barnacles and all other sea damage, and fixed it as good as new. Then went beyond that, to load it with jewels and other presents—"

"I loved her, do you understand!" broke out Rrrnlf unexpectedly above them, his voice for one moment covering all other noise, including that of the approaching Granfer. "We were lovers! But when the old Gods left, Aegir took his nine daughters with him. I never saw her again."

"So Rrrnlf—" went on Carolinus in that same dead voice. Jim saw, to his surprise, great tears rolling down Rrrnlf's cheeks. "Rrrnlf gave the love he could no longer give to the one he had loved, to this figurehead of her that was left. In doing that he gave it some life. Wherever there is love, there is life given. Loved objects become living, to some extent. When Essessili, or some other sea serpent at Granfer's order, stole the figurehead from Rrrnlf and brought it to the kraken, he was able to use that life in it to bring his own magic to a state in which it was alive and acting. Together, they have a magic unknown and invincible."

"No!" cried Jim. "You've brought this kettle alive, the same way. It went to save you. It's alive! You can use that just as well. All you have to do is translate from what you know to Granfer's magic."

But Carolinus remained unresponsive. Something seemed to explode inside Jim.

"Then I will!" he shouted—and in that moment, Granfer broke through the last of the trees on the edge of the clearing, plunging into the midst of the serpents.

He stopped. He had crushed a number of them in coming in among them; but the rest paid no attention. They gathered around him like hounds around their master.

Jim held up the kettle before him with its handle in both hands, between him and Granfer. His mind was busy constructing spells.

He spoke the effective lines aloud to give them more force.

"*Simon says—*" he called out desperately. "*Simon says: Granfer, still!*"

But Granfer was busy speaking to the serpents. Jim's magic did not even make him pause. Jim realized then that his magic had never worked on the other. On the sea bottom Granfer had only pretended to be *stilled*, to hide his own magic from Jim.

Now, his tentacles continued to wave in the air—all but the one that was holding the carved head of Jarnsaxa. He was telling the serpents what nitwits they were to be afraid of the dragons overhead, particularly now he was here. He was telling them that he would lead the way through the walls and through the castle and leave everything open for them to move in, to kill and eat whatever was killable and eatable there.

It was no use. Jim lowered the kettle. Only Carolinus could do it. Desperation drove him beyond the usual limits. He must rouse the other man, even if he made an enemy of him forever. He turned on the magician.

"Damn you, Carolinus!" he snarled. "Do you dare curl up like a worm there, and still call yourself an Englishman and a Mage?"

For a moment it seemed that even these words had not broken through the dark cloud that had come to enclose Carolinus.

But then, suddenly his shoulders straightened with a snap. Once more his erect self, he spun about to face Jim with a face transfigured with fury.

CHAPTER 41

"Give me that!"

Carolinus, his eyes blazing, reached out and snatched the kettle from Jim's grasp.

"Carolinus!" cried Angie.

For Carolinus had taken hold of the kettle, not by the handle as Jim had been holding it; but by wrapping both hands firmly around its sides and base, pressing fingers and palms hard against the metal hot from the near-boiling liquid within.

Ignoring Angie's reaction, he turned to face outward toward the serpents and Granfer. He held the kettle at chest height before him; but his eyes were fixed on Granfer.

He, himself, was now rigid as a figure cast in metal. So rigid, so tense, that he seemed on the verge of quivering with the tension in all his muscles; and his face began to shine with perspiration as he stood holding the kettle and staring.

An old man does not perspire easily. Those standing around felt it; the tremendous effort—not physical, mental, but magical—that Carolinus was making.

His eyes seemed to devour every motion of Granfer, and his hands were rock-steady around the kettle, though the skin of his palms and fingers, where it could be seen, was already beginning to puff up from the blistering and burning that the hands must be taking, out of sight in those areas where they touched the kettle.

The rest were held, motionless. Motionless and silent. Jim felt Angie struggling to say or do something, but his hand which was already on her arm, put there unconsciously to stop her when she spoke that one utterance of Carolinus's name, closed about her arm.

"There's nothing we can do," he said in a whisper.

They stood and watched.

Suddenly, unexpectedly, a thin thread of steam jetted from the spout of the kettle. And the thin, breathy voice they had heard from it before, when it had stood on the table in their Great Hall, calling for help for Carolinus, began to sing. But this time it sang differently.

"Caro—lin—us, Caro—lin—us . . ." it sang softly.

The melody was as simple as a lullaby, repeated over and over; with nothing but Carolinus's name for words. But, like a lullaby, hearing it over and over again did not become tiresome. Carolinus's name, Jim suddenly realized, was the one word the kettle was able to make on its own.

But now it was making it into a little song of love and comfort; and strangely, Carolinus seemed to draw strength from it. He relaxed and appeared to grow at the same time. He not only seemed taller, but broader and stronger. Once more, he showed himself as he had all the time they had known him; in command of any situation in which he found himself, including this one.

In the open area, Granfer's voice suddenly broke off speaking and rose to a high-pitched scream; and the combined voices of the serpents cried out around him.

Looking over the wall, Jim and the rest saw Granfer moving slowly up into the air. For some reason it reminded Jim, who as a boy had seen television pictures of the takeoff of the manned rocket from Cape Kennedy that had first gone to the moon. Like that rocket, Granfer lifted from the Earth, slowly at first, gaining speed gradually as he rose.

He lifted until he was several times his own length above the serpents. He stopped. Then, equally slowly, he began to rotate vertically, like the second hand of a clock, until he was head down.

Head down, he began to drift toward the castle, through the air over the heads of the serpents below, over the dead Essessili, over and above the open ground between all their green bodies and the moat with the castle wall behind it.

Until he hung; enormous, but helpless and screaming in that shrill voice of his, only twenty yards in front of the top of the wall.

"Be silent!" Carolinus's voice cracked out; and it had the same snap to it that it had, until recently, always had.

Instantly, Granfer was voiceless.

Carolinus spoke to him again.

"You know what I want," his voice was sharp and definite.

Fumblingly, with his other tentacles waving wildly as if to reach out and grasp something to hold to, Granfer passed the carved and painted head of Rrrnlf's Lady, still dripping with all the jewels and golden chains that Rrrnlf had attached to it, to a longer tentacle that reached out over the wall to deliver the head into Rrrnlf's waiting hands.

The Sea Devil clutched the figurehead high on his chest. Tenderly he hugged it to him and bowed his head to rest his cheek against the carved, golden hair.

"I'm waiting!" snapped Carolinus's voice again.

From some hidden recess, behind or about him, Granfer brought forth a heavy, black book with gold lettering on its cover. This, too, he passed over the wall, transferring it from tentacle to tentacle, this time into Carolinus's hands.

"Now, sir!" said Carolinus. "I could take vengeance for what you were trying to do; and for what has been done by these serpents under your control. But I will not alter things as they were by changing things as they may be. It was the current of History that allowed you to come this far. I will not tamper with History. So, I will send you back now, and set you down in your own place. But not by your magic— which is inferior—but by mine; for you have no more strength to oppose our strength. Remember that; no matter how many centuries you have yet to live. You have no more magic!"

"I have no more magic . . ." echoed Granfer's shrill voice sadly and almost inaudibly.

"Then go, and your serpents with you, all of you. Begone!"

Suddenly, Granfer had vanished. The gray-green, trodden ground, the moat, was empty, even of corpses, to the forest trees. Only the pathway smashed through the trees, which Granfer had made in coming toward them, remained.

For a long moment, as all those on wall and platform stared at the empty space about them, there was silence.

That silence stretched out; and then, one by one, they began to look up; for the darkness that had been cast over them with the coming of the dragons began to lighten. They looked and saw that the mass of soaring bodies was beginning to thin.

The French dragons were withdrawing to the south, and the English dragons were turning away to go back to their own homes in the west, east and north of Britain.

Jim, who had looked up like the rest, looked down again just as Angie also did. They smiled at each other. Jim became aware that Carolinus was holding out the kettle to him.

"Pull this loose," Carolinus said.

Jim took the kettle by its handle. The metal of its body was now cold when he touched it, and the little singing voice had stopped. But the body of the kettle itself seemed stuck to Carolinus's hands. Jim pulled and it came loose.

"*Carolinus!*" said Angie. For Carolinus's hands and fingers were raw flesh, with the skin completely gone from the undersides of them, except near the edge of the parts that had been touching the kettle, where the bubbles of blisters showed.

"I should keep these to heal naturally, as a reminder to myself," Carolinus said harshly, looking down at his hands. "But I may have use for them."

Suddenly, the hands were as healed and as whole as ever. Carolinus looked up and met Jim's eyes.

"And to you, Jim," he said, "I owe you the deepest of apologies. This was my fault, after all, because I had forgotten something. Strange, how we so often forget what we know best."

He reached out and took back the kettle, holding it by its handle with one hand and caressing its body, now hot again, with the other. But this time the hand that touched the metal did not burn. Jim stared at it.

"Carolinus," he said, "if you could hold the kettle without burning, why did you go through that much pain?"

"There is a time and a use for one kind of pain," Carolinus said, looking fondly at the kettle. "A time for good pain. Good pain focuses, bad pain scatters and destroys."

A wisp of steam came forth once more from the kettle's spout. The little voice sang, once again.

"Caro—lin—us, Caro—lin—us." Then it fell still, although the steam continued to come.

"I forgot," said Carolinus, looking at it, "that love is the one force capable of creating." He shook his head. "That was why Granfer's magic was so primitive. That was why if I had only tried, earlier with all the power at my command, I should have been able to overcome him. But I had let myself fall into a despond, from my sickness and my weakness. And, indulgently, I had let that despond to continue. My kettle worked for me because it had gained life from me; as Rrrnlf's Lady had gained life from Rrrnlf. But Granfer had no love within him; and so no life of his own to give to his totem. Fear and awe are not enough, as our people learned long since. So, in the end, the weaker magic had to go down before mine, with the help of this small kettle."

He looked at Jim and Angie and also smiled. It was seldom that he did so; but when he did the smile was a memorable thing, because a warmth could be felt from it, as from a kindled fireplace.

"So, we won," he said. "And Sir John"—he turned to Chandos—"I do not think the King of France and his army will be trying to land in England now, without the serpents to help them."

"You're right," said Chandos. He too smiled, but a little sadly.

"Heigh-ho," he added, "but I will have some explanations to make, after talking the other captains into sending the army south, to stand as if to bar the serpents from the sea and make them fear that they would be killed, one and all. Armies like not to be sent on a fool's errand."

"But m'Lord—I mean, Sir John Chandos, sir," stammered Secoh. "We heard some time ago—but there was so much else happening I didn't get a chance to tell you. They didn't go."

"They didn't go?" Chandos stared at him. "The army didn't move? But all the captains in council—"

He broke off. Suddenly he burst into a great roar of laughter.

"And so, always, are our captains and armies!" he said. "In the end they make up their minds, and change their minds, and no agreement holds; no one sensible thing is done unless one strong hand drives all! Well, well, it is their way; and this time it's to my advantage."

His laughter was so infectious that the others found themselves laughing with him; and even those farther out along the wall, who had not understood—in some cases not even heard—the interchange of words on the platform, laughed also. It was a laughter of sheer relief after long tension.

Jim suddenly remembered something. He whirled on Secoh.

"Secoh!" he said. "Get that surety back to the French dragons!"

Secoh took off.

Around Jim, the laughter was at last dying.

"ER-HEM!"

It was a clearing of the throat by Brian louder than Jim had ever believed anyone could clear his throat. He looked startledly at his closest friend. Brian, his sword still in his hand, was all but glaring at Jim; with a look that baffled Jim for a moment before understanding came.

Of course, after every victory, there had to be a celebration. In particular, a feast. Brian was always longing to give one of these; only his poverty kept him unable. But in this case, it was Jim's castle; and Brian was in a fever for fear that Jim, who had the wherewithal, would shame himself by forgetting that something like this was due; shame himself particularly in front of Chandos.

"Well now!" shouted Jim. "We must note this memorable day with proper festivities!"

Brian almost slumped with relief.

Jim turned to Angie. "M'Lady! Can we arrange the Hall and have food and drink set up, first for these knightly persons about us, then for the lesser of our people, and finally even some food and drink for those more humble who have come to shelter in our courtyard?"

"Absolutely, m'Lord!" sang Angie, who had probably understood Brian much more quickly than Jim. "All shall be ready in a trice!"

She turned, picked up her long skirt, ran off the platform and down the stone stairs to the courtyard, shouting for a servant or a man-at-arms to carry messages for her, as she did.

Jim watched her go with fondness, then turned back to Carolinus.

"Carolinus," he said, "you'll stay for this, won't you?"

"I think," said Carolinus, touching one of his white mustaches gently. "Yes, I think so. But first, if you don't mind, I would like to be by myself for a while, to collect my thoughts. Do I still have the room you've been keeping me in?"

"Of course!" said Jim. "The room is yours. It will always be ready, waiting for you here. Just go back to the castle and step into it. Call on the servants for anything you want."

"I'll do just that," said Carolinus.

Holding the kettle, he went off down from the platform. As he moved away from Jim, a little jet of steam showed past his right side. Faintly, Jim heard a small, breathy voice singing, as Carolinus moved away from him, until it could no longer be heard. But singing warmly and triumphantly.

"Caro—lin—us! Caro—lin—us . . ."

CLASSIC SCIENCE FICTION AND FANTASY

__THE WOODS OUT BACK   0-441-90872-1/$4.99
Bestselling author R.A. Salvatore creates a world of elfs and
dwarfs and witches and dragons—all in the woods behind Gary
Leger's house. There Gary discovers he is the only one who
can wear the armor of the land's lost hero and wield a magical
spear. And if he doesn't, he can never go home again...

__DUNE Frank Herbert 0-441-17271-7/$5.99
The bestselling novel of an awesome world where gods and
adventurers clash, mile-long sandworms rule the desert, and
the ancient dream of immortality comes true.

__STRANGER IN A STRANGE LAND Robert A. Heinlein
0-441-79034-8/$5.99
From the New York Times bestselling author—the science
fiction masterpiece of a man from Mars who teaches
humankind the art of grokking, watersharing and love.

__THE ONCE AND FUTURE KING T.H. White
0-441-62740-4/$5.99
The world's greatest fantasy classic! A magical epic of King
Arthur in Camelot, romance, wizardry and war. By the author
of The Book of Merlyn.

__THE LEFT HAND OF DARKNESS Ursula K. LeGuin
0-441-47812-3/$4.99
Winner of the Hugo and Nebula awards for best science fiction
novel of the year. "SF masterpiece!"—Newsweek "A Jewel of
a story."—Frank Herbert
